NEVER MIND

THE GENETICS

A NOVEL BY

MEL THORN

ISBN: 0692234381
ISBN-13: 978-0692234389 (Thorn Books)

"Oh, the comfort — the inexpressible comfort of feeling *safe* with a person — having neither to weigh thoughts nor measure words, but pouring them all right out, just as they are, chaff and grain together; certain that a faithful hand will take and sift them, keep what is worth keeping, and then with the breath of kindness blow the rest away."

-Dinah Craik

CHAPTER ONE

In Which a Link is Formed

Only one mile remained before Andrew would know at last if the man he was about to meet would either shelter him or discard him forever.

He would give anything to get a glimpse forward in time, to determine if this charade was worth the trouble. It mattered little that he had spent his entire life waiting for this moment, that he had wished since a child that this event would occur at any point in his future. What mattered now was that he might not get the chance he was hoping to have— to win the ultimate of life's lotteries. This was not how he wanted things to go.

His mother hadn't looked at, nor spoken to him for a while now, and the only reminder he received that she was still in the car with him was when she changed radio stations. Andrew hoped this debacle weighed on her conscience as much as it did on his self-esteem, and his desperation had him almost wishing for a car accident. He might end up disabled, but his mother would get what was coming to her.

It may have been too late to pry her mind of any thoughts whatsoever on the matter, but Andrew had to know what she was thinking. After all, she was leaving him forever, and whether or not that was for the best, he wondered if she had any parting words for him.

"Did you call him?"

His mother took a brief look at him, returned her focus to the road, then shifted her posture upright. Her dazzling scarlet hair fell across her shoulders as she shrugged in apathy. "No. I didn't."

That was something he had already assumed. If one was the type to show up late for doctor's appointments, they were hardly reliable enough to phone someone before visiting. "Why the hell not?"

She looked in the rear view mirror, changed lanes, then leaned back. She passed a scornful look to her teenaged son, whose eyes were protected by long strands of dark hair. "Why should I? He hasn't called *me* in years."

His ears must have deceived him. She couldn't possibly consider that a validated excuse. No rational human being would. "That's a little beside the point, isn't it?"

"Andrew, hush. All right?" Ah, yes. She always had to be the right one, didn't she? Andrew seized the one opportunity he might have to put his foot down.

"What are you going to do, Mom? Just drive up to the door and drop me off?"

"Of course not. I'll make sure he's home."

"You couldn't make sure by calling?"

She sighed— a sound he was well acquainted with. "Andrew, we've discussed this."

"We have? Well, someone forgot to let me know."

When they came to a rolling stop at a solid red light, she turned her volcanic eyes toward his thin face, which was curtained by draping follicles. It was a miracle he could manage to see anything through them. "Don't start. We're almost there, then we'll be out of each other's hair."

"We don't know that for sure, because someone didn't make a phone call," Andrew muttered. She heard him, and he knew she did, but her only reaction was to speed up the vehicle and increase the radio's already-blaring volume. She wouldn't give him the benefit of an explanation, nor would she allow him to question her actions, no matter how senseless they were.

The glare of the sun peeking from behind the ashen November clouds stung Andrew's eyes as he looked out his window at the green sign welcoming them to the borough of Queens. He thought that when he left Staten Island once and for all, he would never miss it, and never look back. Even if his previous dwelling was broken in many ways, it was still a place he had lived in all of his life. Saying goodbye to many of his personal belongings would be the toughest challenge of all that was about to face him.

He wasn't ready for this. He thought he would be when waking up that morning, knowing that the slight chance of leaving his mother for the rest of his life was approaching, but the mere thought of his dreams coming to a crashing halt when struck when the blunt end of reality was all too terrifying. This man might not be the one he hoped and imagined. Time was running out, and there was no going back. This was it.

The road his mother turned onto was one leading into a wealthy neighborhood, one where each of the houses were grand in value, fancy in design and decoration, mountainous in scale, and many of them had more than one garage. A forest of pines and oaks surrounded them, and countless trees and bushes separated each of the yards. His mother dropped the car's speed to a crawl as she checked the addresses, reading them aloud as she passed them.

She slowed more when she spied the address she was looking for: seventy-eight fifty-three Mancante Street. At first glance, the only visible part of the residence was the stretching driveway, which trailed deep through a canopy of trees with branches that could touch the low-hanging clouds. The driveway was more than just a small, paved road, but an infinite journey from the street to the house. At least, it felt that way to Andrew. The longer he had to wait, the more painful the ordeal became.

Finally, a towering structure came into view— a two-story opulent luxury home, built from sandy multi-colored stones, the exterior design modern in architecture. The driveway ended in a roundabout where a small garden of roses bloomed in the center. Through the tall vertical windows, Andrew could see a shimmering chandelier hanging from the ceiling. It might have been the biggest house Andrew had ever been in the vicinity of, or worthy of laying eyes on.

Even his mother, who spent many agonizing moments prattling incessantly, was breathless at the sight. "Holy shit," she whispered. She rummaged around in her purse after parking, and pulled out a sheet of folded printer paper, which she used to confirm the address they were now sitting in the very front yard of. "It's the right house," she said in mystified disbelief.

"Are you sure?" Andrew asked, shaking.

"Yes. Unless…" She muttered something else, mentioned a guy's name that Andrew wasn't familiar with. "No. He wouldn't trick me like that."

"Mom," he choked. "This guy is obviously loaded. I don't think he's going to want me. Look at me." His black T-shirt— faded, over-washed, and blotted with small holes— was at least three years old, and his jeans, which he had owned for four years, was the only pair he had that wasn't ripped in several places. Even his jacket, which was slightly frayed at the cuffs, hadn't been replaced since he purchased it in eighth grade. His wardrobe was in dire need of an update, but he'd consider himself lucky whenever his mother could afford to do so.

"Don't be such a baby, Andrew. We're already here." She opened her door, her mini skirt, which was a bit too "mini," catching in a breeze as she left the vehicle.

Andrew froze in place like a well-carved ice sculpture. He didn't bother unhooking his seatbelt buckle, assuming that it was only a matter of time that he'd be heading back to the house. Whatever laid in wait on the other side of that heavy oak front door, Andrew didn't want to get closer than a yard away from it. What would the house's owner say when his mother told him the truth? How would he react? At this point, he didn't want to find out. Any result was bound to be a negative one.

His mother, on the other hand, had fewer doubts and overflowing eagerness. Unlike Andrew, she was now optimistic at the outcome of their visit. When she saw that her son hadn't left the car, she beckoned him over with a girlish wave, her acrylic ruby nails sparkling.

Andrew didn't come as she commanded, but rather sank low out of sight where he was safe from probing eyes. She would have to confront the man of the house without him. The situation was humiliating enough. He pulled his long hair further over his eyes than it already was, shielding them so that he wouldn't have to see what would happen next.

Andrew's mother went on to the oversized front door without him, to his relief, and rang the bell. Even from where he sat in the car, he could hear its tone, as if an actual collection of church bells were kept in the attic of the home, waiting to ring whenever someone pressed the button.

She fixed her shirt and hair while she waited, checking her reflection in one of the outstretched windows. She waved her skirt down a few times, then stuck one leg out to the side while putting a hand on her hip. She rolled her eyes afterward, hoping the house's owner would soon answer the door.

The first time the doorbell rang, Kevin hadn't heard it. His busy mind was reeling, his fingers rolling across his keyboard at lightning speed. He only had one paragraph left of his first draft, a few sentences away from completing his rough work. Then he could take a cigarette break, his fifth one in the past thirty minutes.

He came to a pause at the final sentence, his mind going blank. He had been hit with writer's block before, but when coming up with a good enough conclusion, he always managed to get stuck. Endings were important to Kevin, as they were to his many readers. It had to wrap everything up perfectly, and to do so in one sentence was still a challenge to him, even after many years of honing his craft.

His pack of menthols were calling him, begging him to be smoked away. He tried his best to restrain himself, to take it easy and to learn to smoke less each day. This was an even greater feat than coming up with a viable ending to a story. He always had an excuse at the ready whenever he got the slightest bit of courage to toss them all into the garbage.

I might be able to think better if I smoke, he convinced himself.

His fingers hadn't yet touched the pack that rested on his desk when he heard his doorbell go off not once, but three times in a row. Kevin left his leather chair, grabbing his cigarettes on the way out of his office, and jogged down the extensive hallway, his socks sliding on the wooden floors. Whoever that was, they had better needed something important from him, and not a cup of sugar, either. He had enough trouble thinking as it was without unnecessary distractions.

He wheezed when he reached the door, hearing the doorbell ring two more times. He jerked it open after pulling his dangling dark hair back with his palm and stared at his visitor, his quizzical cobalt irises shadowed by his crunched brow. At any other time, Kevin was a professional weaver of words, but now, he could not find a single one that properly expressed his confusion.

"Kevin," sighed Andrew's mother, who now wore a forced smile.

Kevin required a moment of quiet thought when presented with the sight of the woman on his front step. He didn't get many visitors, but of everyone that could have rang his doorbell that afternoon, he didn't expect someone he had last seen in high school. "Star?"

Star batted her eyelashes. "It's been a long time." That, Kevin had to admit, was understatement.

Kevin glanced from her to the vehicle in his driveway. He noticed someone sitting in the passenger seat, a young man with his head tucked down and hair in his face. Bewildered, he looked back at Star, attempting to contemplate the proceedings unfolding before him. "What are you doing here?"

She clicked her tongue, and her green eyes rounded. "Kevin! We haven't seen each other in forever and that's the first thing you say to me?"

He once again looked at the individual in the car, who seemed to not only hide from him, but the entire world. "What else do you want me to say?"

"How about 'hello'? What about 'how are you'? I remember you being a lot nicer than this."

"Well, as you said, it's been a long time." He stepped out of his house and shut the door behind him. Now was a good time to light up that cigarette, which he promptly did. "The last time we spoke was when you dumped me. I sort of figured that would conclude our communications." He took a drag, and Star licked her upper lip as she watched him puff. "So this must be pretty important."

She kicked at a shallow puddle with the heel of her shoe. "It is. It's very important."

Gripping his cigarette between his fingers, Kevin turned his head as he exhaled. "You mind telling me how you found my address?"

"A little birdie told me."

More like your little cousin told you, Kevin thought, perturbed. "This birdie didn't give you my phone number?" He parked the cigarette back between his lips, the cherry lighting up as he inhaled.

"He did. I just didn't bother calling. I thought this would be better dealt with in person."

"What would?"

"I'm getting to that." She took a deep breath, her heavy chest expanding. She picked underneath her protracted, painted nails, her eyes rising to the cloudy skies. "Kevin… when we dated, I thought you were kind of weird."

A pause followed her admission, one that Kevin was ultimately confounded by. "Okay?" Smoke wisped from his nostrils. "You came all this way to tell me that?"

"I'm not finished." She sighed, tossing some red hair over her shoulder. "I liked it. You were different. And different is… nice."

He wanted her to get to the point, and fast. The sound of married couples arguing about their sexual shortcomings in public wasn't half as awkward as the conversation he was now having. "Thank you, Star," he mumbled.

"And it didn't matter that you weren't as popular as me, or my girl friends. They told me not to go out with you, but I did it anyway, and I'm glad I did."

He rubbed the fatigue out of his eyes with a circling thumb and forefinger. "Is this going somewhere?"

"Yes, yes, I promise." In their brief silence, the resonance of citrus-tinted leaves falling and clicking onto the pavement was like an oceanic roar. Kevin continued to gawk at her in wonderment, lost in his own unorganized thoughts. "I wanted to say, before anything else, that I'm sorry." Kevin opened his mouth, but she cut him off before he could speak. "I'm sorry about David. It wasn't personal, and I didn't do it to spite you. We were just a better match for each other."

"It's okay," he groaned. How much longer would he have to endure this? "Forget about it. I haven't thought about it, not for a long time. I don't know why you are."

"This is part of my point, Kevin, so just keep quiet for a minute, okay?" Kevin did go quiet, but not without a glare of admonition.

"As you can probably already tell," she continued, "I didn't come alone. I brought someone with me. This will be the first time the two of you meet, and I… I've been preparing for this for so long. I wish I would have done it sooner, but, this is just the way things turned out."

"What are you talking about?"

"After you and I separated, and David and I started seeing each other, I got sick. I assumed I caught a bug that was going around, so I didn't put much thought into it, not until I ended up gaining several pounds. I did a home test, and it was positive."

Kevin hadn't noticed that he had allowed his cigarette to burn all the way down to the filter, but once he caught a whiff of the putrid smell, he dropped it onto the damp pavement. He wiped sweat from his brow with the back of his hand before muttering, "Positive for what?"

"Pregnancy."

She didn't just say that word. He couldn't have heard her correctly. If he *had* heard her correctly, that meant her visit was related to the news she had just revealed, which not only would make no sense, but would prove the existence of miracles. If she really had been there to tell him that the two of them had a child, that would mean she had been keeping it from him this entire time, and no one was that insane.

There was nothing that Kevin could say, or do, that would calm his nerves at this point. Even another cigarette wouldn't do the job. "Are you saying what I think you're saying?"

Star's smile returned, and her eyes stopped fluttering. "You're a father."

He didn't intend to, but he started laughing. A group of young men with cameras were about to spring from the bushes at any moment now, he was sure of it. "You can't be serious."

"I'm completely serious."

"You have to be joking, Star." His laughter dimmed, and his expression darkened. The cameras never appeared, nor did Star tell him a prank was being pulled. "This *can't* be real. How... how is this even possible?!"

"I know what you're thinking. Why didn't I tell you?"

"That and other things!"

"If you want me to be honest... I wanted David to help raise him. For a while, I thought David was the father, but we did DNA tests to be sure, more than one." Her head tipped in a bow of shame. "We knew. We both knew that Andrew was yours. He couldn't have been anyone else's. David was the only other one I slept with after you, and he was my only partner for years. It became most obvious when Andrew developed a lot of your features, and none of David's. It felt like it was too late by then to tell you."

"*Too late?!*" Kevin exclaimed, baffled. "I didn't realize such earth-shattering news had a shelf life!"

"Andrew was already six years old. Telling him at that age that he had a biological father out there somewhere that didn't live with him… I saved it for when he was older." She stopped, allowing Kevin to take a breather, seeing the tension in his muscles. Then, she provoked, "Looks like you didn't need us anyway, moneybags."

"Yeah, I'd much rather have all of this," he grunted while pointing at his elaborate home, "Then I would to see my son."

Star folded her arms, turning to look at Andrew in the car. "Don't take it personally, Kevin, but I thought we were better off without you. I wasn't sure if I wanted you around our son. After your whole incident at school… you know, with your teacher…"

He huffed, incredulous. "What's that got to do with anything? Where did you even hear about it?" That wasn't a question that needed asking, of course. That "little birdie" she previously mentioned was the prime culprit.

Star tossed her hands into the air, palms out. "Fine. We'll drop it." What made her think he wanted to drop it at all? She was the one to bring it up in the first place.

Kevin eyed Star's vehicle again, which was as rouge as her hair, and spied the young man hunching over within it, hugging his own chest. For a kid in their late teens, Kevin thought he looked a bit too fearful of meeting someone new. He had to wonder what was now going through his mind, or what he was told prior to this incident. He calmed, easing into a gentler disposition. "Does he know now? About… me?"

"Yes," Star answered, also lowering her voice. "We told him when he got a little older, when he would understand. Ever since then…" She cleared her throat a couple of times in the same manner one would after swallowing an insect by accident. "He's been wanting to meet you. *Really* wanting to." Her exasperated roll of the eyes told just how much it had been discussed under her roof.

"Then why does he look so horrified?"

She pursed her lips, rocking on her heels. "That's the whole reason we're here. I'd like the three of us to discuss it."

"Please," Kevin voiced with eagerness, holding out his hand and pointing it in Andrew's direction. "Tell him I'd love to meet him." Despite how furious he was at Star, he would swallow his pride to shake the hand of his son.

Star hurried to her car, opening Andrew's door and peeking inside. "Andrew," she twittered, coating her voice with honey as she often did when Andrew needed persuading. It might have worked when she tried to feed him a tablespoon of penicillin when he was seven, but by now, he wasn't so easily fooled. "He wants to meet you."

Andrew sank further into the upholstery. "He looked pretty pissed off."

"I'm the one he's angry at, not you."

Andrew knew that when all was said and done, he had no choice— that she would always have her way, no matter what she dragged him into, though the sheer ridiculousness of being toted around like a toddler as opposed to a full-grown adult never ceased to amaze him. As he climbed out of the car, he felt his guts sink to his feet, and he hid his hands in the pockets of his black hooded jacket.

Though his nerves went haywire, Andrew anticipated this meeting with the excitement shared with opening what few birthday presents he had received in his lifetime. The only evidence he had of Kevin's existence was an old photograph his mother had given him of them standing side-by-side with petulant expressions, which was taken at a dance they attended together. Ever since he learned he had a father he had never met, he wanted to know more about him, but had no assistance on his mother's part. Not until now, as she tried to finagle him upon the man who conceived him without notice.

He found that approaching Kevin took more strength than his body would allow, and that his mouth could no longer produce adequate saliva. Swallowing did little to make it better. Kevin seemed so much bigger than he was in the photograph he had spent years looking at. He wondered if he would be capable of snapping him in two if he so desired. He had to at least been six feet tall, and Andrew's head only came up to his chest.

Andrew's dragging shuffle eventually brought him face-to-face with his father, who surprised Andrew with a beguiling smile and vivid irises. As their eyes met, Andrew lowered his, hiding behind his hair, pulling his jacket further up his neck.

"Hello, Andrew," Kevin greeted, reaching forward for a handshake.

At first, Andrew didn't remove either of his hands from his pockets. Not only would they turn to flesh-tinted icicles in the cold, but Kevin's palms, in comparison to his own, looked to be the size of catcher's mitts. However, after considering that their first meeting was already awkward enough, he wished to do what was polite, and freed his right hand to take hold of a Kevin's. Kevin's palm wrapped around his in a tight grip, and a comforting warmth spread up his forearm. "Hey," Andrew answered him before returning his hand to the safety of his pocket.

"It's nice to meet you. Nice to *know* about you." A hearty chuckle followed this statement.

The corner of Andrew's mouth snuck upwards. "Yeah. You too. I mean… I always knew about you, but… yeah. Nice meeting you." He hunched up his shoulders, his lips tightening around his teeth.

"Why don't you come inside? It's cold out here." Kevin opened his front door and stepped aside, granting Andrew entry.

Andrew peeked into Kevin's home, which to him was more like a castle than a house. If Kevin was anything like Star, he'd bark at him the moment he got dirty footprints anywhere but on the doormat. "Are you sure?" he stammered.

Kevin gleamed again, wider this time. "Of course."

Andrew had little hopes before arriving at Kevin's doorstep, but now they had raised by a small percentage. Kevin didn't seem as bad as he thought he would be, at least so far. Before he placed even one toe over the threshold, his mother breezed past him, knocking into him as she entered the house as she gasped in awe at the size and beauty. She seemed especially interested in the chandelier, which she posed several questions about, ones that Kevin seemed uninterested in answering.

Andrew, downtrodden, lowered his head again and sighed. He noticed that Kevin exhaled in solidarity, and he wondered if they also shared the same thoughts.

"Come on in," Kevin comforted, his deep voice cordial and welcoming. "It's okay."

So far, so good, thought Andrew. Perhaps Kevin truly wasn't the monster his mother happened to be. There was a chance yet that his life would change for the better. With a shred of wavering confidence, he entered what might become his new home.

Andrew, like his mother, was awed by the enormity of the house. In each direction he looked, a long hallway stretched to a room he couldn't see from where he was standing. Framed artwork adorned the walls in the main hall, and several bronze statues of Greek gods stood tall and proud in each corner. They were partnered by potted plants that could just barely touch the ceiling, which had to be thirty feet above them. He wanted to tell Kevin how beautiful it was, but words failed him, and his nerves forbade him.

As soon as Kevin entered, he shut the door behind him, locked it, then stepped up to Andrew. "I'll take your jacket, if you'd like."

"I'd rather keep it on." He hugged it tighter around himself. Over the years, that coat had become more than just protection from rain and cold.

"All right. That's fine with me."

"Thank you." When the words exited his mouth, he meant to say them louder than he had, but it was in a whisper that he managed to utter them.

Surprisingly, Kevin heard him anyway. "You're welcome."

"My god. Look at this fireplace!" Star was like a child on Christmas morning, browsing the décor of Kevin's home as though she intended to buy it. Her buoyant steps bounced over to the mantle, where aromatherapy candles were on display beside framed literary awards. The first thing Star did upon seeing them was take one of them down to get a better look at it. Kevin drew in a sharp hiss.

"Please don't touch those," he commanded, stretching his hands out to catch it if she happened to let it slip from her grasp.

She clutched the award like she had found a wad of money on the ground. "You're an author, Kevin?" A subsequent snicker left her, and she placed the award back on the mantle, allowing Kevin to sneak out a brisk sigh of relief.

"Is that funny?" he asked her, the hairs on his neck raising. She responded with a laugh and nothing more.

Kevin passed Andrew a glace to confirm if Star was alone in her opinion. Andrew felt his eyes on him, and looked up to his face. He produced a shy, crooked smile before shrugging. He wanted to say, "That's the way Mom is," but Kevin seemed to get the idea from the look on his face, and breathed out a slight laugh.

"So, Andrew, you must be seventeen, then," Kevin blurted before Star could change the subject to his net worth.

He nodded. "Yeah. I am."

"Still in school?"

Andrew's head bobbed a second time. "I'm a senior."

"That's good to hear."

"He's been failing his classes a lot," Star butted in. "He's so…"

"Stupid?" Andrew finished beneath his breath.

"I think he fails just to spite me at this point," she continued, ignoring her son's obvious dejection. "I know he can manage. He just won't do it."

Kevin went quiet, and so too did his company. He glanced at Andrew, whose head almost never raised, as though his neck was permanently bent. His son kicked at the floor with his right foot and kept his hands tucked away, perhaps to avoid the temptation of annoying his mother. Kevin estimated that Star's presence kept him from enjoying their first meeting. The discomfort was not felt by Andrew alone.

"Star, why don't we just get to what your plans are?" he sighed, folding his arms over his sturdy chest. "I know you didn't bring him here just to meet me."

Her playfulness dissipated, and the air became as thick as oil. "All right. Fine. Let's sit down." She walked over to the lengthy leather sofa that stretched along the north wall underneath a modern, abstract painting. Kevin headed for his recliner, a twin to the couch that was made of the same material, but didn't sit. Instead, he offered it to Andrew, who initially didn't take it. It wasn't until Kevin insisted with a pleading gesture that he decided to do so, and when he did, he was glad he chose to. It might have been the most comfortable chair he had ever sat on. Its leather cushions were so warm and smooth, and shaped around his torso as he leaned into it. All he wanted to do after sinking into its softness was drift off to sleep.

Kevin sat on an ottoman across from the couch, facing Star. "Now… tell me what's going on, other than the fact that you spent our son's entire life lying to me."

Star crossed her legs, stiffening her posture. "Andrew can't live with me and David anymore."

"Can you elaborate?"

While twirling strands of her fiery hair, she explained. "What can I say? He's a problem. He can't go a day without starting a fight with me about something or other. I can't handle living with his anger anymore. I was hoping… maybe you'd be willing to take him off my hands. He's clearly not very happy at home."

Taking in her words, Kevin stroked his chin as he thought them over. "You want him to live here? We just met."

"I know it's a bit extreme. Believe me, I do. I thought it over a long time before coming here, Kevin. If there was any other option… you're the last person I can turn to at this point."

"I take it from the way Andrew is behaving that this wasn't a consensual agreement between you both." He looked to Andrew, knowing that if he wanted the truth, only one of them would tell it.

"No," stated Andrew. "I wanted to meet you. Someday." His gaze found the statue in the corner, one of Michelangelo's David, half the size of its original counterpart. "But not like this."

"I see," he replied, interrupting Star before she could scoff. "He's seventeen, Star. He's almost done with high school."

"So what?"

"He might have moved out after graduating. You couldn't wait until then? What the hell is wrong with you?"

Andrew's blood heated, as did his radiant face, though he didn't feel he was permitted to express such joy with his mother around. It was rare that someone challenged her. David was too spineless to tell her she was wrong, and would submit to her dominance on situations where it wasn't even necessary simply to avoid arguments. Andrew was the only one who ever confronted her, regardless of how badly he feared the outcome.

Star saw her son's face light up from his father's words, and she delivered a scornful retort. "Andrew can barely make it through high school. Do you think I'm confident that he'll be capable of hooking a job and getting a place after graduating? If I thought he was smart enough to handle it, I would let him." Kevin's disparaging look didn't prevent her from running her mouth some more. "Besides, Kevin. If you must know, living with Andrew is… *difficult* for Dave and I."

"Really," he countered in an endeavor to be wry with her.

"He's unhappy with this and that and will refuse to do what I ask him to. He barely does his homework anymore. He just stuffs headphones on and blasts out his eardrums or locks himself in his room for hours on end blaring that fucking guitar."

Surprised, Kevin looked at Andrew with a touch of optimism. "Guitar?"

His cheeks glowed with more intensity than the sunset burning outside the window. "I play… sometimes."

"That's great!"

Andrew tucked his chin down, the corners of his lips creeping upwards.

Star snorted. "Don't encourage him." They both ignored her, as tough as it was to do so.

Addressing Andrew, Kevin asked, "What do you want to do?"

Speech fled from him, and his breath caught for a moment. Someone was asking him what he wanted? That didn't seem the least bit rational, as he was rarely given a choice in anything he did. "I... well, I haven't given it much thought. This is all a little weird for me."

"You and me both," Kevin agreed. "You're welcome to stay here if you want to, or I could find you a place of your own."

Having options wasn't something Andrew thought of when stepping through Kevin's front door, especially so soon. After being presented with them, he couldn't imagine asking someone he didn't know to pay for his own apartment, even if that man was his father. "If you don't mind it... I... I'd like to stay here."

"All right. Then you're welcome to."

A great moan of relief seeped from Star's mouth. "Thank you."

"Star," Kevin said, this time with a coldness he didn't use with Andrew. "You're not planning to come back." In Andrew's ears, this sounded like both a question and a threat.

Apparently, returning to Kevin's home, whether or not it was to see her son, was of no concern to her. "No."

Though the verbal agreement was made, he doubted her. "This is his home now if he's going to stay here. The only way he's seeing you is if he chooses to."

"I don't *want* to see either of you again, Kevin. I just want my life back. I spent half of it living with my parents so they could help me raise Andrew. For all of the trouble I've went through taking care of him, he's ungrateful to me. If he's not going to appreciate his mother, maybe he'll have a bit more understanding of how hard life is without her."

What could he say to all of that? If things really had been so sour between her and their son, what else went on in their household that he didn't know about? It was a topic all too disturbing that Kevin both wanted more information on, and also wanted to abandon as soon as possible.

"All right," Kevin said, then stood up. He glimpsed at his son, who couldn't keep his eyes on him for more than a couple of seconds before dropping them to the floor. "Did you bring anything with you?"

"Well, I..."

"Just some of his things," Star answered for him. "I'll go get them." She hopped back onto her feet and jogged out the front door without waiting for a response from either of them.

Now that they were alone, Kevin seemed less stern. "How long has she been planning to do this?"

Andrew played with the strings on his hooded jacket as a distraction from his distress. "I think she's been wanting to do it for a long time. She threatened to whenever we fought. It's not entirely her fault. I always told her I'd run away to find you." He sank deeper into the chair, hoping it would swallow him whole. "I told her I'd move in with one of my friends, but she wanted me to go... father away than that."

His tone dropped a notch, and with a tenderness Andrew had never heard an authority figure use, said, "I'm sorry."

He shrugged, hiding his face behind his hair again, which fell back over his eyes as soon as he moved his head. "I'm used to it."

"Used to it? Should you be 'used to' such things?"

Andrew hoped that Kevin's benevolence wasn't temporary. It was refreshing. "It's okay. I mean... she doesn't want to see me anymore, right?" Before saying this aloud, the seriousness of it hadn't hit him. Even now, he was incredulous it was happening.

"Do you want to see her again?"

When he had to take a moment to think it over, he was perplexed at why he bothered. "No, not really, but... she can be pretty forceful sometimes."

"Not with me."

He couldn't remember the last time he felt positive enough to smile as much as he was now, enough to cause the muscles in his face to ache. Before he could express his appreciation to Kevin, Star came back into the house with Andrew's belongings: two duffel bags filled with clothes and various items, as well as a velvet case containing an electric guitar. She dropped them onto the wood floor, and Andrew flinched in horror. He wanted to rush to his wounded instrument, check it for any serious damage, but Star had approached him with her arms outstretched, and he had soon put it out of his mind as he was reminded of what lay ahead.

"Give me a hug," she sighed. Andrew remained sitting, sulking.

He looked away from her annoyed expression to the carpet, his eyes watering. "Andrew, come on," she growled, tapping her foot. "This is the last time we're going to see each other. You can at least say good-bye."

"Good-bye," he whispered.

"Christ," Star grumbled, stomping over to Kevin instead. "He's allergic to peanuts," she added in afterthought, then gave Kevin a farewell peck to the cheek, which he recoiled at. She huffed, "Good luck," then clomped her heels out the door, leaving it ajar on her exit. Kevin followed her, watching her get into her car and drive off, then shut his door and locked it with every latch that covered it.

"Unbelievable," he huffed with disdain. In the calm following the storm, he heard the echo of weak sniffling. When the sound carried through the hall and reached his ears, Star left his mind as briskly as she had left their lives. He headed back to the spacious living room to check on Andrew, whose sobs grew more audible as he closed in. He didn't say anything to him, as he couldn't think of what to say. No advice he provided would make him feel any better.

Hunching forward, Andrew clutched his face, shielding it from Kevin, hiding his weakest spots. He should have been relieved, no, euphoric that his mother was out of his life forever. On the other hand, although she was a harpy, and although they didn't have the greatest relationship, he loved her all the same. All he ever wanted was for her to show a little love back. Every minute he spent vying for her attention led to nothing but wasted time.

He tried to, but couldn't control his weeping. It all hurt so much worse than he thought it would. He was forced to live a new life, stay in a new house, and do so with a new person. There wasn't enough time for him to familiarize himself with his surroundings, not enough time to make peace with it, and definitely not enough time to get to know Kevin before living with him. Buried beneath that pleasant grin on Kevin's face may lie a serpent's tongue. He had no way of knowing for sure.

Why did Star insist on not only treating him like a child, but giving him away in the same manner? Was it possible for parents to abandon their offspring at his age? Even if it had not been, he felt the vulnerability and disadvantages of youth, and the utmost helplessness. Without a driver's license, car of his own, money to his name, or any true friends, Andrew had few options in life, and this one, though better than living with his mother, was terrifying. If his father ended up seeing him as the failure his mother believed him to be, he would have nowhere else to go. Living on the streets was out of the question, as he couldn't imagine scraping the bottom of garbage bins for food, begging for cash to buy an extra shirt without the stink of sweat and decay on it. He would die before he saw himself in such a position.

He wiped his eyes and nose with his hands, shivered and closed his jacket tighter. That's when he felt the sensation of something brushing against his arm. He had almost forgotten about Kevin, and where he was for that matter. Andrew pulled his hands away from his face, blinking the blur out of his vision.

Kevin was kneeling beside him, clutching a box of tissues, passing it toward him. He had placed a consoling hand on his arm, a nurturing gesture that managed to kill his overflowing tears. He took the tissue box from Kevin, yanked a few of them out of the box, then wiped his nose a few times. After arranging himself, he told Kevin, "Thank you, sir."

"You don't have to call me that."

"I'm sorry."

His thick voice trembled with a deep, awkward laugh. "You didn't offend me."

The words "I'm sorry" were ones Andrew used to prevent from being yelled at or hit, though it didn't work in his favor every time. "I… I guess I just thought… because I don't know you very well…"

"You can call me by my name, if that's comfortable for you. No harm in that, right?"

He wiped his nose again. "If you don't mind it."

"Not at all." Andrew's cheekbones raised, despite the tears. "It'll be okay. Really, it will."

Daunted by his pleasant demeanor, Andrew had to ask, "You're really okay with me staying here?"

"Of course."

"I'm sorry Mom did this to you. She has a way with… getting what she wants."

"I would have appreciated she told me about you years ago," Kevin mentioned with a dab of disrespect still lingering in the atmosphere. "But that doesn't really matter now, okay?" Andrew answered him with a nod, and finished wiping his eyes. "What matters is that I know now. As shocking as it is, I can honestly say that I'm excited."

Andrew felt the waterworks starting up again, and he put a stop to them before they got too out of control. "Really?" Kevin affirmed with a dutiful nod. "Thank you. I... I guess I am, too."

They spent a few timid seconds in silence. Andrew had spent his whole life thinking of things to say to Kevin, and now that they were in the same room, those many questions seemed to be stripped from his memory. Kevin, still focused on relaxing him, held his welcoming smile.

"It's very lovely meeting you, Andrew," he told him with sincerity.

"It's great meeting you, too," he answered with a gentle exhale, exchanging tears of pain with those of joy. "I wondered all my life what you were like."

"I hope I'm what you expected."

Andrew sniffed as he loosened his clenching arms, drawing in a deep breath. "You are so far."

"Well, I hope that doesn't change." He was satisfied to see that this put Andrew at ease. "Why don't I give you a tour of the house?"

He didn't want to leave the leather recliner. It had become like a nest to him since he arrived, and he even considered asking Kevin if he could sleep in it that night. Wanting to get to know his parent, he forced himself off of it, knowing he could return to it any time.

Kevin toured him through the house, but spoke of each of his many oversized rooms with shame. He told him he was glad to have someone else under his roof now so that the legroom wouldn't go to waste. Andrew was too awed by how beautiful everything was, and too distracted thinking about how expensive Kevin's bills were to make any comments. His stillness made Kevin nervous, and Andrew didn't mean to put him on edge, but he wasn't skilled with words.

One room that Andrew did speak out on was the TV room: a enclosed, cozy space with a colossal high definition television against the main wall, velvet black sofas covered in silk pillows and blankets pressed against the walls. They could easily fit five large people, let alone one healthy, well-fit man like Kevin. On each of the four walls were shelves that reached the ceilings, all of which were covered from top to bottom in DVDs and video games, with movies on the left side of the room and games on the right.

The moment Andrew spied the labels of game systems on the

spines of many disc cases, he turned to his father, his jaw plummeting. "You play video games?"

"Who doesn't?" Kevin answered with inward joy.

"Wow. You have so many of them. I don't usually meet people your age who are into it."

"What else am I going to do with my time? I don't always work on writing. A man's got to have hobbies, you know."

"Can I...?" He pointed his boney thumb toward the shelf.

"Absolutely!"

Andrew beamed as he rushed over to the shelves. He read each of the side labels, and exclaimed his fascination when spotting a particular title that he thought only he was aware existed.

"I can't believe you have that one!" he told Kevin at the top of his voice, unable to believe how alike their tastes were. "I thought they stopped releasing it into stores!"

"They did," Kevin confirmed, pacing his cave of entertainment, watching Andrew with inclining optimism. "I got that copy right before they pulled it."

Andrew slipped the game, titled *Poison Arrow*, back onto the shelf. He rubbed the back of his neck when he and Kevin looked at one another. "Would it be okay if I played it sometime?"

Kevin parted his hands in an elegant signal of open-mindedness. "Please. This is your home now. You can do whatever you like."

"Seriously?"

"I trust you not to break anything. Not that I couldn't afford a replacement." He winked, then beckoned him over, and Andrew trailed after him like a lost kitten. After walking Andrew back to the living room, he started up the stairs leading to the bedrooms and guest rooms. "Before you ask, yes, we do have a pool. It's in the backyard."

We, Andrew repeated to himself. Something about it sounded natural.

Kevin introduced Andrew to his new bedroom: a well-decorated guest room complete with a queen-sized bed, a large flat-screen television, and a bedside table with a phone and lamp. A glass door opened to a balcony, which overlooked the yard, where the pool and hot tub was. Attached to the room was an adjacent bathroom with a corner glass shower.

"I hope this room is satisfactory enough," he told his son as he allowed him to scope the place out for himself. "If not, I can put you in the other one."

"No, it's okay. This is great. I think I'll be fine here."

It's twice the size of my old room, he mulled over. *I don't think I could handle one any bigger than this.*

Kevin hovered by the doorway, leaning his shoulder against the frame. "Would you like me to help you unpack?"

Andrew wasn't sure how to cope with so much generosity. Never in his whole life had someone willingly presented their assistance with such fervor. "I couldn't ask you to do that."

"You didn't ask. I offered."

"Really, it's okay. You've already done a lot for me. More than I thought you would."

"All right, Andrew. Just let me know if you need anything, okay? Go ahead and make yourself at home." He then turned to leave the room to give him some much-needed privacy.

There was one last thing that Andrew required before he disappeared. "Kevin…" His father stopped, looking back. "Thanks. For taking me in, I mean. It was either this, or… I… I don't know where I'd be now. Where I'd go."

Some speculations arose as to what Star was capable of doing, but those thoughts, Kevin felt, were best left unvisited. "Well, don't worry. This is just as much your place now as it is mine, and it's not your prison. You're free to stay as long as you wish."

Thanking Kevin wasn't enough to show how much this meant to him. He would have to think of a better method of expressing his gratitude, but for now, all he could do was say, "That's very nice of you."

Kevin placed his right palm over his heart. "It's the least I could do to make up for all of our lost time." Though Kevin could sense that Andrew wasn't much for conversation, he could tell that since his arrival there, he was considerably reassured. He wished there was more he could do for him, but he had plenty of time to make up for what Star had done. "Do you like pizza?"

"Yeah. I love it." He couldn't remember the last time he had any.

"I'll order some for dinner. Then we can chat. I have so many questions for you!"

"Y-yeah. I do, too."

"I'll call you down with the intercom when it gets here." He left

Andrew alone when he confirmed with a nod.

Collapsing onto his new bed, staring up at the ceiling, he reflected on the events of the evening, on how surprised Star looked that Kevin allowed him to live there. He imagined what might have happened if he turned him away, where he might now be if it weren't for his hospitality.

Things still had a chance to improve. This was only the first day, and hopefully, many more would follow.

CHAPTER TWO

In Which the Chain is Extended

The kitchen table, which was ten feet long and carved from mahogany, was a bit too oversized in Andrew's opinion, though the antique cushioned seats arranged around it provided adequate comfort. He didn't mind being spaced so far from the pizza boxes that he and Kevin had to pass back and forth, but he did wish they were sitting closer to each other. The lamp hanging from the ceiling gave just enough light for him to see what was on his plate, but it was otherwise too dark. Maybe Kevin liked it that way, but it made it difficult for him to observe changes in his expression— something he preferred doing while engaging in conversation.

Eating in front of Kevin was an anomalous challenge for him. He was sure Kevin wouldn't remark on how he "ate like a fat ass" in the same manner Dave once did whenever he stuffed his face, but he wouldn't risk the discomfiture. When he picked out a slice from the box but hadn't yet taken a bite, this worried his father, and he was torn between eating to make him feel better, and saving it for when he didn't have his eyes on him. Either way, he'd feel like he did something wrong.

Kevin, giving Andrew the personal space he might have needed while getting inured to his new home, allowed him to take as much time as he needed. His appetite had also waned, and his mind was too hectic for him to focus on filling his stomach. "I'll have to register you at the high school," he informed him, wiping sauce from his pinkish lips. "Wouldn't want you missing any classes."

"Do I have to?" Of course he knew that he had no choice, but it was worth a shot.

With a growing smile, he said, "I'm afraid so. Don't worry. I'm sure I'll be able to sort it out." He took a swig from his glass. Andrew eyed his own, which, like Kevin's, was also filled with water. He hated drinking it. It was what you were meant to consume when your kidneys acted up, or if you had a stomach ache. It was not meant to be sided with pizza. "Speaking of school— what's your favorite subject?"

Andrew was aware that other people had favorite school subjects, but he wasn't one of those people. The things he loved and cherished had little, or nothing to do with school. "I don't really have any. I just do what's required to graduate, I guess."

"What about hobbies? Other than your guitar?"

"Well… I really love photography."

"Oh! Cool!"

Andrew had never heard it referred to as "cool" before, but he was delighted that Kevin thought so. "It can be. I keep a portfolio. I want to do it professionally someday." This was the first time he had revealed this dream to anybody. His mother never asked, and he didn't think she cared. Neither David nor what few friends he had gave a damn either.

Pride illuminated Kevin's face. "That's wonderful. It's good to have aspirations, especially creative ones. It's what people seem to be lacking these days." He chuckled, his mouth stretched toward his ears. "My son, the artist. You've definitely got my genes."

Unfortunately, I have Mom's too, Andrew wanted to say.

"What do you like to do?" he asked Kevin, wanting to drive the attention off of himself. "Besides write?"

Kevin finished off a slice, then closed the box, intending to put the leftovers in the fridge. He used his clean hand to brush some of his blackish hair from his eyes. "I collect things. My best friend tells me I do it to fill the social void in my life. I tell him it's because I'm neurotic. I suppose it could be a little of both."

"Social void?" Andrew repeated, once again noticing the distance between them. Such an enormous table, and only two of them sitting at it. "I've been meaning to ask you… why do you live in this huge house by yourself?"

Kevin rested his elbow on the table, holding his chin up in his palm, staring down at the polished wood below him. A sigh breezed from his nostrils. "When I first moved in here, I didn't think I'd be alone this long." Memories of all kinds came to life in Kevin's mind, and saddened silence hit him, leaving Andrew curious. "I know what you're wondering. I moved in here a few years ago. I've been the only resident since then."

Andrew could practically taste his sorrow, depression that came unexpected for someone who appeared so jovial to him. "Forgive me, but… it seems kind of strange to me that someone as well off as you is still single."

"It's a little complicated." He left it at that. The subject seemed to haunt him, and Andrew didn't want to press it if it meant hurting him.

"I'm sorry," he told Kevin, this time with genuine sympathy.

All traces of sadness ebbed away from Kevin's face, and his glow returned. "Oh, it's all right. It doesn't really matter now. Having a son is much better than having a significant other."

"Is it?" Andrew queried, bordering a whisper.

"Yes. With lovers often comes the word 'goodbye'. With family it's— well, it's *supposed* to be different." Andrew had to admire his candor on the subject. Mothers were not *supposed* to say goodbye to their sons the way Star had. "Did you have any friends back at your mother's?" continued Kevin, stepping away from the topic of Andrew's emancipation.

"Some," he answered, breaking eye contact. "I wouldn't call them friends. They tolerated me. I doubt they'll even miss me."

His firm jaw lowered, and his eyes popped. "Why would you think such a thing?"

"Because it's true."

"Do you normally talk about yourself that way?" Kevin wondered. All Andrew could think to do in response was shrug and pick at his food. "You shouldn't," he persisted, seeing that Andrew had stopped participating in the conversation.

Just being honest, mused Andrew, now glum. *I don't expect him to understand.*

"Did you have a photography class at your old high school?" Kevin pondered next.

"There was one at the school, but Mom didn't let me take it." He slipped the remainder of his slice of pizza into the second box and closed it. "She wanted me to keep taking math classes. I'm good at math, but it's not like I love it or anything."

"I can get you into one at the school here, if you want it."

"You don't have to."

"It's no trouble, you know."

"I'm hard to please." When Kevin lapsed into supple laughter, he tensed. He was serious when he said it, and wasn't sure what he found so funny.

"You sound just like me when I was your age."

Crimson spread over his cheeks, and he lowered his head again. "S-sorry. I guess I just keep thinking this is only temporary. Living here with you, I mean."

"I'm not going to throw you out, Andrew. I'm not like your mother."

So he says, Andrew told himself. *Still, a nice thing to hear.*

"So those awards on your fireplace… what were those from?" he mentioned, dodging the spotlight that Kevin seemed persistent at shining on him.

"Contests, some of them local," he said before taking a small bite of pizza. "They helped me promote my first book."

"What kind of book was it?"

"It was a mystery thriller. *The Night Calls.* It was the very novel that jump-started my career. If I wanted to stop writing, I'd still make royalties, and would be able to live off of them. Honestly, I can't stop myself from doing it. Nothing compares to creating a living world with my mind and hands." Following a brief pause, he added, "Except maybe for having a son."

If it was one thing he loved so far about Kevin, it was how excited he was to have him around. It made him hopeful for his future, which before seemed so dim. "Yeah. My photos and guitar aren't as cool as meeting you." When he saw his face brighten, he went on. "I went through every possible scene in my head. You know, of how it would go. All I knew about you was what Mom told me, and even she didn't know much anymore. I imagined you as many things, but I definitely didn't expect… this."

"I look like a total snob, don't I?"

"N-no! You don't."

"It's okay if you thought so. I know this house is too big. I don't *need* these things. They barely keep me happy."

"I don't think you're snobby. You seem cool."

Kevin hoped, no matter what happened, that Andrew would continue to think that. "Thank you, Andrew. You seem very cool, too."

A shade of cherry spotted Andrew's face. "Thanks."

"Are you not hungry?" He gazed at the pizza box, which was still had most of an unfinished meal inside of it.

"Oh. I am. It's just…"

"I know. This is all a little overwhelming. I'm too excited to eat, myself."

"I need some time to get used to things, I guess." He felt guilty for not eating. Kevin bought the pizza just for him, and he had avoided touching it since it arrived. This made his appetite slip even further away from him. "This is going to sound like a weird question… but could we, like, hang out?"

Kevin first sounded his amusement, then replied, "That's not weird."

"I guess not. It feels that way, though."

"Honestly… it would mean a lot to me if we spent some quality time together. Why don't you check out the games? I could watch you play."

Buzzing with excitement, he leapt out of his chair. "Okay." He followed Kevin out of the room after waiting for him to set the pizza in the fridge, and they both disappeared down the vast hall to the TV room.

For many hours, long after Kevin's usual bedtime, he watched Andrew try out game after game, and it became clear to him that it was this very activity that drew them closer. They got to talking about which games were their favorites, and Andrew eventually expressed how awesome it was that he could share something like this with someone older.

"I feel a little *too* old sometimes," Kevin confided, though with a touch of insecurity. He nursed on a chilled, frothy wheat beer that he had retrieved a few minutes ago, but was almost finished with it. He was so distracted chatting with Andrew that the speed at which he emptied it didn't seem to matter.

"You're thirty-five, right?" Andrew asked while his thumbs and fingers glided to and from the controller's buttons. He was playing a horror game that Kevin hadn't picked up in a few years, one that Andrew was swift to get sucked into.

"That's right." He sipped from the chilled bottle in his hand, and only got a few drops. "In other words, I'm old."

"That's not old at all," Andrew huffed.

"Wait until you reach my age. You'll think differently."

"I hope I'm half as successful as you at your age."

He chuckled, setting his empty beer bottle on the table, one that had a stone checkered pattern on the surface. "I guess that's a good way of looking at it. You're right. I have done pretty well for myself thus far, haven't I? There just hasn't been anyone to share my fortune with until now."

As he moved his male game protagonist through a hall of zombies, Andrew voiced with sincerity, "Money's nice and all. I'm just glad we met."

Warmed by his words, Kevin replied with a silken tone, "So am I." When he grabbed his pack of cigarettes from the table beside him, Andrew grimaced at him. Kevin noticed his expression. "What's the matter?" His subsequent breath was perplexed and shaken.

"You smoke?"

He only managed to get the pack open before noticing the comical way Andrew's face was pulled. "Yes. Is that a problem?"

He wouldn't refer to smoking as a "problem," but he wouldn't deny that the very smell of a burning cigarette made him want to retch. Not only did he detest their aroma, but the sight of one perched between another's lips caused memories of those hundreds of Just Say No campaigns to emerge, those that had been shoved in his face all during school. Smoking kills, Kevin. Don't you know that? Doesn't anyone know that? No one wanted to kiss an ashtray, your teeth weren't meant to be brown, and voices weren't supposed to sound like a robot's.

"You do it a lot?" pressed Andrew, with caution.

It became clear to Kevin that Andrew disapproved of whatever he planned to do with that half-open pack of smokes, and now that they had accepted their place in the world, disappointing his son was something he wanted to avoid at all costs. When he came to his own father about how many packs he burned in a day, he was regarded with a scoff, a telltale sign that he was to mind his own business.

Even if it was one small step toward being a better parent than the one he had known, it was a step far greater than any one his father ever took.

"Every day," he admitted. Andrew's expression grew sourer. "That bothers you?"

He never said it bothered him. He was right, of course, but he knew that he had little say in what went on in their domicile. "I'm sorry. I should learn to keep my mouth shut."

"No, I'm glad you brought it up. I've been making a lot of excuses. I think it's about time I had a reason to stop." He lowered the top of the pack, closing it, and rested it on the table.

Andrew had to admit that he didn't expect their conversation to end that way. If he was serious about chucking his habit for his gratification, perhaps this whole parenting thing meant more to Kevin than he gave him credit for.

"Oh…" he uttered, unable to express himself the way he wanted to. *Thank you*, his mind told him to say. *How thoughtful of you. You really are a cool guy, aren't you?* Like always, he found that thinking was easier than speaking. Thankfully, Kevin didn't require his gratitude. His smile said a thousand words.

Here's to a good fresh start, Kevin hoped, crossing his fingers.

Come bedtime, Andrew couldn't sleep. It wasn't the bed keeping him awake; its downy sheets and lavender scent was soothing. Many thoughts, from his life with Star and David, to his worries about whether or not he and Kevin would get along, were loud and constant, and each time he closed his eyes, they refused to stay shut. Usually when this would happen in the past, he would slip a pair of buds in his ears and listen to his favorite albums, but when his mother rushed him out of the house as they left for Kevin's place, he didn't get the chance to grab them. He also left behind several other treasured items, including his CDs and posters, which he hoarded like gold, only to abandon, possibly for Star to pawn or give away. His heart sank at the notion.

In retrospect, he supposed he did trade them for something better. Each fight he and Star got into, he wanted to find Kevin, seek him out, learn who he really was, and beg him to save him from his situation. Things turned out almost identical to his many daydreams, with the exception that he was forced into it, rather than searching for Kevin on his own terms. He felt lucky, and grateful, that things turned out well.

What are you really like? Andrew had no clue as to how many times he asked himself this question, but it had been one floating around in his mind since he first learned of his father. *Do you have any other kids? Are you nice? Would you yell at me like mom does?*

If you met me, would you love me?

Now that he had met Kevin, he had at least some insight into what he was like, and had fewer concerns than he had when ten years old. From what he could tell based upon outside appearances, he wasn't a drunk, an addict, or a lunatic, and his earlier fears were quelled by cordial conversations with him.

It was his mother who told him that his biological father had no interest in getting to know him. As though she had been standing in the room with him, her face contorted in a snarl and her hands perched atop her hips, he heard her say it in the identical manner she had done many times before:

"Why would he want you hanging around?"

It was a question Andrew never thought to be sincere. He knew, even as a child, that she and Kevin didn't speak to one another, and that she hadn't seen him in years. She didn't know a damn thing about what Kevin did or didn't want. Knowing Star, he had to wonder why she invested so much time talking him out of seeing Kevin if she didn't wish to care for him herself. It had been unclear for so long, but now that he was older, he laid blame on her seeing him as nothing more than a cute toy, rather than a son. The older he got, the less she seemed to like him.

"I'm going to find him," he vowed one night after Star had crossed his face with a white hot slap of the palm, following an argument about something he had long forgotten. "I'm going to run away, and you'll never see me again!"

"Go ahead and try it," she had told him. "You wouldn't get ten feet from this house before giving up."

One and a half miles later, it was the police that had eventually picked him up. By the time they found him, he was a human icicle, one too frozen to speak coherently. When they warmed him up enough, they asked his name, where his parents were, and what he was doing on his own.

Don't take me back home, he wished to plead. Instead, he told them,

"Kevin Neil is my dad. Can you find him?"

None of the officers found the man he sought, but they did bombard him with several more questions about his family until he coughed up the information they wanted. When they brought him home, he heard them speaking to Star, who babbled endless excuses as for why her son just walked almost two miles away from home in a snowstorm. Even when a social worker paid them a visit in the weeks following, Star was apt at keeping her slaps and spanks swept under the rug.

Kevin's existence remained to be a mystery, save for the one piece of information Star fed him one day: "He lives in Queens. That's all I know." Neither of them had even known of his literary success. Andrew never watched television, though if he had, he might have seen his father for the first time in talk show interviews, would have at last found out the truth. He spent more time with his camera and guitar than he did reading any books. If he was a reader, he might have found his father's novels on the shelves while searching for a new story to lose himself in. Perhaps fate was the one to steer him from such things, if he chose to believe in it. Maybe, he considered, he wasn't meant to meet Kevin until now. The reason for that was uncertain, but he didn't question it. He was in his life now, and that's what mattered.

If Star hadn't introduced them, he would have continued to make assumptions based upon slight amounts of evidence and his own gut feeling telling him that his true father was out there somewhere, waiting for him. At times, his instincts steered him wrong, but in this case, they had been correct.

It was time now to put regret behind him. Star was out of his life, and change was on the horizon. As he closed his eyes, he dreamt of a positive future, of finding all he had spent his life searching for.

Elliott High School was twice the size of Andrew's previous one, and three times as crowded. The suffocating masses of teenagers swimming in and out of the doors were like swarms of razor-toothed barracudas, and the first walk from the car to the building was his last chance at getting any fresh air, as well as any remaining peace of mind.

Before leaving the house, Kevin asked Andrew if Star left his birth certificate with him. There were two reasons he was so interested in having it: to provide documentation to the high school for Andrew's proof of age, and to see Andrew's middle name, what his birthday was, and where he was born.

"Your middle name is Jacob," Kevin thought aloud when reading it. "Your birthday is... oh, March sixteenth. A Pisces." Andrew never took astrology seriously, but he was amused by his affirmation nonetheless. "And you have your mother's last name." That name was Phillips.

"Y-yeah. They got married after I was born." He wanted to tell Kevin how badly he wanted to legally change it, not wanting to be associated with his mother in any way, but it seemed spiteful, and while getting to know Kevin, he felt he should relinquish that negative side of his personality.

As soon as Kevin saw David's name on Andrew's certificate, he folded it back up, clutching it in both hands as though it was a treasure map. "I wish I could have been there for your birth, Andrew."

This had been one of the nicer things said to Andrew by a parent. "It's okay. I'm sure if you had known, you would have been there. Dave passed out, so I bet he would have traded places with you if he could."

A meager squeak that was meant to be a laugh escaped Kevin's mouth. "Well, despite all that they've done, I'm grateful they took care of you up until this point."

Define 'care'. If his mind could sigh, it would have.

Now within the cramped, confined principle's office, he sat beside Kevin, who was providing the necessary documentation for him to begin his education there. The principal, who had to be in her mid-fifties, couldn't take her cautious eyes off of the young man before her, whose wardrobe consisted of nothing but the color black. Nonetheless, she did add Andrew to the school's records after asking Kevin to fill out a form or two, and acquiring Andrew's grades from his last school via fax. When choosing Andrew's studies, Kevin selected a photography class as promised. Andrew's gratitude was eternal.

Andrew was given a sheet of paper showing where each of his classes were, as well as his locker number, padlock, and combination, and he was to report to his first class, geometry, immediately the same day. Once he was told this, his heart plummeted. He hoped that he'd have more time to spend with Kevin that day, and it was all he wanted to do since waking up that morning. It upset him far more than he thought it should have.

"I'll come pick you up as soon as you're done," vowed Kevin.

Andrew's mood sailed a bit higher. "I won't have to ride the bus?"

Following a snort, he said, "I only live a block away, and I work at home."

Now he had quite a bit to look forward to once the school day was complete. "Cool."

"I'll see you in a few hours, okay? Try to relax. It'll be all right."

Andrew swept his sweating palms behind his back, but it was too late; Kevin already sensed his anxiety. "I... I know. Thanks, Kevin. I'll see you soon."

After a fond farewell, Kevin vacated the school and returned to his car alone. Andrew went on a search for his locker, which his pink slip of paper declared was number 1656. It was at the end of the row, scratched, dented and neon blue in color. He didn't so much mind the hue; it was his favorite. What bothered him was how damaged the handle looked, or how rustic the edges were.

When he approached the locker door, he immediately noticed the leftover residue of stickers that had once been taped to it, ones that looked as though they once displayed radio stations. Andrew became momentarily preoccupied trying to peel off the leftover paper when someone popped open the locker beside him, startling him back to reality.

The young man at the locker beside him stopped what he was doing to gaze upon Andrew with surprise. "Whoa," he gasped. "Who are you?"

That was a good question, one even Andrew had trouble answering. "Andrew." He flicked sticker paper off of the end of his finger, but for a tiny piece of adhesive, it was damn stubborn. He brushed it against his shirt, fighting it off. His voice still hardly raised above a whisper, he said, "You?"

His locker neighbor held out his hand, which was attached to an arm covered in sandy brown hair. Each of his fingers were long and broad, an odd feature for such an average-sized man, though he was a few inches taller than Andrew. Andrew grasped his hand, his own frail and boney, and felt his knuckles crack as they were seized. "Ben," he informed, his square jaw lifting along with his cheekbones.

As soon as Ben released his hand, he tucked it out of view. He didn't mean to brush him off, but he wanted to check the inside of his locker to make sure nothing unsavory dwelled within it before he slipped his jacket inside. When he turned back to his locker and attempted to yank it open, Ben leaned back toward him.

"Are you new, or something?"

A powerful tug with his scrawny arms caused the door to fly open and at last come free from whatever it was stuck on. It jiggled and rattled, and Andrew grabbed it to silence it. "Yeah, I am," he said once he caught his breath, stripping his jacket off. "I just moved here yesterday."

"I'm sorry?"

Andrew couldn't tell whether he wanted him to repeat what he said, or if he was being sarcastic. "I said I just moved here yesterday."

"Oh." Ben nodded, taking a textbook off of the shelf inside of his locker. "You're kind of quiet, you know."

Shrugging an apology, Andrew shut his locker door, looking once again at the sheet of paper listing his classes, and hoped that he and Ben would say nothing else to each other. As he turned away, he heard Ben call to him.

"I really love your style!"

Andrew's style wasn't uncommon amongst teenagers. His dark clothes were matched by leather bracelets and a pair of silver ear spikes, and beneath his T-shirt, one emblazoned with artwork from an album cover pronouncing the name "Drone Diode" sprawled across the top, was one stitched of fishnet that squeezed along his skinny arms, which lacked any sufficient muscles.

Regardless of how long his hair had gotten, and how blinded he was, Andrew kept it hanging in his eyes. In the beginning, this wasn't a style choice, but merely because he was too nonchalant to cut it. His mother began to nag him, telling him he looked too much like a punk, and warned him how he kept people away with how he dressed and behaved. Andrew explained several times that he didn't want anyone to come near him, so he was hopeful that it had such an effect. Star wouldn't see it his way, no matter what he said or did. He decided to keep his hair long in the front just to spite her, and even went so far as to chop the rest of it shorter to emphasize it.

It was when he started wearing black lipstick and dark eyeliner that his mother drew the line, and even David stepped in with his strong, however monotone opinion. He would preach that Andrew was going to school, not "a god damned rave." Andrew would have preferred going to a rave any day, with or without the consumption of toxic substances. Hell, he would have preferred going into a sewer if it meant leaving home.

"Uh... thanks." Having never been in the school before, Andrew had no idea what direction to go in to find his first class. The north hall was lined with classrooms labeled with the letter D followed by two digits. The south was the C wing, and the numbers descended. Andrew's geometry class was, according to the sheet, in a room starting with F.

When he scratched the back of his neck in bewilderment, he captured the attention of Ben, whose eyes never abandoned his sense of fashion. "What are you looking for? I might be able to help you out."

He didn't know whether or not he wanted Ben's help, or anyone else's for that matter. "My geometry class. It's in room F-14."

"The F rooms are downstairs. I can show you where."

"Sure," he agreed, cramming his hands deep into the pockets of his black hip-hugging jeans. Ben swung a backpack onto his shoulder, waved for Andrew to follow, then led him to the stairwell. While they went down the staircase, Ben struck up some friendly chitchat.

"You like Drone Diode, huh?"

Andrew peered down at the T-shirt he had on. Star had washed and dried it enough to shrink it a size, and to cause some of the print to wear off. Still, the name of the band remained bold. "Oh. Yeah. I love them." That was an understatement. Drone Diode happened to be more than just Andrew's favorite band. He practically worshipped them and everything about them, from their playing style, to the members, and followed every one of their albums regardless of the musical territory they ventured into. Even when they added the synthesizer, Andrew still praised them like a number one fan ought to, though he preferred their older work.

"Me too!" exclaimed Ben, walking Andrew down the corridor of the school's lower level. "I was a big fan of Terminatrix for a while, but then I heard Diode, and they're so much better. You ever see them in concert?"

"Nah. My mother wouldn't let me."

Empathetic, Ben nodded at this. "I know your pain. I wish I could go. My parents never let me, either. I'm eighteen now, though. Sure, I live under their roof, and they make the rules, but they can't stop me if a show comes into town." He paused, gritting his teeth. "Unless… I needed them to buy me tickets. Then I'd be screwed, I think."

Somewhat amused, he dictated, "Even when we're old enough to think for ourselves, they never stop seeing us as their babies. I guess they kind of have to. It's nature, and all that."

"If I want to get my jaw broken in a mosh pit, that's my damn business, know what I mean?"

He nodded. "I do." Andrew looked at the door to the classroom he was meant to go into. "I should… get in there."

"Right." Now disappointed, he moved aside to allow Andrew through. "We'll see each other at the lockers again."

"Yeah. I guess we will." He turned his back on him before they could speak any further.

Andrew's classes consisted of the subjects mandatory to carry on from where he was last schooled. While he excelled at math and science, he didn't do as well in social studies or anything involving physical activity. He loathed his gym class above all others, but he was forced to retake it due to a previous failing. This time around, he had no choice but to pass it, or get held back. That meant jogging for a mile, lifting weights that he was barely strong enough to hold, and swimming, which he felt seemed more challenging to him than it was to his peers. Regardless of how habituated he thought he was of running around for miles, he couldn't come out of it without wheezing and coughing. If he had a wish granted upon him, he'd ask not to be so weak. That, and to be able to breathe underwater.

His final class of the day was photography, and his teacher was a charming and welcoming man that was ecstatic at Andrew's interest in the subject.

"Do you have a camera, Andrew?" he asked after the other students prepared theirs for a session on learning how to process film.

"Not with me," he informed. His camera, aged and shabby but still sentimental, was left behind at Star's house. There was little he could do with it today with the newest digital technology, but it had become like a friend to him with how much time he spent using it. For the lack of companions he had, his camera filled the vacant space in his heart, and behind the lens was a great place to hide from things that disturbed him.

"Well, that's all right," the teacher chimed. "I'll partner you up with someone for now. Will you be able to bring a camera tomorrow?"

"I don't know for sure. I'll try."

His teacher, Mister Benson, nodded, then approached a young woman's desk, a girl Andrew overheard was named Sarah, a towering, sturdy young woman with a rounded face and violet eyeliner, which matched her burgundy lip gloss. Independence sparkled in her jade eyes. When told she'd have to partner up with Andrew, she muttered something to the girls sitting near her. The words "emo kid" were whispered with giggles. Andrew's head sank.

Sarah joined Andrew at the desk beside him, not bothering to give him a courtesy glance. Andrew grumbled, "Didn't know this class was patrolled by the Fashion Police."

Caught by surprise, Sarah peeked at him before setting her bag down beside her desk. "Huh? What are you talking about?" Her buddies shielded their mouths to prevent giggles from seeping out, which Andrew glared at.

"Nothing," he grunted, knowing it was useless. Regardless, his blood boiled over like chili in a pot too small to contain it, his face burning.

For the duration of the class, Sarah and Andrew worked together, whether or not they wanted to, and Sarah's demeanor was all too condescending for Andrew to handle. As he was adapted, he endured it until it was over. He would learn something new from the class, and that was the most important thing to him.

Nearing the end, he wasn't listening to Sarah chat about romantic vampire fiction anymore, but was watching the clock. He counted each and every second as it ticked by, his impatient leg bouncing up and down, his knee rattling his desk. He wondered now if Kevin really would be waiting for him outside. It would be refreshing to see him after the long day, to spend time with him, to talk to him, to play games with him. To do anything with him.

Kevin was the only person he wanted to see, the only one he wanted to speak to. Seventeen years was a long enough time to wait. The next five minutes might have well have been an additional lifetime.

Time crawled by, each moment longer than the last. He drummed his fingers on the desk to a tune he made up in his head earlier. He thought of home, the one he wished for when he was young, the one his father welcomed him into. Home was where his guitar was. It was where that massive collection of games was. The fridge was where the leftover pizza was stored. Unexpectedly, he was very hungry for it. He would share some with Kevin this time around and not eat so much like a bird. He just had one more minute to wait, and he could go back to Kevin's house.

The buzzing tone sounded, announcing the end of the day. Andrew rocketed from his desk and was the first one out of the room. He paid no mind to what Sarah and her pals might have been exchanging. All that mattered now was leaving the building.

When Andrew jogged first for his locker to grab his jacket, then for the exit, he didn't realize he had. His legs had a mind of their own, and they guided him toward freedom as fast as the crowded hallway would allow. He might have bumped into a student or two, but didn't have time for apologies.

The winds outside were harsh, but Andrew fought against them, his eyes stinging from the brisk breeze and sunlight. His vision was blocked by the row of buses lined up at the curb, by the crowd of students boarding them, and the many passing cars leaving the parking lot. Through the gap in between two of the buses, he saw it: the sleek, black sports car, parked near the rear of the lot. Kevin was standing outside of it, leaning his back against the driver's side door, checking his watch.

Andrew slipped between the buses, darting through traffic. Tires screeched as a car stopped inches away from him, causing Andrew to almost choke on his own heart after it leapt up his windpipe. A horn bleated at him, and he raised a contrite palm to the driver, a fellow senior student who flipped him off before speeding away as soon as it was clear. If a rock was in sight, he'd consider throwing it at him, despite the blame laying on no one else's shoulders but his own.

When he turned to Kevin again, he was granted the sight of Kevin's fearful eyes stretched, his mouth hanging open. Andrew's pale face brightened as he shuffled up to him, half-smirking and rubbing his neck. He didn't reach the car before his father darted over to him, his shiny, pricey shoes sloshing through a shallow puddle on the way, one he seemed not to notice nor care about.

"Are you okay?" he blurted to Andrew, frantic.

"Yeah," Andrew mumbled with a feigned laugh.

"Be careful, all right? I just got you. I can't lose you already."

Something about these words, no matter how simple they were, swelled Andrew's heart, which he thought was impossible at this stage in his life. "I will." When Kevin looked him over, giving him a cursory inspection for wounds, he smiled. "I'm fine. Really. He didn't hit me."

"He almost did." Andrew turned his eyes and slouched, then bit down on his lower lip. "It's all right. Don't sweat it. I'm just glad you're okay." He then waved for him to get into the car.

Climbing in, Andrew responded, "I'll watch where I'm going from now on. I'm sorry, Kevin." Kevin hopped into the driver's seat, letting him know all was well, that he wasn't angry, and started the engine, which purred as it came to life. Before switching gears, he looked at his son, whose eyes were locked onto him. For a moment, neither of them spoke to each other, and Andrew grew tense at the uncomfortable silence. An aroma of cologne, or perhaps aftershave, filled his lungs, and the longer he breathed it in, the more potent it became. It was the perfect blend of spice and sweetness, and mixed well with the car's air freshener, which was scented citrus. Kevin's slick, black hair was damp and combed to the side, his dark button-down shirt ironed and snug-fitting around his athletic torso, and if Andrew had anything to say about it, he'd admit the look was striking on him. A little too striking, perhaps. This notion would never have come into his head the day before, and he wondered where it came from.

"Seatbelt?" Kevin hinted, amused.

Andrew didn't notice that time had passed since he sat down and looked at his father until Kevin spoke to him. He grabbed the belt and pulled it down into the buckle, snapping it into place. "Sorry," he whispered. *I have no idea what's come over me. For a second, you looked…* looked what, exactly? Whatever conclusion he came to, it would not be an appropriate one.

"All right. Let's go home." Andrew smiled inside, where a warm, fuzzy feeling expanded, when hearing it called "home". "How was your day?"

That question had never been asked under his mother's roof, and it felt surreal being asked it now. "It was okay, I guess."

"Did you meet anyone new?"

"There's some kid named Ben with a locker next to mine. We like the same music."

"That's neat. Maybe you'll end up being friends."

Telling Kevin "I don't know if I want any friends" would have been a lie, despite it being the first thought that ran through his troubled mind. He liked being social as long as he got along with the person, but he rarely found anyone that he related with. He longed for friendship, but the task of finding a person willing to stand him was taxing. "Maybe."

"I got you a new backpack. I noticed you didn't have one this morning."

Floored, Andrew said, "You didn't have to do that."

"I think I did. You don't need to be carting your books around in your arms. That's got to be uncomfortable."

"Okay," Andrew confirmed, giving in. "I needed one. Thanks, Kevin. You're really nice."

"That's my middle name," he stated with pride, then his smile turned lopsided. "Actually, it's Alan."

Each time Kevin looked at him, even for a brief second, Andrew's blood heated a few degrees warmer. It was such a minute amount of attention, but it was the kind he needed from a close relative. "I like your name." Did he mean to say that? It felt so involuntary.

"Thank you. I must also say that your mother chose a good name for you."

Home at last, Andrew walked alongside Kevin into the house, taking his shoes off at the door. Kevin expressed his gratitude toward his consideration.

"Any homework?" he asked, his tone serious now.

"Not today." It was an honest answer. Having received the chance at a better life, he didn't want to screw it up with his indifference. This time around, if he had homework, he would do it. He would pass his classes to the best of his ability and get the hell out of there. "But my photography teacher wants me to get a camera. I left my old one at Mom's."

A swift moment passed as Kevin thought on it. "I'll get you one."

"No." When this word slipped out of his mouth, he didn't think it would sadden Kevin so much. "I could earn one, maybe work for it."

"What? Are you serious?"

What kind of question was that? When was he ever not serious?

"Yeah."

"Andrew, don't be silly. I'd be more than happy to get you anything you need."

"But… but, I…"

Kevin shook his head. "Don't worry about it. Let me take care of it."

"Kevin," Andrew sighed. "It doesn't feel right."

"What doesn't? That I'm trying really hard to be a good parent? I could have given you a decent life this whole time, and I can only now offer it to you. I want my son to live happily. Is there something wrong with that?"

"That's not it. I'm happy you care about me. In fact, I feel great about it. I just want things to be fair. We only just met, and…"

Kevin released a lighthearted laugh. "Andrew, it's not a big deal! It would make me happy!"

"Okay. I'm sorry. I just don't know how to thank you. I feel bad that I can't give you something back."

"No one said you *had* to give me anything back," eased Kevin with a feathered voice.

"It doesn't need to be said."

"Would a hug be good enough?"

At hearing these words, Andrew lifted his head. Digging his teeth into his bottom lip, he nodded. Kevin stepped up to him and pulled him against his chest, and his warm arms draped around him, giving him a tender squeeze. Andrew felt something for the first time in his life: security. The eternal peacefulness brought his eyes to a close as he turned his head to rest his cheek against his pulsing heartbeat, and his arms encompassed his waist. This was what he needed, above all else, and he had been waiting a lifetime for it. Kevin's embrace provided more than serenity, but showed him that people, no matter how he feared and judged them, were still capable of compassion. It gave him hope. Things could get better. His life could improve.

They stood there like that for half a minute, gripping each other like life itself depended on it, saying nothing and never budging. If Andrew so desired, he'd fall asleep there, even while standing. The moment was spoiled by the sound of a ringing phone buzzing in Kevin's pocket.

"Sorry, Andrew," Kevin said, his arms drifting away from him, though it proved difficult for him. Andrew almost begged him not to release him. "I should get that."

Andrew let an unintended sigh flow from his nose. "Okay." Before he could ask how long he would be, Kevin was out of the room, chattering away. That's when his stomach rumbled. Though Kevin had given him cash for his lunch that day, he ended up skipping it due to a lack of appetite. Annoyed by the sting of hunger, he hunted for a snack in the fridge. He discovered the apples in the fruit drawer and munched on one while Kevin tended to his phone call. Whoever was on the other end of the line seemed to not only capture all of Kevin's attention, but also must have been a hell of a wisecracker. Andrew couldn't help but succumb to a sense of isolation, an emotion somewhat shocking for someone who did everything in their power to detach himself from the rest of the world. He suffered through a day of school, and now was *his* time with his father. The caller couldn't wait until tomorrow?

Though he wanted to, Andrew couldn't finish the apple, which despite not being a Granny Smith, tasted awfully sour. He took it to the plastic garbage bin, opening the top by pressing his foot onto a pedal on the bottom, but before tossing the half-finished fruit inside of it, he stared at what he found inside: a full bag of peanuts, one of which had never been opened, and a jar of peanut butter. At the sight of these abandoned, discarded objects, he could only freeze and gape at them in wonderment for some time. After dropping the apple into the bin upon the rest of the garbage within it, he followed Kevin into the living room, where he paced and repeated the words, "No, I'm not kidding" to his caller for the third time.

Just as Andrew took a breath, Kevin said his farewells to the caller and hung up, then faced his son, whom he was surprised to see standing before him. Detecting Andrew's melancholy mood as well as a weather radar predicts storms, Kevin asked, "What's wrong?"

"You didn't have to throw all the peanuts away."

A sigh seeped out of his nostrils, and he pocketed his smartphone. Andrew feared that he might be angry, but his smile said otherwise. "Yes I did."

"I would have been okay with them in the house. I just can't eat them."

"It doesn't matter. I shouldn't have them here if you're allergic."

The very idea that someone would sacrifice something for his sake was a confounding one, and it was a point he thought should be argued. "This is your house. If you want to eat peanuts, eat peanuts."

"This is *our* house. I don't even like them that much. I bought them because I was going to cook something with them, but decided not to. Don't make such a fuss over it. I won't miss them."

He had to take his word for it, and if the two of them were to live under the same roof, he had to start trusting him. "If you're sure."

"Believe me. It's all right." All Andrew wanted to do now was hug him again to show his appreciation for his respect. "That was my friend, Kyle," Kevin explained to Andrew when there was a lull in the conversation. "I told him all about you, and he's coming over to meet you. He's really excited."

Meeting new people so soon? He just got home, and already had to go through the painful process of introducing himself to someone else. "Is he… nice?"

"When he's not drunk," laughed Kevin. Then, after Andrew frowned, he said, "Kyle's been with me since we were kids. Throughout every hardship I had to face, Kyle was there for me. I probably wouldn't be the same without him."

"Sounds like you guys are close."

"We are. We're very close." Andrew stuck his lip out and nodded to an unheard beat. "It should only take him a minute to get here. Feel free to relax for a while until then."

Relaxing was something he could have done prior to discovering that a visitor would be intrusive on the time he hoped to use to get to know Kevin better. All he wanted to do for the rest of the night was settle down in that cozy TV room surrounded by low ambient light and the sound of Kevin's laughter. He had been looking forward to it since he woke up that morning.

On the other hand, if meeting this guy was something that would make Kevin happy, he'd do it whether he liked it or not.

CHAPTER THREE

In Which Strands Begin to Show

There were a few things that Andrew liked right away about Kyle. The first was his abundance of facial piercings. If he hadn't feared needles so much, he'd also have ones in his eyebrows and lip the way he did. It was the kind of rugged appearance he always wanted, but was never brave enough to acquire. The only holes he managed to get punched into his own face were the ones in his ears, and those didn't require as much courage to obtain as a needle through the brow would.

What he also liked was his dark goatee and unkempt, trimmed chestnut hair. For someone with so many piercings, it was a look well-suited for him. His decal T-shirt hung off of him like moth-ridden drapery and his blue jeans required a snug belt just to keep them on his hips. Andrew could have sworn that an aroma of burnt plants followed him around.

What he didn't approve of, however, was the attitude he carried. He had a habit of cracking jokes, sarcastic ones at Kevin's expense, even if he was the only one that laughed at them. Each time he mocked his father with a witty remark, Andrew wanted to tell him off, but Kevin didn't seem as bothered by it as he was. Perhaps, Andrew considered, he was familiarized with Kyle's behavior, having spent so much time with him.

On the other hand, Kevin sounded fed up with his friend for

supplying Star with his address without his permission. "I don't really want every Tom, Dick and Mary to know where I live, if you don't mind," he scolded. "There's a reason I'm not in the phone book. What if a crazed fan wanted my address in exchange for a steak dinner and bag of weed? Would you give it to them, too?"

"Okay, I shouldn't have done that," Kyle told his long-term companion after taking a swig from a bottle of wheat ale. "But aren't you glad I did? Sure, you had to see her again, but you got something much nicer out of the whole thing."

Kevin knew that if he was ever dying from thirst, Kyle could sweet-talk him into drinking the nastiest, muddiest water he would never touch otherwise. He didn't begrudge his friend this talent, but rather cherished it. Sometimes he needed a "designated thinker" on board. "I suppose you're right about that."

"And what a nice surprise it was!" He raised his bottle in toast to no one in particular before finishing it off.

Kevin sighed at the sound of a belch Kyle fired off, then sat down on the couch. It didn't take more than a minute for Andrew to take the seat next to him. As Kevin turned to face him, he uttered, "Andrew, Kyle is your mother's cousin."

A shade of green painted Andrew's cheeks at the knowledge that he and this smartass were related. He turned to Kyle and inquired, "If your Mom's cousin… did you know about me this whole time?"

Kyle, who had been smiling before, looked around the room, his lips pursed as he swayed his head in a robotic fashion. "No. No, I didn't."

"She never once mentioned me to you?"

"No! She didn't!" Under the probing stare of both Kevin and Andrew, Kyle's forehead perspired. "After high school, we didn't exactly keep in touch. She just sort of disappeared on me. When I heard from her yesterday, I was shocked, really shocked." Andrew seemed to accept it, but Kevin hadn't taken his eyes off of him. He swallowed, then smacked his lips. "Honest, Kev. I didn't know."

Kevin gave his friend a look, one that Andrew recognized as "we'll talk about this later." "Anyway… that's how I met your mother," Kevin continued. "Through him. He sort of coerced me into dating her."

"*Coerced* you?" reiterated Andrew, looking to Kyle for clearer answers.

"Kev, come on, that's not fair," interjected Kyle with a folded brow. "I didn't put a gun to your head. I certainly didn't know any of *this* would happen."

While scratching his freshly-shaven chin, Kevin announced, "Your mother and I weren't together very long. At the most, it was two months or so. Maybe not even that. I know this isn't the greatest way to find out, but neither of us were truly interested in one another. We were pressured, I guess you could say, by our friends. It was just something we felt we had to do, despite knowing it wouldn't work out in the end."

Andrew reassured him, "I already knew that. Mom didn't keep it a secret that she thought you were... well, that you didn't like each other much."

This wasn't a surprise to Kevin; in fact, he expected it. However, the very idea that Star might have soiled Andrew's opinion of him before they even had the chance to meet intimidated him. "What'd she tell you about me?"

Andrew's voice dropped a notch. "I... I can't even remember half of the things she used to say." It was a lie, of course. Star's opinion of Andrew varied depending on her mood, but she never ceased to talk him out of his desire to meet his biological father by giving him an assortment of negative labels, none of which he would dare repeat to the face of the man he had come to respect.

"It's okay, Andrew," Kevin eased, even-tempered. "It's not as though I have many good things to say about her, either."

He turned toward the window then, not wanting to look his father in the eye as he spoke these words: "She told me you cheated." What he chose to leave out in this admission was that he believed her.

"Cheated at what?"

"On tests."

"Let me guess. On my literature tests?"

"As a matter of fact... yeah."

"What else did she tell you?"

Feeling threatened, Andrew decided it might be best to back down before he was cornered. The look Kevin gave him, however, was a consoling one. He relaxed in no time. "That you didn't deserve the A you got in that class."

Once Kevin folded his hands together and crossed his ankle over his knee, he leaned back in his seat and breathed deep through his nostrils. To Andrew, his pose looked fancy, but uncomfortable, and he was correct in this assumption. "Did she say why?"

Star did tell him why, but Andrew never thought it was incriminating. Seventeen years was a long time to redeem one's mistakes, and Kevin had become successful on his own terms by now. What he did in the past mattered little to nothing as far as Andrew was concerned. "Yes."

"And?"

"Kevin…" Andrew sighed, his shoulders tensing and his head drooping. "I don't care if it's true or not."

He tried to calm Andrew with a smile, but could see the attempt failing. "She told you about my teacher, didn't she?"

Why couldn't he just drop it? He already liked Kevin. He didn't need him to prove that everything was on the up-and-up. "Y-yeah. But it doesn't matter. Really."

Touched, he told him, "You're sweet. You don't have to placate me. I know she told you I slept with my teacher to pass the class."

"She did tell me that."

"I don't blame you if you believed her." At this point, it was too late to back away from the conversation, though Kyle had already chosen to do so. It was out there now, in the open, exposed for everyone to see. The elephant standing in the corner could now take a much-needed break. "If you wish to know the truth… I *did* sleep with my teacher."

Andrew had to admit that he did not see that coming. If it had been true, what else was his mother right about? "It's none of my business, Kevin."

"It would mean a lot to me if I could explain everything to you."

If Kevin wanted to address it, Andrew wouldn't stop him if it made him feel better. He was curious, after all. Regardless of what words came from his father's mouth, his mind would be incapable of changing its view.

After Andrew nodded his approval, Kevin carried on. "I might have received a passing grade in that class that I didn't earn, Andrew, it's true. But it wasn't the grade I cared about. It was his choice to give me an A. I didn't ask for it. In fact, I tried to talk him out of giving it to me."

Andrew had already been giving Kevin his full attention, but now he was all ears. It could have been that he misheard him when he mentioned that his teacher was male, but he doubted he would make such a mistake. "Why did he?"

The uptight pose Kevin had locked himself into slackened, and he slouched. "It was a gift of mercy, I suppose. For breaking up with me."

"You dated?"

"Shortly after your mother broke it off with me, yes. I think my first and only intimate time with Star was enough evidence she needed that I wasn't very good with women. I couldn't really keep it a secret at that point."

If Andrew had been a few years younger, this information would have shocked him, especially since his mother never mentioned it. "But why? Why did you want to keep it a secret anyway?"

At first, Kevin mistook Andrew's tone of voice to be hostile, but when he next looked him in the eye, he saw an enchanted curiosity there. "When I was your age, Andrew, I was afraid. My father was extremely homophobic. My mother wasn't, but I knew she'd see me differently than before. I tried to convince myself that I just chose to be attracted to guys, and I could change if I wanted to. I didn't want my parents to hate me. As little as my father showed me kindness, I still loved him."

He wanted to tell Kevin that he knew how he felt, but it didn't need to be said. He was certain that his father was already well aware that they shared many of life's complexities. "You had sex with Mom to try to prove to yourself that you're not gay?" What a ludicrous concept. He could never imagine himself fucking a girl just for his mother's approval.

"I'm so sorry," Kevin said to his son through a clenched throat. "I'm happy to have you, Andrew, but I should have dealt with the situation like an adult. Had I known what would result… Christ, I was so selfish, and so insecure. I should never have done something like that. I made a mistake and you ended up in a very unfair situation because of me. It was you who paid the price for my irresponsibility."

"Don't say that," Andrew countered. "It makes it sound like you regret it."

"I don't regret *you*. I regret the awful choices I made. I wish I could have been there for you when you were growing up. If I had known the truth, I wouldn't have run away from it."

"You were there. You were always there. You just didn't know it."

Kevin and Andrew each shared a touched silence, and neither one of them required to define their innermost, deepest appreciation, to express just how satisfied they were with one another's honesty. It seemed, despite the unordinary way they met, that they had already grasped just how much they completed each other's lives, with or without Kevin's parental guidance during Andrew's development.

"I'm going to get another beer," Kyle told them, leaving them alone for the time being, escaping the awkwardness.

Neither of them heard Kyle, or rather, they chose not to. "I was in love with my teacher," Kevin explicated, doing his best to hide any traces of sorrow. "I was a stupid kid, living in a stupid fantasy. I should have known better than to assume it would work out."

Andrew scooted a few centimeters closer to his father, whose skin radiated warmth even at a distance. "What was his name?"

He swallowed. "Damian."

"Are you okay?"

"Yeah, I'm fine. It's not like I miss him. I'm just ashamed of myself, is all."

Andrew wet his lips, which had cracked by now. "We don't have to talk about it. I don't want to upset you."

"I'm not upset. I want you to know everything." He unfolded his hands and tucked them under his arms. "Damian became fearful of losing his job. He was taking a big risk dating me. I was an adult, but it was still against the rules. He almost got caught, and it would have been my fault." As he told his tale, he moved his index finger back and forth over his right eyebrow with his eyes closed. It bothered Andrew in ways that even his screaming mother didn't. "Funny. In the end, I wasn't mad at him. If word had gotten out, it wouldn't have looked good for him at all. I could tell it was a last resort option for him, leaving me like that. When he saw me break down crying, he told me how sorry he was, that he didn't want to hurt me, but he had to. I didn't hate him. It's just the way things had to be."

Picturing Kevin curled up in another man's arms sobbing his heart out injured his soul. If he ever caught someone hurting him like that, there was no telling how violent he'd get. "I'm sorry."

Despite how wet his eyes looked, Kevin grinned at his son and gave him a loving pat on the arm. "I have a good life," he told the room with confidence. "I don't need a man in it. Besides, I ended up with something better. And I couldn't be more proud of the way he turned out."

Proud. Now there was a word Andrew never heard a parent say to him. It felt greater than winning the local spelling bee he participated in during the third grade, one of his only achievements acknowledged by Star. "I've had boyfriends, too," blurted Andrew, failing at the grace he tried to use in informing him of their similar preference in gender. Regardless of his blundering outburst, Kevin was still fascinated by this news.

"Really," he gasped.

"Yeah. We have more in common than I thought. Mom never told me, though. I don't know why."

"I'm sure she neglected to tell you many things."

"I don't doubt it."

With the same entranced expression Andrew had before, Kevin asked, "What were they like? Your boyfriends."

What could he say that best described them all in a nutshell? That they were Assholes? Douche bags? Self-centered pricks? "Not... nice." Good enough.

The grimace on Andrew's face told a more interesting tale than his words had. Kevin had to respond with a laugh, then added, "I see."

"The last one I had was about two months ago. He dumped me because he said I was 'too quiet'. It wasn't that I was quiet, I just never got a chance to talk because he never shut up."

Another boisterous laugh from Kevin, then, "His loss. It won't hit him until too late that he made a mistake."

Stephan might have already learned that lesson, Andrew surmised, when he super-glued the padlock on his locker. He got suspended, as well as screamed at by his mother, but it was worth it. After Stephan told him and his friends that he gave sloppy blow jobs, it was a softer punishment than he deserved. "You're nice to say that."

"Sometimes we let things go on for too long because of how attracted we are to a person. I believe your mother's attraction to me was the only reason she stuck around for longer than a week."

"I can see why she was." He slapped his hand over his mouth as a burning redness covered his face.

Kevin cooed, "Thank you, Andrew."

"I... I meant... from *Mom's* perspective... I can see why she'd..." He glowed brighter.

"It's all right. I'm flattered."

"I wasn't trying to be gross, or anything."

Kevin said nothing, only looked around the room, feigning distraction. To Andrew's relief, Kyle returned to the room to put an end to the humiliating moment, carrying his half-finished beer.

"Have you bored him yet, Kev?" he joked, passing a wink to Andrew.

"On the contrary," Kevin corrected. "My son and I are sharing some quality bonding time."

"Guess you haven't told him about your books, then."

"I'd like to read his books," Andrew stated, enunciating each word so that there was no mistaking them. He didn't need to look at Kevin to sense how pleased he was at hearing this.

"Sure, if you like clichés and predictable plot twists, right, Kev?" He snickered, but was the only one to do so.

"Are you always this rude to him?"

The head from Kyle's beer bloated his cheeks, and a drop of it dribbled down his chin while he stared at Andrew, who looked ready to rip his throat out. He swallowed what was in his mouth, then glanced off to one side. "I'm just teasing him, Andrew."

"Well, lay off of him. He obviously doesn't like it."

Taking a moment to knock the stud in his tongue against his bottom row of teeth, Kyle glimpsed at his friend, who was now grinning. "Got yourself a new bodyguard, eh?"

"Looks that way," confirmed Kevin as he looked to his son, beaming. "Doesn't it?"

When Kyle prepared to leave as nighttime descended, Andrew could finally relax and enjoy the rest of the evening. Before making his departure, however, Kyle pulled Kevin aside to speak to him in private for a conversation that Andrew perked his eavesdropping ears to.

First, Kyle asked, "We still on for this Saturday?" He didn't get a response until Kevin contemplated it along with a deep breath.

"I don't know. We'll see."

"You're not ditching me now, are you?"

"I'm sorry. It's not a good time. I have Andrew now, and…"

"So what? Bring him along."

Kevin whispered something else that Andrew couldn't made out, but when straining his ears enough, he thought he heard him say the words, "To an erotic art show?"

With a scoff, Kyle retorted, "It was just a suggestion. I'm happy for you and all, Kev. But I still want to see you."

"We'll have plenty of time together. This isn't goodbye." Then, all went quiet for at least a minute. Soon after their conversation ended, Kyle was on his way out, bidding his friend farewell, though Andrew wasn't granted the same courtesy.

Now that they were alone, Andrew and his father got to spend time together, the time he had been waiting all day for. Andrew offered Kevin assistance in the kitchen and helped him make dinner, all the while chatting with him and getting to know him. Andrew wasn't a good cook, nor did he intend to be, but if he could lend a hand in any way, he would. Though he misread a measurement and added too much cream to the sauce Kevin was trying to make, Kevin was forgiving. He even said the meal tasted better with Andrew's contribution. Andrew thought him a good liar— perhaps even a little too enthusiastic of one.

Andrew learned many things about Kevin that night: he ran on his treadmill in his spare time; he loved antiques of all kinds, ranging from old telephones to furniture; he cut the tags off of his shirts, no matter how much money he spent on them; lastly, the one thing Andrew adored the most if he were to choose, was how often he hummed and whistled his favorite songs, tunes that Andrew hadn't heard since he was at least seven years old. Kevin's mind was a busy one, but at least content.

Their time playing games together had to come to a close when the hour grew too late, and Kevin suggested that Andrew go to bed in order to get up in time for school. Andrew didn't want to say good night yet. He couldn't remember a time he enjoyed himself this much.

"Can we watch a movie?" he proposed to Kevin, still wide awake.

"I don't know," Kevin pondered while rubbing his smooth chin. "It's almost midnight. You shouldn't stay up on a school night."

"Please?" His bottom lip drooped outward, and at the sign of his wide puppy eyes, Kevin looked away from them, chortling.

"Aren't you a little old to be begging like that?" Andrew continued to pout, and he sighed. "Come on, it's already bad enough you're up this late."

As comfortable and snug as his bed was, it was lonely up there.

"I've stayed up later than this before, Kevin. I was still able to stay awake at school. I'll get enough sleep, I swear. I just really want to hang out some more."

Truth be told, Kevin also wanted to continue spending time with his son, but he knew that if he were going to take parenting seriously, he had to get his priorities, as well as Andrew's needs, properly sorted out. "Do you *promise* to go right to bed after the film is over?"

"Yes, yes, I swear." He placed his right hand over his chest to strengthen his oath.

Following some deliberation, Kevin folded. "All right. Go ahead and pick one out. A *short* one."

The film Andrew chose was a science-fiction action movie that he had already seen before. His father opined that it was one of his favorites, and was pleased with Andrew's decision. Andrew also enjoyed the movie, but he could hardly pay attention to it. All he could focus on was how far apart he and Kevin were sitting.

Something, a feeling that came at quite a surprise, made him want to scoot closer. It might have been Kevin's laugh he enjoyed, or the scent of his overpowering cologne, but whatever it was, it mystified him. Air didn't seem to want to enter lungs properly, nor did his throat wish to stay moistened. His eyes refused to wander anywhere but on Kevin's charming grin, on how happy he looked, how utterly enthralled he was at the time they spent together.

Every moment he was with him, he relished it, savored it as if it were their last. One day, his father might throw him out or give him away just as his mother did, and while he still had a glint of sincerity and kindness to him, he held onto it as tight as could. He had no inkling whatsoever of the consequences in doing so.

Is this what it's like to feel comfortable around someone? Andrew wondered, his heart expanding at the sound of Kevin's chuckling. *To know he wouldn't judge me, or laugh at me, or criticize my every flaw? I bet he wouldn't even yell or spit at me for not passing a class.*

Fifteen minutes of the film had passed, and Andrew no longer paid attention to it. It was Kevin that he focused on now; his face, his shoulders (which looked in dire need of massaging), his button-down shirt that looked way too tight, and the jeans he wore that also looked restricting. Andrew had to wonder how he could breathe when wearing such clothes, as stylish as it made him look. It seemed that style won over comfort every time in Kevin's case, not that Andrew could say he disapproved. His dark hair was combed, almost to excess, slick and smooth, like his broad jaw line. The dryness in Andrew's throat came back when observing his features, as did the sweating and the fluttering beat of his heart.

You like the way he looks, Andrew, he thought, which he then tried to deny. *Oh, you do. Don't try to pretend you don't. What's truth is truth, and by God are you ever telling the truth.*

Outrageous! Ridiculous! And yet, so difficult to refute. Sure, Kevin looked good to Andrew— looked very good, in fact— but Kevin's kindness didn't hurt either. Without his generosity, there might not be anything in his personality warranting an attraction of any type. It wasn't often someone treated him as an equal.

The movie reached the halfway mark, and Andrew still hadn't found the courage to move any closer to Kevin. In his heart, it felt right, but his mind had to strongly disagree, and not just because he was so used to getting struck down by a hand he wished would hold him. Kevin could only draw so many conclusions from their nearing proximity, and Andrew didn't want to push it beyond which was appropriate.

His eyes became too heavy to hold open much longer, and he ended up passing out before he could see the ending. Kevin noticed that he was no longer making comments on the disastrous dialogue, and glanced at his slumping form, seeing his head drooped down toward his chest, his hair draped over his eyes. He didn't want to wake him, but didn't want him sleeping on the couch when his bed was more comfortable.

"Andrew," he whispered, planting his palm on his shoulder, giving him a gentle shake.

"Mmm," Andrew mumbled, twitching his nose. Something tickled it. Likely the strands hair that he refused to cut.

"You should go to bed." Each word tipped towards laughter.

Bed? Wasn't he in bed already? One of his eyes cracked open, and he spotted Kevin there, leaning in close enough to where he could smell his breath, which carried the faint scent of mango juice and menthol. He felt the warmth of physical contact, of Kevin's hand on his shoulder, a touch so much more soft than what he was accustomed to.

"Shit," he whispered, then covered his eyes in embarrassment. "I mean... crap." Kevin seemed more amused than concerned about his strong language. "I'm sorry. Is the movie over?"

"I turned it off for now. We can finish it tomorrow."

"I'll go upstairs." Before he rose to his feet, he smiled at his father, who mirrored it. "I had fun, though."

"So did I."

Andrew staggered toward the stairs, with Kevin watching him to ensure he made it up to the second floor without toppling over. That evening, his sleep was free of nightmares for the first time in months.

At the buzzing of his alarm, Andrew was slow to roll out of his bed, and each subsequent task was done with half-open eyes. Following a hot shower and finding something clean and presentable to wear, he hurried downstairs to see if Kevin was awake, but didn't see him anywhere. On his walk to the pantry to find some cereal, he noticed something on the kitchen counter: a medium-sized box wrapped in navy blue paper with a bow on top, which taped down a greeting card. On the front of the envelope, the words "For my son, Andrew" were written in black ink.

Fresh springs threatened to well up in Andrew's bold, youthful eyes, incredulous at what they were witnessing. A gift? For him? What was the occasion? It wasn't his birthday, or Christmas. Mom wasn't around to hit him and then buy him something in hopes to aid him in forgetting what happened. There had to be a reason it was there, and a damned good one.

Soon he had forgotten all about breakfast as Kevin descended the stairs and entered the kitchen to join him. On his body were clothes in dark colors, a personal taste he and Andrew shared, like many other things they had come to discover. When Andrew turned toward him, it was with a shy smile and shrug of the shoulders.

Kevin greeted his son with fondness, making a mental note of how much cleaner and brighter he looked than the day before. Little did Kevin know, Andrew woke up early and took painstaking measures to make himself look better, including some thorough combing and shaving. Never would he think to fish for compliments from Kevin, but he wouldn't deny how elated he'd be at receiving one.

"This is for you," said Kevin, passing the gift to Andrew. Even though he took it from him, he could only clutch it and stare it down. "Go ahead and open it."

If he chose not to open it, he could hold onto it until a time of sadness, when he needed to be reminded that someone cared for him. It took some thought before he realized that he was no longer living in a shabby, loveless home. He had more to hold onto than just a gift.

Before tearing any of the tape on the sides of the paper that he refused to tear into, he opened the envelope first and removed the greeting card, which was covered in glitter and fancy artwork. On the front, scrawled in curls, was a declaration:

To my one and only son,
For every challenge you face
For every dream you achieve
For every day you wake up to
Know that there is someone who will always support you

Andrew couldn't cease the shaking of his hands, or the stuffing of his sinuses, as he opened the card to read the inner sleeve.

This isn't the best way to make up for all of the birthdays I missed, but it's a start! I hope that this will do you well not only in class, but in the future, when you become a professional photographer.
With hopes of being the best parent I can manage to be,
Kevin

Whatever marvel of a camera was inside of the wrapped box, Andrew felt that it couldn't have been much better than what was written in the card. Still, he proceeded to unwrapping, which took longer than it should have because of the caution he used, until the front image of the box was revealed: a high definition digital SLR camera with a three hundred millimeter telephoto zoom lens included. Gasping with joy, Andrew proceeded to take the camera out of its box.

The black shell shimmered in the kitchen's hanging lights, reflecting the sunbeams streaming through the patio window behind him. The surface had a bumpy texture, its many hulking buttons jutting out on the top and sides, begging to be pushed. The video screen could be flipped out for easier viewing, and even more buttons accompanied it, ones for zoom, focus, start and stop.

Andrew didn't require Kevin's confirmation to know that his gift was valued well over a thousand dollars. All he could think now was to lock it in a safe and never take it out where it could potentially be damaged. "What if it breaks? What if I do something…?"

"It came with insurance. It's fine, relax." Andrew didn't. He did, however, turn his soggy eyes away from Kevin's, doing his best to hide a sniffle.

"Please don't cry," Kevin implored, his exuberance taking a nosedive at the sight of Andrew's tears.

"I'm not sad," he reassured him, then swung his arms around his neck. Grateful for his affection, Kevin returned his embrace, his own just as snug and tight. "This is the best gift I've ever gotten. Second to meeting you, of course."

Smiling both on the inside and out, Kevin said, "I hope it's what you needed."

"It's more than that. Kevin… thank you. Thank you so much."

"You're very welcome, Andrew. Let me know if you need anything else, okay?"

How much more could he ask for? He had everything he ever wanted.

Well, almost everything.

For his lunch that day, Kevin assembled a turkey sandwich that Andrew requested, after first telling him that he preferred them over anything else, something that Kevin vowed not to forget. He'd make sure to buy more lunch meat when he went to the store that afternoon. Entering the school, Andrew had a new backpack swung onto his shoulder, a freshly-packed lunch inside of it, and the carrying case for his camera, which he shielded with his life.

Already at the locker beside his was Ben, who was unloading a few books from the shelves inside. Initially, Andrew said nothing to him, thinking he might not bother to strike up a conversation, but his face lit up as soon as he presented himself.

"Morning, Andrew," he welcomed.

Andrew, who surmised that Ben would have forgotten he had existed since the day before, couldn't believe that he remembered his name. "Oh. Hey. Ben, right?"

"That's me." After packing a book or two into his backpack, he swung the bag over his shoulder and shut his locker door. "No fishnet today?" A grin spilled onto his face.

"Guess not." Giving his locker door a couple of tugs, he struggled to yank it open.

"I thought it was pretty cool."

"Well, I…" With a resonant rattle, the door flew open after some effort, just missing Andrew's skull. He was grateful for his quick reflexes, since he wasn't interested in getting his face smashed before class. "I suppose I wanted to change things up a little." In truth, he thought his favored gothic wardrobe immature, and assumed Kevin would think the same. Kevin had never made any derogatory comment about it, but he didn't want to give him the chance.

Turning toward the hallway where he planned to walk, he gave Andrew one last glance. "Looks good," he complimented, still beaming. Andrew thanked him before also filling his backpack with books and placing his camera, lunch, and jacket inside of his locker. "Have a nice day, Andrew." Then, he strolled away.

"Ben. Wait a second."

He halted before Andrew even finished his request, turning toward him. "What's up?"

"I wanted to apologize to you."

"What for?"

Andrew eyed the floor, rocking his heel back and forth. "For yesterday. I think I was a little rude to you. I'm sorry about that."

A shrill tone sounded— the warning bell announcing that classes would soon begin. Ben straightened his posture, tucking a hand into the pocket of his khakis, leaning his head to the side. His short, sandy hair looked brighter than it did yesterday. "You don't have to be sorry. I didn't think you were being rude. You just don't seem to want to talk much." Andrew's head lowered further. "Nothing wrong with that. I like it. I can't stand when people are too chatty."

Continuing to twist his heel back and forth, he scratched his neck. His short hair in the back was starting to grow longer, reminding him that it needed trimming soon. "Yeah. I think I might know what you mean."

"What lunch hour do you have?"

Andrew had to look at his class schedule to double check. "Second?"

"Me too! You want to have lunch with me?"

He had to admit, it was better to sit with someone and listen to them talk than it was to sit alone, despite how much he enjoyed being on his own. As long as he wasn't mashed into a crowd of strangers, it would suffice. "Okay. Sure."

"I'll meet you at the round table in the back near the window. That one's always empty, so we could be alone and wouldn't be bothered, okay?"

"All right. Sounds cool."

"See you then!" There was a new skip in Ben's step as he strutted to his class.

There was the possibility that Ben did want to be his friend, and that there was nothing suspicious beyond that. To this day, Andrew fought against the persistent notion that everyone wanted to hurt him in some way, and longed to eliminate it. The only way he'd find true friends was to be more outgoing, to show that he had something worthwhile about his personality. If he wanted things to change, he had to make an effort.

Geometry was a class Andrew picked up not by choice, but by demand, and if he wanted to stop taking math classes forever, he had to pass this one and never take another. Sociology came afterward, and following that, history, which wouldn't be part of his schedule at all if he hadn't failed it before. Andrew would claim that the E he received hadn't been his fault, that his teacher assigned the most boring homework he had ever seen; so boring, in fact, that he sketched on it instead of filling it out. He had no rational explanation for his teacher when handing it in, only, "I thought you might like to look at drawings instead of answered questions." Unfortunately, Mister Murray would have rather seen completed work.

Come lunch time, Andrew had a healthy appetite, and looked forward to the food his father prepared for him. He didn't see Ben at the table yet, so he took a seat and ate while waiting for him. Intense flavors of all kinds danced upon his tongue, ones he had only sampled before at restaurants. Was that gourmet honey mustard? Cracked pepper? Fresh tomato? A small strip of turkey bacon? Quite frankly, he had never eaten a sandwich so tasty in his life.

Within the next ten minutes of Andrew indulging in the mouthwatering luncheon, Ben joined him, greeted him, and started snacking on a burger he bought from the cafeteria.

"I didn't think you'd actually sit with me," Ben admitted while chewing.

"Why wouldn't I?" He sipped on a bottle of low fat chocolate milk that was included with his meal.

Shifting his eyes back and forth, Ben muttered, "Oh, I don't know. I'm glad you did, though. I wanted to ask you some stuff." Andrew agreed to his game of Twenty Questions. "Where are you from? You said you moved here?"

"Staten Island. I grew up there, with my mom and step-dad. I live with my biological father now."

"Why the change?"

The milk Andrew nursed on didn't take long to vanish. He finished every last drop it had to offer before tossing it and the empty brown lunch bag into the trash. Now that it was gone, he wished he had more of it. He'd have to ask Kevin to give him two tomorrow. "My mom didn't want to put up with me anymore."

Ben laughed. Andrew didn't. "Oh. Are you serious, or…?"

"Yes."

"Yikes." For a moment, he stopped chewing his food. "I'm sorry. What happened?"

"We didn't get along. We never did. I guess it's just one of those things. Some parents don't get along with their kids."

Now that it seemed safe to do so, Ben took another bite out of his burger. "Did you know your dad before living with him?"

"Not personally. But when I met him, I felt like I had known him forever."

After dabbing his mouth with a napkin, Ben said, "Are you happier?"

"I am so far."

"That's good," Ben answered with a peppy nod. "You'll love Queens. It's crowded and a little noisy, but it's home. If you ever wanted someone to show you around, I could. I know the city like the back of my hand."

Andrew then asked through a soft chuckle, "What would you be showing me?"

"Well… lot's of stuff." He worked his molars, swirling his jaw around like a cranking gear that was about to break down, his gaze drifting from Andrew to the surface of the table, then out the window. "There's the, uh… globe fountain thing in Corona Park. It's pretty cool."

As *cool* as Globe Fountain Thing sounded, Andrew had to turn the proposal down. If it was one thing he learned since his many dispersing friendships, it was to let them grow over time. Never take any trips with anyone you don't know who might abandon you in places, forcing you to walk home or take a cab. If only he could say he hadn't been in that position before.

While he hid behind the curtain of black hair draped over his brow, he let Ben down easy. "I'm sorry. Maybe if you asked me another time, I'd feel more comfortable about that. Right now, I'm focused on settling in and getting to know my father."

"Right. Of course. And that's cool."

"It's kind of you to offer, though. I don't have any friends here yet."

"You do now." Despite his discomfort, the corner of Andrew's mouth raised in a half-smirk at his affirmation. Ben continued, "I hope you don't think that I was coming on kind of strong. I didn't intend to."

"No. Not at all."

A few more dabs with the napkin, and Ben tossed it and the rest of his garbage away in the trash bin. "And I hope I didn't just embarrass myself hitting on someone who isn't gay."

Ben had been hitting on him? How had he not caught on to that? He first blamed him for being too subtle, but then thought better of it, knowing his mind was on other things, as well as on other people. "No. I... I am. How'd you guess?"

Ben coughed. "I have exceptional gaydar."

That couldn't be it, Andrew felt. He must have noticed something. *Do I really 'act' gay? How does one even begin to do such a thing?*

"You okay?" Ben asked, snapping Andrew out his daze.

"Uh... yeah. I'm fine."

Carefully clearing his throat, Ben rested his hands on the table and crunched them together. "I'm going to be truthful, up front and honest with you, Andrew, because I never am with guys, and I always end up regretting it when I miss out on the chance." He first sucked in a massive amount of air in through his nose, then sighed out, "I think you're cute."

"O-oh." Warmth spread across Andrew's neck and cheeks, and he lowered his chin toward his collarbone. "Thank you."

The tone chimed over the loudspeakers. Lunch hour was over for them. Ben, disappointed, gathered his strength to leave the table.

"Guess we'll have to pick this back up tomorrow, won't we?"

"I suppose so."

When Ben dumped his trash out, Andrew did the same, and they each said their farewells. On his way to his next class, Ben's compliment stirred in his mind for some time, curious at how anyone could find him attractive. Anything was possible, he concluded.

An invasive thought poked around in his head: *I wonder if Kevin finds me cute.* Anxious of the implications, he swept it away before it could progress to more unhealthy, addictive notions, as he was prone to submit to.

Equipped with his own camera to bring to photography class, Andrew wasn't required to pair up with anyone to work on his assignment for the day. Getting a good look at his new tool of the trade, Sarah took a newfound interest in working with him. It took a while for him to come around after the previous day's interactions with her, but come to find out, she wasn't so bad. She apologized to him for her behavior the day before, as well as the attitude of her friends.

"This class is super hard to fail," she let him know with a touch of a sneer. "People take it all the time to get an easy passing grade, not because they care about photography. I thought maybe you were one of them. You didn't even have a camera with you and, honestly, you didn't look like much of a photographer."

Puzzled, he muttered, "How do photographers normally look?"

Sarah glanced at her gaggle of friends, who snickered when they saw her sitting with him. "It doesn't matter," she told him this time, ignoring her buddies. "You're here because you care. That's more than what I can say for... some people." She shot her girlfriends another look, curling her nose as though she was served a bowl of worm salad.

At the end of class, Mister Benson asked one final thing of his students: "I have a new assignment for you all. Now we get to the fun stuff. I want you to take pictures. Yes, imagine that, taking photos in photography class." His joke was followed by a quiet laugh from a few of his students. "I want you all to shoot something important to you, but you must convey with camera what it means to you. Keep in mind your lighting choices, whether or not you use zoom effects, the true mood, atmosphere and ambience of the moment. This is what you'll be graded on. It's due the week after

Thanksgiving break, so you have plenty of time."

The task seemed a simple one to Andrew, since there were few things in his life now that had such significance.

Over the course of the hour, Andrew and Sarah got to talking about their favorite types of photos, what they enjoyed shooting, and their plans for the upcoming assignment. At learning of how passionate Andrew was for taking pictures, she let him in on a helpful detail.

"I photograph for the yearbook, and I hear a lot of talk about the club that runs the school paper. If you want, I could help you get in." Then, she whispered, "Their current photographer *sucks.*"

"You'd do that for me?" replied a stunned Andrew.

"Sure. I'll talk to Missus Evans. She's the one that runs it."

"Would I have to stay after school?"

"Yeah, but not for long."

Though he was excited to utilize his talents in a fresh way, and to contribute to something other than his own self-pity, he didn't like the idea of spending more time away from home, or from Kevin. Regardless, he wouldn't pass up the opportunity. The extra-curricular credits wouldn't hurt, either.

With the ring of the final bell of the day, Andrew took his prompt exit, rushing to his locker to retrieve his belongings, including all he would need for homework. He didn't see Ben, but he was glad he hadn't. He wanted to get to Kevin, and didn't have time for embarrassing small talk. Pushing his way past the mass of students, he shoved his way out into the brisk autumn air.

Outside was his father, sitting inside of his black car, smoking a cigarette, which looked halfway burned down. Andrew's heart plummeted into his stomach at the sight of him smoking again, and didn't hide his displeasure when he approached the car with a grimace. When he opened the passenger side door, spiced cologne struck his nostrils, but so too did the sting of smog.

At the sight of Andrew, Kevin lowered the cigarette to a nearby ashtray and mashed it out. "Hey, there!" It didn't take long for him to notice his son's churlish frown, and his smile fell. "I know. I'm sorry, Andrew. I told myself, 'Just one today, Kevin. Just one', and then one turns into two and three, and..." Disapproving of his own actions, he mashed the cigarette harder into the tray attached to the dashboard, crushing it to dust.

"It's okay," Andrew calmed, seeing him become visibly agitated. "I'm not angry." Quoting Kevin from the day before, he stated, "I just got you. I don't want to lose you already."

"It's not okay. I should be trying harder." Once the cigarette turned to pulp from his stabbing and grinding, he cracked open the windows. "I'm going to throw them away when I get home, and I'm going to see my doctor about it."

"I'm sorry," a nervous Andrew stammered as he climbed into the passenger seat, worried he might have stirred up an oncoming storm. "I didn't mean to upset you. I know it's hard to quit."

"I'm not upset with you," Kevin told him, softer now. "I'm upset with me. I'm glad it bothers you. I'm glad I have a good reason to quit. Regardless of how hard it is to give it up, I don't *want* to smoke anymore. I do it because I feel like I have to. When I was living on my own, it was a different situation. Now that I have you to care for, I shouldn't be so willing to die, and polluting your air in the process. No. I'm quitting. For good this time."

Moved by his pledge, Andrew swore, "I'll help you. Just tell me what I need to do, and I'll do it."

Kevin's smile said a thousand words, but he could only think of a handful of them to respond with. "You help me when you show that you care. And I can see that you do."

Once they were home, Andrew shared with Kevin all about his day, how he made friends in unexpected places and how he might soon be working on the school paper. Kevin told him what a great idea it was for him to work on something to get his mind off of his stress, and it would give him incentive to hone his skills. Andrew didn't state how disappointed he was at the idea of staying after school, wanting to spend as much time with Kevin as possible, but in his mind, it sounded clingy, and he knew that wasn't a personality trait that should be exposed.

"My photography teacher wants us to take photos of something really eye-catching," he told his father during dinner, which was a type of thick, saucy pasta that Andrew had never eaten before. Whatever it was, it tasted amazing.

"Oh? That sounds fun. What did you decide to shoot?"

A noodle he forgot to chew slid down his throat and he washed it down with water. Kevin's chewing slowed while he waited for him to answer. "Well... if it's okay... I wanted to take some of you."

"Of *me?*"

"Y-you're photogenic, I think."

"Really!"

Andrew's cheeks turned as red as the pasta sauce on his plate. "I mean… if you don't want me to, that's okay."

"No, no, no, I'd be happy to be the model for your project!"

"You… would?"

"Absolutely! I'm just…" Kevin placed his elbows on the table, then covered his pleased smirk with his hands. "Surprised you'd pick me for that. You flatter me."

Andrew's joints locked, and beads of sweat collected near the rims of his ears. "Don't take it the wrong way or anything."

"What's the 'wrong way'?"

Come on, Kevin, dwelled Andrew. *You know damn well what the 'wrong way' is. Or maybe you like to pretend not to.*

Still, Andrew couldn't bring himself to say it. The *wrong way* didn't seem so wrong to him anymore.

"Andrew, really," Kevin continued with a soft sigh. "I'd be honored to do it for you."

"Thanks, Kevin. It'll be fun to work with you." He told him he had until after Thanksgiving, so they could do it whenever Kevin was ready. Kevin said he'd like to look his best for the shoot, and not so exhausted.

They finished watching the science-fiction film after supper, but Kevin unfortunately let him know that he had work to do, despite wanting to dismiss it for time with Andrew. Andrew, disappointed, told him he understood, and took the opportunity to practice his guitar. Before long, he formed a tune, which he prepared to write lyrics for. As each of his fingers plucked and pulled at the strings, his stress melted away, all of his fears evaporating. It was more than an instrument for music, but an instrument of therapy, a tool that Andrew considered more useful than any modern commodity. He was one with himself, and it was the only time he could obtain complete and total peace of mind.

Now it had sunk in. This was home. He could be himself, and nothing more would be expected of him. He could just be Andrew.

CHAPTER FOUR

In Which an Extra Rung is Added

During the next couple of weeks that followed, and the days leading up to Thanksgiving break, Andrew and his camera became better acquainted— as did he and his father.

The school paper was a small, unimportant project compared to working for an actual newspaper, but Andrew didn't mind that. After all, his job wasn't to do any of the writing. He was told what things to shoot, and he photographed what he was assigned. The school's football team seemed bewildered to see a skeletal young man dressed in all black watching them with a camera from the bleachers. Their snickering didn't deter him, though it was tough to ignore.

Still, the club working on the paper thanked him for the shots, and told him they were perfect for the article. Whatever article that was, Andrew didn't bother to ask. His day was long enough as it was, and he wanted to get home already.

Kevin, like he did every day, picked him up when he was done, and just like every day, Andrew was excited to see him. He would tell Kevin all about his day, from his classes to how well his camera was working for him, and Kevin never once interrupted him. Regardless of the topic, Kevin always listened, was attentive and responsive.

They formed a routine for their evenings, one without verbal acknowledgment, a practice that came as natural as their flawless conversations. Andrew would do his homework while Kevin prepared their dinner, they'd eat and chat, then play games, watch a movie or two, and, on the nights Andrew especially loved, they'd talk to each other for a couple of hours. Relationships tended to be a common subject during their discussions, though not on accident.

Every day had been the same as the last, until that Friday afternoon, when something happened that drew them closer and indefinitely secured the link that had come to tie them together. It began as soon as Kevin picked Andrew up from school and told him about an auction he won earlier that day for an antique he fell in love-at-first-sight with. Never in Andrew's life had he seen anyone filled with so much childish wonder at the prospect of owning something so old.

Not until Andrew arrived home with his father did he see the new addition to the house. At first glance, Andrew mistook it for a piano, and congratulated him on it. Kevin had himself a chuckle before correcting him.

"It's a harpsichord," he informed. "From the seventeenth century! Can you believe that? They said that an Italian opera was composed on it during the Baroque era. I couldn't let it go. It called to me, and I had to have it."

While walking around the aged instrument, Andrew scrutinized its wooden finish, its many keys, which had recently been cleaned of dust, and at the interior of the lid. All sides were painted, though faded over the length of time, with weaves and curls of silver wrapping and twisting around each other. The inside of the lid also displayed artwork: a bushel of multi-colored roses on the left, and a band of dancing skeletons encompassing a bonfire on the right. For such a brilliant piece of history, it brought with it a sense of despair and darkness that Andrew couldn't explain, and yet couldn't help but feel grip at his insides.

"It's gorgeous," he complimented, brushing his fingertips against the fine, wooden keys, mimicking a play style he himself could never accomplish. Regardless of its grim aura, he found it easy to connect with it.

"Isn't it? I thought you'd appreciate it. I admit that when bidding on it, I had you in mind."

"You got this for me?"

"I figured it would suit a musician." Andrew's warm, affectionate smile was all Kevin required to know how grateful he was. Giddy once again, Kevin cupped his muscled hands together. "I already know exactly where I want to put it. Andrew, would you be so kind as to help me move it into the basement?"

"Sure," Andrew confirmed, grabbing one end of the harpsichord, watchful of its pointed edges, as Kevin lifted the opposite end. Together, they hauled the antique down the basement stairs with care, taking it to Kevin's sanctuary for all things ancient, a glorious display of hundreds of items, all from another time. Though Andrew had seen it before, Kevin couldn't stop himself from repeating tales of their origins to Andrew, who regardless of hearing them ten or fifteen times, was just as enthralled as he was the first.

At Kevin's request, Andrew aided him in moving the harpsichord to the center of the room, where a black and gray rug was sprawled. He claimed that the harpsichord deserved to be the centerpiece, the main attraction, and Andrew had no arguments. It truly did hold the room together.

Upon setting it down once and for all on the soft rug, Andrew thought he had a better hold on it than he did, and the corner began to slip from his sweating palm. "Shit," he muttered under his breath, drawing Kevin's attention. Attempting to catch the instrument before it fell from his hands, he readjusted his grip to tighten it, only to cause the side of the instrument to slide downward out of his hands. Not only did he manage to drop the extravagant prize, the edge of the wood punished him for his mistake by slicing his palm open.

With a agonized groan, Andrew grabbed his hand while hissing inward and outward breaths. Kevin was then unconcerned with the state of the harpsichord, which after its revenge seemed well-satisfied sitting alone on the rug, though a fresh coat of blood now mixed with the paint job on the sides and top of the lid.

"Are you okay?" asked Kevin, coming to Andrew's side.

"Yeah," sighed Andrew while Kevin inspected his wound. Burning embers spread over his face as Kevin held his injured hand, succumbing to the strangest of tingles moving along his arm when Kevin's thumb coursed over the edge of his palm. "I've had worse."

"Still looks a bit on the nasty side. Come on." With Andrew's hand still in his own, he took him back up the stairs, Andrew following his every step in perfect synchronization. Where he took him next was the bathroom, and once inside, he popped open the medicine cabinet where he fished around for a first aid kit.

You really don't have to, Andrew thought to protest. *I'll be fine. You should have seen the gash I got falling out of a tree when I was nine.* But he didn't want to tell him to stop. In fact, he would make up injuries if it meant being tended to by him if he lacked the dignity to do so. Whatever Kevin wanted to do to help him, he allowed it, and then some.

First, Kevin asked Andrew to wash the cut in the sink, then after drying it, he applied antiseptic to it before lightly wrapping it with gauze. It was more than what was necessary, as Andrew would have simply settled for a adhesive bandage, but he also couldn't deny how enamored he was at Kevin's cautionary approach to his medical care.

"Good as new," Kevin announced when finished, giving Andrew's forearm a few loving pats.

For a moment, Andrew stared at Kevin's patch job, turning his hand around to see it on all sides. By now, the pain had seeped away, if there had been any to begin with. Then Andrew pressed his bandaged hand to his chest near his heart, but that alone couldn't express his gratitude.

"Thank you, Dad."

In the instant these words struck Kevin's ears, he had almost been knocked off of his feet. "Dad" was such a strange word to him. He and his own father were so detached that he had called him by his first name, thus he had accepted Andrew doing the same. Being addressed as the term had altered everything he knew about fathers and sons, and it was a change he had already learned to love.

With his emotions thoroughly stirred, Kevin patted Andrew again, only this time on the shoulder. "You're welcome, son." They shared a smile, as well as a serene moment of clarity.

Clearing his throat to kill the uncomfortable silence, Kevin reopened the medicine cabinet and placed the first aid kit back inside with Andrew watching his every move. With the door open, Andrew could see the contents scattered along the shelves: antacids, extra-strength headache relief (at least three bottles of it), and an abundance of cough drops and syrup. On the top shelf sat several prescription bottles that Andrew had to squint at to read. The labels were bolded with a brand name "Malanex"; an antidepressant.

Before Andrew could register what he laid eyes upon, Kevin shut the cabinet. "Any homework today?" Boy, was he ever crafty at changing the subject.

"Sociology."

"Need help?"

He didn't, but he enjoyed every minute they spent together. "I could use a little."

"All right. Well, I'll get dinner started." He made his way toward the door, but Andrew blocked his path. He strained out a broken chortle. "What's the matter?"

"Nothing, I just..." No words could convey his thoughts or feelings well enough. Instead, he draped his arms around Kevin's neck and clung to him as tight as he could manage. Though Kevin's face wasn't visible to him, felt it light up. He was engulfed with an embrace just as tight as the one he commenced by a strength and adulation foreign to him, but all too sweet to pass up.

No one's ever held me like he does, Andrew both delighted and worried over. *And I've never wanted it so badly.*

"I hope you're happy here, Andrew," said Kevin, continuing to clutch him to his collar.

"I've never been happier."

"Really? I'm so relieved to hear that."

"Could I help you make dinner?"

"Certainly!"

Once again, they returned to their routine, though this time they did so with the knowledge that they had made a home for one another, a place where they could both be happy, and no matter the task they carried out, it was with an unyielding devotion that was both a mystery to them and the answer to life they had spent their lives looking for.

On the last day before Thanksgiving break, Andrew had obsessed over his appearance, ever since Kevin complimented him on it. If he worked hard enough, he'd hear him say it again: "Well, don't you look good this morning?" He was grateful to him for noticing, as he had spent almost an hour preening and grooming.

That morning, he began with shaving his chin and jaw, running a comb through his long hair, and smacking some aftershave on his face. Following the procedure, he leaned over the counter and stared at his reflection with a now sinking stomach.

"What the hell are you doing?" he asked himself. "Look at yourself. Is he really going to care?"

His reflection, which sparkled only a second ago, nauseated him. Taking a second to question his bizarre behavior, he sat upon the closed lid of the toilet and clutched at chunks of his ebony hair. He could take all the time in the world to pretty himself up, but it all led to the same thing, something that even Andrew couldn't deny was wrong. No matter how hungry he was, how juicy it looked, how delicious it must have tasted, it was a fruit not meant to be picked.

Nevertheless, the craving to take a bite was too strong for him to fend off.

Regaining his composure, Andrew finished his grooming by brushing his teeth and dressing in tight, black clothes. Once Kevin told him he actually liked the intricate design of his fishnet shirt, he made a habit of wearing it again, underneath his T-shirts. In addition to the fishnet, he alternated various earrings he had available to him, most of them spiky and the length of claws. There's no way Kevin could go without commenting now. He had to say something.

Now ready to go, he raced down the stairs, hearing the coffee pot bubbling. Kevin was sitting at the counter on one of the barstools, eating toast and reading the Elliott High School paper, looking through Andrew's many photographs. Kevin greeted him like he always did— with a joyful, "Good morning, Andrew!" Never did Andrew grow tired of that lovely voice.

After telling his father good morning, he leaned on the counter. Kevin was preoccupied staring at the paper, and Andrew thought he might look at him if he drummed his fingers. He did not. "You see my photos?" he asked Kevin, placing his arms on the counter and sticking his rear out as he leaned forward.

"Yeah, they're terrific! You're very talented."

What a wonderful buzz Andrew received then. Kevin thought he was *talented*. "Thanks." He pointed to one photo in particular of three girls smiling while standing in the hallway next to Student of the Month plaques. "This one's crooked."

"I didn't notice," Kevin chuckled. "It looks perfect to me."

"It's definitely not."

"Oh, hush. It's fine." He folded the paper up, and Andrew's blood electrified. Soon, he would look; he would notice his handiwork. "You hungry? We've got time to have a balanced breakfast."

Is he going to look, or not? Andrew's boney arms grew sore at leaning them on the counter's surface.

"Actually, I'm not really that hungry," he responded. "I just want to get school over with, you know?"

"Today? Or in its entirety?"

"Well… all of it, of course. But today, especially. I get two free days for Thanksgiving break. A four-day weekend."

"Oh, I see. That would explain your…" He turned his head and at last gave Andrew's appearance a thorough examination. "Excitement." Kevin's lips then eased into a smirk, one lacking any innocence that a parent should have when smiling at their son. "Nice outfit."

Andrew, assuming that Kevin was mocking him, asked, "Really?"

"Yeah. You look good."

"I wanted to put black lipstick on, but I wasn't sure. What do you think?" Andrew then drew a finger across his bottom lip, tapping it with his tongue.

"I…" Kevin cleared his throat a couple of times. "I think it would help."

"Do you think it'd look good?"

"It would certainly complete your ensemble." At the sight of Andrew's protruding lower lip and weak nod, he was then a bit more honest. "Yeah. It'd look good."

"I'll go put some on, then." His cheeks hurt from smiling so wide for so long, but it was out of his control, as were his feelings. He raced up the steps, found the lipstick in his drawer, then smudged some onto his top and bottom lips, wiping off some that managed to streak. When he came back down, Kevin was pouring himself coffee, and he interrupted him by showing off his now obsidian lips, puckering them.

"Cute," Kevin giggled, then hid his magenta face by raising his mug to his mouth.

Cute. The cloud Andrew sat on only sailed higher.

"I don't want to go to school," Andrew confided in his father, who avoided eye contact after the compliment he paid. "I want to stay home." *With you.*

Kevin gave the suggestion a serious moment's thought. Then, he decided, "You'll have a four-day weekend after this. You can stomach it, Andrew."

"Damn. Thought you were going to let me for a second there."

"Well, you already dressed up. Surely you can't let all of that hard work go to waste."

"But…"

He rocked his head back and forth. "It's school. You have to go." Andrew's frown induced laughter from him. "Don't make that face. I'm not falling for it."

"But it's so boring."

"It's supposed to be boring. If it was like an amusement park, you wouldn't learn anything. I'll be here when you're done. Then we'll have some fun."

Although he knew that he had to, Andrew couldn't wait for the school day to end.

Leaving Kevin's vehicle was troubling for more than one reason: a torrential downpour had rolled through and flooded the streets, and he didn't want to spend six hours sitting in class when he could be at home spending time with his new best friend. Once at the school, Kevin drove up to the curb to prevent Andrew hopping into a fresh river that had accumulated. He stalled his good-bye, already tasting lemons as the words touched his tongue.

"Have a good day, Andrew."

Andrew could have sworn he heard "I'll miss you" in that tone he used. "You, too, Dad."

Kiss his cheek, offered an impulsive voice. *No way!* he argued, shrinking toward the car door. He jumped out, into the drumming rain, dashing for the entrance to avoid getting soaked, and he wasn't the only one. Joining the swarm of students, he followed the traffic to his locker. As he expected, it wasn't only Kevin's attention he caught with his apparel that morning.

"Hey, Andrew." Ben's suave voice and elegant swagger, borrowed from the cheesiest of actors in contemporary romance films, didn't gather the awareness from his friend he might have wanted. At seeing Andrew continue to stock his locker without a moment's glance in his direction, he planted a hand on his locker door.

"Hey, Ben," Andrew answered, his wary eyes now fixed on his face, which seemed to be leaning closer.

"You look good today." His eyebrows twitched.

"Thanks." It would have been a nice compliment had it not been meaningless. Ben made a habit of paying it every other day.

Ben offered his hand, but Andrew didn't take it. Another of his long frowns decorated his young face. "Can I walk you to class?"

Geometry class was right downstairs, so they'd only get a moment to talk. Andrew agreed to it, at any rate. "All right. If you want to."

Realizing that Andrew wasn't going to touch him, his hand drifted back to his side. "Sweet." He walked alongside him as they traveled down the hall to the stairwell. When they were alone inside, Ben cleared his throat and turned to Andrew with his eyes focused on the floor. "Wait up a second."

Andrew didn't want to be late for class. It was bad enough that he had missed a couple of problems on his homework the night before. "Okay?" He stepped back, joining Ben underneath the stairs where he had ducked off to.

"Andrew..." Ben struggled to find the appropriate way to approach the matter. Andrew checked the clock on the wall. Class would start in the next minute.

"Ben, I'm going to be late," he warned him.

"What are you doing for Thanksgiving break? Do you have any plans?"

"Just hanging out with my dad."

"Would you maybe want to hang out with me sometime?"

He's asking me out. Andrew sucked his cheeks in and bit on them. *I should have seen this coming.*

"I... uh... well, my dad and I were really starting to get to know each other. I was looking forward to doing something with him." Andrew could understand the confused half-smirk Ben was wearing. He didn't need to be told that his attachment to Kevin was a bit on the odd side.

"You see him every day."

"I like seeing him."

"You can't take a break from him for a few hours? Just to see a movie or something?"

"I don't like going to the movies. Honestly, I don't like going anywhere."

Ben's brow settled, his mouth tightening. "What do you like?"

The loudspeakers rang with the start-of-class bell. "Shit. Can we pick this up at lunch?"

With a languid droop of the shoulders, he told him, "Sure."

"Okay. See you later, Ben." He rushed out the stairwell door after hearing Ben say farewell. Thank goodness the bell interrupted them. If they stood there any longer, they'd become stammering, petulant statues.

When lunch arrived, Andrew wasn't looking forward to it, or the conversation he planned to have. Was there even a polite way to say, "I don't like you that way"? There had to be. Not all relationships were built upon the premise of two people hating each other for years, wishing they had better. He wouldn't be like his step-father and take what he could get. He was an adult, and was old enough to choose who or who not to be with.

As Andrew came to the table in the cafeteria, their usual spot near the window, he saw that Ben lacked a lunch that day. He didn't blame him for not eating, for his stomach was also in twenty different knots of all sizes.

"Were you late for geometry?" asked his friend with regret.

"No, I made it."

"I'm sorry I cornered you like that. Looking back, I shouldn't have done it. Did I make you uncomfortable?"

Andrew withdrew his gourmet turkey sandwich from the bag, but didn't yet bite into it. "A little."

Ben's palm met his face, and he grinded his thumb and forefinger against his eyes. "Shit. I'm an idiot."

"It's not your fault." He picked at the corners of the bread, dropping crumbs onto the plastic. "I'm not used to it. People have liked me before, but… I always figured they were just teasing me."

"I'm definitely not teasing you, Andrew."

"Still…" He shrugged.

"I shouldn't push it, though. I don't want to screw everything up before I even have a chance."

"About that…" Andrew paused to glance at Ben, who had a mixed expression of trepidation and hope etched on his face, his beady, brown eyes wide. "I know you like me." At first, he couldn't continue that thought. He didn't want to hurt him in any way. "And I'm really flattered by that."

Dread now shadowed Ben's previously joyous mood. "You're not attracted to me."

"It's n-not that you aren't a cool guy. You are. I like you. I just… don't really want to date you."

"Andrew. It's cool. I get it."

There wasn't much time for Andrew to talk him through the ordeal. Ben stood and turned his back on him. "Ben, I'm sorry."

When Ben faced him, he couldn't hide his humiliation. "What are you sorry for? You feel what you feel. I can't make you change your mind."

"Can we still be friends?"

"I don't know. I think I've embarrassed myself enough."

A crack splintered the center of Andrew's heart. "I understand." Just like that, he was alone again, looming over his picked-at lunch, his chest and eyelids heavy. He didn't blame Ben for parting ways. He might have done the exact same thing in his position. Regardless, he had lost another friend, and no matter how many times it happened, he couldn't get familiarized with it. No other word had felt so threadbare from overuse than "goodbye," but he was conditioned to expect it around every corner. Nothing special ever lasted. Things ended, hopes shattered, and dreams died, and you either got used to it, or died along with them.

Andrew couldn't focus during his next few classes, replaying the events at lunch in his mind a hundred times over, wondering how different things would be if he had just kept his mouth shut. He had a friend, a fun companion to chat with every day, and had put his own feelings before him.

That's life, he reminded himself. Sometimes, it didn't go as planned. Sometimes it had surprises, and more often than not, they weren't pleasant.

During photography class, he and Sarah worked together on photo editing software, fixing up her picture she took for the upcoming project. Andrew complimented her on her shot of an elderly couple sitting in the park, and told her that the scene gave a lifelike perspective.

"They looked so happy," she cooed to Andrew while adjusting the hue of the photo's pixels. "I couldn't pass up the opportunity."

"It's good that you took the photo and not me. Older people tend not to like me."

"I think you might scare them."

Apprehensive, Andrew glanced down at his sunken chest, which was wrapped in his tight, black shirts. "Do I look scary?" She winced, and Andrew detected the answer in her expression before she stated her opinion. "It's okay, Sarah. You wouldn't be the first to give me the whole 'you must be Death in disguise' lecture."

"Oh," she sighed, relieved. "Not that I mind it, you know. It reminds me of Conrad." She broke off to sigh in pining. *Conrad.* She must have mentioned that name before. It sounded like one he had heard a thousand times; maybe more. "He's a vampire," she confirmed. Ah, that's right. Her favorite TV show. She had indeed mentioned it before, perhaps in a valiant effort to take his ears off to protect them from hearing any more bullshit. "But not like one of those old, gross vampires. He's from modern times and is in love with this girl who works at a bar…"

That's when Andrew stopped listening. He eliminated his boredom by scratching at the granite tip of his pencil until the undersides of his nails were blackened. Sure, his hands were now filthy, but it was better than talking about "Blood Hunt" for the fortieth time.

By the end of the day, sweat dampened Andrew's forehead when he neared his locker. Ben was at his own, yanking things out of his backpack, shoving them into the cabinet. A scowl had curled his features, exasperated sighs wafting out of his mouth. Andrew wondered if it might be best to forget his jacket and go without it to avoid confrontation, but he knew he wouldn't be able to keep that up every single day.

As he sidled up beside Ben at his own locker, he once again fought with the handle on his door to open it. For a moment, Ben watched him struggle like he had just found an animal caught in a trap.

"Let me help," he guided, his frustration ebbing away. Andrew stood aside, and Ben jiggled the handle a few times before pulling the door open. It creaked louder than it had the day before, as though it had been dying from a painful illness. Whatever the problem was with it, it wasn't getting any better.

"Thanks," squeaked Andrew, much like the metal door had.

"You're welcome." Ben slammed his own locker shut, then merged with the crowd, following it to the school's exit.

Andrew grabbed his jacket and hurried it on, chucked some books into his locker, then chased after him. He didn't know exactly what he thought he could accomplish by talking to him. He could only make matters worse. What else could he possibly say, anyway?

"Stop following me, Andrew," Ben grunted, keeping his eyes on the doors he planned to escape out of.

"Ben, please. We can't talk about this?"

"What's there to talk about? I like you. You don't like me."

"I *do* like you!"

"Not in that way. I told you, I don't want to embarrass myself anymore. This is just the way it has to be." He pushed past a few more students, and then Andrew lost him in the crowd.

Enduring the loss, Andrew dragged his heels across the parking lot. Seeing Kevin would lift his spirits. It always did. He spotted that familiar black sports car, parked across the lot near the back, and he picked up his pace as soon as he noticed it. Before he knew it, he was sprinting across the vacant parking spaces, kicking up water, which soaked through his rubber-soled sneakers. At the sight of the smile on Kevin's face when they laid eyes on each other, his heart soared, and the rest of him almost took flight with it.

Someone else was in the car, sitting in the passenger seat— *his* seat. On closer inspection, he saw that the occupant was Kyle. With a curled lip and nose, Andrew opened the door to the backseat, climbing into the one behind Kevin.

"Hey, you," Kevin cheered, his thick voice full of respect. Andrew said hello to him, but his eyes were on Kyle the whole time. "How was your day?"

"It wasn't all that great," Andrew answered with his eyes burning into Kyle's back.

"How come? What happened?"

"There was some drama between me and a friend. I'll tell you more later."

"Nice lipstick, Andrew," snickered Kyle.

Clenching his eyes in a narrow squint, he wondered, "What are you doing here?"

"Your father and I were spending some time together and he asked me to tag along while he came to pick you up." Kyle's silver-studded face turned toward him as he looked behind his seat, the seat Andrew felt belonged to him. "I hope that's not a problem?"

"Dad can do whatever he wants. He doesn't need my approval." Kyle didn't address how Andrew neglected to answer his question.

"He's going to join us for Thanksgiving tomorrow," Kevin added, not hearing the subsequent gentle exhale from his son. "And I'm going to introduce you to your grandmother. Don't worry, it'll just be the four of us."

"Sounds fun." At least, it would if he hadn't known Kyle would be joining them.

Kevin caught his dismal attitude, which was substantial in every word he spoke. "I'm sorry you had a bad day, Andrew. We'll have some fun tonight and you'll feel better."

"I look forward to it." Despite Kyle's presence, Andrew would relax.

On their arrival home, Kevin took Andrew's jacket like he did every afternoon, hanging it up in the coat closet. Andrew removed his shoes to avoid stamping wet footprints on the carpet.

"Homework?"

Andrew had almost forgotten about their "routine" in his angst. "Just the photography assignment that's due when I get back."

"We'll get that done this weekend." He crossed his heart with his index finger. It was such a simple gesture, and yet one that immediately shattered the dreary frown that sculpted Andrew's face. Kyle interrupted the moment, however brief, and brought his best friend a beer, also carrying one for himself. Kevin thanked him, and they each cracked them open.

"Want one, Andrew?" offered Kyle with a Cheshire grin.

"Don't offer my son alcohol!" gasped Kevin.

"Kev, he's almost eighteen. How old were you when you started drinking?"

"Age is *hardly* the point!"

"I don't like the taste of beer anyway," Andrew interjected. Dave let him try it once. He never dared to drink it again.

Kyle didn't let up, despite Kevin's wishes. "What about vodka?"

Andrew didn't have time to answer before Kevin blurted, "That's it. Out. Out of the kitchen."

With raised eyebrows, Kyle strolled away, sipping from his glass bottle. They went to the TV room, where Kyle fired up one of the many game systems, passing the second controller to Kevin. Andrew sat next to his father on the couch, close enough to where their shoulders touched. Though Andrew played this move with caution, he saw that Kevin enjoyed their closeness, and had leaned against him, enough to where Andrew could feel the pressure of his weight. Many waves of delight followed, ones that spread through his entire body like wildfire.

Something about watching Kevin play anything, whether it was a racing or fighting game, enchanted Andrew, just as many things about Kevin did. That grin on his face when he was victorious in a battle, that playful cheer when he'd win a race, made Andrew's troubles fade. Better still was when he held his hand up to Andrew for a high five every now and then, which he would slap with vigor. He was just as excited as Kevin was when he beat Kyle.

"I'm on a roll tonight," Kevin sang with pride. "Your ass is going down, buddy."

"Wait until I get a few beers in me," Kyle argued. "Then we'll see about that."

"If you start beating me, I'm going to have Andrew play against you. I bet he wouldn't have a problem."

"Oh, I'll be glad to take that bet."

Why did Kevin have to make that arrangement? Now he'd have to prove himself to him, and he'd feel terrible if he failed. He knew Kevin wouldn't give two shits about losing a video game and was only including him to give him something to do, but rational explanations didn't help him.

Over the course of the evening, he got to see what his father was like when tipsy. Before that evening, Andrew had already assumed Kevin to have a childlike spirit, but when under the influence, he was twice as fun. Everything entertained him, made him laugh, made him cheer, and he spewed hilarious taunts and insults that Andrew would have never imagined him saying when sober.

The greatest benefit, however, was how much more *touchy* he became.

Andrew had no complaints, but Kevin had a habit of wrapping his arm around him and grappling him against his chest. Each time he did it, Andrew got a whiff of his clean skin and the detergent imbued in his clothes, and breathed it in as deep as he could manage before he'd let him go. The wonderful high he got from it was only heightened when he'd say sweet things like, "Greatest son in the world," and that he was a lucky father.

The hours ticked by, and Kevin eventually lost interest in playing. He passed the controller to Andrew, who took it with shaking fingers. Kyle stared him down like a rhino about to charge, or at least would try to if it could walk straight. Andrew stepped up to the plate, holding the controller in his sweating hands, and played a game or two against Kyle. Seeing that his tactic was "mashing buttons," Andrew did the same until one or the other's character was dead.

"Shit," Kyle huffed, wiping sweat off of his neck. "What the hell, Andrew? Do you spend all day practicing or something?" Andrew's pale cheeks turned rosy, his eyes shifting.

"He's not piss-ass drunk," laughed Kevin, who was sliding down the couch, his back dragging along the cushion. Andrew tried not to pay attention to how wide his legs were spread, or at how the top two buttons of his shirt had somehow popped open.

"Hey, it helps me focus! And shut up, you're drunk, too."

He blew a half-hearted raspberry. "So?"

Another few rounds, and Andrew continued to beat Kyle until he got frustrated enough to toss his controller down. "That's it. I give up. I'm done." He didn't bother to look at the immense grin Andrew produced.

"I told you!" cheered Kevin, then hugged his son again. A just reward, in Andrew's heart. "That's my boy!"

This was the perfect time to act. Another chance like this might never come up. Kevin was intoxicated, and would likely forget all about it in minutes. Andrew planted his lips on his cheek and gave it a wet smack, leaving a smudge of black on his skin. A tinge of pink spread over Kevin's face.

"Aw, how sweet," he told Andrew, then returned the kiss to Andrew's right cheek, which glowed and tingled. Andrew could hear his every rapid heartbeat in his ears and felt his fingers go numb. Even the high he got when wailing pitch bends on his guitar wasn't half as tremendous as the one Kevin just gave him.

Kyle didn't share the sentiment. Instead, he stared at them with a cocked eyebrow, clutching his unfinished beer. "Want to go out to the garage for a smoke, Kev?"

Brought back to reality, Kevin turned to his friend, away from Andrew's bright crimson cheeks and shaking breaths. "Sure." He glanced at Andrew, whose buzz was numbing from Kyle's interruption. "I'll be back in a little bit, okay?"

"I thought you were going to quit?" whispered Andrew.

"Well…" Kevin, who had never dealt with this experience before, had no idea how to tell his son that cigarettes weren't what they planned to smoke. He didn't want Andrew exposed to it, though he likely already had been at his age, and he didn't want him to know.

What might he think of his father if he told him he did this? "I am. I *did*. See?" He yanked up his right shirt sleeve to surprise Andrew with a nicotine patch. Andrew was speechless. "We're just going to have a little chat."

Whatever "chat" they would have, Andrew knew it must have been of a private nature if he wasn't invited along. This led to him to picking up objects off of the coffee table and rolling them around in his hands to ease his stress. What would they be saying that he wasn't permitted to hear?

To ease his discomfort, Kevin tossed his hair with an affectionate stroke to the head. It seemed to do the trick to loosen his muscles and unclench his jaw. He smiled at his son, who mimicked it, trading silent fondness with him. Such acts of love and devotion were not meant to be craved, to become addicted to, but Andrew succumbed to the sensation just as one accepts all rules of life and death. He wanted nothing more than a touch or glimpse from his father. As fearful as he was of such an emotion, he allowed it to seep into his very soul, where he would nurture it until it grew to an unbreakable size. Kevin lingered for some time in the uneasy silence, eyes locked with Andrew's, until he could no longer face it. After a final pat to Andrew's shoulder, he vacated the room and joined Kyle in the garage.

Already Kyle was lighting up a joint he had earlier prepared. He took a hit off of it, then passed it to his friend, who hit it as well while leaning against his car. For a time, they were quiet, other than the coughing and wheezing. The air thickened, and not just from the heavy clouds they puffed into the air. Even though the temperatures were dropping outside, he felt heated under Kyle's laser stare. The silence unsettled him, but he had no idea what to say, for he had no clue as to why Kyle looked so intense.

"How are you and Andrew getting along?" His question carried an accusation.

"Wonderfully." He took the joint from Kyle and inhaled deep, then passed it back. "He's great."

Kyle didn't answer him until after he puffed. "You two are becoming close?"

"I think so, yeah." He puffed next, holding his breath.

"I can tell."

Kevin could no longer handle his steel gaze and cryptic hints, and got to the point. "Is there something wrong with Andrew and I being close?"

"No." He lowered his eyes. "Not at all."

"Then what's your problem? What's with that look you're giving me?"

"I'm not giving you any look, Kevin."

"Yes you are!"

"*Should* I be giving you a look?"

Once he passed the marijuana cigarette back to his friend, Kevin stated, "I don't know what you're talking about."

Exasperated, Kyle took a larger hit to calm himself down. "Weather's looking shitty." Kevin already knew the direction this conversation was headed in, and tossed Kyle a lazy nod. Kyle puffed some more, his tension evaporating. "They said a snowstorm was coming tonight." Another nod from Kevin, who refused to play with hints. Get to the point, Kyle, and get to it fast. "And I think I... drank too much. With the roads and the beers... I probably shouldn't... you know."

"Drive home," Kevin finished with a sigh.

"Right. Right."

"You want to stay the night."

A cough, then another, heavier than the last. Then, riotous laughter. "I'm not subtle, am I?"

Allowing the weed to take over, he burst into cackles. "Never were."

"You don't mind?"

It took longer than usual for Kevin to come to a decision in regards to Kyle sleeping over. Before Andrew came around, he did more than permit it; he invited him to join him in his bed at any time he wished. Now, something prevented from delivering his usual "of course not" to him, something he was unclear on. The deliberation caused the smile to fall from Kyle's face. Kevin knew he had been wanting this for a while, and shunning his advances any further felt wrong to him.

"No," Kevin answered at last, swallowing as his cottoned tongue stuck to the roof of his mouth. "Y-you can stay."

Elated once again, Kyle put the joint out by pinching it and placing it into the plastic bag it came in, then engulfed Kevin's neck with a powerful tug while driving his tongue into his mouth. It had felt like forever since Kevin had any kind of intimate contact with another, though he and Kyle had many shared nights to speak of. He proclaimed his desperation by embracing him and kissing him back.

"I missed you," whispered Kyle. Though they had seen each other on multiple occasions since Andrew came to live with him, Kevin knew exactly what it was he missed.

Once the arrangement had been made, they retreated into the house. Kyle headed for the stairs first, passing the TV room on the way, and bid Andrew good night. Perplexed, Andrew watched as he climbed the staircase without another word, then turned his eyes to his father as he too entered the room.

Seeing Andrew, Kevin greeted him, then said, "It's getting late. I think I might turn in for the night." The air turned to ice in the moment these words were uttered, a chill originating from Andrew's sullen expression. "Is everything okay?"

"Yeah." He swallowed, which felt impossible to do. He hated telling him lies, but what else could he say?

"I'll see you in the morning, all right?"

"Is Kyle... staying here?"

There was no denying now that this was the very topic that had frozen the air between them. Kevin didn't enjoy it any more than Andrew did. Regardless, he said, in a rather dry monotone, "Yeah. Weather's supposed to get pretty bad."

"I see." He looked away, gazing at the television screen, staring through its backlight and pixels until his retinas burned. For a while, Kevin stood there behind the sofa where Andrew sat, releasing light coughs and kicking at the floor, his hands in his pockets.

"Well... good night, Andrew."

"Good night, Dad."

Kevin vanished from sight, and then Andrew was alone. Why on earth did this upset him so much? Had he really not assumed before that Kevin and Kyle were fucking? Even if they were, why should it matter? Kevin had a life, and Andrew knew he had no right to tell him how to live it. For all he knew, he might have had several sexual partners. It wasn't too far-fetched of a concept, considering that there were hundreds, perhaps even thousands of people that had known and read about him for much longer than he had.

All the same, he hurt in places he didn't even know were in him. Closing his eyes didn't help. All he could see behind his eyelids were short films of Kevin and Kyle in bed together, rolling and tumbling and belting out lust-filled cries. This whole new overpowering, prolonged jealousy had bewildered him, and none of his feelings made any sense to him.

He was in deep, too deep to dig out. Kevin meant more to him than just a parent— that much he could finally admit to himself. What he wanted from him at this point remained uncertain, but he could not deny that it was there, that feeling of desperation, of longing. To be crushed against his chest, to be wrapped up in his strong arms, to be told that never again would he be abandoned. To feel that electrostatic kiss to his cheek, to feel it even in other places, would be a heaven he couldn't beg for enough.

Shutting down the game console, then turning off the television, Andrew followed his father up the stairs, and as he climbed toward the top, soft laughter echoed down the hall from Kevin's bedroom, a sound that tossed a partially-digested dinner around within his stomach. He ducked away into his bedroom, dropped onto his bed and tried his hardest to forget everything.

As he stared at the ceiling, his hands upon his chest, his fingers intertwined and writhing, he heard the faint sound of moaning coming from the other side of the wall, which only increased in volume as the eternal minutes rolled by. Within a few gut-wrenching moments, he heard the voice of Kyle groan his father's name. This had to be the equivalent of Hell.

Andrew knew then that he had to accept the inevitable: there were things he wanted that he could never have, and Kevin was one of them. If he continued acting on his emotions, he might push his father away, and lose him forever. That would be tougher to cope with than hearing him fuck his best friend in the next room.

His nose drizzled, and he sniffed, his vision blurred by shadows and rivers of tears. Kevin could have anyone he wanted, anyone who wasn't related to him. Why would he go for him? What made him think that someone like Kevin would even be remotely interested in a scrawny punk like himself? Even if he did want him, it'd be wrong in several ways. He didn't deserve someone like Kevin, and Kevin didn't deserve to be stuck with him.

As he whimpered, the thumps and cries continued, and the more repulsed Andrew was by his own reaction to it. The sound of Kevin in throes of passion would have been enticing had it not been mixed with Kyle's, who apparently loved to make it clear just how pleased he was at Kevin's maneuvers. Andrew rolled out of bed and went into the bathroom, turning on the shower, which blotted out the sounds of ecstasy. With the water running, he decided to step under it for a while to calm his sparking, flaming nerves, and to stop his hands and knees from shaking. For a time, it soothed him, but not enough. He wanted to sleep, forever if he was capable.

He wrapped a towel around himself when he got out and collapsed onto his bed. Thankfully, the moans of delight had stopped, only to be replaced with sounds of talking and light chortling. Andrew could picture them, Kevin on top of him, kissing him, whispering to him, and both of them with wide, goofy smiles. He closed his eyes, desperate to think of something else, anything else, to get his mind off of it. School. Math problems. That was boring enough.

After hanging his towel and slipping on a pair of boxers, Andrew returned to bed and shut his eyes for the last time that night.

I'm not afraid of the fact that you're my father. I'm afraid that I want you all to myself.

And I'm afraid that I'm okay with that.

CHAPTER FIVE

In Which Molecules Expand

While in the car, this time in the passenger seat where he belonged, Andrew was quiet. Kevin had a good time chatting with Kyle about people they used to know in high school, but he had nothing to contribute with. Though he loved being with Kevin on his first day off of school, all he could think about was the night before.

Ever since they made eye contact that morning, Andrew hadn't been able to say much to him, and even if he wanted to, he didn't know how. Telling himself to abolish his attraction to Kevin overworked his mind and body, and it was better to shy away from him while he went through the healing process than it was to tell him what he was going through. Upon seeing Andrew's melancholy state, Kevin attempted to cheer him up by telling him humorous stories. Andrew wanted to laugh just to make him happy, but he couldn't even manage that.

The past two weeks he spent with Kevin— sharing meals, movies, games, stories, memories— were the best of Andrew's life, but now he felt something he didn't intend to feel. He had come to a crossroads, where on one side, he continue with his infatuation, allow it to develop to see if Kevin ever felt something in return; or, on the other side, he dismiss it, forget he ever had it, and hope it melted away.

The latter was the healthier choice, but at this rate, Andrew was clueless as to what was "healthy" for him anymore. The reality of the situation said that moving as far away as he could from his over-attachment was the right thing to do. On the other hand, Andrew didn't always do what most people considered "right." What *felt* right was Kevin holding him. What *felt* right was that kiss to his cheek.

Oh, what he wouldn't give to feel that a second time. No amount of gifts or treasures measured up to the incalculable bliss he felt in the moment Kevin's lips collided with his face.

No, not now. He promised himself he'd try to forget about it. It was wrong. *So* wrong, on so many levels. Nature indicated they weren't meant to be lovers, and Andrew would heed nature's advice, no matter how stubborn the notion was. What mattered most was that Kevin was in his life, and he wouldn't give that up for anything. It was time to understand where his priorities lied.

The trip to Kevin's mother's house felt like it lasted an eternity, especially with all of the love songs playing on the radio. He would change them, but Kevin seemed to not only know them well, but enjoy them, which made matters worse. He couldn't be more grateful to Kevin for killing the engine, and eliminating the weepy, sentimental tunes along with it, when they parked in his mother's driveway.

Andrew was the last to get out of the car, trailing after Kevin and Kyle, who walked side-by-side, chattering and chuckling. He could no longer picture them as best buds— not after what happened last night. He wondered why they weren't also holding hands. It could have been that they were restricted only to a friendship, but Andrew found that hard to believe after hearing the way Kyle groaned Kevin's name.

Resisting the urge to stare at his father wore on his willpower. Kevin's attire was formal for such a small event: a black suit with a raspberry necktie, including a black dinner jacket and shoes to match. His dark hair was smoothed to the side, some of it lingering over his sapphire eyes and thick eyebrows, giving his gaze a mysterious allure. It was...

Breathtaking, Andrew summed up, then swatted the thought away like an irritating fly. He had to work harder to fight it, or it would never go away. That is, if he wanted it to, and he wasn't so sure anymore.

Kevin glanced behind him when seeing Andrew spacing himself

from the others, his head low and his heels dragging, his hands hidden away in the pockets of his hooded sweatshirt, which was black with a blue skull emblazoned on the front. It was unbearable for him to see Andrew in pain, to feel that he was completely helpless. He wanted to ask him what was on his mind, but Andrew would only tell him he was fine. The very idea that there wasn't much he could do to make Andrew feel better tortured him. At a loss, he had no choice but to wait until Andrew was ready to open up.

Dianne, Kevin's mother, had a one-story brick house with an elaborate garden out front, adorned with daisies, tulips, and lilies, but what stood out the most was the bright, blood-red rose bushes, which encompassed a babbling koi pond, where massive speckled fish swam. Andrew watched them with childlike fascination for a few moments while Kevin stepped onto the front porch and rang the doorbell.

The woman who answered the door had more freckles on her face than Andrew could count, and they stood out on the her small, pointy face, which was decorated with light makeup to cover up her wrinkles. Her hair was thick and dyed a dark brown, which was fading at the roots where a deep gray was present. Her posture was straight and proud as she cheered with joy at the sight of her only child.

"Hi, honey," she chirped, swinging her arms around her son, who stood at least a foot taller than her at his statuesque six feet. Kevin passed her a salutation, as well as the pie he brought. "Oh! You brought dessert! You didn't have to!"

"I know how much you love Dutch apple," said Kevin, doting and accommodating.

With appreciation, she sighed, "Thank you, dear." That's when she noticed her son's best friend accompanying him. "Kyle! What a surprise!"

"Miss Malone," answered Kyle. "How's the beading going?"

"Oh, it's been fun. Doctor asked me to stop because of my arthritis. How could I do that? I'd be bored out of my mind if it weren't for my crafts." Before Kyle could supply her with a response, she changed the subject. "So where is he?"

"Andrew." Kevin's call, sugary sweet, stroked Andrew's ears, hitting a nerve. "Come meet your grandmother." Andrew strode toward his father with his head low. "She won't bite you," his father comforted. Getting bitten had been far from Andrew's greatest fear at the moment.

Andrew pulled his blanket of hair aside so that Dianne could see his eyes when they met, and pushed his hand forward so that she could shake it. "N-nice to meet you."

Dianne didn't take Andrew's hand. Instead, she smashed him against her chest and squeezed the breath out of him. "Hello, sweetie!" she sang. Andrew gasped at being suddenly smothered by perfume and breasts, two things he could have done without. Hearing him release a heavy cough, she released him before he suffocated. "Oh, honey," she cooed to Kevin, pride welling in her blue eyes. "You look so alike!"

"I would hope we do!" rang Kevin.

Kyle snickered. "He's definitely got my cousin's nose, though. It's got that weird curve. You know the one." He pulled the tip of his nose upward with his index finger, then elbowed Kevin in hopes it would get him to laugh. Andrew bowed his head, sliding his hair back over his face to block his unappealing nose, his collar warming.

Smoke drifted from Kevin's nostrils when he cast a heated glower at Kyle. "Stop it," he growled.

"I'm just messing, Kev," he retorted on shaken breaths, wiping his sweating palms on the back of his jeans.

Nervous at the threat of Kevin and Kyle locking horns, Dianne interrupted them. "Come in, boys. Kevin, help me in the kitchen for a while. I need to make the stuffing."

The men entered the home, a sparkling clean abode that smelled of fresh linens and pumpkin spice. The living room had a small fireplace, which crackled and gave the atmosphere a cozy ambience. A tiny, round oak table stood in the middle, and a recliner and couch rested against the wall. As they neared the dining room, Andrew got a whiff of the feast he and his family would be indulging in. Despite his sadness, his appetite was strong. Turkey happened to be one of his favorite foods, and he looked forward to it.

Kevin disappeared into the kitchen as he was asked, and Andrew began to follow him. Before he could set foot in the dining room, he was brought to a halt by Kyle's firm voice.

"Sorry," he muttered. Andrew looked at him, but said nothing. "About the nose thing," he clarified.

Don't get angry, Andrew told himself. *Maybe he really is sorry.*

"It's…" Was it really okay? Under his mother's roof, he had already suffered enough humiliation, and he thought he had parted from it once and for all. He grit his teeth, swallowed his pride, and released a sigh. "It's okay."

"It just still hasn't sunk in, that's all," Kyle explained. "Kevin with a son. It blows my mind."

Is that all on you my father blows? he loathed to consider. "I guess it hasn't really sunk in for me that I live with him, either."

"He seems pretty excited. I'm happy for him. Don't get the wrong idea about me, Andrew."

"What idea would that be?" His hair slid back over his right eye.

"That I'm an asshole."

The urge to not only bark, but bite, filled him from the bottom up. Lowering his voice, he asked, "*Are* you?"

Kyle raised his palms in a defensive pose. "I can see this isn't a good time to talk. I'm going to check if they need any help in the kitchen."

He cursed himself under his breath. Kyle set him off, and he wished he hadn't. Since he was Kevin's friend, he wanted to like him, but whenever he tried to, Kyle gave him more reasons to change his mind. If Kyle's methods of bonding with him included making fun of him, he hoped he thought of new ways to get along with him.

After waiting for about five minutes, and dwelling on his situation, he heard that syrupy call again, his father's deep voice beckoning: "Andrew!"

Andrew moved toward the sound of his voice like a moth to a bright light, a magnet searching for its opposing partner. The feast displayed on the dining room table was not Andrew's primary focus, but finding Kevin, who must have been in the kitchen. He brushed past Kyle, who was laying out silverware and passing him worrisome glances as he crossed rooms.

Andrew strode into the kitchen, where he saw Kevin licking the end of a spoon. Each of his toes froze and stiffened as he tongued the roof of his mouth and swallowed, hypnotized by the visual gift bestowed upon him. When Kevin slipped the spoon away from his mouth and set it down in the sink, Andrew resisted the impulsive desire to spout, "No, please, don't stop."

"Dinner's ready," he announced. "Are you hungry?"

"Very."

"Have a seat at the table."

"Are you sitting there, too?"

There was concise pause as Kevin studied his son's expression. "Yeah. You can sit next to me, if that's what you want."

That was indeed what he wanted, but if he were going to abolish his attraction, he couldn't act on every whim that entered his mind. "Just wondering." He huffed out a gentle cough.

A withered frown touched his older face before he nodded. "Okay. Well, go ahead and have a bite. I'll join you in a moment."

Andrew shuffled back to the dining room and sat, the scent of turkey and biscuits filling his nostrils, initiating a bellow in his stomach. He grabbed a fork and stacked food onto his plate, all while Dianne and Kyle piled food onto theirs as they shared a friendly chat the likes of those had by old friends who had known each other for many years.

Kevin entered the room next, and without question or conformation, took the seat beside Andrew, who glowed at his presence. Once Kevin began to eat, so too did Andrew, without either of them uttering a word, but each obtaining the same feeling of comfort.

Dianne and Kyle joined them at the table, their conversation dying down. Dianne, now that they were seated, scoffed at her son, who was already stuffing his face. "Kevin!" He lowered his folk at the sound of her sharp tone. "Before grace?!"

With a shrug, he mumbled, "M'hungry," with his mouth full of stuffing. He couldn't help but grin when a giggle slipped through Andrew's tightened lips.

"Goodness. I didn't raise you without manners."

Kevin sighed, lowered his fork, then wiped his mouth off. "Sorry, Mom. Go ahead." He sipped from his glass of wine, passing an amused look to his son, whose face filled with color when their eyes met.

Dianne reached her hands out on both sides of her, Kyle to her right, Kevin to her left. Kevin and Kyle each took her hands. Then, Andrew felt a hand grasp his own, resolute and warm, if not a bit damp with sweat. He snuck a peek at his father, whose eyes were closed while Dianne said her prayer.

Andrew turned his hand in Kevin's until the surface of their palms met, then clenched. What he expected to receive was a reproofing glance, perhaps even to be shooed away, but instead he felt Kevin's hand also tighten around his own. He peered at Kevin with his eyes cracked open, and there upon his face was a radiant gleam of satisfaction. Andrew continued to watch his face as he too opened his eyes, and glimpsed into his son's with silent approval. His palm squeezed around Andrew's once more, tighter, and he spread his four fingers to allow Andrew's to snake between them. Andrew took the invitation and allowed his own knuckles to wriggle between each of Kevin's until they were linked together. There was a gentle massage in the webs between his fingers as Kevin started stroking them with the tips of his own, a slow glide back and forth, rhythmic and soothing.

If there was anything that felt better than this, Andrew couldn't conceive it.

When Dianne finished grace, Kevin's grasp loosened, their bond severed, and he turned away while clearing his throat, his eyes wandering around the room. Andrew felt that sting of desire again, pining for that moment to return to him. He had never felt so good in his whole life. *Do it again*, he beseeched from the very depths of his aching soul. *Please. Don't be afraid to. I like it more than you think I do.*

At this thought, he deliberated that perhaps Kevin did understand how much he enjoyed it. He couldn't have been the only one to see the dangers inherent in any kind of romantic attachment to someone of blood relation, and Kevin didn't seem the type to be so blind.

With a sardonic tilt of the head, Kevin inquired, "Can I eat *now?*"

"Slowly," Dianne advised. "I know the way you are."

"Parents," Kevin jested to Andrew with a wink.

"Heh… yeah," added Andrew through compressed molars. *Parents*, indeed.

Many topics arose around the table, most pertaining to Kevin's career and when his new book was scheduled for release. Kevin explained to his mother, with a hint of exasperation, that he was "working on it," to which Kyle replied:

"Haven't you *been* working on it?"

"Believe me, Kyle," Kevin addressed, refilling his glass of wine. "My editor gives me the same lecture. I'm not just going to forget about a book that's in the middle of a series. Would I let my fans down so readily?" He took a sip from his glass, smacked his lips, then said, "I've never had a problem meeting a deadline in the past."

"You should ditch the publisher, anyway. They own your ass. Art should have some freedom to it."

"Sure, they own me. But in a way, I sort of own them, too. I'm the best thing that's happened to them in years. They practically do the advertising for me at this rate."

"Yeah, and they take a huge chunk of your royalties while they're at it."

Shaking his head, Kevin clicked his tongue. "I took an advance. Not quite the same thing. Besides, it's all part of the game, Kyle."

With a snort, Kyle concluded, "Shouldn't games be fun?" Kevin had no answer for him.

Dianne had something else on her mind, unrelated to Kevin's work. She now had questions regarding Andrew's separation from his own mother, a subject Andrew would have preferred remained dead and buried along with his hundreds of inhibitions.

"Your mother just left you with Kevin?" she questioned after swallowing some stuffing. "That's it? She never wants to see you again?"

"I'm happier living with Kevin, anyway," Andrew reassured. "As a kid, I wanted to be with him— uh, live with him." He ignored the quick glance Kevin gave him out of the corner of his eye. "She tried to convince me he wouldn't want me. To this day, I don't know why she did that. She hated me."

"I'm sure she didn't *hate* you," Dianne eased, exchanging troubled glimpses with her son.

"No," Andrew perpetuated. "She hated me. After so long, I'm clueless as to why she kept me around, just to make us both miserable. She could have found my father any time, could have let me have a better life. Why did she wait until now, when I'm old enough to think for myself? I don't know, Miss Malone. I know the way she thinks, but I couldn't tell you why she thinks the way she does."

Andrew hadn't intended it, but the room dropped to a dead hush once he had spoken his mind. He wished they'd say something, change the subject already. Then he felt a graceful hand dress his shoulder. *It'll be okay*, the touch signaled. *From now on, everything will be okay.*

Kyle was the next one to speak, switching the topic to football, something he knew next to nothing about. As the mood in the room lifted, Andrew got comfortable enough to ask Dianne, "Where's Kevin's dad?"

Dianne first looked at Kevin, whose expression of shame was enough to tell her that he hadn't given Andrew many details regarding his own parents. "We're divorced, sweetie," she said without batting an eyelash. "We've been divorced for many years now."

"I'm sorry," Andrew empathized, both with her and Kevin.

She cut a piece of turkey in half and poured gravy on it. "Don't be. Kevin's father... your grandfather... didn't approve of Kevin's life."

"What about it?"

Her face fell, and Kevin tapped the teeth of his fork on the edge of his plate, leaving half of his food unfinished. Dianne first sighed, then explicated, "He didn't like the fact that he enjoyed the company of men." Kevin followed up with this comment with a taught-lipped inhale, saliva squealing against his teeth. Andrew tensed at his palpable distress. "We had one too many fights about it," Dianne continued. "When Steven told me that he'd rather disown him then..." She paused as Kevin dropped his fork.

"Could we not talk about this?" he offered in the politest manner he could.

"I'm sorry, Dad," whispered Andrew, though he couldn't convey that he had more than one reason to be.

Softer, he said, "It's okay. I'm sorry, too. I would just rather not even mention him on such a nice, happy evening. We're all here, together, having some good food, relaxed and content, and it doesn't need to be sullied by such drab discussion."

Dianne did her best to calm her son. "I know he still loves you, Kevin."

Growing ever more frustrated, he croaked, "You'd be the only one."

"He does love you, Kevin. You know the way he is."

"That's exactly my point, Mom." Kevin then turned his injured eyes to his own son, all scars exposed. "My father and I don't speak. That's all you need to know."

Now the picture came in clearer for Andrew. He glanced at Kevin for a moment, who was busy poking at his plate, pretending to be more interested in the food he wasn't eating. He wanted to tell him that it would never be that way with them. He couldn't imagine them getting so angry with one another that they'd stop speaking. When it came time to say it, he couldn't form the words the way he wanted to. They didn't seem enough to get across how he felt.

"Excuse me," Kevin told the room, carrying his empty plate to the kitchen to get away from prying eyes. As he rinsed the plate with hot water, cursing under his breath and rubbing the back of his aching neck, he heard footsteps enter the kitchen. He raised his voice loud enough to be heard, but not with the energy of affection he had when first arriving to the house. "Need something, Mom?"

"Are you okay?"

Hearing Andrew's voice, he turned at once, shutting off the hissing faucet. "Yeah. Of course. Why wouldn't I be?"

Andrew could sense his dishonesty, no matter how mastered he was at hiding it. "No you're not."

Kevin's chuckle, fake but practiced, echoed across the kitchen. "I'm fine, Andrew. Don't worry."

That was asking too much of him. "Can I ask you something?"

He dried his hands with a nearby towel, then faced him and gave him his full attention. "Anything you wish."

"Do you love your father?"

This question was not one Kevin expected, though Andrew looked to be full of probing inquiries. He figured he might also have quite a few if they had traded places. "I did. Once upon a time."

"Did you ever do anything with him? The kind of stuff you and me do?" Kevin shook his head and shut his eyes, the same way Andrew did as a child in hopes it turned him invisible. "You were never close? At all?"

"No. Unless 'close' means him working his life away while a TV kept me occupied. Sure, we'd talk, but usually about my failing grades and how disappointed he was in me." He shrugged, looking off to the side and crossing his arms. "And how he hoped I wouldn't turn out to be a 'faggot'. So, if that's what 'close' means, then yeah. We were like this." He crossed his index and middle fingers over each other.

There it was— the vein Andrew struck when it was most vulnerable. He didn't mean to cause Kevin any pain by opening it. If Kevin wanted to forget his father, the way he wanted to forget his mother, he would let it lie. "Sounds like me and Mom."

Kevin slackened his posture and leaned against the counter. "Your mother is worse. My father didn't abandon me until I was older than you are. I had plenty of time to live on my own before I bid him farewell." Andrew couldn't argue with him on that. Silence passed between them for a moment. "Do you love your mother?"

In all honesty, he didn't know anymore. After so many fights, so many screaming matches, he had assumed those had been the meaning of life. He thought parents were meant to hurt their children. After meeting Kevin, that all changed. "I guess I do. Just not the way I used to when I was a kid."

Kevin articulated with care, "I'm glad you're in my life, Andrew."

"I…" There was so much Andrew wanted to say, none of which could be summed up in a short time. His hands trembled, and he tucked them into his pockets. "So am I, Dad. I'm really glad."

"I won't make the mistakes my father did, or the wrongs your mother was responsible for. I'll always be here for you. No matter what it is you need."

Andrew held back the tears that were determined to flow. "It's really nice to hear someone say that to me."

Now would have been the perfect time to tell him. Why couldn't he gain the courage to spit it out? Just say it, Andrew. Tell him the truth. It could be as simple as breathing.

I'm attracted to you. I'm so very attracted to you, and everything wonderful about you. I want to give you everything we never had.

And yet, just as he thought he would confess it all, it shrank to the back of his mind where it was safe alongside his desires and fantasies, where he would seal it away with a combination lock. Fear of rejection was one thing, but another fear more prominent took charge.

I can't lose you. Not now. Not after this.

Kevin placed a hand on Andrew's shoulder and stroked it with his thumb. "Did you get enough to eat?"

"I did. That pie you brought, though… I could go for some of that."

"Great! You'll love it, I guarantee it."

He did, in fact, love it when he got to try it. It had the right touch of homemade cooking Andrew adored when eating anything Kevin made for him. The taste of cinnamon was a tad overpowering, but it was otherwise delectable with vanilla bean ice cream.

Dianne told them that they could stay for as long as they liked, and the men took that opportunity to watch the football game. Neither Kevin nor Andrew seemed to follow it with the same passion as the present company, so they had a conversation of their own. Kevin had been the first person Andrew had known to actually laugh at his jokes. Each time he heard him burst into hearty cackles, it inflated his confidence, something he lacked prior to coming into Kevin's life.

Kyle's confidence, on the other hand, diminished at the sight of them sitting on the couch together, carrying on like they were in their own private club, their voices low, their faces lit up like Christmas trees. He had seen Kevin smile like that before, namely when they were in bed together, but hadn't seen it that vivid in months. As Dianne spoke to him, he did his best to pay attention to her, but his eyes couldn't part from the scene of Kevin and Andrew whispering and giggling, alone in their own world, a world he wasn't accepted into.

"Want to head home, Kev?" he proposed, speaking over the commentators of the game. "It's getting a little late."

Kevin rolled up his sleeve to look at the face of his silver wristwatch. "It's only nine."

"I have to help my friend move tomorrow. I'm the only one he knows with a truck, I guess."

"You've failed to mention this until now."

"Well, you seemed distracted, so…"

"*Distracted?*"

"I have to get to bed soon anyway, honey," chimed in Dianne, hoping to defuse the ticking bomb that was the growing tension between her son and Kyle. "Go on. And take some leftovers while you're at it."

With the aid of both his friend and son, Kevin wrapped up some food to take home with him. Once he kissed his mother goodbye, he took his leave along with the others. Andrew snatched the passenger seat before Kyle could steal it from him, which Kyle protested with a low grumble.

Striding into his abode, Kevin reset the alarms, took Andrew's coat and hung it in the closet, then stripped off his own. Kyle grunted his disdain at Kevin when he saw that his friend had no interest in taking his coat so generously as he had his son's. Kevin, lost in a chat with his first and only born, paid him no mind, or perhaps hadn't heard him.

During an energetic talk between Kevin and Andrew about a favored science-fiction film they both enjoyed (and even quoted), Kyle could only take so much more. Were they doing this on purpose just to annoy him? If so, they were successful. Exasperated with being shoved into the background, he alerted Kevin to his plans of going home for the night.

Neither of them could hear him over the "pssshow" sound effects they imitated. "Oh, man, I love that part! When he was like, 'Frank, my wife is dying, you son of a bitch!'"

"He was so good in that movie."

"He was *so* good."

"*Guys!*" Kyle shouted, gaining Kevin's wide-eyed stare and Andrew's sensitive flinch. "Home. I'm going home."

"Oh," gasped Kevin, as though this was news to him. "Oh, okay. You want to take some turkey with you?"

"No thanks." Ruffling the folds of his jacket in a irritated huff, he headed for the door.

Kevin excused himself from Andrew's presence for a moment to chase after him, stopping him before he could step outside. "What's the matter? Are you mad at me?"

That was a difficult question to answer. It might not have been Kevin he was flustered with, but the situation. "No, Kev. I'm just tired and want to be alone right now."

"Are you sure? Because it kind of, sort of seems like you're mad at me."

"I'm not mad, Kevin, for fuck's sake!" He clamped his mouth shut, bowing his head. When he next looked up, he saw the childlike pout on his friend's face and sighed. "I'll call you tomorrow."

Glancing over Kevin's shoulder, Kyle saw Andrew enter the room, perhaps to inspect the commotion. Then, he grabbed Kevin's face, going in for a deep, passionate kiss, complete with tongue. Kevin complied, but with a look of infinite surprise. Kyle had kissed him on many occasions, but not with such intensity, or with such aggression. As kinky as he might have considered it on any other night, he could only find it bizarre and unwarranted in this case. Not until he placed his hands upon his shoulders and pried their lips apart did Kyle cease his throat diving. Embarrassed, Kyle turned for the door, bundling up and meeting the cold as he left the premises.

Once the door was shut and locked, Kevin spun around to see Andrew standing there before him, kicking at the floor and nibbling on the inside of his cheek. Andrew's eyes only rested on his face for a moment before lowering in a look of blended discouragement and shame. When Kevin approached him, he took a slow step back.

Now tense, Kevin tried to kill the silence. "He's, ah... zealous sometimes."

"I can see that," mumbled Andrew, shifting from one foot to the other, rocking to an unheard rhythm.

"He doesn't really do that a lot."

What made him think he cared? He did, of course, but he wasn't aware Kevin knew that. He shrugged, hoping it gave off the illusion that he didn't mind either way, but then he worried it made him seem indifferent. Unable to resist the temptation of the carrot dangling in front of his face, he asked, "He doesn't?"

"Not really."

Andrew couldn't prevent himself from blurting, "Not like I care."

"No. Not that you would. I'm just... saying."

"Kiss him all you want."

"Okay."

They both nodded, looking anywhere but at each other. "So..." Kevin said first. Andrew, hopeful, looked up past his obsidian drapes of hair.

At least fifteen seconds passed before either of them said anything else. "That movie we were talking about..." Andrew began, and Kevin's eyebrows peaked. "You want to watch it together?"

"I'd love to."

"Cool. I'll go start it."

"I'll make popcorn!" And then Kevin was off, booking it toward the kitchen like it, or his ass, was on fire. Andrew had to wonder how he still had room in his stomach for more food.

With popcorn on the table, the sci-fi film blaring its bold title on the flat screen, Kevin and Andrew sat beside each other on the couch. Despite there being plenty of room for the both of them to space out, their shoulders were centimeters away from touching. At the thirty minute mark, Kevin left the TV room to take a bathroom break, but when he returned and took his seat, he felt a generous weight pressed on his side as Andrew leaned against him.

Initially, Andrew didn't intend to collapse onto Kevin the way he had, having been too withdrawn to even consider touching him without invitation. However, when Kevin dropped down onto the cushions like a launched cannonball, Andrew's light body went momentarily airborne— at least, it felt like it had. The result was him falling into his father's shoulder.

Andrew knew that it might have been better to shift away, offer an apology, and brush it off as "totally weird, right?" The decision to do so would have felt even more ludicrous to him than loving Kevin more than he should. If his head was already on his shoulder, why not just leave it there? Maybe he could progress it to further physical contact that might never again fall into his hands. As long as Kevin didn't move away.

Kevin didn't budge, except to look at his son, whose mouth crept up in a steady incline, though it looked more like a wince than any kind of grin. Kevin, who had been surprised by the turn of events, had no complaints yet. In spite of his chest rising and falling with a heavy sigh, he gave in and not only accepted the closeness, but welcomed it. Offering his shoulder as Andrew's pillow was only the first of many things he would enable throughout the evening. At some point he pressed his cheek against the top of Andrew's head, nuzzling his hair.

Eventually, Kevin draped a blanket over Andrew when he began to shiver, and Andrew proceeded to sprawl his body out over the length of the sofa, his head still fused with Kevin's arm. Completely relaxed, he let out an unintentional moan, curling under the blanket's warmth and the arm that suddenly came around him.

High with delight, Andrew buried his face into Kevin's chest, bumping him with his forehead like an amorous feline. Kevin, silently rejoicing their intimacy, tugged him a bit closer and squeezed him. The sounds of happiness emanating deep from Andrew's chest and throat told Kevin that his affection would not be squandered; it went to someone who soaked in every bit of it, loved each moment of it, and held onto it as tightly as the many trinkets he held dear in his antique shrine downstairs.

Why can't we do this every night? wished Andrew, knowing all too well that he'd be sleeping alone that evening. *If I died right now, it wouldn't be so bad. At least the moment would last forever.*

Though neither of them would admit it, they no longer cared

about the movie, or the hilarious lines of dialogue within. Their snuggling had been the only thing on their minds, and while they enjoyed it, though they sought more than just hugs, they both knew that it had to end. The very concept of giving each other something such as a kiss goodnight— feasibly one with the same vigor Kyle shared with Kevin— was preposterous. Would it even give them the reconciliation they needed in the first place?

As the credits rolled, Kevin and Andrew stared at the scroll of text with the same diffused mood, and even as the final special thanks and soundtrack had passed and the DVD returned to its menu screen, they remained glued to their seats, and to each other. The hand Kevin had rested on Andrew's shoulder tapped a few times. Andrew couldn't tell if it was a gesture of comfort or warning.

"You should get in bed, Andrew."

"I'm not tired."

"Still… you really ought to."

Lowering his voice to the edges of a whisper, Andrew said, "I don't want to."

"Andrew." Kevin sucked a large breath through his nose and dragged a hand through his dark hair. "It's not like we won't see each other again. We live under the same roof. I'm not going anywhere."

We might never sit together like this again, though, Andrew understood. *We both know that's what's making this so difficult.*

Andrew answered him with a solemn, "Yeah. I know." With that, he stood and stretched his back and neck, expanding his chest and rising his hands toward the ceiling. When he next looked at Kevin, he thought he saw sweat on his brow. "I guess I'll see you in the morning, then."

"Right," whispered Kevin, swallowing. He still hadn't gotten off the couch. "Good night, honey." He squeezed his eyes shut, turning pink. "I mean, Andrew."

Andrew, still in a delicate voice, replied in both adulation and amusement, "Good night, Dad."

So, into separate rooms they went. In separate beds they each lied awake for another hour, staring at separate ceilings, separately pining with separate thoughts of loneliness.

Separate they had been for years. It was separate they had to stay.

Whether they wanted to be or not.

The sun hid behind rain clouds the next morning, and there was talk of thunderstorms on the weather station, a channel Andrew didn't normally spend his free time watching, but felt forced to when nothing better was on. For having hundreds of channels available to choose from, having a satellite dish seemed less interesting than he thought it would be. The flat screen television mounted upon the wall in the kitchen kept the room from falling too quiet while Andrew fried a batch of eggs and bacon. It was his first time attempting it, and it already wasn't going very well.

He made one batch previously, one that he managed to burn, and had cleared out half a carton of eggs. This time, he got it right, and felt a sense of pride when he did. Never in his life had he been capable of cooking something properly, but he discovered how simple it was when taking the time to learn.

While letting the bacon crackle, he put the coffee on for Kevin like he did every morning. He poured two glasses of pulp-free orange juice, then set the table, each plate loaded with a sizeable, nutritious breakfast. He then poured some fresh coffee into Kevin's favorite mug, where he added two heaping spoonfuls of sugar and three tablespoons of cream, just the way he loved it.

Over the course of the night, Andrew had trouble sleeping, and Kevin never once left his mind. Not only did he consider sneaking into his room many times over, but wondered if he too went through the same torment. He knew it was a bad idea to be so hopeful, but their relationship had reached a point he never thought it would.

Unlike Andrew, Kevin slept in, but not with ease. He also spent a good amount of time tossing and turning, troubled by his thoughts. When he woke, it was with sleepless eyes and a cloudy, groggy head— the closest he could come to having a hangover. He pulled on a pair of black jeans and matching silk shirt, one which he didn't bother buttoning all the way up, then shambled down the stairs with his hair standing in all directions.

On the final step, he stopped. A luscious aroma lured him toward the kitchen, and as it hit his nose, his stomach reacted with a short-tempered growl. He followed the scent to the dining room, where he saw two plates lavished with fresh breakfast, sided with orange juice and... was that coffee?

"You're up," chimed a gentle voice, which Kevin turned toward. "I feel like I've been waiting ages."

Kevin looked at the food on the table. Then, he looked back at his son, his tired eyes no longer pressed into a squint. "You made breakfast?" he confirmed, astounded.

"Yeah." Andrew shoved his hands into his pockets. "It's my first time doing it, so I hope it's good."

Touched, as well as stunned, Kevin added, "And you made me coffee."

"Two sugars, extra cream. Right?"

All of the proper words of grateful kindness failed him. The only times anyone ever made him breakfast was when his mother prepared it or he ordered it at a restaurant. "Oh, Andrew," he sighed. "You're so…" Andrew's heart fluttered for a moment. "Thoughtful."

The wavering of Andrew's heart paused, but it would be back. It always came back. "Sit down and eat. I'll go get the mail."

"Forget that now." Kevin pulled out a chair, fixing his messy hair with his palms. "Eat with me."

He was hoping he'd say that. Andrew took a seat across from him at his own plate, taking a bite. He felt something crunch between his teeth, and he grimaced. A piece of egg shell, no doubt. After a second and third chew, a burnt flavor twirled against his tongue. Ugh. This was *horrible*. He couldn't take a fourth bite, preoccupied with whether or not Kevin would agree with his opinion.

Before giving Andrew any clue regarding his view on the meal, he took a few bites. Andrew sat in suspense while sipping his orange juice. Then, their eyes met. Kevin nodded and gave a thumbs up. "S'good!" He took another bite. His face then contorted, looking like someone who was struck off their feet by a speeding vehicle. "Real good." Something crunched against his molars and his nose twisted as he bit into it.

"Really?" Once again, Andrew heard the fraudulence in Kevin's encouragement. Why did he have to lie like that? The eggs were several degrees of disgusting if he had to judge them.

"Oh yeah," he uttered with a cough. "Satisfying." Kevin no longer took small bites. He shoveled his food in, filling his stomach as fast as he could, swallowing before the flavor could touch his taste buds. "Thank you, sweetie."

Sweetie. Andrew's blood warmed. *At least he cares.*

While munching, Kevin kept his eyes on the weather displayed on the television, but every so often they drifted back to Andrew. Each look had an indication of torture in it, something Andrew was familiar with by now. "I was thinking of doing your photo shoot today."

"Sweet. I can't wait."

"What would you like me to wear?"

"That's… up to you." It might have been quite the treat if he had worn nothing at all. Whatever grade might his teacher award him with if he turned in naked photos of Kevin Neil?

"I'll find something nice. Wouldn't want to look shabby for your pictures."

Andrew, exhausted from holding back, thought it time to test the waters after what went on the night before. If there was a spark, a uniting of crossing stars, it required verification, regardless if the hints were subtle and they had to fumble in the dark for any clue as to the statute of romantic notions between them. Facts had to be exposed, and if Kevin was going to hide from them, he had to jump in first.

"You'd look good in anything," he complimented with a seductive smile, arching his shoulders back.

Kevin slipped his fork out of his mouth, his lips puckered as food sat inside his bloated mouth. Giving Andrew's comment to float around the air for a moment, he began chewing. "I would?" Flattery traced his words, and he looked to be holding back a smirk.

Andrew nodded with serious certainty. "You would."

"Oh. Thank you." He chewed a few more times, dabbing his mouth with a napkin to hide his satisfied expression.

A piercing silence followed thereafter, the both of them chewing, sipping, moving about in their chairs. Kevin cleared his throat, and Andrew chugged his orange juice until the glass was empty.

"I think you look good, too," disclosed Kevin.

The uneaten bacon on Andrew's plate was moved aside for more important matters. "You do?"

Kevin's head bobbed up and down to a slow tempo. His gaze fixed on the items on the table, on the television, even on his smartphone plugged in on the counter, as long as it was anywhere but on Andrew's face. A tinge of cardinal swarmed up his sternum, and he plucked at a strand of his dangling hair.

Andrew tested things beyond a point that might not have been wise, but he no longer cared. He not only wanted Kevin to know, but the whole world to be in on the secret. "What do you like most about me?"

"Everything." The maroon tint on Kevin's neck spread up to his cheeks. Andrew's chuckling, a sound Kevin not only found adorable, but heavenly, worsened his glow.

"Really? Everything?"

In a velvet, silken inflection, he reiterated, "Everything." When seeing that Andrew was the next to blush, he no longer hid his smile from him. In fact, he showed it off with pride.

"I do too. I mean... about you. Think that. Yeah." A snort filled Andrew's abrupt cackle. After a second or two, Kevin joined him, both of them erupting into a song of shy, lovesick giggles. Then, as if caught in a snare, they both stopped when realizing just what they were doing, who they were, or rather, who they were meant to be, and their flirting died just as soon as it started.

"Um..." Kevin uttered, looking away from Andrew's guilt-stricken eyes, his own filled with sickened regret. "I, uh... have to call my editor. She's been begging me to get on the horn with her about the new release. I told her a million times it'll be ready by next month, but for some reason she just doesn't trust me, you know?"

"That's too bad," murmured Andrew as his nose twitched.

"You don't mind, do you?"

"Course not." Dropping his head, he watched his hands for a while as he twisted them together. He didn't want to feel ashamed of himself— after all, an attraction was an attraction, and there was little he could do to bury it— but an attachment of this sort to his parent could only result in tragedy.

You should know better by now, Andrew scolded himself.

Kevin didn't leave the table for a short while, observing Andrew's saddened state with crushed spirits. What could he offer him that would be of any help, other than the obvious? He then set his napkin on the table and departed, shuffling toward the kitchen while watching the floor.

After Kevin's "phone call," which Andrew didn't believe for a second actually took place, Kevin offered to model for Andrew, hoping it would mend their stress and give them something else to think about. Andrew agreed to it, curbing his depression with more positive outlooks. Kevin told him he'd return after taking a shower, and Andrew was once again distracted, this time with thoughts of Kevin wet, naked, and covering his smooth skin from head to toe in water and suds.

Feeling a new, persistent growth in the crotch of his pants, he cursed under his breath. Why'd he have to wear jeans that were so damned tight on him? The strain against the fabric was unbearable. In an effort to calm his nerves and lessen the swelling, he readied his camera to help keep his hands busy. The attempt was unfortunately in vain. Kevin was upstairs, running his strapping hands over his taught stomach, soap streaking toward his groin, where he may or may not have a tall, proud growth as powerful as the one Andrew suffered through, and not even the Jaws of Life could get that image out of his mind.

"Fuck," Andrew hissed as he adjusted his length around his pant leg (though it lacked any adequate "length" to speak of), hoping to get it out of sight before Kevin came back. If he couldn't see it when glancing down, he knew he was successful. For good measure, he draped his long T-shirt over it. A job well-done… that is, until the bottom of his shirt started rolling up. What the hell? It never did that before.

When Kevin came back downstairs, he was fully dressed, drying his trimmed, black hair with a towel while carrying a comb. Andrew rolled his shirt back down, flattening it with his hands until it no longer curled. From where he stood, he could smell Kevin's same zesty cologne again, and all signs of stubble were gone from his chin and jaw line. When Kevin tossed the towel over a chair, he gave his straight locks a thorough combing. Andrew picked up on how rehearsed this seemed for him. Did he do this every morning?

"I'm ready for my close up," Kevin sang. "Try to show off my good side. I've got a reputation to keep."

"That won't be a problem," Andrew voiced with confidence, adoring that radish tint that revisited Kevin's skin. Taking hold of his camera, Andrew approached Kevin with an off-beat step. "Take a seat on the couch for me… uh, please."

Kevin did as he was asked, silent and waiting for further instructions. Seeing Kevin do his bidding so willingly was too much for him to handle, and he tried his best to keep his excitement under control. Flipping open the tiny screen, he focused the image, centered it on Kevin's face and upper body. "Give me your best professional pose."

Kevin crossed one leg over the other, draped his arm over the back of the couch, tilted his head to one side, and looked into the distance as though nothing in the world mattered to him. It was the perfect likeness to suit models in men's catalogues, ones that Andrew was sure Kevin looked through hundreds of times.

He snapped three high quality photos of Kevin in that position in different angles. No matter where Andrew stood, Kevin knew what direction to look in. Even after he was done, and thought those photos probably would have been great enough for the assignment, he didn't want to stop there. He wanted more.

"The camera loves you," Andrew informed with pride.

Kevin's upper row of teeth glinted as he gleamed, and he dragged his hand over his mouth to get its overbearing size to shrink. He could no longer pull off the "serious businessman" look. Andrew snapped another of him, thrilled at the opportunity of capturing his father's joy for a lifetime. Pleased with Andrew's approval, his smile grew twice its original size. He could no longer look at the lens, but instead stared at his dark-painted walls.

Soon, Kevin struck poses for him Andrew didn't ask him for. He snapped so many pictures of Kevin, his memory card filled up. When the session came to an end, Andrew collapsed onto the couch beside him, and breathed deep for a minute or two, letting his heart calm down from its pounding. Kevin sighed, "I could use a cigarette," then leaned back in his seat, sprawled and stretched out, releasing a moan of relaxation.

"Good for you, too, huh?" Andrew joked, and Kevin laughed. That sound never got old, nor did the way Kevin arched his back. He'd rather watch that all day than go to school.

"Will that be enough?" his father asked.

"I don't know. I might need more."

"I think you had plenty."

Are we talking about the same thing? wondered Andrew.

"You're good with the poses," he mentioned, leaning closer to Kevin. "You should be a model. You know, a professional one."

"It's not that I'm good. I'm used to it. I dated a photographer once. He loved taking pictures of me. I modeled for him many times."

"What was he like?" Andrew wanted to know, seeking to make comparisons.

"Nothing like y..." He paused, his mouth twisting, as he considered what he was about to say before rephrasing. "He was...

okay."

"Was he a good photographer?"

"Oh yes. He worked for a magazine, had his own studio, published a few books. He was quite talented." Andrew's bottom lip sank, and Kevin, amused, added, "But his personality was unfavorable. He was a bit of a cheapskate."

"Why'd you date him, then?"

"I was an idiot. I followed my dick, not my head."

There were fewer words Andrew loved hearing Kevin say than "dick." "Do you do that a lot?"

"No!" he exclaimed, studying his son's face. "I mean, not anymore. When I was younger, I made a lot of mistakes. I wasn't the same person then as I am now."

"What about Kyle?"

"Huh?"

If he was to address this matter, he had to do so with caution. He had no right to oppose Kevin's relationship with Kyle, and he knew it. "Aren't you... boyfriends?"

"*Boyfriends?*" Kevin repeated, bemused. "Wherever did you get that idea?"

"I... heard you. In your room the other night."

"Oh God," groaned Kevin, palming his face. "Shit, Andrew, I'm sorry. That must have been awkward."

Awkward? That didn't even begin to scratch the surface. "It's okay."

"Look," Kevin went on, rubbing the creases upon his face. "Kyle and I... it's complicated."

"Complicated?"

"Yes. We're not boyfriends. I know it seems a bit on the odd side, but we're just close." He sank farther back in his seat, leaning against Andrew, who pressed back. "I might have wanted something more at one point, but... Kyle has this way of handling difficult situations. And by that I mean, he doesn't deal with them at all."

Puzzled, Andrew asked, "What do you mean?"

"If he felt something for me, he hides it well. Kyle says he wants to remain friends, so, that's what we continue to be. By now, I've made my peace with it, and if he's too afraid to admit things like that, then I don't think we belong in any sort of relationship."

"And you have sex?" Andrew added, unable to force the last word out without feeling nauseous, as though the very idea had been a virulent plague.

"Sometimes. Usually after we've had one too many beers. When we're in the mood, we just go at it. Have to satisfy the urge somehow, right?"

"And he likes that?" he asked, his voice ripe with jealousy. "Having that with you?"

Kevin planted his cheek on Andrew's boney shoulder, feeling and hearing his breath quicken in the process. "He must. In fact, it seems to be the only reason he spends time with me now. As you can imagine, it's a little hollow."

"Maybe he thinks you'll leave him if he tells you the truth," Andrew insisted, refusing to look his father in the eye. His every muscle seized when he felt Kevin's warm breath on his neck.

"He knows I would never do such a thing."

"Does he really? If he knew for certain, he wouldn't hide it from you."

Taking a moment to think on it, Kevin counseled, "Maybe he doesn't know what it is he wants. Maybe he's just as confused as I am."

"And maybe he's worried you'll hurt him, like everyone else does."

Shocked, Kevin went quiet, and so too did Andrew. Following the brief, frozen silence, Kevin whispered, "I would never."

"You can't know that. You couldn't possibly know that."

"I know I would do everything in my power to prevent it."

Hoping he could calm himself, Andrew bit down on his own lip. It did him no good. If anything, it exacerbated his anxiety. "That's what you say," he answered. "That's what she said, too."

Unsettled by the direction of the conversation, Kevin pondered in a shaky voice, "Who?"

Andrew scoffed, much like his mother. "You know who."

The truth was that Kevin did know who Andrew referred to, but acknowledging it would mean the end of whatever silly game it was they were playing. Quick, Kevin. Change the subject. "Andrew, I can tell you're upset. And I don't want you to be. I want you to be happy. If there's anything I can…" How on earth could he finish that sentence? He knew what it was they both wanted, and drawing attention to it could be disastrous.

Unable to handle the discomfort any longer, Andrew rose up off the sofa and skulked away from him, incredulous that they continued to tiptoe around the subject when things were so painfully obvious, but even more frustrated that fantasy would have to remain fantasy.

"Andrew, wait," Kevin called to him, also standing up, but his son was already out of sight, rushing up the stairs to his bedroom.

Already Andrew began to feel immature for abandoning the conversation in the manner he had, and concerned that he might have hurt Kevin's feelings. All the same, he needed to be alone. There were problems of his own he had to make peace with.

More importantly, there were dreams he had to say goodbye to.

Chapter Six

In Which the Ladder Extends

Space was what Andrew needed, so Kevin gave him plenty of it. For hours on end, Andrew remained holed up in his room, practicing his guitar to take his mind off of all that ailed him. When Kevin vowed never to hurt him, he believed him— and that was the problem. No one else ever made him feel as safe as Kevin did, and no one else would compare to him. No matter how long he tried to deny that, it was a reality that rang all too loud in his ears, even in pure isolation where he spent the majority of his time.

Andrew didn't want Kevin to think he was angry with him, because he wasn't. Far from it, in fact. With the both of them under the same roof, spending so much time together, it complicated his ability to rationalize. It was moments like these that he treasured his privacy, and cherished how little it was invaded when he needed it. Let him think things through, and everything would be fine.

Having spent many evenings working it out, Andrew finished the tune to the song he had been writing. Now he only had to complete the lyrics, and make sure they sounded right. It would only take him a couple more days, but he would save it for Christmas time. Until then, he would practice it until he knew it inside and out. It would be the first true song he had ever written, and its purpose would be just as vital to him.

The intercom on his wall spoke in an electronic tin can voice that made Kevin sound a few years younger than he was. "Dinner's ready, Andrew, if you're hungry."

Dinner? Had he really been cooped up in his room that long? The heavenly sound of Kevin's gentle words reminded him that he didn't have to be alone, and he didn't have to spend the whole night brooding over what he didn't have. He set his guitar aside, then walked to the intercom and hit the "Call" button. "I'll be right down."

During dinner, discussion hadn't been an option, for neither of them had the will or strength to carry on a topic. At the sight of Kevin's long face, Andrew wanted to erase it and lighten it up again, but he could tell that it would take more than a few bad jokes to do so. He understood his pain more than Kevin might have assumed.

Kevin was the first to vacate the table, taking his dishes to the sink where he rinsed them off. Andrew soon followed, bringing his own plate and silverware to the counter, and Kevin glanced at them before picking them up and washing them as well. Andrew retrieved the wet plate he set down on the drip tray and dried it off with a towel.

"You don't have to do that," Kevin told him with mixed amusement and dismay.

Firmly, Andrew replied, "I want to." Kevin nodded, and they quietly washed plates for a minute or two. "Dad... I'm sorry."

"For what?"

"For..." The games had to stop. They weren't children, and he was tired of not only acting like a kid, but being treated as one. "For comparing you to my mother."

"Oh," Kevin breathed, relieved by his honesty. "Well, that's... that's okay, Andrew."

"No, it's not. You're nothing like her, and I shouldn't just assume you'd turn out like her. I should be getting over it, and her, by now."

"I know how you feel. Don't be so hard on yourself."

Someone had to be hard on him. If he wasn't, who would there be left to scold him for his mistakes, to belittle him in front of others? That was part of life, wasn't it? If that wasn't life, why then did he have to go through it?

Kevin shattered the insecure shell Andrew had built around himself by paying him a compliment. "I heard you playing. I've heard you play on other nights, too. You're good."

A compliment from Kevin was a multi-million dollar lottery

winning. "Thank you. I guess I was taught by listening to so much music."

"Drone Diode. That's your favorite band, isn't it?"

Andrew went speechless for a moment, surprised that Kevin bothered to pay attention to such things. "Yeah. They're my idols."

"Have you ever met them?"

"I always wanted to go to one of their shows. I never got to, though. I'd always have these daydreams of playing out jam sessions with Christian Maccrum. He's the most incredible guitarist I know of. I've been trying to mimic his style for years, but I just can't do it. It's *his* style, you know what I mean?"

"Style is pretty important in art. It makes one piece unique from another."

"I know that now. When I grew up, I started trying to do my own thing. It's not nearly as good as anything Christian Maccrum does… but it's okay, I guess." He took another dish that Kevin passed to him, dried that, then slipped it into the cupboard with the rest.

"Sounded more than okay to me."

"Thanks, Dad. It matters a lot to me what you think."

"Me too. I mean, about what you think. Of me."

Andrew chewed his inner cheek, Kevin grinded his teeth, and for a while, the only sound was the running water and squeaking of cloth against glass.

Then, as they reached the final dish, Andrew grew exasperated of their tongue-tied introversion. He had a lot to say, and even more to get off of his chest. Kevin wasn't his therapist, but he was the next best thing.

With an elongated breath, he started. "When I was a kid, I did more than dream about meeting you. Of course, when Mom told me about you, I wanted to seek you out for years. Part of me thought she made you up to screw with my head, but I didn't want to believe that. In my heart, I just knew you were out there.

"But Mom didn't tell me much else. Every time I asked her questions about you, she'd keep things from me. I wanted to know where you lived, if you knew about me, what you looked like… but she'd hide everything, told me that it didn't matter. I always thought, 'Why? Why did she tell me about you, but keep so many things about you a secret?' Until now, it didn't make any sense. But I think I get it now.

"She used my desperation to meet you as a possible payment she never gave me. Whenever she wanted me to do something for her, she'd promise me…" his throat clenched as he revived the memories, but he pressed on while Kevin gave him his full, undivided attention, however melancholy he seemed now. "She'd promise me she'd take me to see you if I did 'this one thing' for her; sometimes it was cleaning up after her, and other times she wanted me to stop 'acting up'. One time she told me to paint a whole room, and I got nothing for it. She offered this so many times that I no longer believed her, and each time she did I… I lost hope. I knew I'd be stuck with her forever. I would never get to meet you. And I wanted to. I needed to. She knew I needed to, and she didn't let me have the chance. It was her way of punishing me."

"*Punishing* you?" affirmed Kevin, haunted by the implications.

"I wasn't kidding when I said she hated me," Andrew explained. "I know this because she told me. She told me how she wished I…" he struggled with these next words, as he had sworn he would forever try to forget them. "She wished I hadn't been born, and that she should have aborted me." Though he noticed Kevin's horrified jaw nearly touch the floor, he didn't give him the chance to speak. "And sometimes I wish she did, too. If she had, then I wouldn't have had to go through it all. If she had chosen to get rid of me sooner… I wouldn't have lived like I did. Instead, she had me, and punished me for existing."

As Andrew spoke, he hadn't noticed the dampness on his face. He had shed so many tears that by now they felt almost customary. However, this time, he wasn't the only one. When glancing at Kevin, he saw the redness around his eyes, heard his quivering breaths. It was unbearable to witness.

"I held on, though," Andrew comforted him. "I had to grow up early so I could take care of myself, but I kept going. Every wish I made was to meet you, hoping and praying that you were nicer than her and not as careless as David. The only way I got through her abuse was imagining you rescuing me from her— kicking the door down, telling her off and carrying me away. One time I tried to run away from home, just to find you. Obviously, that didn't work out.

"But then she brought me to you. I can't tell if that was her way of apologizing to me, if that was her last act of mercy, but I can honestly say that I'm grateful for it. At first, I was terrified, thinking you'd turn out to be nothing like I imagined. But you did. You were all that I wished for."

Turning to Kevin's tear-soaked face, he declared, "You're the best thing that's ever happened to me."

"Andrew," Kevin managed to squeak out, but it was all he could muster. Before Andrew's wounded heart could react to the sight of Kevin's sobbing, he was tugged into his father's arms, which clenched him. "You are, too, honey. You are, too."

For the remainder of the night, they watched the science-fiction movie marathon that ran since Thanksgiving, once again taking their places on the couch in the TV room, a blanket around them with Andrew's head on Kevin's shoulder. Once or twice, Kevin gave his face and head gentle kisses, acts of both love and reassurance, healing Andrew's every scar.

During all of Andrew's Thanksgiving break, he and his father were attached at the hip for every activity. When Kevin went shopping for groceries, Andrew came along. When Kevin did laundry, Andrew helped him. Not once did Kevin think to object, nor did he ask Andrew to leave him be. Andrew's company was all he wanted.

When the four-day weekend came to a halt, Andrew begged Kevin to call in sick for him. Kevin clicked his tongue, shook his head, and said:

"You know I can't do that, Andrew."

Andrew cupped his hands together. "Just one day?"

"It's only school. You'll survive."

"Can we play games later?"

"Of course. Once your homework is done."

Many students at Elliott High School shared Andrew's somber expression when returning to class, missing the excitement of the long weekend that passed before anyone had a chance to enjoy it. Joining the crowd, Andrew headed to his locker, backpack and camera case in hand.

The damn handle got stuck again. No matter how much he pulled, it didn't wish to separate from the cabinet. It squealed in defiance, fighting against his every yank. Then, after about a minute worth of playing Tug Rope with it, it ejected, knocking Andrew a step back. He thought he heard a chorus of giggles behind him, though his imagination had always concocted such things in the past, as he picked up the items that managed to fall from his locker after the door seceded.

Ignoring the murmuring and chuckles for now, despite how little he wanted to, he put his textbooks back on the shelves where they belonged, but saw something else had fallen out with them: a folded sheet of loose leaf. He snatched it up off of the floor, unfolded it, and saw hasty writing in blue ball point ink.

I was too embarrassed to face you in person. I'm afraid you might be mad at me. I've been acting like kind of a jerk to you. I like you as a person, Andrew, and I'm sad at the thought of not speaking to you anymore. I'm sorry.
If you forgive me, sit with me at lunch. If not, I'll understand.
~Ben

Of course he forgave Ben. Before their last conversation, he had enjoyed getting to know him and learning of his interests. Their taste in music was identical, their choice of books and movies were alike, and they even loved some of the same food. A friend like Ben was hard to come by for Andrew. Regardless of his choice not to date him, he liked him.

At lunch, Andrew sat at their table, the one that they reserved every day. Where Ben had been sitting since their parting was a mystery to him, as he never saw him in the lunch room anymore. It was possible that he was sitting with other people now, and had blended into the crowd, but he considered that implausible.

Andrew kept his eyes peeled for Ben, who after ten minutes or so approached the table, hunched over. At seeing Andrew sitting and waiting for him, joy painted his face. He then took his regular seat across from him.

"I thought for sure you wouldn't do it," Ben admitted. He didn't have a lunch with him that day, which Andrew figured was due to a lack of appetite. "I'm glad you did."

"Why wouldn't I?"

"I wouldn't, if I had been you."

"I didn't see a point in avoiding you."

Ben nodded at that, relaxing his posture, easing his arms onto the tabletop and folding them. "You're right. Neither did I. Andrew, I like you a lot. I'm not denying that. But I didn't even give you a chance to know me much before putting the moves on you."

"I know enough to think you're cool," Andrew verified, gnawing on his sandwich. Damn, was it ever good. Even better than the last one he ate. "And that I like talking to you."

"Yeah, but I'm eager. When I like someone, I get too excited. I think I scared you."

What Ben didn't understand was that Andrew wasn't afraid of him. The real issue at hand was much deeper than that. "No, not really."

Maddened by more than just the conversation, Ben sighed. "I know you're not into me. I'm okay with that. I've made my peace with it. I just want to know why that is." Andrew looked apprehensive, and Ben calmed him with a tip in his voice. "You won't offend me. I know I'm not attractive."

For some reason, Andrew felt the need to whisper. If anyone was listening, why did it matter? "I have... a type. I mean, we all do, don't we?"

"Standards. I got you." He nodded, his shoulders tightening.

"Not even that. There's nothing wrong with you, Ben. You're just not my type."

"What *is* your type?" A trace of frustration edged his voice.

All color faded from Andrew's cheeks. "I guess... I like them a little older?"

Ben's bothered tone escaped him when he answered, only to be replaced with a hint of revulsion. "Older? Like, how much older?"

Andrew's shoulders raised toward his ears. "Like... thirties?"

"*Thirties?!*"

Andrew shut himself up with a bite of his food. He didn't think Ben would understand when he revealed this fact, but he also didn't think he'd look so grossed out.

"That's a bit out of your age range, isn't it?" continued Ben, pulling on the collar of his shirt.

"A bit."

"Why?" he laughed. "Why do you like them so much older?"

"I don't know. I just do. Do I need a reason?"

Clearing his throat a couple of times, Ben responded with, "Well. I guess I can't make myself age quicker." Andrew cranked out a weak smile. Ben twiddled his thumbs. "If I was older... would you have liked me then?"

Andrew rested his hand on his cheek and his elbow on the table, studying Ben for a moment. "It's a possibility." His heavy sigh said otherwise.

"I guess when I hit my thirties, I should try again, eh?" Indignant laughter quaked out of his mouth.

"Worth a shot…"

"In the meantime, I'll do my best to find a time machine so I can tell my older self to come back for you."

That's the corniest line I've ever heard, Andrew thought with a shake of the head.

"Doing anything after school?" Thank goodness Ben changed the topic.

"Doing a photo shoot for the school paper. They want some pictures of the drama club." He nibbled a bit more on his sandwich until it was finished, then tossed his empty lunch bag into the nearest bin. When his eyes locked with Ben's, he saw that they had darkened. Disturbed, Andrew muttered, "W-what?"

"You don't listen to a word I say to you, do you?"

"Wait, what? What are you talking about?"

"I've told you at least three times that I was in drama club."

"I, uh…" Had Ben really told him that? He never heard him bring it up, not once. "I'm sorry, Ben, I… I guess I forgot."

Ben grunted beneath his breath, "Forgot."

"I told you I was sorry," scowled Andrew, sterner than before.

"Doesn't matter." Apparently it did matter, because his face remained scrunched.

With an annoyed sigh, Andrew stood up. "I'll see you then?"

"Yeah, if you can remember."

Blowing off his combative statement, Andrew stormed off, hot under the collar.

For photography, Andrew brought in a printed photo of Kevin to class, one of him sitting cross-legged on the couch and staring into the distance. Upon inspecting the pictures everyone else brought in, he noticed a few students had touched their photos up with graphics programs. He hoped that wasn't a requirement.

Mister Benson took the photographs from each of his students, setting them in a pile on his desk. He assigned his students with darkroom work while he looked them over and graded them, and Andrew and Sarah once again found themselves pairing up, chatting with each other about what they did over their break. Sarah mentioned seeing her whole family, which of them she didn't like, and how much she hated leaving town. Andrew told her about how strange his weekend was as well, and how close he and his father were getting. He neglected to include details on how much closer he'd like them to be.

Near the end of the class, Mister Benson handed the pictures back to his students until Andrew received his. The front of the photo was untouched, but a message was on the back in blue marker:

Great model, but you should learn to utilize light better! B

It wasn't an A, but it wasn't one of the Ds or Es he was accustomed to receiving when living with Star. For once in his life, he felt proud of himself and his work. Above all, he couldn't wait to show his good grade to Kevin, who he was certain would be proud.

The steel doors to the performing arts center creaked open when Andrew pushed them, and he eased his head inside to get a peek of the auditorium. Straight ahead was the stage, and on it stood many students of various races, heights, and weights, each of them holding playbooks and standing in a semi-circle around two who were reading their lines aloud to one another. Ben was one of them. Before him stood an actress, a young woman with coffee hair and a slightly round face that Andrew didn't recognize.

"You can't do this, Adriana!" Ben cried, reading the lines from the book he gripped onto. His features were warped into fictional aggression. "I'm not responsible for what happened!"

"The sickness began with you!" shouted the brunette opposing him, also looking up and down from her playbook. "It was you who spread the disease, Richard! It is you who carries it! Look around you at the mass of death and tell me now if you lack sorrow!"

"How dare you accuse me, wench! If anyone carries disease, it is the men with which you lie!"

Andrew, who did his best to slip into the room as to not interrupt their rehearsal, crept down the middle isle with his camera in hand. Just as he zoomed his lens in to Ben and his acting partner, the door he came in slammed. He flinched at the heavy reverberation, then all of those upon the stage stared in his direction, the recital coming to a pause. Andrew passed them all a nervous wave, and some of them giggled.

"Andrew!" exclaimed Ben, the pretend rage fading, though Andrew would have preferred it over his sardonic sneer. "Everyone, this is Andrew, he's taking pictures for the school paper."

Some waved, others said hello, though dryly. A few did nothing. With so many unknown eyes gawking at him, Andrew shrunk toward the nearest shadows. The instructor stepped down off of the stage and beckoned Andrew forth before telling him, "Hello, Andrew. Why don't you take a seat in the front row there?"

"Yes, ma'am," he said with a nod. He did as directed, sitting in the middle of the row where he had the best view of the entire stage.

Soon the only sounds in the room were the two actors reciting lines and the clicks of the shutter in Andrew's camera. Soon, more students got in on the action, playing out their parts as piano music began. That's when they started to sing.

Andrew had a hard time wrapping his mind around the concept of Ben singing. He never pictured him the type to sing about anything, especially not so well. The tune was not a happy one. Its lyrics told a tale of loss and sorrow, of struggling times, and the shift in mood was abrupt and unsettling.

When the song came to an end, Andrew applauded, many actors breaking into a contagious smile. Ben took a bow to his spectator, oozing with pride. The instructor told them they were finished for the afternoon, and Ben hopped off the stage, dropping into the chair beside Andrew.

Following a short breather, Ben asked him, "What'd you think?"

Andrew picked underneath one of his nails, which were painted black. "The club is full of really talented people."

He snorted. "Not about them. About me."

"You're in the club, aren't you? I was including you."

"Ah. Well, thank you, then." Ben lifted his feet, resting them on the edge of the stage while folding his arms behind his head as Andrew looked for an excuse to make a quick getaway. "This is just the start of my acting career, you know. After high school, I'm going into an arts college. You know what they say about actors?"

Playing with a silver bracelet around his wrist, Andrew mumbled, "That they do a lot of drugs?"

"Hah! Heh-heh. Andrew. You're amusing." Whether or not he

was being sarcastic, Andrew couldn't tell. Perhaps he was a good actor after all. "No, not that they do drugs, silly. That a lot of directors start out as actors. Directing is what I really want to do."

"Are you sure directing a film is what you really want?"

"Absolutely. It's been a lifelong dream of mine. I'm in the film club too, you know. I've actually been meaning to ask you, since you're so familiar with cameras, if you'd like to film something for me."

"I can take photos," Andrew clarified. "That doesn't mean I can film well."

"Still objects, moving objects… is there really a difference?"

"Yeah. There is, actually."

"What if I told you the project would be really fun, and one of a kind?"

"I don't think I have time for it, with my homework and the school paper…"

Ben tapped his index finger on the armrest of his seat. "What else?"

He knew what he was asking, but Andrew didn't say the D word this time. "Ben. I shouldn't."

Stung by the rejection, he closed his eyes and took a deep breath. "That's fine. It'll only be the best independent film in the whole school, and your name would be on it, and I thought you'd appreciate being a part of it. But that's fine."

Someone's confident, aren't they? Andrew griped. Packing his camera into its case and draping the strap over his shoulder, he stood up and scooted toward the middle aisle.

"Oh. Andrew?" Andrew halted and peered over his shoulder at him. "When the projects are finished, they're shown to an audience, and we get special awards. And the parents always come to the show."

Andrew's intrigue was captured. "They do?"

Grinning from ear to ear, Ben nodded. "Oh, all the time. In fact, they're encouraged to show up. I bet your dad would love to see something you filmed."

"Yeah," agreed Andrew, giving the room a thorough examination as he contemplated it. "What do I have to do?"

Cheering inside that he hit pay dirt, Ben leapt out of his chair and bounded to Andrew, wagging his tail. "It's easy. You just follow my directions. Because I'm the director, you follow me?" With a glare, Andrew's head bobbed. "I'll give you the script to look over, and I'll tell you what to shoot, and you just shoot it. Hell, you could even use some of your photographer intuition, if that's even a thing."

"How long are you planning to work on this?"

"No less than a week is my estimate. So…" Rubbing his hands together, flashing his teeth, he asked, "Are you in?"

Releasing a woebegone sigh, Andrew shrugged. "Okay. I'll read the script and see what I think, but no promises."

"*Yes!* Thank you, Andy."

Frost coated Andrew's stare. "Don't call me Andy."

Ben's knees trembled. "Okay, okay. *Andrew.* Sorry."

Ben walked Andrew backstage through a rickety door, taking him to a rehearsal room where everyone's belongings were stashed. He grabbed his coat, then his backpack, which he then unzipped and reached inside of. When he withdrew his hand, it was holding a thick notebook with a black and red cover. Taped to the front was a slip of paper that read:

The Final Star
A screenplay by Ben Erickson

Stretching his head to the ceiling in a bold stance, Ben passed the script to Andrew, the tendons in his hand bulging as he offered it. It took Andrew a few moments to realize that Ben intended to pass it to him, and he seized it after Ben waved it back and forth like a flag of victory.

Andrew flipped the cover back, the title page staring him in the face with enormous font and bold lettering. On the next page was Ben's name again, also filling the length of the paper and dwarfing the word "screenwriter." He hid an eye-roll from him, then flipped that page as well.

The only line Andrew had the time to skim over was, "In a distant galaxy, one so far away that we're not even aware it exists…" Ben clapped Andrew's hands together, shutting the notebook in the process.

"Tell you what," Ben recommended. "Why don't you take it home with you and read it, then you can call me and tell me what you think?"

"I guess I could," Andrew replied with uncertainty.

"You'll love it, though. I already know you will. I can feel it. You were meant to work on this project with me."

Taking an offbeat step backward, Andrew squeaked, "Sure. Well, I'd better go. Dad's waiting for me."

"Course. Can't keep Daddy-O waiting." The sycophantic manner in which he said this wasn't the only strange thing about it; the raising of his right eyebrow suggested that Andrew might not have been very accomplished at keeping his own feelings toward Kevin a secret. Ben grabbed the notebook, slipping a pen out of his bag, and wrote his number down on the back sheet before placing it back into Andrew's diminutive palms. "Talk to you later, then."

Sweating from the stuffy air inside the tightly packed room, Andrew zipped out after bidding him a curt farewell, then sped to his locker to retrieve his things and made haste for the exit. Bundled in his jacket with his backpack and camera in hand, he dashed through the snow to Kevin's car, hopping into the passenger seat.

As he did every day, Kevin gifted him with a sweet salutation and asked him about his day. This time, he noticed the unfamiliar object resting in Andrew's hands.

"What's that?" he asked, tilting his head to get a view of the front cover of Ben's screenplay.

"My friend Ben wrote a script, and, well, this is it. He wants me to film a movie for him, or something."

"That's neat. Are you going to?"

"I'm considering it. I think I'll check out this 'screenplay' first." Taking a moment to think it over, he confided, "I've never filmed anything before."

"I bet you could do it," Kevin encouraged. "With how easy you make photography and the guitar look, I'm sure it'd be a breeze for you."

"Thanks." He rolled his hands into a ball upon his lap, flattening his chin to his chest. "I, uh…" He coughed a couple of times. "Missed you. Today."

"Did you?" His rejoinder was not one of confusion, but surprise, as if the idea of being missed by anyone was absurd. When he gave Andrew a quick peripheral once over, Andrew's rosy face bounced up and down, and he cracked a warm smile. "I missed you, too,

Andrew. All I could think about all day was playing video games with you."

"Me too." In addition to other things.

"I can't wait to spend the evening with you."

"I can't either." The glow upon Andrew's face burned brighter.

At home, Andrew set Ben's written work aside to complete his homework, which he would later admit to rushing through. He showed Kevin the grade on his photo, and he launched into a speech about how he deserved an A.

"Thanks, Dad," Andrew told him. "But I don't mind the B. It's much better than the grades I'm used to getting."

"It's A work," argued his father, twisting his nose around like a foul smell had entered it.

"I could have done better, you know. I could have touched it up on the computer. I really should be using my full potential." Kevin looked at him as though his son had just swallowed a wasp and might need immediate medical attention. Puzzled, Andrew perpetuated with, "It's okay. I'm not upset about it. You don't have to love everything I do."

At this, his posture slumped. Letting out a gradual exhale, he said fondly, "I know. I'm just… trying to be…"

"A good parent. I get it, Dad, it's okay."

"I really do love it, though."

"I know you do. And I know you care about me. You wouldn't be bothered by my reaction if it didn't matter to you how I felt. But you can be honest and still be a good father." Saying this, it struck Andrew like a sack of stones that Kevin had just as many worries pertaining to their separation as he did, and his devotion to him expanded thrice its original size. He paid him some soothing words. "I won't be mad at you for telling me the truth."

Conflicted, Kevin looked into the eyes of his first and only born, then down to the photograph he had handed him, then back to his son. "You're a good photographer, honey. But really… you could have used some light effects." He shrugged, bit the corner of his lip, and squeezed his eyes half shut as if awaiting a shrieking retort.

Rejuvenated, Andrew took a breath of fresh air. "Thank you."

"I, I'll hang it on the fridge!"

"You don't have to."

Kevin did anyway, but Andrew didn't object. What he did wish to do was tell him how much he loved him. The timing, however, didn't feel appropriate to him. When the moment arrived, he had a feeling he would know it.

"Your cooking could also use work," Kevin informed, again with a weak inflection.

"I know," Andrew agreed. "That's why I leave it to you." They shared a supple laugh.

Killing a few hours before dinner, Andrew took the time to read Ben's screenplay as Kevin attempted to get some work done in his office. The total length of pages included in the notebook ran up past the seventies, and every one included details about how exactly he wanted his actors to pose and express themselves.

The story was abysmal, that much was positive, but not for the lack of sufficient prose. Something about it seemed familiar to Andrew, as though he had read it elsewhere or seen it on television. It could have well been the abundance of clichés that scored such a review from him, and he didn't wish to accuse Ben of plagiarism if the idea had, in fact, been original, but when he came to the final page and the screenplay's crashing conclusion, it became clearer than ever that it had to have been copied from another source. It was all too predictable.

A second opinion was required on something like this. Hauling himself out of bed, book in hand, he took it down to Kevin's office, where he heard the sound of frantic fingers gliding over keys. Like it always had been, the office door was wide open, Kevin hunched over his keyboard, typing at a speed Andrew considered unfathomable.

"How's it coming?" he butted in, and Kevin turned in his immense leather chair to face him. He stuck the end of a pen into his mouth, one that already looked threadbare from being gnawed on.

"Great. A couple more adjustments and I can finally send it to my editor, then she can get off my back about it." He slipped the pen away from his molars and set it on his desk, where many other chewed writing utensils lied. Looking at Andrew, he noticed his son's bemused interest in them. "When I quit smoking, I…"

The situation had explained itself. "Oh," Andrew giggled.

"What's up?"

Holding the screenplay up in both hands, Andrew presented it to his father like a Holy Grail. "I need your help with something."

"Name it."

"It's about Ben's screenplay. I read it, and I got kind of a weird vibe that I'd seen it before. I wasn't sure, so, I thought... because you're an author..."

"I'll take a look at it." He reached his hand out, and Andrew placed the book into it, brushing their fingers together. At the sensation of their skin touching, they each faked coughs and pretended to scratch non-existent itches.

"Th-thanks. I wanted to be sure, you know?"

"Yeah, absolutely. It's, uh... no problem." He picked up a pair of reading glasses from the desk and slipped them on, then grabbed a pen that didn't yet have thousands of tooth-shaped craters all over it, then like a teething baby began to bite into it as he opened the notebook upon the surface of his desk.

A page turned. Another, then another. "Mm," hummed Kevin as he flipped them. "Hmm. Huh." He didn't get halfway through it before closing it, sliding the glasses off of his face. "He wrote this?"

In a joking manner, Andrew said, "I guess that's what I'm trying to determine."

"It's *very* familiar."

"*Right?*"

"The whole thing about the slaves and the mines and the end of the world thing. I've seen that before. I know I have."

"I know! I feel the same way! He totally ripped it off."

"Wait a second. We don't know that for certain. Maybe he doesn't even know he did. To be honest, I can't pinpoint what it is he's duplicating. I've seen so many sci-fi movies, it's difficult to narrow them down. Maybe no one else will notice."

"Dad," Andrew snickered, folding his arms across his chest. "If you and I noticed it..."

"Andrew, really. Even if he did, it's just a school project. I doubt he plans to make millions off of this idea."

"So... what do I say to him? I wasn't too keen on working with him to begin with, but now I can't see myself filming it and deceiving him."

Kevin stood out of his chair and passed the screenplay back to Andrew. "Tell him what you think, but try to be diplomatic about it. It's not easy to share writing with people."

"I don't want to hurt his feelings. He annoys me a little, but he's still my friend."

"If you can handle me being honest with you, Andrew," Kevin reminded him, "Then I'm sure he can take a little criticism from you."

Ben and I aren't the same person, Andrew almost told him, then decided not to. "You're right. I'll give him a call and talk to him about it. Nicely."

Approving with a nod, Kevin placed his hand on his shoulder, sliding his thumb over the bone of his collar. The two of them were caught in an awkward silence, the brilliance on their faces fading into profound awareness, their matching cobalt irises somber, tempting one another to proceed to forbidden, hallowed ground that no one was meant to tread upon.

Kiss me, begged Andrew, his toes curling inside of his socks, grabbing clumps of carpet in them as he tried to inch himself taller. *For the love of fuck, kiss me.* Saliva snaked down the corner of his mouth as desperation took hold of his every nerve. Kevin's eyes drifted to Andrew's shaking bottom lip, which was glazed with spittle, and his only thought was how delicious it might taste, if perchance it might even rival sugar in its delectable sweetness.

"Let me know if you need anything else, okay?" Then Kevin was back in his leather chair, suddenly fascinated with his keyboard as if a tragic accident had just taken place on it.

Andrew wanted many things from him, but none of which he'd confess to. Dismayed that they continued to dance around the clues they threw at each other day in and day out, Andrew withdrew from the scene and headed up to his room.

As Andrew took his leave, Kevin watched him go, his heart sinking toward his grumbling stomach. In regards to Andrew's photography (and his substandard cooking skills), he had been up front and honest with him that day, but the ultimate declaration was of greater significance. Andrew deserved to know the truth about this budding, discreet passion that came as little surprise to him, but with the force of a thousand tons. Finding the right method in which to address it was a bigger issue.

Not in so many words could Kevin convey a decree such as "I'm in love with you," but even in the mind of one familiar with words and their meanings, he could produce few that were good enough for Andrew's ears. Love was a complicated matter, but when it came to Andrew, it made too much sense. Things like this, especially when it came to his son, had to be handled delicately. He wanted nothing more than for Andrew to know, but all would be lost if he were to scare him out of his life. His career meant half as much to him as his son did.

A migraine threatened to sweep in. By this stage in his life, after having suffered through hundreds of them, he could sense them approach from the second they prickled at his sinuses. He left his office and strolled to the bathroom, where he ate a few pills in hopes they would kill the headache off before it worsened. He then retired to bed to rest both it and his thoughts away.

In his own room, Andrew had dialed Ben on his cordless phone, and waited through five rings before getting a voicemail message. The second he hung up, the phone bleated its electronic ring, and Andrew answered.

"Neil residence," he told the caller.

"Neil?" repeated Ben. "I thought your last name was Phillips."

"It is." He pinched the bridge of his nose. "Neil is my dad's."

At hearing the sound of that D word again, Ben was quick to change the subject. "So did you read it?"

"I did. Ben, I have to be honest with you."

"You hated it, didn't you?"

"No, not exactly. It's just that it…" At first, Andrew thought the line went dead, but when he heard Ben's shallow breathing, he figured the suspense was too great for him. Andrew sighed, then said, "I loved it."

"Really? You did?"

"Yeah. When do we start filming this thing?"

"Oh, man, you have no idea how excited I am! It's going to be awesome. You're going to meet my selected cast. They're all friends of mine. They all wanted to be 'in' the movie, so of course they didn't want to film it themselves. You'll be saving us so many problems."

Andrew had little doubt that Ben milked the opportunity for all it was worth. "Cool. I have a question, though. Judging by the events in the script, it sounds like the production value is kind of… beyond our reach. Are you going to be able to afford the budget?"

"Greg is our designer, and he's got a lot planned for special effects. He's buried up to the neck in graphics programs, and he's good with them too."

That didn't quite answer his question, but Andrew accepted it nonetheless. "It sounds like you have everything properly planned out."

A smarmy chuckle echoed down the line. "If there's one thing you're going to learn about me soon, Andrew, it's that I'm the man with a plan of action. Get it? Because directors say 'action'. Do you get it? Andrew?"

Andrew picked up his pen and bit on it. Hard.

CHAPTER SEVEN

In Which Chemicals Stir

"**Cheryl**, this is Andrew. Andrew, Cheryl Dawes."

Cheryl, a woman that to Andrew looked two years too old still be in high school, gave him her hand, which he then shook. Her wrist was adorned with beaded bracelets of various warm hues, which matched her multi-colored nails. Her extensive hair was dyed violet, the same tint as her lace shirt, and her triangular face was thankfully a welcoming one.

In a voice as smooth as cream, she expressed, "Nice to meet you, Andrew."

Andrew could only work out two words: "You too." Then Ben wedged between them.

"She's going to be playing Jeny," he interrupted, and without giving them the chance to say any more to each other, he introduced Andrew to Greg, "the designer," whose bleached white T-shirt looked a size too small on his colossal, rotund teddy bear gut. On his sizeable face was an auburn beard that reached his jugular, complete with bushy mustache.

"Heard a lot about you," mentioned Greg, a comment that Ben reacted to by dropping his face into his palm.

Andrew looked from Ben to Greg, wary. "Good things, I hope."

"Mostly about your butt."

A pop resonated from the corners of Andrew's jaw as it nearly detached from his skull. Peeking once more at Ben, he saw the hand around his face had tightened.

"As you can already tell," he snarled, "I have some very prudent friends."

"It's okay, Ben," Greg eased, only to increase his friend's tension. "A great ass is worth discussing."

"Holy *shit*. Shut your damn mouth already."

Andrew tried to relax Ben with a laugh, but on its way out, his lungs compressed and only a dry, heaving sound was heard. Ben, grumbling nonsense to himself, next introduced Andrew to Matt, a kid whose style could not be more dissimilar from his own. Complete with a backwards Yankees baseball cap, baggy blue jeans that even a belt couldn't hold up, and a mysterious contradictory Mets T-shirt, Andrew had to wonder how a lad like Matt ever became interested in film. He usually saw his type hanging around in the parking lots of fast food joints.

"S'up." A professional salute if ever there was one. Matt did not only shake Andrew's hand; he slapped it, gripped his fingertips, then pounded the top of his hand with a balled fist. "Nice to have someone around who actually wants to use the camera."

You all joined film club and none of you wanted to film anything? The plot thickened, as well as ripened.

"Nice style, bro." Whether Matt was honest or sarcastic was difficult to decipher. Andrew was willing to bet the latter.

If there was one thing Andrew loved more than spending quality time with his father, it was going through his closet and dressing himself up, which was now easier with someone special to show his selections off to. That day he included lipstick and a shadow of ebony eyeliner, or what Dave once referred to as "guyliner." Over his eyelids was also a shade of black, lighter then that underneath his lower lids. Applying the makeup to his face had already been fun for him, but it was Kevin's encouragement to his avant-garde movement that made it more than just a daily process and something the two of them could enjoy together. For the first time, Kevin helped him out with his facial decoration in front of the mirror, assisting him in lining his eyes with pencil and brush alike, all the while basking in the glorious moment of them standing toe-to-toe, faces inches apart, with Kevin's hand upon his taught face.

"You're the pinnacle of all that rocks," Kevin had complimented him while painting his nails with polish. In that moment, Andrew could sprout wings and sail to the moon.

Distracted by the resurfacing memory, smiling both inside and out, he hadn't noticed that Ben had taken him through a full tour of the spacious, tidy living room.

"And Garret…" Ben surveyed his kingdom, the Erickson abode, a modest-scale home big enough to house three people and not enough room to contain a party of their size, looking for the absent member. "Is missing. What a shocker. Oh well. We can rehearse a few scenes while we wait for him. Andrew, would you like a drink?"

"You didn't offer *us* any drinks," sneered Matt.

"There are only so many to go around."

"It's all right," Andrew told them both. "I'm not thirsty."

"Suit yourself. My parents should be back home by five, so let's try to get as much work done as we can." Ben walked to the corner of the room, where a tripod was set up. Atop it sat a video camera, one that Andrew assumed belonged to their director. Noticing that Andrew hadn't joined him, Ben waved him over.

Ben asked him if he had ever a used a camera like his, to which Andrew replied that he hadn't, but could figure it out in no time. Ben then arranged his actors around the room while handing them copies of his script to read from while they rehearsed, and took a seat next to Andrew and his camera in a chair he dragged from the kitchen.

Telling the performers that they were going to go over a scene in particular for practice, he told Matt and Cheryl to pair up. Having already read the screenplay, Andrew surmised that Matt had been cast into the role of the story's villain, Vrek. As far as Andrew knew, "Vrek" was not a real name in any galaxy, but Ben seemed to take to it as well as any other implausible chunk contained within the tale.

As one would expect, Matt's acting skills were as rusty as corroded nails, and Cheryl outshined him by so much that Ben had to interrupt them several times to get Matt up to her speed. With how many cuts, takes, re-takes, and frustrated grunts by Ben, the entire film looked to become more of a comedy than the blockbuster science-fiction action film Ben made it out to be. The script was already enough to tell Andrew not to take it seriously, but in the fraction of time he spent with the ham-fisted crew responsible for its production, it had become an entertaining, however laughable, effort. A slew of obscenities defiled any dignified moment on film due to Ben's lack of patience, and soon the movie's main lines of dialogue included "fuck off" and "go fuck yourself."

At his wit's end, Ben told them to take a break, then sat down in his "director's seat" (a wooden chair taken from the dining room), sighing at his cameraman, whose smirks and giggles couldn't be suppressed.

"You find it amusing, do you?" Ben confronted, not appearing the least bit humored.

Andrew admitted with his head down and hand over his mouth, "I do."

"I've spent a month writing this thing. Somehow I pictured it going differently. Not this… mockery."

Andrew first thought to say, *it's better off this way,* but rather than stoke the flames, he tried to think of what Kevin might say. "Well… even famous directors have to go through it. Some scenes take hundreds of tries to get right."

"I was hoping this might help me get into a good arts college. Now I just feel like an idiot."

"It's not totally hopeless, Ben."

"Sure it is. I never get the things I want." His eyes ran from Andrew's face down to his waist.

Unnerved by Ben's probing, hungry leer, Andrew leaned away from him and clamped his boney knees together. A sound of rubber crunching across dirt and gravel reverberated from outside the window, and Ben tossed the curtains aside to inspect the view of the driveway. Andrew also turned to look out, seeing a spotless silver car parked in the drive. Climbing out of the driver's side was a slick-haired, smooth-skinned young man, dressed in a gray jacket. In spite of the cloudy skies, he wore sunglasses, which Andrew guessed had a high price tag.

Out of the passenger seat came a pencil thin blond woman, dressed in red, who came to the side of her driver and followed him to the front door of the house. Whoever the man was, he couldn't carry on a conversation with his female friend in a volume other than eardrum-rupturing. To call it obnoxious would have been a compliment.

Ben left his chair, anticipating the ringing doorbell. Andrew followed at a distance to watch from afar, expecting to shake hands with yet another actor from film club. Swinging the door open, Ben greeted their final member, inviting him inside.

"Garret," Ben growled. "You're two hours late."

"Dude, I'm sorry." Garret, flashy from top to bottom, stripped his long coat off and passed it to the host, who took it with a disgruntled frown. "First the car wouldn't start. I had to ask my folks for a jump. Then, Caitlin calls. You know how she is."

Ben said, "Sure," in that indifferent sort of way.

"She just started some medication. Like I care, right? But no, she talks my damn ear off for an hour and a half about side effects and shit like that. Then I had to talk to Jesse about the money he owes me."

The blond standing beside the loud, yammering Garret withdrew a phone from her pocket and started punching letters on the keypad, disinterested in the conversation, not that it had any relevance.

"I'm just glad you're finally here," Ben addressed, derision in his every word. "The others are taking a quick break, but we're going to get back to work once they get done fucking around. You're going to be playing Mark, Jeny's boyfriend, and Cheryl is playing Jeny."

"She is? Nice. Will I get to kiss her?"

He scoffed. "I don't know, maybe." Andrew's coughing knocked the repulsive image of Garret and Cheryl kissing out of Ben's mind. "Uh, Garret, I'd like you to meet Andrew. He's going to be filming."

Andrew sidled up beside Ben with his hand extended, forcing himself to smile despite the discomfort. "Nice to meet you."

Only a few seconds passed before Garret snorted out a tight-lipped guffaw, but slipped Andrew his broad, lanky mitt with a grip so loose that it would have been more polite to do without it. At the sound of his snickering, Andrew backed away a few steps.

"So, uh... where'd you find Satan's Little Helper?" joked Garret to Ben, whose look of horror protracted with each sound out of his mouth.

Andrew, on the other hand, was far from horrified. Being teased was nothing new to him, whether it was at home or on the playground. On the other hand, it was a wound he thought he had stitched a long time ago and a pain he thought he had sworn off. In that instance, it returned to haunt him, turning his blood as black as his wardrobe.

Ben wasn't letting his visitor off easy. "He's my friend, Garret. Don't be a dick."

Garret wheezed. "I'm sorry. It's just ridiculous. Someone tell this kid that Halloween ended two months ago." He bellowed out another cackle. "I don't think he knows!"

Andrew didn't give Garret another opportunity to use him as a human dartboard. He turned and left the room, finding the cordless phone inside the den on a small table next to a lamp. Garret was too busy losing his mind to notice that Andrew had disappeared, whereas Ben picked up on it immediately. Leaving Garret to his mania, Ben chased after his companion, seeing him with the phone pressed to his ear and talking softly into it.

"I'll see you soon," were the only words out of Andrew's mouth that sounded happy. After hanging up the phone, he and Ben traded glances.

Pointing his palms to the ceiling, Ben made several harsh gasps of incredulity. "What, you're leaving now?"

Andrew breezed past him, heading for the front door. "Yeah. I am."

Following his every footstep, Ben hunched over with his palms clasped. "Andrew, please. Garret's a total asshole sometimes. I just put up with it because I have to."

"That doesn't mean I have to, Ben."

"Andrew! Come on, I need you on this!"

"No you don't. You could film it yourself. It's your screenplay."

"But... but I wanted..." He halted just before Andrew opened the door, bracing himself on the frame. "I wanted you to do it with me."

The ways in which Andrew could interpret that phrase were limited, but evident, eliminating any leftover desire to work with him. "Good luck." Andrew didn't wait for his father to drive up to the house. He began his journey down the soggy dirt road to meet him part of the way, putting as much distance between him and Ben's house as possible.

Inside the house, Ben lingered by the door, his forearms quaking, his back to Garret, who by now had ceased his cackling. As soon as Garret saw that Ben had little interest in joining him in his taunts, he also noticed that Andrew had left.

"Where is he?" he wondered.

Ben's hands rolled into fists. "Gone. He went home."

"What? Are you serious? What a crybaby."

As these last few words hit his ears, Ben swung around to stand off against his so-called friend, who became restless at his incendiary gaze. "This was my one chance, Garret." On a nearby phone table sat a yellow book as thick as a block and just as heavy, which he then scooped up in his flexing hands. Before he could get a reply, he dove at him, flailing the book like a rabid madman, slamming it into his shoulder and back. "You! Fucking! *Asshole!*"

Garret raised his hands in self-defense of the incoming blows. "What the fuck?! Stop it!"

He didn't stop. He beat Garret with the phone book until several loose pages flew out of it and the cover ripped in half. "My one chance! You fucked it up! *You fucked it all up!*"

"What is wrong with you?!" hollered Garret when he got the chance to finagle the book from his attacker. "Fuck him! And fuck you!" Chucking the damaged phone book across the room, Garret motioned for his girlfriend to follow him outside, and he too disappeared, bringing Ben's dream project to a crash and burn, much like the conclusion of his epic saga.

Muddy, charcoal water filled half of the sink, swirling from the disturbance of the washcloth Andrew dipped into it again and again. With each wipe across his pale complexion, he removed more of his makeup, some of which ran in streaks down to his jaw. His face was almost clean now, though not as cheerful as it had been before he left the house.

At the outset of washing the colors from his eyes and mouth, it had been like any other time he did so in the past. As more of his actual face revealed itself after each individual scrub down, it became harder for him to look at himself in the mirror. Garret was nobody to him, someone he had met only once and would likely never see again, and yet his words had affected him. Regarding the joy he received when doing up his face, it mattered little to him what others thought. He would go on doing it, because he liked it. No one could convince him otherwise.

All the same, he felt a vulnerability at Ben's house that prior to then he only felt living under his mother's roof. He was a child again, backed into a corner with no way out. As happy as he was now living with Kevin, she would always be there, in the faces of those who made him confront his weaknesses.

Now that his face had been vacant of any colors save for his peach skin tone, he twisted the cloth to wring the water from it, watching the obsidian liquid drizzle into the pool below. Kevin had spent so much time helping him apply it, and all he could do now was wash it down the drain.

He supposed he didn't have to remove it all. Kevin wouldn't have minded if he left it on. Hell, he might have liked it if he had. Kevin's opinion was the only one that mattered to him after all, and he wasn't one to ask him to change. Nevertheless, he couldn't bear to see it now, remembering how much fun Kevin had helping him with it. Garret hadn't only clamped his ample claws into what he loved, he dug them into who he loved, tearing both joys of his life asunder. He had dismissed him as an asshole, but he had done more than insult his fashion sense.

Andrew grabbed a dry towel from the rack behind him, smashing his face into it, consoled by its softness and lavender scent. As he dwelled on all that occurred that afternoon, he heard a gentle rapping upon the door.

"Come in," he said while hanging the towel back where he found it.

The bathroom door drifted open, Kevin on the other side of it. "Hey. How are you doing?"

"I'm all right."

As Kevin entered the room, which like their choice in clothing had a black color scheme, he took a long look at Andrew's bare face. "You took your makeup off? How come?"

Any reason Andrew gave him would have made little sense to either of them. "I don't know. I guess I felt... weird."

Kevin sat down on the lid of the closed toilet, resting his elbows on his legs, folding his hands together. "Did what he say to you bother you that much?"

"It's bothersome, yeah. But I'm used to people saying stupid things like that. Honestly, I didn't want to film the movie anyway. It's not really him I'm thinking about right now." He leaned his back against the counter, tucking his hands into his tight pockets.

"What's on your mind, then?"

With his eyes glued to the rug on the tile floor, he fiddled around with the lint in his pockets. He could choose to give him any number of answers: Ben had reached new heights of brazen courage when coming on to him, and he only blamed himself for that; he had an upcoming sociology test he hadn't done an ounce of studying for; his next task for the school paper was photographing the swim team, and he hadn't made much of an effort to visit the pool. Any of these would have been true, but a claim that they had taken up most of his thoughts would have been bullshit.

Then, as if his mouth had a mind of its own, he blurted, "How long has it been since you last had a boyfriend?"

"U-uh…" Kevin rubbed his palms together, his shoulders weaving. "Why do you ask?"

"I just want to know."

"A couple years. I like to blame it on being too busy with my work, but… that'd be a lie."

"Do you want one?"

He dragged the back of his hand across his glistening forehead. "Yes. I do. But right now, I care more about you."

"I care about you too, Dad. A lot." Andrew's eyes rose to his father's face, which stared back at him. "You make me happy."

"Andrew," cooed Kevin. "You make me happy too. Very happy."

Andrew's flat chest lifted and fell as his breaths staggered. "I…" As he struggled with his next few words, Kevin waited in elevating suspense. "I'm not good at this," he then mumbled to himself, cursing under his breath.

"Neither am I."

Caught off guard by that remark, Andrew studied him for a moment. "What do you mean?"

"What do *you* mean?"

"N-nothing."

"I see." Rising to his feet, Kevin stepped toward Andrew, whose knees buckled as he drew closer to his face until they were less than an inch apart. "Seems we both have a problem with 'nothing,' don't we?"

"S-seems that way."

Andrew's breath quickened, as did his thundering heartbeat, when Kevin dragged his warm, smooth palm along the back of his neck, his soft fingertips feathering the follicles of his slick hair. Every nerve on Andrew's skin reacted with satisfied prickles as he clasped his eyes shut, savoring every second Kevin caressed him, concerned that it might be temporary. A nervous tremble quaked Kevin's wrist as he moved his warm, dry hand over Andrew's right cheek, brushing it with the edge of his thumb. The stiffness in his arm settled as Andrew pressed his face tighter against his palm, inviting him to bring his other hand to his left cheek.

Andrew ached to show him all that brewed and simmered in his heart for the past month they had spent together, exhausted of the hints, the disastrous flirting, the tripping and falling over their own emotions just to get some kind of solace from each other that everything would go well if they gave it a shot. He grew tired of speculation. It was time to face the truth before either of them changed their minds.

Wary, but confident, Andrew draped both arms around Kevin's neck, pulling him closer to his radiating body. Kevin's Adam's apple bobbed, uneven breaths skittering out his nostrils, eyes stretched. The sight of Andrew wetting his lips sent his nerves into overdrive, craving nothing more than to crush his own mouth against his son's. At first, he thought to engulf his waist and tug him closer, but he cursed under his breath and lowered his arms to his sides.

"It's okay," whispered Andrew, his arms tightening around his father's shoulders. "I want you to."

"Andrew, I…" He sucked on his upper lip, commanding himself from within to control his own behavior, an impossible feat at this point. "I'm sorry."

"Why?"

That was an unanswerable query, as it meant acknowledging the multitude of wrongs he had almost committed. With great care, he took hold of Andrew's forearms and unhooked them from his neck. Heartbroken, Andrew watched Kevin back away from him. Unable to look at the hurt in Andrew's gaze, Kevin fixed his to the floor.

"I'm so sorry," Kevin reiterated, inching toward the door.

Andrew voiced his desperation in a final plea of both forgiveness and longing. "Dad… it's okay."

Repulsed by his desires, Kevin slipped out of the bathroom, sliding his hands over his hair and pulling at it, all while Andrew called to him like a lost, familiar echo.

It took Kevin and Andrew hours to face each other again, and when they had, they were unable to find the courage to discuss what went on between them earlier, or to admit their connection to one another. As powerful as their attraction was, evidence remained ever stronger that the kind of relationship they sought was not easy, nor was it considered normal. There were so many things Kevin wished to tell his son, some of which stemmed from loneliness, but the facts were loud and clear that Andrew had just as many secrets pertaining to him— some of the most exciting kind.

And thus, Kevin thought it best to discard the emotion before it could get any larger. Whether or not Andrew was willing, accepting, and just as head-over-heels as he was, it was not acceptable.

Andrew was his son, and he aimed to keep it that way, regardless of the daggers that pierced him when doing so.

In the weeks prior to Christmas break, Andrew joined Ben at lunch following an apology he delivered on Garret's behalf. Andrew didn't believe for a second that Garret wanted to speak to him, let alone apologize, but he accepted it from Ben nonetheless. When asked if he found another individual to film the movie for him, Ben mumbled something incoherent and dodged the question by changing the topic of discussion to Andrew's work on the school paper. The manner in which he questioned him was not as friendly as it had once been, which came as little surprise to Andrew.

The arrival of Christmas marked a turning point for Andrew, and while he didn't care much for the holiday before then, his point of view changed when he had the excuse to give Kevin the gift he had been waiting a month to give him. That morning, he scrambled out of bed and dressed, then grabbed his guitar, a pick, and mini amplifier. His fingers itched to play that tune, to have Kevin hear it, and soon he would.

When he came down the stairs, he smelled crisp, fresh breakfast. Kevin was already awake, and had been spending a good deal of time in the kitchen making a mountain of waffles for them. He hadn't yet heard Andrew come in over the sound of cracking and stirring, but Andrew was glad he didn't. He wanted to surprise him. On the television hanging on the kitchen wall, a holiday film played that Andrew wasn't familiar with, one with cheery songs and animated animals.

While Kevin's back was turned, and while his attention was on the food he prepared, Andrew plugged his amplifier into the nearest socket, then connected it to his guitar, and they both hummed with electric life as he flicked the switch on. He then sat upon a dining room chair, facing the kitchen where Kevin toiled away, pulling the strap of his guitar around his neck and resting the instrument in his lap. Then, he strummed the low E string, and the dining area filled with the bellowing echo of a rumbling twang. Kevin leapt nearly a mile into the air and spun around to check the source of the noise. After planting a relieved hand over his chest, they laughed in unison.

Kevin stepped away from the counter and entered the dining room toward Andrew, pocketing his hands. "What's this?" he asked, both curious and joyful, taking a seat in one of the chairs at the table beside him.

"Your present." Andrew began to play, his skilled fingers sliding over each string. The chords started in minor keys, a sad melody that carried into one much sunnier as the chorus arrived.

Andrew sang more than just a song to Kevin. He told him a story. In this tale, he had gone back to his younger self, and had told him to hold out a little longer, to endure the pain, because something good would happen to him if he waited. He would meet Kevin, his best friend, his savior; he would be given a home, a better place, where he was loved and respected; He sang about how times were tough now, but eventually, he would be happy.

At the conclusion, Andrew pulled the strap off and set his guitar down, immediately grabbing Kevin around the neck and holding him, tight. He felt an almost painful squeeze from Kevin when his arms swung around his waist and crushed him against his torso. "Merry Christmas, Dad," Andrew wheezed.

"Just when I thought you couldn't get any sweeter," Kevin spouted through occasional sniffles.

Andrew shut his eyes as he mashed his cheek against his. "I love you," he whispered. A series of soft kisses from Kevin met his cheek and temple, each of their skin growing warm.

"I love you, too," Kevin vowed as he cradled him. "With all my heart." As their link was broken, they swapped misty-eyed smiles, and Kevin bumped his forehead against Andrew's. That's when an overpowering aroma of blazing ash arrived at their noses.

Andrew was the first to notice it. "What's that smell?"

"Shit," Kevin gasped, releasing Andrew and sprinting to the kitchen. Before reaching the waffle iron, a cacophony of hoarse coughs splashed from his throat. Worried that he was hurt, Andrew started to rise from his seat. As his wheezing died down, he switched off the waffle iron, which had burned some of the batter he had put on it. Andrew settled back down when he realized all was okay.

"Sorry, honey," Kevin said when he got the chance, waving wisps of smoke away from his face, though it didn't alleviate the stench.

"It's okay. I like them a little crispy."

"Well, you're in luck. These are pretty well done."

Andrew helped Kevin in the kitchen after putting his guitar away, and also set the table with him. He made coffee for him, and Kevin poured him orange juice. Every move they made was systematic, yet rhythmic, natural and graceful. Kevin turned off the television and used the same remote to turn the radio on, Christmas tunes blaring over the speakers strung up around the house. They sang along, their voices harmonious without any need for indication.

They shared breakfast, which Andrew couldn't even begin to eat half of. Kevin made so many damn waffles, enough to feed two armies, and just three was enough to pack his taught stomach. Still, it was delicious, and Kevin seemed happy that he was satisfied.

"Now," Kevin said after dabbing his mouth with a napkin and drinking some coffee. "Your gift." He left the table, waving a finger for Andrew to follow. Andrew didn't need to be asked twice to follow Kevin anywhere. When they entered the living room, Kevin walked to the tinsel-laden tree and sat beside it. Andrew sat cross-legged in front of him. Kevin handed him his package, which Andrew knew before opening it that it was a CD, but whatever disc it could possibly be boggled his mind.

In one quick rip, Andrew tore the paper off, curiosity getting the better of him. There, in his hand, was a first edition, rare Drone Diode album, one of their first prior to signing a recording contract with a major label. The album that Andrew now held in his hand was limited in copies, and as far as he knew, there were only ten known of in existence. On the cover were four signatures. Only four! That meant the album was made before Sam Dennison joined the group, and if Andrew knew his Drone Diode history, that must have been a very long time ago— at least six years.

The biggest signature belonged to that of Ross Helvette, lead singer. It overshadowed even Christian Maccrum, his musical hero. He recognized Ross's signature, that just-barely-legible scribble that had unnecessary curls to it. A tiny heart was etched beside it.

"Oh my god," Andrew finally said after letting it sink in. "Dad… where did you get this?"

"Online auction. Had some pretty ambitious competition for it."

"Do you have any idea how rare this is?"

"The lead singer was the one selling it. He talked it up pretty well on the site, so I had *some* idea."

"Ross Helvette sold this to you?!"

"He thanked me when I bought it."

"No way," Andrew laughed, too excited for proper words. "You spoke to him?!"

Kevin beamed, both on the inside and out. Just the look of happiness on Andrew's face was enough of a gift. Then he nodded.

"Wow! What'd he say?!"

"He told me that because my bid was so generous, he'd send me a bonus package. That's your next present."

Andrew trembled, his hands shaking and wrists twitching. He bounced up and down, something he hadn't done since he was a child, while Kevin reached under the tree again. He chanted, "Oh my god" over and over until the words had lost all meaning.

"I guess this isn't really a gift from me, but I think you'll still appreciate it, nonetheless." Kevin passed him a tiny wrapped box with a red bow. Andrew shredded it like a tornado hits a house, and popped the top off of the box. All that sat within it was two laminated cards connected to straps with the Drone Diode logo printed on each with writing at the bottom, scrawled in black ink, that said, "Limited Access – VIP". On the back was Ross's handwriting, stating, "Thanks for the contribution".

"No…" Andrew gasped. His eyes moved from the passes to his father. "No way. Backstage passes?! I'm going to meet them?!" Kevin nodded again, smiling wider. Andrew's hands fluttered as though he were about to take off in flight. "Oh my god!" He grappled Kevin, sharing another of their warm hugs. "Thank you! Thank you so much!"

"We'll go together," Kevin let him know, giving his back fond strokes. "Just the two of us."

"I'm so *excited!* Feel my hands!" Kevin took his hands and clenched them, chuckling at the shaking jolts coming from them. "I'd better go put the CD in a safe place."

For the day, they played a few games, and Kevin found it tough to let go of Andrew, even for a moment. Andrew's casual flirting had progressed to the stage of innuendoes. Each time Kevin laughed at one, then suggested one of his own, he wondered how much longer they'd go before ripping each other's clothes off and diving for each other there on the couch.

Come nightfall, Andrew again fell asleep on Kevin, wrapped in that cocoon of blankets. Kevin couldn't bear moving him, or getting up himself. Andrew's hands on him, his breath against his skin, was all too wonderful to abandon. When he too closed his eyes, he had many dreams, all of which Andrew starred in, and none of which were innocent.

At New Year's Eve, Kevin was invited to a party, which he declined in favor of watching the countdown with Andrew, who struggled to keep his eyes open for it. Kevin woke him in time for the fireworks show at Rockefeller Center broadcasted on television, then let him go back to sleep. Neither one of them were interested in sleeping in their beds anymore, for then they'd have to be away from each other, and what was the point of that? Still, they did what they had to do, knowing there were fewer options.

After New Year, Andrew had to return to school, with a heavy heart. When Kevin dropped him off that day, there was a deafening silence between them, one that even a padded room would consider too quiet.

"You have to go, honey," Kevin advised, parked by the curb.

A groan rattled Andrew's throat. "The day is too long."

"It'll end. I'll be here when it's over."

"That's hours away."

Kevin chuckled and gave Andrew's head a soft stroke. "We can stand a few hours apart."

Maybe you can. With a sigh, Andrew popped the door open and turned to look at Kevin before leaving. After an exchange of the L word, Andrew left the vehicle while he still had the nerve to do so. Now more than ever, Andrew couldn't wait for that school year to end, the final year he'd ever have to put up with.

Ben was ready to greet him at their lockers, and told him he'd have a present to give him later.

"You got me a present?" Andrew asked, bewildered.

"Of course I did!"

"But… I didn't get you anything."

"You don't have to, Andrew. I'll be honest… the gift is for both of us."

Oh, please be something simple like matching friendship bracelets, he begged. "That's sweet of you."

"I'll give it to you at lunch. That way you can guess all day what it is!"

"I look forward to it." His locker door must have resented him. He had never seen an inanimate object act so stubborn. "I've got to talk to them about this locker. I can barely even open it now."

"Let me," Ben offered, and as he did once before, opened it for Andrew without a hassle. "All set."

"How are you doing that?"

He raised his arm and curled it, flexing his bicep. "A little bench pressing goes a long way."

Andrew found it hard to believe that it was simply because his arms were too weak. "You must know some kind of secret to opening it."

"Come on, Andrew. Wouldn't I tell you if that were the case?"

Would he? Andrew wasn't so sure. "I guess. Thanks for the help." He stashed his belongings inside while he had time.

"No problem. I'll see you later." Ben strolled away like strutting down a catwalk.

When lunch eventually came, Andrew saw Ben sitting at their table. Ben had rushed to the cafeteria as fast as he could, wanting to get there before Andrew, so they could waste no time.

In Ben's hands was an envelope with Andrew's name on it, which he held onto for dear life until Andrew was fully seated. Before giving Andrew a chance to speak, he slid the envelope toward him, and Andrew's first reaction was to stare at it. Not that he wasn't intrigued by the card, but the heart sticker Ben had stamped on the back was a bit too much for him.

The sticker tore in half when Andrew ripped open the envelope and removed the card inside. On the front of the card was a printed illustration of reindeers nuzzling. One of them had a pink nose, the other black. The words "Thinking of you this holiday season" shimmered in glitter underneath. At that point, Andrew dreaded opening it, but he knew he had little choice. Drawing in a deep breath, he flipped it open. There, sitting inside of the card were two thin, rectangular pieces of paper. In a typewriter font, the paper proclaimed: Queens Energy Theatre presents **Drone Diode**, **Blue Ecstasy Tour** with the date of the concert printed next to it. The date was the exact same as the backstage passes Kevin gave him.

Andrew cupped a hand over his mouth, but not for the reasons Ben thought he did.

Ben, seeing the look of shock in Andrew's eyes, lit up like the tree ceremony in Rockefeller Center. "They're for us," he explicated, grinning from ear to ear. "So we can go together. This is my first time going to a concert and I'm so excited."

"Oh, God," Andrew moaned.

"I know! Right? It can't come up any quicker. I seriously can't wait."

"Ben… I…"

"You don't have to thank me, okay? I'm really looking forward to taking you. I already got something to wear all picked out. I think you're going to like it. The style is right up your alley."

"Ben, listen," Andrew interrupted, setting the card and tickets down on the table. Ben watched them like a hawk. "Shit. This is kind of hard."

"I know what you're thinking," Ben said to him, softer this time, reaching across the table for his hand. "You think it's an attempt to win you over. I promise, Andrew, it's not like that. I wanted to give you something special, something we'd both remember, even just as friends. I just know how much you love Diode, and I…"

"It's not you. It's the tickets, they…" Ben watched as Andrew's face twisted into a look of guilt. Already, he felt something terrible was about to come forth. "My Dad and I were going to go together." Andrew tensed as Ben slid back, sighed, and cracked his neck. "He surprised me on Christmas with backstage passes. That Ross Helvette actually sent us, and… even signed." He paused, waiting for Ben to speak, but he only shook his head, hissing steam rolling out of his nose. He didn't look sad about it; hardly so. He looked infuriated. "Oh, God, Ben, I feel *terrible*."

"Do you have any idea how much snow I had to shovel to earn those passes?!"

"I… I'm sorry!"

"I worked for two whole days after Christmas for my parents!

Into New Years! Trying to get you these tickets!" He slapped his hand onto the table, making Andrew flinch. "My parents argued with me for days about me going! I had to beg like a fucking dog! I had to *beg* my own parents to buy my friend a Christmas gift, like I'm a god damned child! And you're turning it down?!"

"How was I supposed to know that you and my dad got me the same gift?! I can't read your fucking minds!"

Ben, quivering, shook his head back and forth. "I am so sick of your dad." He reached for the envelope and snatched it away from Andrew, his seething, molten eyes locked on him. "Every time I want to do something for you or with you, he's there, hovering around in the conversation. Now he's even one-upped me on a fucking Christmas gift!"

"It's not *his* fault!"

"Andrew, give me a break. It's because of him that you don't have time for me. It's because of him that I can't even give you presents!" When Andrew gaped in horror, it only made the problem escalate. Fellow students seated at nearby tables began to stare, burning Andrew's cheeks brighter. "This was really important to me! Do you even give a shit? Instead of saying, 'why don't you come with us, Ben?' You tell me to fuck off! It's as close to a slap in the face as you could give me!" Ben, who didn't think he would be spending his lunch hour yelling at his friend, shoved the tickets back into his book bag and gave the timid Andrew another scathing look. "Why do I even bother?" he asked.

"What do you mean?"

"First you turn me down every time I want to hang out. Then you walk out on me and my movie after you said you'd help me just because my friend teased you. Now this. You can't be bothered to accept a gift, an *expensive* gift, by the way, because you'd rather be with your daddy." At the sight of Andrew's head lowering in shame, something occurred to him, something he hadn't considered in the past. "Are you in love with him?"

"Who?" gasped Andrew.

"You know who I'm talking about."

"N-no I don't."

"If you were, it sure would explain how attached-at-the-hip you are with him. The starry-eyed look you get when you talk about him. Andrew, for fuck's sake, it's not normal."

"Maybe it's *you* that's abnormal!" spat Andrew, and right away his scathing remark left lasting scars. "Maybe you should stop trying to get into my damn pants when I've already made it clear that I don't like you that way!"

Ben sprouted out of his seat, glaring poison-tipped daggers at his playmate. "And maybe I don't want to be your friend!" Before letting Andrew come up with a retort, Ben grabbed his bag and hauled it over his shoulder. "I'll find someone more deserving for those tickets." Then, he hauled ass for the exit, spacing himself as far as he could from Andrew, hoping he didn't see the tears of anger and regret in his eyes on the way out.

With so many eyes on him now, Andrew was too embarrassed to stick around. He also grabbed his bag and rushed out, stressed beyond belief. He wondered if it was better this way. Their friendship hadn't been a very solid one to begin with, and Ben was interested in more than friendship, something Andrew couldn't give him. This might have been their only option.

Going to his classes required a bit more energy than usual now. He should have been used to losing friends. It happened all the time. Still, every time it did, he couldn't handle it. How many more would he lose? Would he lose Kevin, too? That was something Andrew couldn't fathom. If that happened, he might implode. He was already about to just from temptation.

At the end of the day, he was thrilled to see Kevin, but found it difficult to hold a smile for long. Kevin picked up on it right away.

"Everything okay?" he asked when driving home.

Andrew wanted to forget the horrible day, to be done with it and to focus on other things, but he didn't want it boiling inside of him. "Ben and I got into a fight."

"Really? About what?"

"He got me tickets to the show you were going to take me to. I didn't know what to say to him. I feel so bad. Now he's really mad at me because I'm going with you."

"Oh, gosh," Kevin sympathized. "I'm sorry. Maybe he needs some time to cool down. If you guys really are friends, he'll come around."

"I was thinking... maybe we should invite him along."

Kevin recoiled at this suggestion, gritting his teeth and wrinkling his brow. "Uh... well..."

"I mean, he bought those tickets for *me*. He seemed so excited to go. The whole thing feels wrong, Dad."

"You're very sweet to think of him, Andrew, but... I don't think that's a good idea."

Andrew sensed a transition in his speech. "Why not?"

"Because..." His eyes darted back and forth. "I sort of wanted it to just be us. You know, alone. I'm sure Ben didn't want your old man tagging along with you."

Andrew wanted them to be together, too, more than anything. All the same, he remembered times in his life when friends of his hurt him the way he let Ben down, and couldn't stomach being the very monster he detested. "He got two tickets. Maybe we could take him and Kyle, or something."

"Andrew," Kevin sighed, fidgeting. "Normally, I would say yes. But I was looking forward to doing this with you. I wanted it to be... you know, special." *Like a date*, he wanted to add.

Andrew's guilt dissipated somewhat at Kevin's hints. "I... I do, too. I just feel bad because I know he's into me."

The corners of Kevin's mouth tugged down. "*Into* you?"

He tossed some of his hair aside to get a better look at his father. "He's got a little bit of a crush on me."

For several seconds, Kevin sucked on his lower lip, twisting his tongue around in his mouth. "I didn't know that."

"I didn't think to bring it up. There was never any reason to."

While Kevin was stopped at the light, he attempted to address the matter civilly. "How long has that been going on?"

Andrew chewed on the nail of his pinky finger. "Pretty much since I met him, I think."

Kevin's head bobbed in a stiff nod, his fingers releasing and gripping the steering wheel. "And... how do you feel about him?"

Moisture coated the air, their heavy breaths fogging the windows. When Andrew next spoke, he did so with devout tenderness. "I'm not interested."

Kevin's forearms slackened, the crease in his forehead relaxing. "How come?" Relief washed over his voice.

"I like someone else."

One of Kevin's knuckles popped as he flexed his hands, attempting to relax the tendons in them. "Who would that be?" As he looked at his son, he saw the almost seductive, surreptitious smile that crept onto his lips.

"That's a secret," he whispered.

After the light beaconed green, Kevin drove off and turned down Mancante Street. Matching his son's tone, he also lowered his voice. "Is that so? I would hate for you to spill secrets to ears that shouldn't hear them."

"Maybe I'll mention him in my sleep."

"Sounds like you dream about him a lot."

"My whole life."

Both of their mouths curled into furtive smiles as Kevin parked into his garage. Kevin opened Andrew's door for him, as well as the door connecting the garage to the house. Andrew tipped in a half-bow, and they both giggled. Now home, Andrew was happy again, even happier when seeing how excited Kevin was. Kevin might have been correct about Ben; if given some time, he would come around. Until then, he would let him be.

"Seriously? He didn't want them?"

Garret, a young man who Ben discovered early on in film club had more ingenuity than he did, had been the first one he called after coming home. It was their third year together, a friendship that while on some days shaky, showed its true strengths whenever Ben had a problem. Garret's compelling ability to excel in areas Ben was incapable always gave him a feeling of inadequacy. He felt it even when his aura of smugness wasn't in the room with him. On the other hand, Garret sometimes set his own bullshit aside to listen every once in a while, which was rare, but welcomed.

For ruining his pet project, Ben could never truly forgive Garret, though he had told him he had. "I didn't know you had a crush on that weirdo," Garret had explained after his apology. It must have been Greg that informed him. He had learned long ago not to involve Garret in any of his romantic quests.

Still, there Garret was, on the other end of the phone line with him, listening to him complain. It was times like these Ben was glad to have him around, even if it meant hearing him gripe about people and things he didn't approve of (which was a list too extensive to pay attention to). "Nope. He just tossed them back in my face, said he was going with his father."

"His *father*? Who the hell goes to concerts with their father?"

"Andrew does, apparently." As Ben chatted with him, the phone pressed against both his ear and shoulder, he scrolled over several websites looking for a place to sell the tickets. As a last resort, he asked, "You wouldn't maybe... want to...?"

"I can't. I have a test coming up I should probably study for." Garret was a bit too quick to answer, quicker than Ben found normal, even for a man whose mouth shot faster than a firearm.

"You're going to pass up Diode for a test?"

"Maybe if I had been the first person you asked," he indicated.

"You know why I asked Andrew!"

"I know you've got a hard-on for the kid, but that's a lousy excuse, man. We've been talking about going to see Diode since the start of their tour. You always made excuses. Then some boy in guyliner bats his eyelashes at you..."

"Fine. Then I'll just sell them. Sorry I even suggested it." Ben had his thumb on the red button, ready to hang up, until he was stopped short by Garret's grunting.

"Wait, wait, wait. Look, I'll... I'll go."

"Are you sure? Don't back out on me at the last second, Garret. I need you here."

"No, I won't. I want to go. Really."

Ben hung up when their call came to an end, once more looking down at the tickets in his hands. Simply laying his eyes on them again brought the painful memory back. He hadn't only planned to take Andrew to the concert, but out to dinner beforehand. Andrew not only turned him away, he crushed his heart beneath the heel of his rubber-soled, black and white shoe. All he wanted was to show Andrew that it didn't matter if he was eighteen or in his thirties—that they could still have a good time, that he still had admirable qualities, and that he was still boyfriend material.

Whatever way their roads would lead them, Ben imagined them sitting and talking after a long day of his shooting an independent film, and a day of Andrew's photo shoots, sharing a meal and holding hands. Andrew's eyes would brighten when he'd tell him about the type of cast he'd obtain for his movie, and he would laugh when Andrew told him about the kinds of people that would come into his studio. They'd call each other sweet things, talk about "taking that next big step" of moving in together after seeing each other for years, and they wouldn't fight the way they were now. Things would be harmonious and perfect, for the both of them.

Though the dream was a happy one, his imagination was cruel to him, and included a scene of Andrew's cell phone buzzing, which he would interrupt the conversation to answer. He'd chatter with who was obviously Kevin, tell him how he couldn't wait to come home. And then, even in his mind, Andrew would tell him their time together would have to wait because his father wanted to see him.

Perhaps, Ben assumed, Andrew had dreams of his own. Maybe in his mind, the scenario was different. In Andrew's mind, he might be sitting across from Kevin at that same table, sharing with him his day, holding his hand and laughing, and Ben didn't get invited.

Ben's head collapsed onto the surface of his computer desk, which he hugged with his arms. Why did things always go the opposite of the way he intended? Regardless of how hard he tried, how hard he aimed to prove himself, he ended up a failure. If Andrew had in fact wanted to spend all of his time with Kevin, there was no way he could stop him from doing that.

He supposed he could have moved on from Andrew. There were plenty of fish in the ocean. No— the seas were not as plentiful as others made them out to be. None of the fish he met were as colorful as Andrew was, and they always swam with schools, whereas Andrew loved to float in his own pond. He loved that about him. Not even he could change him, and he wouldn't want to. He didn't flap a fin because the other fish were doing it. He did things his own way.

Not since junior high had he met someone that stood out so much. That's all he wanted to show him, to tell him. He was special to him. He was special, period.

Too little, too late, nagged Ben's mind. Chances, however slim, fell through his fingers every time he'd try to grasp them. Andrew was the kind of guy he always wanted, and he couldn't manage to keep him around for long. Failure, in Ben's eyes, was a lot harder to swallow than being rejected. He had failed at many things, but none so hard as his friendship with Andrew. If he had just called him and asked what he got for Christmas, or asked him what he would like, they might not have had to part ways.

Then there was Andrew's father. What was his name again? Calvin something? He had no idea what the man looked like, but he pictured a debonair, tall, dark and handsome suitor gorgeous enough for Andrew to drool over, and it only made his fury more palpable. Sure, he couldn't have seen it coming that Kevin would buy Andrew only the greatest gift he could possibly attain for him, but what kind of world did he live in where such coincidences took place? Andrew was right when he said it wasn't Kevin's fault, but how could he not loathe him at this point? Why couldn't he share Andrew once in a while?

Having enough of the gentle sobbing, he dried his eyes and crawled into bed. A nap might have calmed him, and in the morning, he'd fake sickness. His parents would buy it; they always did. He didn't want to see Andrew, and hopefully he wouldn't at the show, either. The crowd would be packed, so he knew it was unlikely. After all, his father got him backstage passes.

Ben stuffed his face into his pillow and whimpered.

CHAPTER EIGHT

In Which the Ladder Twists

On Friday, the night of the Drone Diode show, Andrew and Kevin were full of energy and hopped up on something greater than even the most potent pharmaceutical.

They had hours to kill before the doors to the venue opened, but their night out was all they could think about. Andrew, preparing Kevin for what he was in store for, played him most of Drone Diode's discography while they prepared. Nothing made him happier than to hear Kevin exclaim, "Wow, they sound pretty good!"

Andrew rummaged through his closet, searching for the best outfit he could throw together. One of his favorite shirts, a black one with long sleeves adorned with small chain links and rings scaling up the arms, was his first choice. He would complete it with black pants decorated with chains, zippers and belts that went down each leg, ones that seemed to be a little bit tighter in the waist than they had been more than a month ago.

Having trouble with his size zero waist band, he scooted into the bathroom and yanked his shirt up. His flat stomach had an extra inch to it now. He frowned and placed a hand on the new bulge in his gut, sucking it in. After some thought, it might have been a good thing that he wasn't nearly starving anymore. Since living with Kevin, he got his appetite back. Kevin always made him the stuff he liked, and plenty of it.

One thing Andrew always wanted to do that he wasn't permitted to at his previous home was dye his hair. He liked his natural color, but sometimes he liked to change things up a bit. Kevin had proved so far that he was the opposite of Star, so he might give him some leeway on the matter. He decided to ask.

Kevin was in his own room, but the door was cracked open; a rare occurrence. Even so, Andrew didn't wish to disturb him without knocking. "Come in," the silky voice of his father called. Andrew obeyed his beckon and entered, drinking in the scenery of the sacred room for the first time.

Upon Kevin's immense bed were black blankets with matching ebony sheets made of silk. A small fireplace adorned the wall in front of the bed, a flat screen mounted on the wall above it. Bedside tables, also painted jet, were on either side of the mattress: one topped with a tablet and MP3 player plugged into the wall to recharge, the other covered in hardcover books from various authors, sided with a pair of silver reading glasses. A window overlooked the expansive wilderness outdoors, lined with dark curtains. Along the walls were framed film posters, all from different genres and periods of history, and a massive stereo stood left of the fireplace. The most notable object in the room was on the wall at the head of the bed: an ultraviolet light, one that Kevin must have purchased or "borrowed" from a bar.

None of these items surpassed the glory of the skylight built into Kevin's ceiling, wide enough for beams of moonlight to illuminate tiny particles of dust that drifted through the air, tinting the modern décor with a cerulean glow.

This was the room of Andrew's dreams.

On entry, he didn't see Kevin anywhere, but he heard the sound of hangers rattling from Kevin's deep walk-in closet. He followed the sounds, creeping up to the open winged doors, and inside he found Kevin, wearing only a pair of dark jeans. Andrew had seen him shirtless before, but underneath the radiance of his dim closet light, which added shadows to the curves of Kevin's muscles, nothing else in the world looked more appetizing to Andrew than he did in that moment.

Standing there staring at Kevin's toned upper body, saliva glistening on his lip, he had forgotten the reason he came in. Something about hair? Was that it?

"What's up?" Even Kevin's perked eyebrows flirted with him.

"Uh… oh. Yeah. I was wondering… if maybe you could… get me some hair dye?"

"Sure!" Then, his hardened chest was covered with a shirt. Andrew's penetrating, laser-like eyes never moved away from its tightness. It was made of a leathery fabric, had metallic silver buttons down the middle, and a foldable collar. The most distinguished feature was that it had no sleeves. Kevin went for his dresser next. "What color are you going for?"

"Blue. It's my favorite. Well… after, you know." He gestured to his raven attire.

Kevin reached into a drawer and removed a blood red tie. "If that's what you want to do, I don't see why not. As long as you don't regret it afterward."

"I won't regret it. I know what I like."

Finishing the knot in his necktie, Kevin turned to face him, and he got to take a good look at Andrew's getup. "Wow," he gasped.

He looked down at his clothes, thinking he had articulated his distaste. "What? Is it too much?"

"No! You look…" He cracked an enamored smile. "Good. You look very good."

Redness flowed up Andrew's neck. "So do you."

"Well, don't we just look good together?"

"Yeah. We do."

Every step closer Kevin took, Andrew felt uncontrollable tingles race throughout the rivers in his veins. Words formed on the tips of their tongues that neither one of them had the nerve to come out with. An impassible line split between them, keeping them separated, a line that no matter how badly they wanted to step over, knew that they might set off a series of deadly traps if it was crossed.

Whenever I look at you, I'm reminded of how beautiful my creations are, Kevin wanted to say, *needed* to say, but that cautionary line always butted in. How tired of it he was. To him, it was a dilapidated wall with holes and cracks, one that he could easily tear down if he just grabbed it and shook it with all his might, if only he wouldn't hurt Andrew— who stood on the opposite side— with falling debris in the process.

A wad of saliva slid down Kevin's throat when he and Andrew once again reached kissing distance. Andrew's eager, ready breathing pushed him nearer to the edge, especially when he could feel it on his face. "Let's go get that hair dye for you."

Andrew shut his eyes, teased by the dangling prospect of resolve, but he smiled at his father nonetheless. "Cool."

While out buying Andrew's dye, Kevin also refilled his gas tank, as well as bought himself and Andrew raspberry frozen beverages tinted a blue color that Kevin deemed "appropriate." Andrew was impressed at how delicious it was. It also gave him an intense buzz that had to have been a contender for cocaine. As they sipped, and their mouths turned bright cyan, Kevin stuck his tongue out to show it to Andrew, wiggling it around. Andrew giggled, showing him his now neon teeth.

"Ah! The drinks are radioactive!" He laughed, in harmony with Andrew. "We're going to have superpowers now."

"I want to shoot ice from my hands," Andrew revealed, reaching his hand out and making a *froosh* noise.

"Hey, I want to do that," Kevin protested.

"There can only be one ice-thrower, Dad. Maybe you can be a rainmaker."

"Sure. I could make it rain, then you could turn the water to ice. We'd be the cause of every traffic accident."

Now at home, their teeth sticking together, Andrew stood alone in his bathroom, reading the instructions that came with the dye. It being his first time, he was a bit of an amateur, and the words on the sheet seemed more complicated at a glance than they really were.

Andrew didn't get a lot of time to go over and understand them before he heard a knock. Stepping out of the bathroom, he rushed to the door, narrowly avoiding a collision with the table his TV sat on.

As if Kevin could hear his mind cranking from outside, he asked, "Do you need any help?"

"Actually... that'd be great." He figured the instructions would be left for Kevin to construe, and he would get to spend more private time with him. He allowed Kevin into his bedroom, and Kevin followed him to the adjacent bathroom, where Andrew handed him the papers and toolkit. Kevin took a moment to look the directions over, then ran his eyes over Andrew.

"You might want to..." He scratched his neck. "Take your shirt off?"

A shy grin poked Andrew's cheeks up toward his ears. "Why's

that, Dad?"

"Just so none of the dye gets on it. Of course."

With a tug of the sleeves and pull at the bottom, Andrew stripped his shirt off and hung it on the towel rack, his scrawny chest out in the open for Kevin to see. He had seen it before, once when Andrew went down to the laundry room to find a clean shirt, but Andrew never ceased to feel ashamed of how weak he must have looked. Kevin was built so much better, and spent a lot more time in his gym than Andrew did, and he hoped that it was enough to satisfy anyone, let alone his father. Kevin said nothing to him, but his approving grin said all he needed to.

First, Kevin grabbed a towel and wrapped it around Andrew's collarbone, draping it over his neck and shoulders. Andrew felt a soft trace of wandering fingers down his shoulder blades, and he stiffened in several areas— including the most important one. "Try not to let it slip," whispered Kevin, and Andrew nodded, wondering how many ways he could interpret that phrase.

Andrew watched with curious eyes as Kevin prepared the bottle of bleach included with the kit, then set it down on the counter for a minute while he left the room, telling Andrew he'd be back. What, Andrew fretted, would he see on his way out? Hopefully not Used Tissue Mountain accumulating in the small trash bin next to his bed. When Kevin returned, the room filled with his amusement.

Oh God, what'd he find? he worried.

Whatever it was that he saw, he didn't make any sort of comment on it. Kevin set a container of petroleum jelly on the counter and cracked it open. It looked half-empty from where Andrew was standing. He scooped out a finger full of the gooey, smelly stuff and smeared it along Andrew's forehead. Initially, Andrew thought to object, thinking he was trying to pull a childish prank. Then, Kevin was mindful enough to clarify: "So it doesn't stain your skin."

Moving his slimy finger around the frame of Andrew's face, Kevin did it much slower than was necessary. Andrew shivered, turning to putty. Once finished, Kevin slipped on plastic gloves and grabbed the bleach bottle, starting to shake it onto Andrew's head.

"You won't have my beautiful black locks anymore," Kevin warned.

"They'll come back." For a moment, Andrew doubted it. "W-won't they?"

"They should. Don't worry."

If Andrew could wipe his brow, however sticky it was, he would do so. Other than Kevin's aquatic eyes, his hair color was the one thing they shared genetically that linked their appearances, making them a verifiable part of each other to common observers. It was something that could be disregarded by others, but in his opinion, it defined their intangible bond.

Completing that step, Kevin leaned against the counter and folded his arms. "Have to wait thirty minutes."

Andrew took a seat on the edge of the whirlpool bath and crossed his legs to prevent Kevin seeing the activity going on below his waist. For what felt like forever, they were both quiet. Andrew wanted to say it all, just tell Kevin how crazy he was for him. Kevin desired to do the same, but could only click his tongue against the roof of his mouth. This was the longest thirty minutes of their lives.

"So."

"So…"

"The venue. Is there a bar in it?"

"Probably."

Kevin nodded. Andrew did too. An eternal pause drifted between them.

"This weather."

"Yeah. I-it's… cold."

They shared another awkward nod. Kevin drummed on the countertop, looking all over the room. Andrew rocked his foot against his knee. Andrew thought he heard a cricket chirp.

"What are you going to say to Christian Maccrum later?"

A fit of butterflies fluttered in his gut. He had forgotten that he would be meeting him that night. "I hadn't thought of that yet. I'm too excited."

Chirp. Chirp.

"Dad, this is killing me."

"Oh, God, I know. Me too."

"The bleach, I mean. It kind of itches."

"Oh. Right." He forced out an anxious chuckle, then came to Andrew's side. "Looks ready. Time to rinse it out." Kevin reached around Andrew's back and turned the bathtub's faucet on. When he leaned away, their noses almost touched. Staring into Kevin's eyes, Andrew wanted to grow enough balls to kiss him already. Their constant pensive tiptoeing was unbearable. "Duck your head under the faucet," Kevin requested, tearing his eyes away from Andrew's before he lost control, and Andrew did as he was told.

While the lukewarm water rushed over his scalp and neck, Andrew felt an amorous hand moving over his head in all directions. It not only removed all of the sticky bleach from his hair, but massaged his skull and the back of his neck. A second hand rested along his spine, keeping him balanced, but following his vertebra up and down.

When his hair was thoroughly rinsed, Kevin took a blow dryer to it. It felt amazing against his skin, which was still somewhat damp, though not nearly as amazing as the hand running through his hair. Throughout the whole drying procedure, Andrew's eyes partially closed like someone who had one martini too many, satisfied and at ease with everything in his life. Kevin mirrored that young smile, loving him without words. If Andrew had to choose a favorite time in his life, this, with absolute certainty, would be it; both of them silent, Kevin stroking his scalp, grinning like lovesick fools.

After Andrew's hair was dry, Kevin started applying the actual dye, laughing as more and more of Andrew's hair turned sapphire. "You look like a blueberry!"

Thinking he was teasing him, as Kyle was wont to do, he stammered, "Is that bad?"

"No. It's adorable." He separated Andrew's hair into sections while spreading dye all over it. "It's you. I love it."

The dye now fully applied, they had to wait again before Andrew could rinse it. They went back to their silence, trying to think of appropriate topics that didn't include romantic and physical attraction. It was tougher to manage than they speculated.

"All right," Kevin said when the time was up. "Have a shower and rinse that off."

"You're not going to rinse it in the tub?" *You don't want to put your hand on my back? On my neck? You don't want to hold me the whole time you're doing it like you did before?*

"I don't want it to stain. You should be all right. Just come downstairs when you're ready."

Just say it. You want to say it. He wants you to say it. He wants to do it. Someone needs to make the leap. Do you really think he's going to?

"Kay," Andrew answered, holding his tongue for a moment.

Kevin took the gloves off, tossed them in the wastebasket, then opened the bathroom door.

"Get in with me."

Kevin twisted around, his head missing the door frame by a few centimeters. They gaped at one another, each of them dripping buckets of sweat. Kevin chuckled, but it didn't sound like the laugh of someone who was amused.

"Andrew," he gasped in awe and bashfulness. Andrew's chest singed auburn. "I…" Kevin dragged his palm over his face. "I don't know. I probably shouldn't." His captivated smile disagreed.

Not that he doesn't want to. Just that he shouldn't. Andrew learned that making the first jump wasn't as bad as he thought.

Though Kevin denied him, he lingered, hovering around the doorway, ambivalent. Andrew told him, "I was kidding anyway." Kevin frowned at that. "I'll be down soon."

"Take your time." He breezed out before Andrew could make any other arousing suggestions.

Kevin did everything he could to distract himself for the next hour or so from what just happened, until Andrew came down the stairs, his hair fully dyed, fully dressed, and ready to leave.

"We'd better head out," he told his father, whose eyes were secured on him. "We only have about twenty minutes. I want to get in the doors early so I can take pictures."

Kevin took his suggestion and slipped his shoes on alongside Andrew, who was bothered that Kevin didn't want to speak to him now. He hoped the rest of the night wouldn't progress in this way. Little did he know that it was the first evening that marked the rest of their lives.

Outside the venue stood a line that reached all the way around the building and curled toward the crammed parking lot. As he and Kevin joined the queue at the very rear, Andrew was disappointed that he might not get to be in the front row, but he could take some good shots from near the back of the crowd with the zoom lens he had. Standing outside in the blistering winds, Andrew realized all too late that his jacket wasn't enough to keep him warm.

Kevin, watching his son as he stood in the cold and shivered, sighed and beckoned him forth. "Come here." He unbuttoned his long overcoat, and Andrew scooted in as Kevin wrapped the extended folds of black cashmere around him, closing him inside of it like a well-packed tortilla. Andrew's arms then snuck around his waist.

"Is that the only coat you have?" teased Kevin. "Jeez, I'm falling down on the job, aren't I?"

He tucked himself tighter against Kevin's chest. "You're keeping me warm enough." He nuzzled into the base of his neck, inhaling his clean scent and cologne. The placid rise and fall of Kevin's chest picked up in speed.

"You're driving me crazy," Kevin moaned in a voice ripe with angst.

The line shifted. The doors must have opened. Andrew, ecstatic, nudged his father in the direction it was moving, and he guided him while trying to keep Andrew locked into the insulated coat. When they reached the burly bouncer with the shaved head and wide gut, he gave the blueberry-haired Andrew a suspicious look.

"ID?" he requested.

A freezing wind struck Andrew's cheeks, and with how still he had become, Kevin thought he had turned into a human popsicle. "I... I'm sorry?"

"ID," reiterated the bouncer, who now focused on Kevin. "This is an eighteen or over show."

Andrew closed his eyes. "No. You're kidding me."

"He doesn't have ID," Kevin explained. "But I'm his father. He's only a couple of months shy of eighteen."

The bouncer looked from Kevin to Andrew several times. His sardonic roll of the eyes slapped a frown onto Kevin's face. "Sorry. No ID, no getting into the venue."

Andrew turned to his father. "What do we do now?"

Kevin leaned closer to the bouncer, who put a hand up demanding he take a step back. Kevin eased back again. "How much do I have to pay you for us to get in there?"

The bouncer's face scrunched. "Are you kidding?"

"No, I'm not kidding."

"Get lost, pal."

"I'll write you a check."

The bouncer took an intimidating step toward Kevin, and he and Andrew inched backward. "You're not getting me. No ID, no entering the venue. *Period.* Now, please, kindly take your... son... and go, so I can get these people in. You're holding up the damn line."

"Dad…" Andrew sighed, taking his father by the crook of the arm and leading him away. "It's okay. Really."

Kevin, who wasn't accustomed to being turned away, followed his son's guidance. "I'm sorry, honey," he told him as he walked him back toward the parking lot. "I guess I should have thought this whole thing through. I feel awful."

"It's not the end of the world, right?" Andrew wouldn't deny how upsetting it was that he wouldn't get to meet his idols that night. He had been looking forward to it all week, not to mention years. "At least we get to keep the passes as memorabilia."

His son wasn't skilled at hiding his disappointment. It soaked his every word. "I know how excited you were. I let you down."

"No you didn't. I had fun tonight. Even if we didn't get to go in."

Kevin's steps slowed, his head dangling. "But this was important to you."

"Not as important as the time I spent with you."

Hearing that only made him feel worse. "Andrew…"

Andrew stopped, released his arm, and faced him. "I'm serious. I loved being with you."

"You would have loved meeting Drone Diode, too."

He was right. He would have. Regardless, he wouldn't trade their night together for any other. They were closer than they had ever been, and one of the greatest highs he had ever received was when Kevin's fingers were moving through his hair. If he had to choose between that and seeing a live show, he'd pick the former every time.

Unbeknownst to Andrew, they were being watched. Ben, idle beside his friend Garret (who insisted on wearing the loudest shade of yellow that even piss would scoff at), spied Kevin and Andrew shuffling in the opposite direction the line was flowing. A light had dawned— they were going back to the parking lot, and from the looks on their faces, he could tell that it meant they wouldn't be seeing the show.

"That's Andrew," Ben gasped, jabbing Garret with his elbow, who spun around. He squinted to focus on the man walking with him, assuming it must have been Kevin, the man Andrew couldn't go a day without shutting his trap about. "They're leaving."

"Maybe your little boyfriend is too young." Garret guessed.

For once in his life, Ben felt victorious. "Andrew!" he called, invoking snickers from Garret. Both Kevin and Andrew turned to the sound. Ben pulled the tickets from his pocket and waved them in the air. "Going somewhere?!"

Kevin's lips creased. "Hmm. I take it that's your friend?"

"Yeah." Scowled Andrew. "That's him." Andrew, while not appreciating Ben's gesture, didn't want to fuel the fire. "Let's just go. Ignore him." Still, he couldn't control the shaking of his fists as he turned his back on Ben.

"Can't get in, Andrew?!" Ben shouted again, drawing the attention of onlookers. "Aw, that's too bad! I could have gotten you in if you came with me!"

Dismissing the fact that this claim was hardly believable, Andrew still couldn't hold in his growing aggravation. He wiped his aqua hair back and tugged on it. Kevin put a hand on his shoulder to calm him, and edged him away from Ben's sight. "I'm getting really sick of his attitude," Andrew growled. "I'm this close to flipping out on him."

"Like you said, just ignore him. Let's go home."

Fed up, Andrew kicked a rock across the parking lot. It clanged against a car. Kevin, shocked, leapt back. "How was I supposed to know?! I didn't know you'd both give me the same present! I would have gone with him! I would have! Now he's mocking me?!" Andrew hadn't intended to snap, but his fuse was cut shorter and shorter after any interaction with Ben. In spite of his rage, it was a cathartic release.

"Andrew…" Kevin calmed, stepping over to him and mounting his hands upon his uptight shoulders. "It's not the end of the world, remember?" His stroking hands relaxed him and slowed his heavy, enraged breathing. "Just let him have this one. Don't let it get to you."

"I… just… I just want to—"

"Andrew. Let it go."

Andrew dropped his face into his hands. Kevin was right, but it felt so difficult. He couldn't blame Ben. If he had been in his place, he might have mocked him, too. In that regard, he was happy for Ben, and glad he got to go. Maybe now, he'd feel satisfied enough to move on from him. Perhaps this was just the way their kinship was meant to conclude.

"Can't wait to see this show!" Ben egged on from around the building. "Can't wait to have Ross Helvette sign my CD!"

Andrew turned on his heel and started toward him again, his feet smashing the icy ground beneath him, balling up his hands and ready to swing them as steam hissed from his nose. Kevin grabbed him by his bicep.

"No, Andrew."

"Dad!"

"Forget him."

It was so much easier said than done. Ben was like salt inside of an open wound. So many eyes were on them now, all of them belonging to the lucky fans of Drone Diode who would soon be getting their eardrums blasted out by their industrial-electronic rock tunes. Kevin's eyes also followed him, and they were fresh with culpability. Andrew couldn't bear that injured stare, and tried to calm himself down for at least his sake. He hadn't lied when he said he treasured their time together.

On their way to Kevin's car, Andrew stopped in his tracks, slipping his camera case from his shoulder. "Wow. Dad, look. That's their tour bus." Near the very back of the parking lot stood a jet black bus with artwork sprawled on the side along with the name of the band. The windows were tinted, but Andrew could see that shades draped over the interior. The bottom compartments under the floor were opened, and visible luggage and music equipment was tucked away inside.

Never having seen the bus belonging to his favorite band before, Andrew readied his camera to take photos. He and Kevin walked closer to the mastodon-sized vehicle, Andrew snapping pictures of the bus at all sides. "It's so big!" exclaimed Andrew, his mood lifting. "I wonder what it looks like inside!"

One or two more shots from Andrew's camera roused the attention of some men in the distance who were gathered by another bus nearby. Andrew only noticed them when one of them started heading in their direction, a man wearing a thick, puffy green coat, a backwards baseball cap, and an oversized shirt with the band logo on it.

"Hey," he called to them, his stance reproachful. "You shouldn't be back here."

The moment Andrew caught a glimpse of him, he gasped, almost dropping his camera to the ground. "Terrance Hayworth?!"

Terrance, who only a moment ago looked ready for confrontation, took a step back in surprise. His wide, hazel eyes filled his face, and his cap almost flew off. "Yeah. Do we know each other?"

"You're the guitar tech! For Drone Diode! Oh man, it's awesome meeting you."

Stunned that someone not only knew his name, but was actually excited to meet him, Terrance's expression eased into that of charmed affability. "Really!"

"Hell yeah!" Andrew cheered. "Can I shake your hand?"

Terrance was more than happy to allow him. They exchanged a powerful handshake. "Didn't realize anyone followed the road crew."

"Are you kidding? You're the guys that make it happen! The band would be nothing without you!"

"Can't say I hear that one every day." Terrance produced an exceptional grin. "Usually people want to ask me all about Diode."

Andrew gazed at the group of men milling and smoking near the other bus. A couple of others, all wearing that same T-shirt, streamed in and out of the back door to the venue with equipment. "You guys have your own bus, too? That's awesome!"

"It's not as cool as theirs. We get sleeper beds, you know, like bunks. But they get actual bedrooms."

"What? Why don't you guys get that stuff?"

"We're not the band. The band is usually a lot more spoiled than we are."

"That doesn't sound very fair."

"You hit the nail right on the head, kid." Terrance eyed Kevin for a moment, then glanced back at Andrew. "I take it you guys are here to see the show?"

"We planned on it," Kevin notified. "Andrew here is just barely eighteen."

Terrance pointed at the laminated cards hanging from their necks. "You have VIP passes on."

"They still wouldn't. He doesn't have I.D."

"Man, I'm sorry. That sucks. I'd get you in if it didn't mean my ass."

"That's okay," Andrew said. "I got to meet you. That's better than nothing."

"If only Ross and his disciples showed the roadies as much respect as you do."

"Before I go, could I get a picture?" Andrew showed him his

digital camera, and Terrance's face changed from pale and cold to ecstatic and fiery.

"Absolutely!" he sang. Andrew stepped up beside him to pose while Kevin snapped the photo for them, and Terrance bid them a good night. It was a great one, Andrew felt. One of the best.

Upon opening the front door and entering the house, Kevin punched a number on the alarm keypad mounted on the wall, hung up his coat, and turned up the thermostat. For a while, he was uncomfortable and speechless. Andrew, concerned he was angry with him, followed him upstairs in hopes of discussing it with him. He didn't give him the chance to slip into his bedroom before confronting him on it.

"Dad. Are you okay?"

He nodded. "A lot on my mind."

"Did you want to talk about it?"

"It might be best not to."

Haunted by his inhibited demeanor, he pushed for answers. "Was it what I said at the venue? What I did? I didn't mean to upset you."

"I know, Andrew. It's not that. I'll be downstairs in a minute." He stepped into his room and shut the door afterward.

Andrew sighed, went into his room and changed his clothes into something more comfortable to relax in for the rest of the night. He was the first of them to come downstairs, and the first to enter the TV room, where he watched a few minutes of a show before Kevin joined him. Now dressed in a plain gray T-shirt and loose-fitting jeans, Kevin dropped onto the sofa near Andrew, but not beside him as he usually did, rubbing his forehead and crossing his ankle over his knee.

Whatever bothered him, Andrew had an inkling of, but wasn't clear on. Anything that upset Kevin did the same to him. "I had fun with you tonight."

"So did I."

"Really? You had fun?"

He nodded, as well as smiled. "When I saw how happy you were…" He didn't finish that thought, but he didn't need to. Andrew knew just how it felt.

Andrew scooted another centimeter closer. "I'm happy when you're happy, too."

The fingers around his knee flexed. "I thought for sure you were going to start a brawl with Ben."

Andrew laughed, but softened his voice to a smooth whisper. "I probably would have if you weren't there to stop me."

"I was worried. I didn't want you getting hurt."

Scooting closer by a few inches, Andrew saw Kevin's shoulders lock up. Still whispering, he told him, "I can take care of myself."

"I have no doubt of that." He at last turned to face him. "You surprised me. You can be a little spitfire, can't you?"

Tucking his chin down toward his chest, Andrew chuckled. "Sometimes. Guess which side of the family I get it from."

For the first time in hours that night, Kevin broke out into one of his deep laughs. When his smile vanished, he traced his knee with the tip of his finger in thought. Andrew also went quiet. "Your buddy sure seemed... excitable."

Letting the air reach a thickness that could be tasted, Andrew shimmied a few inches toward Kevin, closing the gap between them. He thought he felt a tremble quake Kevin's forearms. "Yeah, he's like that. When I told you he had a crush on me, you looked like you were going to throw up."

He swallowed. "Did I?"

Andrew struck while the iron was hot, and made sure it continued to burn. "You did. Why did it bother you so much?"

Kevin's throat became a desert, his tongue a dry riverbed. Suddenly the blank, forest green wall in front of him seemed a lot more interesting to look at. "That's left for interpretation, isn't it?" When uttering these words, he didn't recognize his own voice.

Andrew slid closer to his father, pressing their shoulders together. "I want you to tell me."

"Andrew..." He sighed, his hand shaking, which he brought to his brow. A palm flattened against his leg, gripping it in an act of comfort. Rather than calm him down, it inclined his stress.

Andrew wanted more than solace regarding the status of their relationship. He wanted answers. "Why are we pretending not to feel this? I'm tired of lying to myself, and to you. Why should I have to hide what I'm feeling? Why should you?"

"I don't know what you're talking about." Whatever you do, Kevin— do not look your son in the eye. Keep staring at that wall, and all of those DVDs that you've collected over the years.

Andrew was no longer decisive, but fearful. "Yes you do."

"Andrew, please..."

"I thought you were going to start being more honest with me."

"I... I am." A heavy, sorrowful sigh shot from his mouth and nose.

"It's okay, you know."

"No, it *isn't*. It's far from okay."

This was what he had dreaded happening in the event of such a conversation. If he couldn't convince his father that their feelings were natural, they would never again have this discussion. "We're always trying to tell each other, to show each other what we want. It's okay if you're afraid of it. I am too. But I'm not going to go on acting like I don't feel it. It's ridiculous."

"Andrew," Kevin snapped. Seeing the look on his face killed him, rendered him helpless like a turtle on its back, exposing his every sensitive area for him to dig into. "There are rules. We might not like them, but they're there. Sometimes the things we..." He stopped and placed a hand over his eyes to hide them from Andrew to prevent exposing too much. "Sometimes, even things that seem right for us aren't possible. Loving you that way... it's not possible."

"You don't believe that," Andrew argued, firm. "I can hear it in your voice."

"What do you want me to do, Andrew?" Lowering his hand from his face, he slapped it onto the armrest of the couch. "Do you want me to just act impulsively? Say 'fuck it' and jump in without giving it a second's thought?"

"You don't think we've given enough thought to how we feel?"

"It doesn't matter what I feel. What's wrong is wrong."

Andrew wasn't about to let it go, not this soon. "Do you think you'd hurt me?"

"Of course I do. If I pursued anything with you beyond father and son, what kind of parent would I be? How would I differ from a predator?" When Andrew reached for his hand to hold onto, he withdrew it and got up off of the couch, pacing. "If some other older guy wanted to be with you, I'd have a problem with it. If I allowed myself to prey on you like that, I'd be no different than them!"

Quiet tears streaking down his cheeks now, Andrew stabilized his voice the best he could, fighting off a need to scream at him. "It's not like that. I don't believe for a second that you would do anything to

170

hurt me, Dad."

"It *is* like that! If someone knew about it, what do you think they'd say?! 'Oh look how cute they are together'?! No, they'd slap handcuffs on me and stuff me in a jail cell! What we want isn't always the right thing! I have to do what's right for you, Andrew. And looking at you as anything but my son and friend isn't right." He turned away from Andrew's torturing tears. It ripped his every emotion in half.

"You're acting like I'm a child. I'm an adult, too, you know. I'll be eighteen in two months, for fuck's sake. I'm almost old enough to vote, old enough to decide whether or not I want to smoke, old enough to watch porn. I think I'm old enough to choose who I want to be with and who I'm attracted to."

"Do you think that matters? I don't."

"Yes, it does!" Andrew stood as well, facing his father with determination. "It doesn't matter if I'm seventeen, eighteen, twenty-two, or your age. I would still feel it. I'd still want you. It's not a phase. It's not some childish fantasy. You're my best friend. Dad, you're everything to me."

Kevin bowed his head, knowing exactly what he meant. Andrew came to his side and wrapped his arms around his neck, clinging to him. He felt Kevin's arms drape around his waist, his hands stroking his back. Now whispering as though rubbernecking outsiders could hear them, he whispered into Andrew's ear: "You are too."

"I love you. I love you more than my guitar. I love you more than my camera. I love you in ways I never thought I'd love anybody."

"Andrew... I love you, too." Drying his eyes on his ash-tinted shirt, he sighed, "How do you do this to me?"

He leaned away from Kevin's clinging arms and moved his hands to the back of his neck, giving it a slow caress with his thumbs. Kevin swallowed, tentative. Before he could protest, Andrew brought his mouth to Kevin's and instantly felt it widen, not only accepting the connection of their lips, but moving his in time with the gradual, rhythmic motions. Andrew's entire body surged with radiating heat, his nerves on fire as he shook with the greatest sensation of ultimate euphoria. Everything had fallen into place: every horrible browbeating he suffered, every friend he had lost, every relationship that failed, each resulting in this; each ending the way they did to bring him to this most heavenly point in time, this moment in destiny. It had all been worth it.

For at least a few minutes they stood in the silent TV room, embracing each other with mouths coupled, smacking and sucking at one another's lips, releasing delicate moans every now and again. Andrew fought for extra room in Kevin's mouth, which he complied, stretching it wider to give him space. Taking advantage of the opportunity, Andrew slipped his tongue in, snaked it around Kevin's for a few turns, until he felt his shoulders tightly clench. Initially, Andrew thought it was a reaction of arousal, but he had been wrong. The passionate kiss, the feeling of togetherness, was then broken. Kevin, aching in his every muscle, took a step away from Andrew.

Faced with the jarring reality of what they were doing, Kevin said, "I can't," though shaking his head as if disagreeing with himself.

"Dad," begged Andrew. "Please. Don't walk away."

"I can't do this. *We* can't do this."

"Why?"

Any answer Kevin gave him would be just another excuse to run away from the situation. In his cluttered assortment of go-to reasons, he couldn't find a single one that made any sense to him. Andrew was simply the one; his soul mate. There was no running away from that.

Unable to come up with anything Andrew could believe, he instead listened to his reflex to fly rather than fight, and escaped by slinking off to the staircase, jogging up to his bedroom.

Andrew, now feeling one of the worst senses of rejection in his life, sat back onto the couch, hunching over with his head down. It wasn't as though he imagined that ever going well, but he at least had some hope that it would. Kevin seemed so enthusiastic about loving him in that way, then he cowered from it. Maybe he was right about it being wrong.

But why, then, did it hurt so much?

CHAPTER NINE

In Which Molecules Collide

Whipping winds howled outside the window of Kevin's bedroom, every so often interrupting his thoughts, all of which were stuck on Andrew and how badly they wanted each other.

What was it about their courtship that seemed so important? Whenever he considered telling Andrew to ignore any romantic attachments they had developed, another notion entered his head that doing so would be regrettable— that they were meant to love each other the way they did, and it was not something they could just forget.

Get in with me, he remembered Andrew suggesting in the bathroom a few hours ago. He almost took him up on the offer. Good lord, what if he had? Would he have been able to look at Andrew again afterward? Or, alternately, would they have spent the rest of their evening in carefree content knowing that they no longer had to hide from each other?

No doubts lingered in his mind regarding his love for his son, but that kiss, and how amazing it felt to do it, forced him to think differently. Maybe he wasn't the best father, if he enjoyed having that with Andrew so much. Oh yes, he enjoyed it, quite possibly more than any kiss he had ever shared with another man. Something about it contained the power of fifteen glorious lust-filled nights, doubled over and extended into infinity. A blast of the most deadly bombs, but most satisfying to hear explode, even if the reverberation deafened him. To say he had never felt a kiss like that would be honest.

Right was how it felt. Yes. Right.

In the same thought, he imagined him and Andrew having a relationship in secret behind locked doors, hiding it from Kyle, from his mother, from his legions of fans and the outside world. They wouldn't enjoy the thrill of being open about their feelings for each other in the presence of others. That would frustrate him to no end. One thing he loved to do when starting a new relationship was share the joy with others, and he certainly hated the idea of acting pensive and timid with Andrew when they had company, only kissing and hugging each other when they were out of sight of prying eyes.

They could make arrangements, couldn't they? Work around the problems; that's what couples did. They worked together, and kept each other happy. On the other hand, that might not be what Andrew wanted. Perhaps he didn't wish for their relationship to stay discreet. After all, he was the one who had the bravery to start talking about it when Kevin was far from ready to admit it to himself.

Echoing in his mind now was Andrew's declaration that his age had nothing to do with his feelings. While that might have been true, it also stood that Andrew was missing the eighteen years of experience Kevin had since conceiving him. Unlike him, and the many relationships he had to suffer through, Andrew had never been in a serious one before, and Kevin was all about getting serious. With their agreement to be together, he'd have to face the fact that Andrew came with a sense of naivety that he himself had long ago outgrown. It was true that Andrew was an adult, and could make his own choices, but did he really know what choices were best? As a parent, Kevin wanted to say no. As a partner, he longed to say yes.

He tossed, turned, kicked blankets off of himself and groaned. Struggling to fight off deep-seated feelings, ones that had been blossoming for several weeks now, was a battle Kevin lost. Alone, in his dark, satin room, all he could think of was Andrew lying beside him, curling against his chest, smiling up at him like he always did when they reached the pinnacle of happiness with one another.

Andrew, his heart cried out. *You want this so much, don't you? We both do. I can't lie to you, and so I can't deny you. Eighteen years ago I was irresponsible, an empty-headed fool with no sense of time or future. I hadn't considered my mistakes. Would it really be a mistake to let you love me? To love you back, the way I so badly want to? To hold you, to feel you, to cherish you? If we're both in pain when apart, why should we be?*

Because he was Andrew's father. There was no denying the facts. However, even that was tough to wield as an argument against how they felt. If anyone should love him, it should be him. No one else was more right for him.

Even if for a while, he would dismiss genetics altogether. They weren't a permanent set of directions meant solely to steer him and Andrew away from each other. If anything, it heightened the passion of their link, reinforced their bond, and only steered him closer to that which he knew belonged to not only his being, but his blood. No union would be more perfect in essence.

Kevin leapt out of bed like it had been sitting atop an active volcano, then slipped out of his room and moved next door to Andrew's. He steadied his quaking hand and knocked three times on the door. There was no answer. He begged that there was still a chance to fix things. If he had upset his son too much, humiliated him in ways he didn't think possible, the process might be irreversible, and he would only have himself to blame.

He knocked again, this time twice. "Andrew?" he called, his voice as gentle as wind. Still, no answer. He turned the handle and nudged the door open, taking a peek inside. Andrew wasn't in his bed, nor was he in the bathroom. Curious, he shut the door, then headed downstairs to search for him. He wasn't in the kitchen, nor the living room. If there was one place Andrew might be, Kevin knew where.

Before Kevin reached the TV room, he saw Andrew there, sitting alone and dejected on the couch, his head low, his hands holding it down. He pulled at the back of his neck, shaking with light sobs. Kevin realized that he must have been in that position since he left him there an hour ago.

Andrew hadn't heard his father enter the room, his attention centered on relieving his own pain. Kevin didn't allow his torment to continue any longer. He circled around the couch, taking the empty seat beside Andrew, who was startled at his sudden appearance, glancing up at his face with red, puffy eyes and a runny nose.

All of the burns and scars in the world couldn't possibly hurt Kevin as much as the sight of Andrew crying. He placed a hand on his aquamarine head, brushing strands of his long bangs out of his wet eyes. He dragged his thumb across his cheekbones to dry his tears, but this only caused more of them to fall. He grabbed a box of tissues and started wiping and dabbing them away while Andrew remained still and dazed.

Andrew didn't say anything, but he placed his palm on the surface of Kevin's hand as it caressed his face, curling his fingers around his wrist, tying them together. Kevin inched closer to Andrew's quivering mouth, his heart racing, his lungs pumping out carbon dioxide faster than he thought them capable. Andrew trembled beneath his touch, but was more than willing to direct his mouth closer to Kevin's, panting each inch they drew closer.

When their lips finally connected, all of their sadness faded. This time, Kevin didn't pull away from him, he didn't run, and he didn't hide. Instead, he welcomed the glorious sensation that filled him from the bottom up, accepted at last that this was it. Nothing felt greater than to at last release all of their inhibitions and to give in to what they had for so long fallen victim to. Andrew's crying stopped, replaced by youthful, pleased moans. This was what satisfaction was all about.

Andrew swung his arms around Kevin's neck, climbing into his lap and straddling his hips, surprising him, but enticing him all the same. Kevin's hands moved up and down his back while he kissed Andrew, their tongues writhing, their lips glistened with each other's saliva, and each of their heavy breaths equal in their power. As Kevin's hands snaked up Andrew's back, they slid beneath his shirt, stroking the bare skin of his spine and shoulders. Andrew felt it difficult to contain his boyish moan of delight.

He didn't know how far to take his necking with Andrew. He was most definitely ready to have an intimate relationship, but he wasn't sure where Andrew's comfort lied. "Would you like to go upstairs?"

Color flushed from Andrew's face. In short, he did want to go up to Kevin's room, and he wanted to do all manner of naughty things there. However, the time didn't feel right. If they climbed into bed together before letting it sink in that they were now emotionally fused, they were more likely to regret it afterward. "A-and do what?"

A deep chuckle escaped his tight mouth. "Whatever you like."

"Do you want to... have sex?"

Kevin suppressed an amused grin. "Only if you're ready."

"C-can we wait before we do? I don't want to, you know, rush into things."

"Absolutely."

"Really? That doesn't bother you?"

"Why would it bother me?"

Andrew shrugged. "I know how much it sucks to have blue balls."

His full laugh resounded throughout the room, the one Andrew held just as dear to his heart as Kevin himself. "I'm pretty sure I can handle it. I just want you to be happy."

Andrew draped his arms around his neck and clung to him, feeling Kevin embrace him back with a hug as hard and fierce as a bear's, squeezing the air out of his lungs. He loosened his grip when he squeaked out a wheeze. "I am. I'm so happy. I don't think I've ever been this happy before."

"I'm happy, too." He kissed Andrew's face, then released him. "Whatever it is you want to do tonight, we should get in bed soon either way. It's getting late."

"Can we…" Andrew paused, thinking this question was childish, but he soon changed his mind when he realized that they have come too far to get coy now. "Can we sleep in the same bed?"

"Of course."

"In your room?"

"Sure. I'd like that."

Now feeling he might be too excited to sleep, Andrew hurried off the couch and up the stairs, Kevin close behind. Kevin opened the door and strolled in, pulling his shirt off over his head and chucking it into a hamper in the corner.

Andrew entered, but kept his shirt on, at least for the moment. He shut the door behind him, bathing the room in darkness. Kevin turned on a tableside lamp, then took his jeans off, kicking them across the room. The crotch area of Kevin's black bikini briefs was expanded and tight, but he wasn't shy about it. Andrew could look all he wanted. And boy, did he ever.

When Kevin pulled the sheets down, he climbed into bed, and Andrew was snapped out of his hypnotic daze as soon as Kevin's nether regions were out of view. Wiping drool from the corner of his mouth, Andrew fumbled with his shirt as he pulled it off, then wormed his way out of his pants, which proved more difficult than usual with how tight his boxers felt. The tent that sprung up when he managed to slip his jeans down drew Kevin's attention, and he planted his hands over it, embarrassed. Though Kevin smiled at the sight of it, he didn't consider himself as desirable as Kevin might have.

Andrew dove into the bed next to Kevin, hiding his erection, turning all shades of red. Then, Kevin shut off the light, and the room was once again covered in shadows. A still followed, though neither of them had quite been able to fall asleep. After a few moments, Andrew turned to Kevin's silhouette.

"Kiss me good night?"

Without question, Kevin leaned over Andrew and brought their lips together. The incredible feeling of being kissed by him, with them in nothing but underwear, covered by silk, was immaculate, better than any orgasm he achieved on his own. At the finale of their kiss, Andrew wished he was ready for sex, and wasn't so afraid of scaring Kevin away. He almost lost him once. Andrew curled an arm around him and moved his fingers against Kevin's scalp, scratching at the fine hairs on the back of his neck, causing him to moan happily.

"Dad... what are we?"

"Hmm? What do you mean?"

"Other than... different."

Kevin slid an arm around his waist and rested his hand on his back, giving it firm strokes. "What you want to know is if I'm your boyfriend." It didn't sound like a question. Andrew nodded, but said nothing else, relaxing at his touch. "I think 'boyfriend' is too frail a term. You're a lot more than that to me."

"You are, too."

"You'll always be a part of me. Nothing would ever change that." He sighed with adulation as Andrew curled against his chest and nuzzled the nape of his neck.

"I like being a part of you," Andrew whispered, drowsy.

Kevin continued to pet his back while he drifted to sleep, cradling him tight. "So do I." He planted a gentle kiss to Andrew's forehead, then joined him in dozing off.

During the weekend, the two best days in Andrew's lifetime, Kevin took him to Manhattan and walked with him through Central Park, then shared a pricey, but delicious lunch at a café. When Kevin asked if Andrew would like to go ice skating, Andrew was a bit on the apprehensive side. Skateboarding might have been his thing when he was younger, but sliding around on a sheet of ice didn't sound too fun.

In the evening, Kevin read some of his own mystery-thriller novels to him, elated at how suspenseful Andrew considered the plot and twists, and Andrew played a few requests on his guitar in exchange— most of them from the nineties. They wrestled in Kevin's bed when their hands were free, rolling and play-fighting with one another, and stayed up chatting for a while.

"What about Kyle?" Andrew asked Kevin out of the blue after Kevin stopped tickling him, which he was grateful for. He thought if he laughed any longer, he might puke on his father's silk bedspread.

"What about him?" confirmed Kevin, plucking goose down from Andrew's hair.

"You and he... used to..."

"I haven't spoken to him in a little while. Even if I had, we wouldn't be having sex anymore."

Andrew got the sense he was now coming between Kevin and Kyle, and that felt unfair to him. "Wouldn't he notice that something was wrong?"

Kevin rolled onto his back and Andrew rested upon his chest. "I'm sure he'd pick up on it. But what can I say to him? That me and my son are in a relationship? I don't think he'd take it very well. Christ, he's probably already sick of me."

"Your friendship with him isn't going to suffer, is it?"

Kevin comforted him by stroking him on the head. "No. We'll be fine. Try not to worry about it."

That was like asking Andrew not to breathe. Of course he would worry about it. How could he not? Kyle and his father had been friends since childhood, and he only came into Kevin's life almost two months ago. In a way, he felt he didn't have a right to claim his father as his own. He didn't like Kyle very much, but he knew that Kevin did, and he wanted Kevin to be happy.

However, he said nothing more on it, especially when Kevin kissed his stress away. It would be left for a later time. For now, he basked in the bliss of their intimate time together.

On Sunday afternoon, Kevin took Andrew to a natural history museum, giving him a broader education beyond high school. Andrew was fascinated, bubbling with childlike curiosity at every display he ogled. The star charts and planetary timelines captured the majority of his intrigue.

"Look at how small we are compared to the rest of the universe," he mentioned to Kevin in awe, who observed the many models of planets made by college students. "Just some tiny little speck in the middle of infinity."

Kevin stepped up beside him and leaned down to the chart. "I wonder how much we haven't discovered."

"We might never know. The universe constantly changes. Like we do. Look at the dinosaurs, for example. In an instant, they were wiped out." He snapped his fingers. "Just like that."

Straying from the theme of Earth's doom, Kevin said, "I'm going to name a star after you."

Andrew argued with a grin, "I don't think 'Andrew' is a very cosmic name."

"That's the beauty of it. It'd be as special as you."

Warmed by his words, Andrew clasped him in his arms. "I'm having fun today."

Kevin smashed him against his chest, loving on him with discreet smooches to the face. "I am, too."

For the remainder of the afternoon, they engaged in a rowdy snowball fight in the front yard, which ended with the two of them tumbling to the frozen dust, tossing clumps of snow onto each other. By the time they finished, they were covered from head to toe in white flakes, soaked and trembling from the cold. Kevin insisted they retreat indoors to warm up, and he made them each a cup of gourmet cocoa while they curled up in front of the fireplace, exchanging humorous stories of youth.

Kevin still hadn't heard from Kyle, nor had he bothered to call him. He wouldn't convey it to Andrew, but he knew something had to be wrong. Kyle was angry with him, he was sure of it. About what, however, he had no clue. He longed to share with him how happy he was now, how he and Andrew were closer, but like so many of his ideas, it only worked out in fiction. Kyle would handle it about as well as his own mother would: by cursing and asking a plethora of questions that might or might not have answers to them.

Kevin would give him time, whatever he needed it for. When Kyle was ready to talk, he would. He only hoped he'd do it sooner rather than later.

Much to Andrew's dismay, the weekend finished, and he had to return to school. Just as he did every morning, Kevin drove him, but unlike mornings in the past, they snuck each other a kiss on the mouth, and it was twice as difficult for Andrew to leave his side. Kevin almost had to push him out of the vehicle to get him going, telling him that it would be like any other day, and as much as he loved him, it would be unhealthy for the two of them to be chained together all day.

Andrew wouldn't have minded being chained to Kevin, but he still understood his point. He entered the school as he did every day, but this time with a high so powerful that it would laugh ecstasy away. As he strutted to his locker, he saw that Ben wasn't there, and breathed a sigh of relief. The last thing he wanted after such a magnificent weekend was an altercation with a former friend.

After cranking the dial of his padlock to the numbers of his combination, the lock, which normally popped open, stayed secured. Frowning, Andrew tried it again. Nothing. Had he really forgotten his own combination over the weekend with everything that happened? He couldn't imagine being that absentminded. He set his backpack down and found the slip with the padlock combination on it. It was the same set of numbers he had been trying.

What the hell is going on here? pondered Andrew, scratching his head. *Maybe the lock is defective.* He remembered Stephan's padlock— the one he glued shut. He then omitted that from the list. *Unless…* He glanced at his neighboring locker with widening eyes. *No. He wouldn't.*

Andrew stepped over to Ben's locker and tried his own combination on the lock hanging on the handle. With ease, the lock snapped open. Stunned at what he had learned, Andrew stood and contemplated it. Normally, he would have wondered how Ben came to find out his locker combination, but having a locker right next to him gave him all sorts of opportunities. In this case, he really wished he had paid any attention to what Ben's combination was— he had no chance of opening his locker without confronting him.

"You son of a bitch," he muttered, opening Ben's locker. Inside were textbooks, a coat, and photographs taped up to the inside walls. Andrew recognized some of them as the photos he snapped of the drama club for the school paper. Discontented, he thought about ripping them down. Then, he thought differently. Not only was Andrew against tearing any photo, regardless of its meaning, but he didn't want to alert Ben to his knowledge of the switch of padlocks. He decided to make his invasion a bit more veiled.

Andrew grabbed one of the paper workbooks off of the top shelf, one filled with assignment sheets for biology, and pulled a pen out of his backpack. He opened the front cover, making sure he was out of sight of the other students, and started sketching in bold black ink. He covered most of the title on the front page, as well as Ben's handwritten name, which was sloppy and barely legible. Satisfied with his artistic work, he slipped the workbook back in, tucking it exactly where he found it as though it had never been disturbed.

Andrew's next stop was the office, where he got them to give him a new padlock when he told them his was sticking. He also informed them that his locker door was having problems and wanted to get a new locker as soon as possible. He was told it would be addressed. Andrew was grateful, no longer wanting to see Ben in any circumstance. Though he was rather annoyed that Ben had taken the severance of their friendship to a level he didn't predict, he hoped he made his point.

Biology was Ben's third class of the day, and by far his least favorite. Sociology was the one he preferred, if he were to choose. Few things were more fun to him than studying the behavior of human groups. A single person on their own was fascinating enough, but the mind became twice as complicated when thrown into a crowd of several others. Unfortunately, he had to get through biology to reach sociology, which was his fourth class, and came after lunch. He looked forward to a relaxing afternoon, which he knew would be spent learning about emotions and preservation of self as developed since day one of a person's time on the planet.

As he approached his locker, he glanced at Andrew's with a wry smirk. He wondered how poor Andrew's morning had gone, if he struggled even more than usual with that insufferable locker door. What a slap in the face it must have been for him to return to school only to find that his combination didn't work. He would have loved a report on the look that likely landed on Andrew's world-weary face.

Sometimes things just don't go the way that you want, he gloated with pride. Opening his own locker, he grabbed his biology workbook, textbook, and paused for a moment as he stared in at the photos Andrew took of him and his drama class. The words typed underneath were what he always loved most about them:

The very talented Ben Erickson rehearsing with our drama club.

He truly wondered whether or not Andrew meant that, or if his compliment was as empty as their friendship. He liked to think he was being honest, that he did find him talented, and he recalled just how proud he looked and sounded at the rehearsal that day. Proud of *him*. Not even his father was proud of him.

Fewer things made Ben happier than to hear that applause from his companion, to see that pleased glow on his face when the song ended, the song he was the leading voice for. Perhaps he really had meant what he wrote.

He paused, staring at the ground, looking back on the way he behaved on Friday at the show. The look of hurt and rage on Andrew's face when he taunted him satisfied him then. Now, it only nauseated him. He wished he could take it all back.

What had he done? What kind of self-centered prick had he turned into?

Now overcome with depression, Ben shut his locker door, but unhooked Andrew's padlock and brought it to the locker it belonged to. He twisted the dial of the lock on Andrew's locker door, knowing the combination as his own, but somehow, it didn't work. The padlock remained shut.

He must have asked for a new one, he realized. *I hope he doesn't know I did it.*

Ben considered apologizing to him later if he saw him. He hoped he would forgive him. For now, he had to go to class. With his book bag swung over his shoulder, he headed to biology.

Studies for that day involved photosynthesis and plant growth, which Ben found tedious and snooze-inducing. Before the start of class, Ben, along with the other students, handed in his workbook for the teacher to grade, then sat down with his lab partner. For the hour, she helped him with most notes they had to take for an upcoming test, which he found tough to follow, while the teacher graded the student workbooks.

At the end of class, the teacher handed the workbooks back to the students, but gave Ben a discerning, reprimanding look instead of his booklet. Puzzled, Ben stared back at her, but heard her say, "See me, right now."

Giving the other students time to file out before approaching his teacher at her desk, Ben stood before her while she slid the workbook toward him and flipped open the front cover. He glanced down at what appeared to be a drawing of a detailed, anatomically correct penis in fluid black ink, complete with veins and wrinkles, and his mouth and eyes popped.

"You know that's highly inappropriate, Benjamin," scolded his teacher.

"I didn't draw that!" he defended. "I can't even draw that well!"

"If you didn't do it, then who did?"

How could he possibly explain that? Andrew could have been the only one, and he didn't share the class with him. Even if he told her the truth, she wouldn't buy it.

"You know I have to give you detention for this," she continued, pulling open a drawer containing slips.

"Great," grunted Ben, his nostrils flaring and lip twitching, waiting for her to write out a slip for him. She passed it to him, and he snatched it from her hand. "Thanks a lot." She then passed him a new workbook and told him to fill that one out from now on.

Storming down the corridor to the lunch room, fumes and steam leaked from Ben's ears. Detention. Of all things. His father was going to be livid beyond belief. Apologize to Andrew? What was he thinking when he came up with that plan? The next time he saw him, he'd do a lot worse than change his locker combination.

Andrew debated entering the cafeteria. Despite the snow falling in blinding sheets outside, he almost considered eating out at the picnic tables set around the courtyard. He'd freeze his ass off, but at least there was no risk of seeing Ben. It didn't take him long to change his mind.

Why should I have to change my life around because he feels the need to act this way? I didn't do anything wrong.

Thankfully, Ben was absent from their usual table, and he could sit alone and eat his meal in peace. Carrying his regular brown paper bag filled with Kevin's handmade lunch, he crossed the room with a brisk stroll, hoping to reach his table before Ben noticed him, though he stuck out like a sore thumb with the way he dressed. He couldn't wait to fill his growling stomach, especially with his daily dose of love and turkey. It was just the thing he needed to cheer himself up. The day started out somewhat on the poor side, but it didn't matter. He had home to look forward to, now more than ever.

Andrew didn't have time to figure out what happened. He had made it halfway across the room, toward his table, before his footing gave way. In slow motion, he dumped the items in his hands onto the tiled floor, spilling the contents of his lunch bag. The small bottle of chocolate milk rolled across the floor and underneath a table, and his sandwich, wrapped in cellophane, hit another teen's shoe.

His kneecap and right hip throbbed, fiery pain coursing up his waist, making the struggle to return to his feet an exigent task. Pressing his weight on his wrists, he hauled himself to a kneeling position. That's when he noticed his treasured lunch sprawled across the floor. All he could do was close his eyes, grit his teeth, and utter quiet obscenities.

A symphony of giggles surrounded him near the table where he tripped. He turned toward the sound, and laid eyes on Ben, who watched him from over his shoulder, a smug leer painted on his face.

"Whoops," he sang to Andrew, generating further jollity from the others sitting at the table with him, people Andrew had never met before. He still had his right foot sticking out, even waved it back and forth, showing it off to him. *That's right, you little punk,* his shoe taunted. *It was me.*

Fuming, Andrew regained his strength and climbed back to his feet, charging at Ben with balled up fists. Ben saw it coming and stood before Andrew had the chance to jump him. Now that they were facing each other, Andrew hesitated, remembering that he was half Ben's size, but he was too furious to back down.

"You want to hit me, Andrew?" snarled Ben.

He did want to, but knew it was a fight he would end up losing, and he might not have a recognizable face afterwards. Instead, he grabbed Ben's food tray in one hand, and with his eyes locked on Ben's, he turned it upside down, sending the half-eaten burger and fries down onto Ben's white shoes.

The two of them froze in a deadly staring match for a few moments before Andrew whispered, "Whoops."

A hush fell over the audience seated at the table. Ben grabbed the collar of Andrew's mesh fishnet shirt, scowling, his face flashing to the color of a ripe tomato. For a moment, Andrew panicked. Maybe

Ben really would finish what he started.

"Hey!" A member of the school staff, a tall man in a white shirt with a radio tucked into his pocket, approached them just as spectators around Andrew and Ben became both awed and uncomfortable, many of them ignoring their meals. "Break it up, boys," he warned, firm. "Now. Back away, back away." In case they didn't get the message, he waved his hands back. They did as they were commanded. He asked them their names, and they told him. He beckoned for Andrew and asked Ben to sit down, who smirked at his former friend and shrugged. Andrew's glare didn't seem to faze him.

"You," the man in the white shirt bellowed. "With me. Now."

There was no reason to argue that he didn't start the fight, or that the staff member likely picked him out because of his choice of apparel. Andrew went with his mouth shut and hands up, as he was taught to when submitting to authority.

The staff member, who didn't supply Andrew with his name, lead him to the office, where he informed the principal of Andrew's behavior. According to the looks the principal gave him, he wouldn't be getting off easy. Why couldn't he have worn white that day? The convictions might have been less severe.

Andrew knew exactly where this was headed, having gone through it before. "So, do I get detention, or what?" he asked before the elderly principal could deliver her punishment.

"Yes," she confirmed, her hands folded upon her desk. "Half hour after school." She wrote him a similar slip to the one given to Ben earlier, and passed it to him.

"Great," sighed Andrew, taking the form. "Thanks a lot."

The first thing Andrew dreaded when the final bell of the day rang was telling his father. What might Kevin think of him? When living under Star's roof, she expected a detention every once in a while. He couldn't stand disappointing Kevin. A "spitfire" was what Kevin called him the night of the Drone Diode show, but he had no idea just how true it was.

Now, it was too little, too late. He had to find out sooner or later, and it looked as though it would be the former. At the end of the day, he walked out of the school to the parking lot where Kevin waited for him as usual. When he didn't enter the vehicle as he did every other afternoon, Kevin knew something was up.

"Dad…" He chewed on his lip.

"Are you okay? What's wrong, what happened?"

"I sort of…" A brief pause, then, "Kind of… got detention."

"*Detention?*"

That look of surprise on Kevin's face was enough for Andrew to want to lay down in front of his car. "It… it wasn't really my fault… I just…"

"Did you get into a fight?"

He bowed his head. "Sort of. Was about to."

"Andrew…" He sighed. "Why?"

"I won't do it again, I promise," he assured, repulsed at the thought of letting him down. "I was just so angry, and…"

"We'll talk about it later. You'd better go."

Fighting back fresh tears, Andrew shut the passenger door and left the lot, jogging back inside the school. All he could think about on the way to the detention room was Kevin's face. Prior to that day, he must have thought his son a good boy who could do no wrong. Without effort, he managed to crush that in such short time. The face of his disappointed father was by far a worse punishment than staying a half an hour after school.

Upon entering the detention room, Andrew noticed three other students, only one of whom he recognized. Ben sat in the far corner of the room, sulking, reading a book.

Guess he didn't get off scot-free after all, Andrew noted, handing the teacher his detention slip and taking a seat far away from Ben, who hadn't yet seen him enter. Andrew started working on homework, glancing up at Ben now and then.

Feeling eyes on him, Ben looked across the room and saw Andrew hunched over one of the far tables. Curious, he raised his head to get a better look at him, seeing just how miserable he appeared to be. Fulfillment elevated his previously poor mood.

Maybe detention wasn't so bad after all.

A half hour later and Andrew was free to go, and he didn't wait another minute to make his leave when the chance became available. On his exit of the school, he hoped Kevin was still outside waiting. He wouldn't have blamed him if he had left him there and forced him to walk home. He wouldn't have been the first to do so.

When he opened the passenger door, Kevin looked up from some notes he was writing in a composition book, which he then stuffed into the glove compartment. The engine purred and heat blew from the vents, keeping the car warm enough until Andrew was done with detention. Kevin said nothing at first, letting Andrew get in and buckle up.

"Are you mad at me?" Andrew peeped, apprehensive.

"No, honey." He put the car in drive and turned onto the main road.

"Are you disappointed in me?"

"Andrew. I'm not upset. You served your time. Nothing I do or say is going to make the situation better."

Andrew shrunk deeper into the seat. "Ben was just getting to me. I don't know what his problem is."

"I know it's hard, but you can't let it bother you. There will always be someone that doesn't like you. We can't make everyone happy."

"I just want it to be over, Dad."

"This is your last school year. You won't have to deal with it anymore once you're finished." Kevin pulled onto their street. "Just get through it the best you can. And try not to get any more detentions."

"I…" He palmed his face. "I'll try. For you, at least." He calmed at the feeling of Kevin's hand gliding over his shoulder and neck.

"Everything will be okay," Kevin vowed.

Andrew wished he could believe that. Still, Kevin meant enough to him that he would stay hopeful. They both entered the house, and Andrew finished what was left of his homework while Kevin spent some time on the phone with his editor. The call was lengthy, so Andrew had a lot of time to kill. He played games in the meantime until he was done, though they seemed dull without Kevin playing with him.

Once finished with his call, Kevin appeared in the TV room, and took a seat beside him, draping an arm around him. Andrew paused his game so that their imminent conversation would go without interruption. "I was wondering…" Kevin was all ears. "Would Friday be okay?"

Kevin, blinking, queried, "For what?"

"Um… the date? You know, for…?"

"Oh! Well, yeah, if that's what you'd like. As a matter of fact…" He pulled his smartphone from his pocket, opening the calendar and checking to make sure he didn't make any other plans on Friday. "I could take you out that night, too. This week, I have a book signing to attend, on Wednesday."

"Can I come with you?"

"You'll be at school."

"But I want to see you sign books. Call me in sick."

Kevin chuckled. "There will be plenty more, you know. After I publish this next one, I'm going to have to go to another, I'm sure of it. That should be after you graduate anyway."

Andrew plopped his head onto Kevin's shoulder. "School ruins everything," he pouted.

"Don't make that face. I'll have to kiss it." He leaned over him, but Andrew launched his mouth onto his before he got the chance. They seized the opportunity to make out for a minute or two, and it was somehow more extravagant than the first time they had.

Andrew's jaw began to tire out, and his groin ready to explode. As excited as he was to take things to a level beyond kissing, he still worried that their first time might be the last. "You're taking me out?" he asked his father when their smooching ceased. "Where are you taking me?"

"That, my dear, is a surprise." Kevin left the couch to find the nearest phone book in order to make reservations at whatever mystery restaurant he planned to take him to.

Andrew glowed with positivity. "I'm going to be spoiled in this relationship, aren't I?"

Leaning over the frame of the couch, with Andrew's head tilted back, Kevin kissed him on the mouth. "Spoiled rotten, young man." He nuzzled his nose, bringing a smile to Andrew's face. He grabbed hold of the phone book in the drawer of the side table. "I'll be back, and then we can play a while."

Just as they did every night, they fell into their routine: playing games in the evening, having dinner, watching movies, then retired to the same bed where they slept together. Andrew always had problems falling asleep in the past, but whenever Kevin stroked his head and back, he drifted off instantly. This was where he belonged: asleep in Kevin's arms, stilled by his slowing heartbeat and breathing, curled into a ball beneath layers of silk and warmth. Nothing in the world felt better than to be held by someone he loved, someone who loved him in return.

Andrew was new to relationships, Kevin was aware, but he also looked forward to the future. When holding Andrew, everything fell into place, pieces of a puzzle that have been missing for so long, now snapping together. When Star had told him he was a father, he panicked that he would do a terrible job, or that Star had already damaged him beyond repair. Since Andrew had entered his life, he couldn't remember being any happier— happy that he had someone to look out for, happy that he'd have a life to share with another, and happy that he could offer Andrew a life he couldn't have before.

When Kevin closed his eyes, he wondered if Andrew's feelings for him would last, if they might sour as they got older. If it were to happen someday, and Kevin was sure it would, he would make the best of things until then. Every chance he got, he would give Andrew all he needed, and then some. He would be the best father he could, the best lover he could, and above all, the greatest friend.

CHAPTER TEN

In Which the Strands Fuse

While covering his padlock with his hand to prevent Ben seeing his new combination, Andrew cracked into his locker now without any problems, save for the trouble he continued to have with the door. It wasn't as though he could turn to Ben and ask for his help, as Ben's demeanor made it pretty clear that all discussions between them were forbidden ground.

It wasn't until Ben slammed his locker door shut, and with a touch of pride in his voice, chimed, "Later, daddy's boy," that Andrew knew there was no hope whatsoever in fixing what was broken— and what he really wanted to break was Ben's nose.

No, he can't possibly know about us, can he? Andrew convinced himself, though the accusation alone was troubling. *Right now he's just taunting me.*

During lunch, Andrew watched the ground like a bombardier, making certain no feet would dart out and surprise him. He stopped partway across the room when he saw that a group of students had taken residence at his usual table, and among them was Ben, who seemed lively and chatty with those he ate with. He recognized one of them from the day before, the one who laughed when Ben tripped him. He had a similar smile on his face now when he laid eyes on him, seeing him standing and staring in awe at the surreal exhibit before him. A few of the others he acknowledged were from Ben's drama club.

"There's a seat left for you, Andrew." Ben's manner seemed less welcoming and more like an anglerfish attempting to lure organisms in with its photophore.

Andrew said nothing to Ben, but turned his back on him and walked away. There were no other empty tables, so he plopped down into a spot between a group of upbeat girls, quaking and hunching over as he was crammed between them, half of them sending text messages on smartphones. One of them looked up from her busy typing to comment on Andrew's arrival.

"What are you doing?" she probed, evidently put off by Andrew's sense of style.

"Look, I just want to eat my lunch," Andrew stammered with trembling hands. "You don't have to talk to me, or even look at me."

Tossing her hair back, she sighed, "Whatever," and forked some salad into her mouth. She engaged the other girls in conversation about films that had "retards" in them, and whether or not they should feel guilty for laughing at them. Andrew wanted to tear his ears off by the end of the lunch hour.

At least when his time in the cafeteria was through, he didn't have to see Ben for the rest of the day.

The end of the pen Kevin chewed on had been crushed to death, but his oral fixation only worsened as the days passed. He tried chewing gum, but he hated the stuff. The nicotine patches were doing him all right, but they never gave him the full satisfaction of taking a long drag from one of his menthols.

Maybe he could purchase a pack and hide it. Andrew wouldn't have to know. *I can't do that to Andrew,* he decided, though it wasn't a choice made simply.

Writing usually took his mind off of it, but his concentration was lacking, even when he got up and paced to get the blood flowing to his brain. He needed a cigarette. He needed several hundred cigarettes.

"Come on, Kevin," he pep-talked to himself. "You can make it. Just keep holding out."

He smacked his lips, tasting the fresh mint, feeling the sting of smog in his eyes, that glorious after-dinner treat that hung in the air even hours after he had smoked one. His office was once the identical scent of a cigarette factory, and it calmed him when his mind was hectic. Now it smelled of… well, truth be told, he couldn't tell. His sense of smell seemed to have diminished over the years.

Click, click, click went his fingers on the keyboard as he grinded the pen between his molars. A cracking sound declared he had broken the plastic. Not wanting to get ink in his mouth, he chucked it into the wastebasket, a proverbial fountain pen graveyard, and searched for another object to stick in his mouth.

The doorbell rang. As far as he knew, he wasn't expecting any visitors. He left his office, his fingers twitching as he approached the front door. Kyle was on the other side, bundled up in his tan suede coat, greeting him with a crooked, hollow smile.

Not only was he surprised to see his friend, but pleased. "Hey!" He invited him inside, taking his coat and hanging it up in the hall closet. Kyle gave the gesticulation silent approval. "Where have you been, huh?"

Kyle shrugged, following his friend into the living room after removing his steel-toed boots. "Working my ass off, that's where I've been." He took a seat on the burgundy, velvet lounger, raising his head a few inches as he sniffed the air. "Did you clean?"

"Not recently." Unlike Kyle, Kevin didn't sit. Instead, he shoved his hands into his pockets and stood over him, watching his buddy with interest.

"Smells good in here."

"Oh. Thank you."

A breeze rattled the screens on the windows as bits of snow and ice rained against them. Kyle folded his hands in his lap, clearing his throat every ten seconds or so. This went on for at least half a minute.

Unsettled by the stillness, Kevin pressed for any sort of conversation, regardless of the topic. "Want a drink, or something?"

"No thanks." He twirled his thumbs together.

Growing agitated, Kevin coaxed him. "How was the move?"

"The what?"

"Your friend. He asked you to help him move?"

He mulled it over for a moment. "Oh, that. It was all right." Silence once again filled the room.

"Kyle… is there something you wanted to see me about?"

"I'm getting to it, Kevin. Okay?"

Kevin checked the silver clock hanging on the wall. Andrew would be done with school in an hour. "All right." He sat on the leather recliner, crossing his ankle over his knee.

"How are things going with Andrew?"

"Great. Really great." He bit down on the nail of his index finger.

"I figured I'd come by when he wasn't around so I'd have your undivided attention." When Kevin didn't reply, he perpetuated. "Kev... when you first got your publishing contract, I was really happy for you. I never told you that I was a little jealous of you, too." This wasn't surprising news to Kevin, who reacted with a passive nod. "But, you shared so much with me, gave me so much when I wasn't doing well, and... shit. This is harder than I thought." He scratched at the goatee on his chin, delaying. "Maybe we should have some beer first."

"You can't say this while sober?"

"It's hard, Kevin. I need to loosen up. You want one?"

"I don't even have any beer in the house."

"Well, you've got vodka, don't you?"

"No. Kyle, whatever it is, you can talk to me. I'm not going to throw you out, or anything."

Kyle stood up anyway. "I *know* you have vodka."

"Well, I don't want to drink with you!" He toned his voice down when Kyle cast him an indignant, soul-piercing stare. "Um... right now. It's one in the afternoon, and I still have to pick Andrew up from school later."

"All right. Fine." He sat back down on the lounger, tenser than before. He rubbed his hands together, taking many extended breaths. "When you signed on that contract, that was the last time I felt jealous in regards to you. Until I saw you with Andrew."

"You were jealous of me and Andrew?"

"I don't know, maybe 'jealous' is the wrong word. When I saw you both giggling and whispering with each other, I felt like I was losing you to him. I know that's utterly ridiculous. You're still here, talking to me."

From a mile away, Kevin saw the direction their chat was headed in, and his craving for nicotine ascended. "I'm just excited to have him in my life."

"It's okay, Kev. After thinking it over, it was unfair to get upset with you. It's not your fault, or Andrew's. My point is... Christ, I can't believe I'm doing this." He rubbed his drooping, exhausted eyes. "When I saw how… I don't know… *close* you guys were getting, it made me feel sort of…" He shrugged. "Rejected. You were acting like you were enamored with each other."

Kevin placed a hand over his mouth. "It's not what you think."

"I know." Though he said this, he didn't sound the least bit convinced. "I guess I was just hoping, deep down, things between us wouldn't change. Because I've really come to love what we have together. Our closeness, I mean." He didn't elaborate, but his spreading eyes and jagged tilts of the head gave Kevin a few hints.

Please don't, Kyle, begged Kevin. *Please don't do this. Not now.*

"Haven't you enjoyed it?" asked a now hopeful Kyle.

Kevin, scratching his brow, shifted back and forth in his seat. "I… yeah, of course. But we've sort of been going at it for a while now, haven't we?"

The light on Kyle's face faded. "Well, yeah. I guess that's my point. You would date a guy, it wouldn't work out, you'd cry to me, we'd hold each other and… then I'd ease the pain in our own way. I'd date someone, it would end, and same thing would happen. Every time we had a break-up we were back at each other. It was more than just therapy I think, Kev. Maybe it's something else. Maybe it's meant to be us."

Oh, God, no, Kevin's soul screamed. *Why? Why couldn't you have done this a year ago? I would have been all for it.*

"Uh… maybe. But, maybe not." The spirits he crushed within Kyle were impossible to face, and he turned away from him. "Has it really been that harmonious between us? Think about it, Kyle. There's a reason we remained friends for so long."

"What do you mean? I thought it was going really well."

"Please," Kevin whispered, hiding his eyes. "Don't take this to mean I don't love you, because I do, and I always will. But think of all of the times we actually had sex because we wanted to be close, and how many times we did it because we were drunk. I'd say ninety percent of the times we fuck are when we're loaded." Kyle bowed his head in shame. "I can't be getting shit-faced every time I want to be held, you know? It's not exactly good for my liver, or my heart. I want love, when I want it."

"You're right. I know. That's my fault. I was still sort of in that, you know, denial phase. I knew I liked what we had, but I didn't want to admit it. But I want to change things. I thought this all through for days on end. I don't want to be a fucking coward about it, Kevin."

Kevin had to fire off using some different ammunition. "Well, we don't really get along as well as we used to, either, Kyle. We argue more than we do anything resembling fun."

"I can't help that! You've been in my life so long. I've forgotten how to respect you. I should. The way you respect me."

Kyle could win the Contrite Olympics at this rate, in Kevin's opinion. "What do you want us to have, exactly?"

"I guess I haven't worked that out completely." He left the recliner and walked around the living room, picking up random items on the coffee table. He sniffed one of the aromatherapy candles. "I know it's probably safer to stay friends, but I'm sick of playing it safe. I want to take a few risks. After we had sex, even if I was drunk, it felt really nice when you held me all night. I think that's what I want us to have."

"Kyle," Kevin moaned, dropping his forehead into his sweating palms. "I don't know. We're alike, sure. And the sex, from what I can even remember of half of it, is pretty good. I just think the timing is sort of bad right now."

Kyle disapproved with a dubious snort. "Timing? What, is summer better for you?"

"No, that's not what I mean. With Andrew here and all…" He couldn't finish that thought. Whatever he came up with would probably be a lie.

"He's your son, not your watchdog. You guys can still have some bonding time while you and I are together. I don't see why this would be a problem."

"Kyle, *please*. Do me this one favor and listen when I tell you that… I love you to death…" His eyelids compressed, preparing for the worst. "But it wouldn't work."

"Do you have someone else that you don't want to tell me about? I'm a big boy. I can handle it."

Desperate, Kevin switched gears. "Where is this all coming from all of a sudden? You're always teasing me and making fun of me for one thing or another. I never, not once, got the impression that a relationship beyond friendship was something you wanted."

"Teasing you!" Kyle repeated with a gasp. "It's friendly banter! And it's my…" He placed his hands on his hips, clicking the stud in his tongue against his teeth. "It's my stupid little way of flirting."

Feeling somewhat nauseous, the beer that Kyle suggested earlier was starting to sound better and better. "Teasing me," he uttered, incredulous. "That's *flirting*."

"It used to make you laugh. You always knew I was kidding. Jeez, Kev, suddenly you have this huge issue with it. If you were offended, I certainly had no idea until now."

"You thought I'd laugh at you insulting my writing?"

After taking a step back, Kyle lifted his palms in defense, waving the white flag of surrender. "Okay. I get it. You're right. I'm sorry." Kevin didn't answer, but his temper simmered. "Sometimes I'm not the greatest friend, I admit it. But I can change that, Kev. If you want me to. I can be better if you let me."

Beyond this point, Kevin had no idea how to approach the matter any longer. "Kyle, we have fun together. If we had this talk a while ago, I might have wanted it then. I hate to be an asshole about it, but it's a little late." When Kyle snapped his gaze away and watched the floor, Kevin regretted being harsh with him. He had never seen him so humble before. This was the first time he had heard him address any issue with such passion.

"I understand," he whispered, then shuffled to the coat closet, cursing under his breath. "I don't know what I was thinking. Christ, I'm an idiot."

Now overcome with guilt, Kevin left the leather chair and jogged up to him. "I'm sorry. You mean the world to me, Kyle, you really do. It's just that…"

"You don't have to explain yourself. If you don't feel something… well, you just don't feel it. It's not your fault."

"Yes. It is."

Kyle didn't answer, other than with a gentle kiss farewell to Kevin's mouth. A heart-splitting sting followed, one that Kevin tried to ignore, but its pressure was overwhelming. "It might be a while before you see me again. I need a little space now to think things over."

"You'll call me, won't you?"

For a few moments, Kyle went quiet. Then he nodded. "Eventually. See you around, handsome." Kevin didn't get the chance to say his goodbyes before Kyle stepped out and shut the door behind him. As he sauntered with a hanging head down the driveway, Kevin clutched his chest, which throbbed.

Will I tell Andrew? he wondered, watching Kyle drive out of his life for who knew how long. *I shouldn't. He'd feel like he was responsible, and I already upset one person today.*

He went back to work, craving cigarettes even worse than he had before Kyle stopped by.

Neither Kevin nor Andrew were in good moods when they met up in the parking lot, which was made clear by Andrew's weighted sighs and Kevin drumming his thumbs on the steering wheel.

"I don't know what Ben is up to," Andrew said after a few minutes. "But he seems really determined to make the rest of my school year a living hell."

"Send him to me," Kevin joked, trying to keep a light attitude. "I'll take care of him."

Taking him seriously, Andrew shook his head. "Nah. He'd just use that as another excuse to fuck with me."

"What exactly is he doing?"

"It's tough to explain. I guess you could say he's harassing me, but not bad enough to tell anyone. I hope it doesn't get to that point."

"Don't wait until it does. I don't want you getting hurt."

"I know, Dad. I'll be all right."

Upon entering, Kevin turned up the thermostat, knowing Andrew liked it a little warmer in the house than he did, and Andrew worked on his homework with Kevin's help. While using Kevin's aid to do a math problem, the house's cordless landline rang.

"I'll get it," Kevin told him. "Just keep repeating that process." Andrew only drummed his pencil on the table in concentration. "Hello?" He said into the phone once answering the call. Kevin glanced at Andrew, who hadn't looked up from his calculator and compass. "He's here. Who may I ask is calling?" Andrew glanced up from his notebook paper and geometry textbook, listening in on the conversation.

Lowering the phone from his ear, Kevin planted his palm over the mouthpiece and got Andrew's attention, who seemed mystified. "It's Ben," he whispered. "You want me to say you're busy?"

Andrew reached his hand out. "No. I'll talk to him." Hopeful that Ben might want to reconcile, he caught the phone when Kevin tossed it to him and pressed it to his cheek. "Ben?"

"You have my original screenplay," harped an icy voice on the other end. "I want it back."

Andrew first rolled his eyes in Kevin's direction, then gave his caller an answer. "You couldn't ask me for it while we were in detention?"

"I think it was best we stayed at a distance from each other."

With a rigid, arched lip, he sneered, "Right. So what would you like, for me to mail it to you?"

"Drop it off at my locker. I'm sure you know the combination, seeing as how you defiled my biology homework."

"Maybe you shouldn't have switched our padlocks? Idiot?"

Face-to-face interaction wasn't necessary to feel the flaming malevolence of their words or the venom in their voices. Ben, after first hissing in a deep breath, said, "Maybe you should learn to be a better friend."

"Sorry I don't reach the social standards of your good buddy Garret."

"He only points things out that look incredibly ridiculous. Rightfully so. And he returns things loaned to him."

With feathers now adequately ruffled, Andrew snapped, "Why do you want it back anyway? Your little 'screenplay' was about as original as a plaid shirt. It was horrible."

Ben's voice turned from forceful bitterness to a furious bark. "Fuck you."

"Don't call our house again." Without giving him the chance to retort, he hung up and clutched at his curtain of hair to relieve his stress.

Heading toward the table where Andrew was sitting, Kevin, in a pillowed voice, asked, "What'd he want?"

"He wants his stupid screenplay back," explained Andrew, returning to his homework. "I'll give it to him tomorrow and we can end this bullshit."

Kevin lowered into the seat beside him, draping an arm around him, feeling his muscles relax at his touch. "Maybe you should take it into consideration…" Andrew's shoulders tightened at these words. "That he might not know what he's doing wrong. We seem to have little perspective of right and wrong on some things…"

"What do you mean by that?"

"Not... *us*. I just mean, as individuals." He grit his teeth, then squeezed his mouth over them. Regardless, Andrew couldn't relax again. "You should try to have a serious talk with him about your friendship, see how he feels. There might be a chance to fix things with him."

"I appreciate you trying to help. And you're probably right. But I think it's too late. After this, I doubt we'll ever look at each other with respect."

"Andrew, it's better to have fair-weather acquaintances than enemies. Right now, you're acting like enemies."

"I can handle it, Dad. Really."

Giving in, Kevin dropped the lecture for now. Instead, he continued to help Andrew work, though not without the tingles of anxiety flowing through him. If experience taught him one thing, it was that leaving a freshly kindled fire unattended was unwise. Before long, it could burn down several acres of life, leaving only ashes in its wake, and all one could do in the aftermath was watch it fade into nothing.

The next day, Andrew delivered the

(*Horrible*)

screenplay to Ben as promised. When handing it over, he did so with the assumption that he'd get nailed in the jaw, but on the contrary, their transaction was quick, silent, and with even-tempered demeanors. It was the most professional Andrew had seen Ben portray himself, though it wasn't without the flawed grace of two "enemies" that Kevin had referred to them as.

For the remainder of the week, Andrew avoided his locker and kept his books inside of his bag at all times. It was a lot heavier, but it seemed capable of withstanding the load. He asked Kevin not to make him lunches, to which Kevin replied much like a parent would, stating that he needed to eat lunch every day. He made them for him anyway, and told him that he could save it for later if he couldn't eat in the lunchroom.

Andrew missed Kevin's lunches all week. They were usually the highlight of his school day, and now being without them kept him in a darker mood. He returned to the office to once again request a new locker, and they insisted that he would have a new one by the following week. He crossed his fingers on that.

Friday couldn't have come fast enough for him and Kevin. Despite the gloom Andrew felt regarding his battles with Ben, he looked forward to his night with his father, and being with him in every way. The upcoming weekend also excited him. He wondered what they'd be doing together for the two days he had off of school, and whether or not it would involve what he hoped it would.

Come Friday, he did all he could to prevent the afternoon from being ruined by Ben. He didn't stop by his locker all day, he didn't go to lunch, and he had jovial chats with Sarah in photography class, who talked with him about the Drone Diode roadies he met at the show. She, in exchange, told Andrew about her favorite groups, most of which Andrew had also never heard of, but was grateful to hear about.

The last bell. Yes! Finally! Andrew grabbed his bag and scurried out the door before anyone else, bolting down the hallway. That day, he didn't give two shits about Ben, about having to miss lunch, or about how his locker still hadn't been moved. Today was his and Kevin's day, one unlike any other, and he would make the most of it despite recent events.

With a skip in his step, Andrew crossed the parking lot to meet his father, who seemed just as elated to see him. They shared a passionate kiss, one extended beyond the usual ten second mark, before Kevin took off.

"I'm so excited," Andrew twittered.

Hearing his son's enthrallment thrilled him. "Are you? Me too."

"You're still not telling me where we're going?"

"Nope. You're only finding out when we get there."

Andrew cupped his hands together and squeezed them. "Give me a hint, at least!"

He hummed, then, "They have some of the best house wine you can get."

"You aren't going to give me any other hints?"

Kevin tapped on the steering wheel a few times. "It's a five star establishment."

Fluttering his eyelashes and perking his head, Andrew chirped, "Oh, high rollers, are we?"

"Quite," Kevin agreed, lifting his chin and pursing his lips.

When they strolled into the house, spirits soaring with anticipation, Kevin set the alarm, then hung up his and Andrew's coats. Andrew started toward the kitchen table with his book bag to get his weekend homework out of the way, but Kevin called him back.

"We'll work on that tomorrow," he advised. "Tonight's ours."

Andrew was more than happy to dismiss his homework for the time being, so he was thrilled that his father was willing to do the same. "What time are we going out?"

"The reservation is at seven. We've got some time to kill." He reached for his son's hand, beckoning him forth.

Andrew came to his side with a bashful smile, taking his hand and clasping it tight, their fingers interlocking. Kevin guided him up the stairs, opening his bedroom door and walking Andrew inside. The floors were a bit cleaner than when Andrew last saw them, and the sheets appeared to have been washed and turned down. Various bottles of clear liquid in all shapes and sizes were sitting on the bedside table, and lastly, Andrew saw that the light indicating the cordless phone was on had dimmed, while Kevin's smartphone had also been turned off and set aside.

Though no one else lived in the house, Andrew closed the bedroom door for security, then followed the grinning Kevin into his bathroom. As soon as he entered, he saw the elaborate display of candles set up around the room, which Kevin began to light before turning on the faucet for the whirlpool bathtub.

While testing the temperature, Kevin asked, "How warm do you like your water?"

Andrew shrugged, his face and neck glowing. "Warm?"

"Good answer," Kevin chuckled. For a few more minutes he ran his hand under the faucet until the heat was adequate, then stopped the drain to let the tub fill. In the meantime, he stripped his shirt off and hung it on the rack upon the wall, its obsidian hue rendering it invisible against the black towels.

Andrew, standing before him with a thundering heart and trembling breaths, never took his eyes off of him, or his sturdy chest and happy trail of blackish hair inching down toward his waist line. He bit down on his inner cheek, trying as best as he could not to get overexcited.

Kevin unsnapped his black jeans, and sweat began to form under Andrew's arms, which quivered as he crossed them over his chest. He watched him undress every night when they went to bed together, but Kevin was now doing it at an unbearably teasing pace, giving him the show of a lifetime. After dropping his jeans to the ground, Kevin also hung them on the rack. Then, he grabbed the waistline of his black briefs, which were a bit on the forbidding side.

"Wait," Andrew gasped, and Kevin paused. For a moment, he assumed Andrew had second thoughts, but when he saw him trace his upper lip with his tongue and stare down at his crotch, he realized that might not have been the case. "Can I?" Kevin's grin might have been all the permission he needed, but he only came to him when he nodded. Andrew grabbed the top of Kevin's black underwear and pulled them down an inch every second, until they were down to his ankles.

Andrew was greeted with the tool of his creation for the first time, and hadn't seen any other like it. Kevin's, unlike his last boyfriend's, was lengthy, but slender, and the longer he stared at it, the faster and fuller it grew.

"I'm a little embarrassed," Kevin confessed, poppies speckling across his face.

"Why?" wondered Andrew, baffled. He felt honored to be graced with such a delectable vision.

"I didn't expect to get turned on so quick."

"I'm glad you are," Andrew comforted, draping his arms around Kevin's bare collar, pressing against his nude body. A moan escaped Kevin's parted mouth. "It shows me how much you really want me."

"More than anything," Kevin assured in a hushed voice, dragging his moist lips around the nape of Andrew's neck.

Andrew sighed, delirious with joy. "Undress me. All the way."

With ease, he pulled Andrew's T-shirt up over his head, placing it on the rack, then proceeded to kiss underneath his chin, all the while Andrew hummed in delight. As Kevin's tender touch rippled down his arms, then his waist, he shivered with anticipation at the waves of tickles cascading over every inch of his skin. Kevin undid Andrew's tight jeans, and with care slid them down to Andrew's ankles, allowing him to step out of them. While kneeling upon the bathroom rug, Kevin slid Andrew's boxers down, again to his feet.

Andrew attempted to control his enthusiastic breathing when Kevin met his erection face-to-face. One part of him wished Kevin would shove it in his mouth, and another wanted the erotic, picturesque moment to go on longer before any sex came into it. He twitched beneath Kevin's burning stare, which seemed to be giving his genitals a thorough look.

"You've inherited more than just my hair and eyes," he observed, proud of the notion.

In spite of having done it more than a hundred times, Andrew couldn't look him in the face. "That's good, right?"

"It's very good."

Kevin stood, removing his gaze from Andrew's crotch. Andrew was a tad dissatisfied that Kevin didn't fellate him, but he had later to look forward to. They embraced and kissed, tongue-wrestling while the tub filled up. When the water rose to a suitable level, Kevin shut the faucet off and climbed in, holding Andrew's hand as he joined him.

Kevin sat, resting his back against the edge, and Andrew lowered in front of him, his spine to Kevin's chest. Kevin's arms came around him, soaking him in warm water with a washcloth, applying gentle smooches to his neck and shoulders while he grabbed a bar of soap and moved it over his skin. Every time he slid the bar up and over his back, Andrew shook with ecstasy and tilted his head back, shuddering as he squeezed the cloth, sending more rivers down his chest and stomach.

After covering Andrew's upper body in soap suds, he rinsed him off with the cloth until he was as shiny as a polished shoe. Following that, he massaged Andrew's shoulder blades with the edges of his thumbs. Andrew, soothed, sank into the cradle of his arms, resting against his breastplate.

As a comfortable silence surrounded them, Andrew dictated with pride, "No one's been able to make me feel this good before." Kevin tightened his embrace. "I know I've only been in a few relationships, but it's still significant to me." He looked at Kevin, whose eyes were closed in respite. "How many boyfriends have you had?"

There was a delay while Kevin thought about it. "You would be my ninth."

"Wow. I expected you to have more than that."

"It's difficult to find a quality guy who's willing to commit for a long time."

"How long is a long time?"

Kevin opened his eyes, and in the room's low lighting, they resembled grayish chalk drawings upon solid white paper. "The rest of my life." His heart swelled when Andrew snuggled against his chest and pressed his face onto his shoulder as Kevin smoothed his damp palm over his back.

Life. Such a simple word, and yet so complicated. To have Kevin for the rest of his life was a concept Andrew had accepted, but understood the repercussions of. He had not forgotten their age difference, nor had he dismissed what little time they had together on earth. With this awareness came a decline in his joyous mood, mourning the loss of one who had not yet left him. A love like theirs was meant to last forever, wasn't it? "I don't ever want you to die."

Kevin squeezed him and used a chipper voice when responding. "Why are you thinking of that?" Andrew didn't have an answer for him. "It's too soon to be worrying about it."

Reminded of his father's smoking habit, he checked to make sure he still wore his nicotine patch. He sighed with relief when he saw it stamped to his arm. "Keep taking care of yourself. Please."

"I'll be all right, honey. I'm not leaving you sooner than I have to. Unless I can't help it." Andrew didn't remark on how frightening that idea was, not wishing to cast a gloom over the remainder of the evening.

After they were scrubbed down well enough, they got out of the bath and Kevin dried Andrew off, then himself. Kevin went to his closet and dressed in presentable attire, and Andrew did the same to the best of his ability with what he had to choose from his wardrobe. They killed their extra time with a couple of movies, the plots of which could not tear them away from their heavy necking, until Kevin checked his watch and told Andrew their date was imminent.

Corvino's was indeed the upscale diner Kevin talked it up to be, but what Andrew didn't expect to see inside was the quartet of men in black suits plucking at string instruments upon a dimly lit stage, blocked off by a rope barrier made of burgundy velvet. As they provided the dining public with historic scores of yesteryear, Andrew was drawn in by their accurate skills, watching their taught, aged hands drag hair-lined bows across thick strings, vibrant tones of minor keys sailing over the abnormally high ceiling of the restaurant.

Marveling at the amazing sight, as well as soaking in the glorious sound of classical music, Kevin interacted with the greeter, a man with a dazzling grin full of blinding, bleached teeth as pearly as his button-down dress shirt. Kevin confirmed their reservation, and also paid the young man a tip, which he tried to turn down. Kevin insisted, grateful to him for his pleasant, upbeat attitude. The greeter then took it, thanking him until the word lost meaning, then showed them (with an even broader smile) to their designated table: an isolated booth adjacent to the string quartet, where they could hear each note with clarity.

Andrew was speechless enough at the scenery, which was adorned in their preferred dark hues, but the table was another spectacle altogether. Upon it sat crystal wine glasses, silverware rolled in cushioned fabric and tied with red ribbons, a vase containing a single rose, and the cleanest plates Andrew had ever had to privilege to stare at. Had he gone back in time to tell his younger self that he would one day eat in a place this ritzy, his child counterpart wouldn't believe a single word of it. Really, young Andrew! I think the silverware might be made of actual Sterling!

"What do you think?" The baritone of Kevin's voice put a stop to his thoughts, bringing his full attention to his father.

Hearing the quartet come to the end of a piece they were playing, a familiar number by Bach he might have heard in a film or on television, he inhaled through his nostrils, taking in the scent of baking bread and burning oil. "It's incredible. I've never even been inside a place this nice. Never thought I would get to, either."

With a debonair wink, Kevin assured, "Plenty more where it came from. Really, though. I'm glad I could bring you. This is my favorite restaurant. I've only brought one other guy here, and he wasn't much of an Italian fan."

"I'm glad you brought me, too. But you know you didn't have to take me on a date before we... did anything."

With a nonchalant shrug, Kevin said, "I know that. We've already discussed sleeping together. I'm not buying you a meal to get you in bed with me. I like taking my partners out, spoiling them a little. However, there's an exception with you."

"Besides the obvious, I'm assuming?"

"Yes, yes, besides that. What I mean is that, the men that came before you were pleasant. They weren't bad guys. Many of them were actually quite delightful to be around. But I would be lying if I said I was blameless for the deaths of those relationships. Back then I blamed them, and I was wrong to. Each time I fell in love with someone, I felt as though they had no reason to love me back. I wanted them to, so badly, but I saw nothing in myself, and thus expected them to also see nothing. I thought that by constantly buying them gifts, they might love me for that instead. But rather than buying their love, I bought their guilt.

"I gave so much, and thought it was to make them happy. But when our relationships went on without them getting me anything in return, I began to resent them. I accused them of being cheap, called them awful things, without realizing that my generosity made them uncomfortable. It never hit me for so long that I wasn't endlessly giving everything up to make them happy— I was bribing them to stay with me. Several of them I accused of cheating on me, even went so far as to check their cell phone records. I was so paranoid and insecure with myself that I turned everyone I was with into a liar. And none of them had done a thing to me. Many of my failed relationships, Andrew..." The slow breath he took was unstable and broken. "Were all my fault. And I wish I could take it back."

Andrew found it difficult to believe that Kevin would be so desperate. A man like him could have anyone he wanted and didn't have to stoop to buying someone's affection. "Don't look on it with regret. You didn't know what you wanted. Sometimes it takes a few failures to know what works."

With a few stiff nods, he added, "You're absolutely right. But, Andrew... I don't want to fail you like I failed them. I want nothing more in this world than to provide you with the best life a father and lover can give you, and then some. If I have to sell my soul to give that to you, you'd bet I would do it in a heartbeat."

Though Andrew had smiled at him with sincerity, traces of sadness lingered in it. He wanted to tell him that he believed in him, had faith in him to love him, but he feared he might cry if he spoke. Rather than make an emotional scene, he stretched his arm across the table, palm open, and Kevin placed his own larger hand into it.

"Son, I would sooner die than see that I've caused you pain, for any reason at all," Kevin went on. "Should you ever decide I'm not treating you well enough, I want you to let me know. Even if I'm incredibly overbearing."

"Dad," squeaked Andrew. "I don't think you'll have to worry about that."

"I do have to worry about it, Andrew. There's more at stake

between us than a possible break-up or astringent end. If I lose you, I lose more than a partner. I lose my son, and my friend. How could I not worry about pushing you away?"

"I trust you with my life. After all, it was you who gave it to me."

Kevin squeezed Andrew's palm, who clenched it back in gradual pulses. "Andrew," he sighed, afloat with lovesick joy. "You've given me so much hope. With you beside me, I feel capable of anything I aim to accomplish. It sounds silly, but with you I feel immortal, like I could take on the world."

Their hands squeezed together a few more times, timed with their beating hearts. "It's weird you say that. I feel the exact same way. Whatever happens… I'm always going to love you."

Kevin slipped his other hand beneath Andrew's so that it was sandwiched between both of them. "So will I."

While they shared a significant moment of tenderness, their waiter arrived, presenting them with menus. Kevin ordered wine right off the bat, as well as their classic cheddar garlic bread for them to split. Another classic score echoed from the chambers of the stringed instruments on the small stage, aiding digestion.

Their meals were large, and they ate to their stomach's content. They didn't need to ingest much to fill themselves up, for the portions were sizeable and worth their price. After finishing their food, Andrew squeezed into the seat beside his father and listened to the remaining half of the concert while tucked under his arm.

Don't, Kevin almost told him when feeling him snuggle against him. *Someone will see us.* But he didn't let him go. He only pulled him tighter against him, loving him and his warmth. While protected by the shadows, Andrew leaned in begging for kisses, which he supplied him with.

Far east from their booth was a young man who did, in fact, see them. Had it not been for the boring concert his girlfriend, Beth insisted on watching, if it hadn't been for what she called their "three month anniversary" she felt needed celebrating, and if it hadn't been for the hundred dollars he asked his parents for to spend on a dinner he thought pointless, he wouldn't have taken several minutes to observe the other patrons and simply walked out of there, girlfriend in tow, thirty minutes ago. There was something familiar about the raven-haired men cuddling and kissing each other in that seat over there; he had seen them before, somewhere else.

Satan's Little Helper, his memory snapped. *That's Ben's boy toy.* Who was that sitting next to him, kissing him? It looked a lot like the guy he saw him outside the venue with, the one Ben said was his father. No, it couldn't have been his father. That was too strange, even for someone like him. Bizarre or not, he saw it with his own two eyes.

He leaned toward Beth, still focusing on the canoodling couple. "Beth," he whispered.

"*Shh!*"

"Don't fucking shush me!"

"*SHH!*"

"Will you just give me your god damned phone?"

Beth spared her boorish significant other a glare of admonition, though one could hardly resist looking at Garret in such a way. "What the hell do you need it for?"

"Mind your business and give it to me."

While shaking her head and scowling, she yanked her purse open and ripped her smartphone out, slapping it into her boyfriend's open hand, then turned back to the show while he slipped away, muttering slurs. His next task was dialing Ben's number as he trudged through the breezeway, pacing back and forth as it rang.

"Ben," he said as soon as his friend answered with a yawn. "I'm at Corvino's with Beth. You'll never believe what I just saw."

Most of the bedroom was covered in shadows, save for the moonlight streaming down through the skylight upon the ceiling and the lavender burn of the black light that faced the bed where Kevin turned the sheets down. Andrew had to hand it to him for preparing for the event so well, as he was sure his father also had the same inkling that it might make or break their relationship.

Andrew took a seat on the fresh, clean sheets as Kevin removed his dinner jacket and hung it in his closet. Since coming into the room, neither of them had spoken. Whether it was out of nervousness or guilt, they didn't question it. It was up to them to relax and enjoy themselves, as well as each other, and leave all of their fears outside the door.

When Kevin left his massive closet, clasping both doors shut, he came to Andrew with his dress clothes still attached, his steps offbeat and wobbly, then sat on the bed beside him, pecking his neck and shoulder with the very edge of his lips. When he felt Andrew tense up, he released him and scooted back as though he were a spider about to lunge for his face.

Careful, Kevin. This isn't just about you. This is Andrew's night too, and he's not some trick you pulled out of a bar for a good time. If he's not ready, neither are you.

Spotting the fear on his father's face, Andrew chuckled, taking his hand and pulling it into his lap, holding it there. "It's okay," he promised, though Kevin swallowed. "I'm just really nervous."

"Me too." He wiped off the sweat that streaked down his neck. "I don't know how many times I've had sex, but... this is like my first time all over again."

"What do you think is going to happen?"

"I don't know. What usually happens during sex, I assume." His eyes came to a close as Andrew draped his arms around his neck. "I'm afraid of hurting you." Their shaking mouths gradually closed in.

"The only way you'll hurt me is if you turn me away." His tongue swirled over Kevin's bottom lip, sneaking up toward the space between his rows of teeth. Kevin accepted his intrusion and curled his tongue around Andrew's, making out with him until they both relaxed.

A soft click resonated as their mouths separated, and Andrew said at once, "What if I screw up?"

Panting, his blood and groin flaming, Kevin shook his head as he smiled. "You'll be okay."

"I don't want to disappoint you." He kissed his father again, this time with more enthusiasm.

"Never," Kevin huffed between their smacking. "You never could."

Andrew released a pitiful whimper. "I love you." Another few collisions of their lips, each one fiercer than the last.

With a power and truth he had never before used in these words, with Andrew or otherwise, Kevin declared, *"I love you,"* clutching Andrew's face in both of his sturdy hands. He engulfed him in his arms, swarming him with affection, sucking on his neck until it turned bright pink. Andrew succumbed to the ecstasy of his touch, his embrace, and in return lavished him with just as much adoration.

Soon, they were tearing clothes off of each other, lying in bed in nothing but their underwear, which were so restricting by this point that their erections could have torn a hole straight through them, all with their tongues fighting each other's. When Kevin stopped for a quick breather, and to rearrange himself, he glimpsed down into the desperate face of his son lying beneath him.

"Please," Andrew whined, clutching at his father's stiffened back, dragging his nails over his shoulder blades, lifting his hips toward Kevin's in desperation. "*Please.*"

Kevin didn't need to be asked twice. He slid his hands down Andrew's waist, toward his writhing lower half, and yanked his boxers down his legs, chucking them somewhere off into the dark where the rest of their clothes were located. Next to join that pile was his own briefs.

As eager as they both were to get to the main event, they didn't neglect the carnal satisfaction of foreplay. Kevin had the ultimate pleasure of tasting every inch of Andrew, which to him was sweeter and more divine than any glass of the richest chardonnay available. Before hearing Andrew's bellowing moans, he thought the sound of rain spattering the window was his favorite. How wrong he had been. The Lord's heavenly choir couldn't strike his ear with the same beautiful chords as Andrew's gasps of lust. Rising and falling oceans could never compare to the sound of the word flittering upon his young pallet: "*Fuck.*" The sight of Andrew grabbing handfuls of silken sheets like he was crushing grapes, his head thrown back onto his pillow, his eyes clasped shut and his mouth yawned in a permanent O shape, was more golden than any sunset.

Neither of them had the patience to draw it out much longer. Kevin mounted Andrew, feeling the instant gratifying sensation of his loving hands curling through his locks, his breath against his neck, his legs propped onto his hips. Kevin's approach was not without care— he used almost an entire bottle of lubricant to ensure the act was without agony— but Andrew would have accepted him no matter the conditions.

Kevin's entry pinched him at first, but it was a temporary pain, one that was eased away by his father's sweet nothings and encouragement, accompanied by a tight embrace and soft kisses throughout. Exchanges of doting words took place every few minutes, making the encounter so much more pleasant in Andrew's view. This was just how he imagined their lovemaking to unfold, and he couldn't ask for more.

Every thrust of Kevin's hips, every groan croaking from his mouth, and every inch he accepted into him, Andrew felt the peaks of wondrous exhilaration. To at last share the most meaningful and congenial time with Kevin was more than a dream come true— it was a tie that needed to happen, what they felt should have happened since they day they met. Andrew swore with his body that it was his father he belonged to, and only him. With how perfectly they fit, it was like it was meant to be.

As the culmination ensued, it came as no surprise due to Kevin's warnings, each rising into a crescendo of concurrent lament and bliss. *Not now,* Kevin scolded his own insubordinate body, which was rampant with shivers implying the surge of adrenaline. *Longer. Just a little longer. Forever.* Forever.

Naturally, the same thought raced through Andrew's mind, but all he could do was squeeze him with his thighs and grab onto his forearm for dear life, the life of which was given to him in this very manner almost eighteen years ago, though he doubted it contained as much passion when done with the woman who birthed him. Kevin braced himself by pressing his hand onto the headboard of the bed, only for Andrew's hand to trace his arm up, never letting him go, digging his nails into his skin hard enough to leave indents.

Kevin began to withdraw, but Andrew tugged him back onto his sweating body, locking them together, begging him to retain their connection all the way to the finish line. In those last few throes of passion, Andrew heard his name, twice, in the most breathtaking, fervent cries before Kevin collapsed upon him, heaving and wheezing.

With the fire in his loins sufficiently burned out, Kevin cradled Andrew and smothered him with kisses, all while Andrew clutched him around his neck. Andrew assumed that their fun would end with Kevin's climax, but he proved him wrong when he lent him a helping hand in reaching his own, which he was quick about.

Taking the time to allow their heartbeats to return to normal, Kevin relaxed on his back while Andrew rested upon his chest, his entire body singing and sparkling in the streams of moonlight through the windows upon the ceiling. In the buzz of their electrostatic afterglow (and following the time Andrew took to clean the sticky mess off of himself), Kevin held onto him as though he might drift out of his arms and into space without warning. Andrew didn't complain about how tight his grasp was. It was what he needed after the exertion.

Andrew was the first of them in fifteen minutes to speak. "We're going to do it again. Aren't we?"

Kevin laughed. "Now?"

"No, not right now. I mean, this isn't going to be the only time we have sex."

"Of course not. What made you think I wouldn't want it again?"

"I don't know, Dad," he sighed. "I was afraid you might feel... weird."

"Honey, I don't even know what that word means anymore."

"Are you sure?"

Opening his eyes, staring up at the smoky clouds above as they rolled over what few stars could be seen in the winter, he cracked a smile of resolve. "Positive." He peered at Andrew, who was also observing the migrating sky. "Why? Are you... feeling weird?"

"Yeah." Seeing the horrible impact this response had on Kevin, which was evident in his panicked, heartbroken expression, he quickly explained himself. "Not like, in that way! I feel good, really good. I mean that it's weird that I feel this good about it. I should feel grossed out or something, right?"

"Not necessarily. You should love what makes you happy."

Andrew buried his face into Kevin's neck, inhaling every fiber of him. "I do."

Kevin smooched him on the head, caressing his back, which he saw was putting him to sleep. He decided to catch a few winks as well, turning onto his side and draping an arm around Andrew, feeling his heartbeat in his palm, one that he not only was responsible for creating, but for filling with so much jubilance.

A craving for cigarettes invoked a headache that crept in to pester him, but he swatted it away as easily as one would a flea, for tonight he would get the best rest he had ever experienced in thirty-five years, and he would do so with one who enriched his life in all ways possible.

CHAPTER ELEVEN

In Which Particles Dissolve

In the early morning, Kevin woke an hour after Andrew had, and when he stirred, he saw his son's face beacon with hope— hope that he would finally stay awake and the two of them could spend time together.

"Morning," was the first thing Kevin said to Andrew, rubbing the sleep from his eyes. "How long have you been up?"

"An hour," he told him, snuggling against him, engulfed by Kevin's swinging arms.

"You could have gotten out of bed, you know."

Andrew pouted. "I wanted to be here when you woke up." He purred as Kevin's palm traced his cheek.

"I'm glad you stayed." Andrew dove for his mouth to kiss it, but Kevin leaned back. He explained before Andrew could get the wrong idea. "I don't exactly have the freshest breath right now."

"I don't care." He kissed Kevin anyway, bringing the first smile of the day to their faces.

"Let's hop in the shower."

Titillated, Andrew agreed to this, hoping it might lead to another sensual encounter between them. He jumped out of bed, followed by Kevin, who gave his naked rear a spank on the way, evoking a laugh, squeal, and scamper. Kevin chased after him into the bathroom, cornering him before jumping him with a playful tackle, lifting

Andrew off of his feet, all while he cackled boyishly.

During their warm shower, Kevin gave Andrew a thorough scrub-down, chatting with him about their plans for the weekend. Andrew desired to stay indoors, particularly in bed with Kevin for most of the day, but Kevin wished to take him out for lunch and shopping. Andrew told him they'd meet in between and compromise, which Kevin was satisfied with.

Lunch was shared at a reputable diner where Kevin ordered some of the saltiest pasta Andrew had ever tasted. He was at least able to get a turkey sandwich for himself, which came drenched in gourmet sauces. It wasn't as good as his father's cooking in his opinion, but it did add a new touch to the meal.

Kevin took Andrew to one of his favorite antique shops, where he seemed to become one with its ancient atmosphere. There was an armoire he fell in love with the moment he saw it, and made a special order for it to come to the house. They told him it would take up to a few weeks before it would be shipped out. Andrew loved seeing his father so happy, but he couldn't stand the musty basement smell floating around the place, and could hardly wait to get out of there.

Andrew was graced once more with Kevin's prosperity when he bought him some non-fiction he wanted at the local bookstore. The titles he chose centered around working with high-end cameras and professional photography, as well as a few books on astronomy and psychology. He was more than excited to stuff his nose in a book that wasn't assigned to him in school, and Kevin was pleased to encourage such a healthy craving to learn.

They relaxed most of the afternoon playing games before retiring once more to bed, where Andrew couldn't keep his hands off of his father, who complied in the best way possible. The second round of their lovemaking was tremendous enough, but when Andrew requested another, he wore out every last fragment of Kevin's energy until he passed out. Surrendering to the inevitable, Andrew did the same.

Come Sunday, the two couldn't bear to be away from each other, if even for a moment. Kevin seemed above all torn about the weekend coming to a close, wanting Andrew to stay home with him on Monday. Andrew almost consigned to it, but he knew he had a test to take, and if he wanted to get out of school forever, he couldn't fail his classes. When explaining this to Kevin, he agreed with him, and told him he'd be fine, but there was a heartache in him that Andrew found difficult to turn away.

They didn't waste the day on worries, but spent it on their favorite activities. The weather was unusually warm that day, so they were able to take a long walk together, quality time they used to discuss their future together and their plans for the long term. Their concerns rested on discretion, and whether or not they could keep it a secret forever. Someone would find out. Someone always finds out.

Come Monday, when Kevin dropped Andrew off at school, they swapped a kiss while out of sight of others. "I love you, Andrew," Kevin enunciated. "So much."

Andrew slid his arms around Kevin's neck. "I love you, too, Dad." Kevin embraced him, and hung onto the moment while it lasted.

"You should probably go."

Andrew groaned, but he released him nonetheless. "It's just school. I can make it."

"Just like every other day."

"Yeah. Just like it."

Andrew left Kevin's car, and his arms, and shut the door before Kevin could convince him his studies weren't as important as a day in bed with him. If he had, Andrew would have taken him up on the offer.

In spite of his salutation, his day would, in fact, not be like any other. His stroll was with a raised head, a skip in his step, and a smile on his face. Before Kevin came into his life, the world was tinged gray, and he thought nothing would ever lighten it. He never would have guessed that his father would be the one to paint his life with such brightness, but now, he would select no other to hold the brush. With love to give, and adulation returned to him, he could take on any obstacle that faced him.

Better yet, the office informed him of his locker relocation. He took it without hesitation, and moved his belongings there immediately. As he filled his locker, one which opened with greater ease than his previous, he thought he heard the sound of chortling near him.

The giggling wasn't something Andrew found out of place— so much laughing went on within the halls of Elliott High School that he often wondered if they were pumped with nitrous. Therefore, he thought to ignore it on any other occasion. However, he felt something about it was odd, and not just the furtive way his peers kept it under their breath; it was how hard they were staring at him.

First, Andrew peeked at them in his peripheral vision, not wanting to alert them to his awareness. Two guys, one dressed in a jersey, the other in a polo, stood with two girls clad in pink and white, all of which had eyes locked on him— and grinning.

Andrew shut his locker door and secured it, escaping the scene before it got any creepier. *What the hell was that about?* he fretted with a thundering heart as he went to his first class.

The haunting moment hovered around in his mind through all of first hour. After being assigned some geometrical problems by his teacher, and after opening his textbook and working on them, he once again felt it: eyes burning through him, staring into his thoughts.

He turned and looked at his classmate, Dylan, who twisted his head away just as their eyes met, but his grin never faded. As they sat side-by-side, he couldn't escape the confrontation.

"What are you looking at?" provoked Andrew.

Dylan didn't lift his head, but continued to stare down at his paper, pretending to work. "Nothing."

"Doesn't seem like you're looking at nothing." Dylan only answered with a laugh, stoking the cinders within Andrew. "What the hell is your problem?"

"Something you want to share with the rest of the class, Andrew?" his teacher asked, killing the silence.

Curling his paper under his clenching fist, Andrew turned back to the work on his desk. "No," he growled.

People didn't normally pay this much attention to him (unless they fed him the usual 'go back to your coffin' comments), and it was one of the many signs that something had gone horribly wrong over the weekend, something he wasn't privy to. At the bell, he packed his things and hauled his backpack onto his shoulder before barreling out of the class.

Andrew's honed perception started picking up all sorts of signals from various strangers, usually those in his classes, and almost always men. One young man in particular made a fellating face with his eyes rolled back and mouth hanging open. As immature and silly as it looked, it initiated a chain reaction of extreme paranoia in Andrew. What did they know?

Things didn't improve at lunch time, where even while he sat alone, he was probed at by the gazes of several students he had never met before, ones that would glimpse away when they saw him looking. Andrew wanted to break down at that point, perhaps run home, run to the only person who hadn't treated him like shit all day. He could sneak out the lunch room, trudge through the snowy sidewalks to Mancante Street, which was just around the corner. It was so close, and yet, too far away.

He had only taken a few bites out of his sandwich before a familiar foe, Ben, caught his attention. He had been staring him down for the past few minutes while gobbling his lunch, his jaw grinding in slow motion as his brow pressed down over his eyes, a scowl of immense proportions creasing his curled mouth. Andrew didn't have the stomach to return the evil eye, nor did he have it in him to finish his lunch.

The pieces came together, but didn't quite match up. Ben must have told their peers something about him, but what could he have possibly said? Simply that they were fighting recently? That wasn't enough to warrant so many knitted brows and sinister laughter. Clues to how this predicament commenced were limited, as everyone who insisted on looking at him refused to tell him why.

For the first time, he dumped his lunch into the trash, unable to even look at it now, speed-walking out of the lunchroom. As soon as he tossed his food, he regretted it, felt guilty for it, but he had no other choice.

For the duration of his next few classes, the looks didn't cease. Some were of amusement, some were revolted, but all were invasive. It wasn't until photography class, his final class of the day, that he got any sort of insight into what was happening to him.

Sarah, his last remaining companion other than his father, didn't speak to him or look at him for the entire hour of class. When he tried to get her attention, she'd glance over, would open her mouth as though she wanted to say something, then turn back to her computer.

"Sarah, please," Andrew whispered. "What's going on? Why are you ignoring me?"

She peeked at Mister Benson, who was grading assignments at the teacher's desk, checking if he could hear them. Then she leaned toward him, keeping her voice soft. "Is it true?"

Andrew's throat clenched and swelled. "What? Is *what* true?"

"About you and…" She lowered her voice even further. "Your dad."

His bottom lip retracted, and he bit down on it in a sour grimace. "What did you hear?"

"People say you're…" She couldn't utter the next word without a touch of bile coating it. "*Fucking*."

"You believed them?"

"At first I didn't. But then…" She brushed some of her blonde hair behind her ear, averting her eyes. "Garret told me he saw you making out with him. At Corvino's."

Garret, Andrew stored into his memory, holding back the bile he wanted to retch.

"People talk shit all the time," Andrew dismissed.

"He's my friend. He wouldn't lie to me."

"I thought we were friends, too. You're not even going to try to listen to my side of the story?"

"I'm sorry, Andrew," she told him, sounding just as hurt. "I've known him a lot longer than I've known you. Maybe you really do those things. It's just wrong. Really wrong."

On the verge of tears, Andrew spouted, "Well, I don't give a shit what you, or anyone else thinks." At that, Sarah turned away, and Andrew refused to look at her for the remaining ten minutes of class.

The bell rang, and Andrew hurried down the winding corridors as students swarmed them, passing the area where his old locker used to be. Ben was there, chatting it up with Garret as if they were none the wiser to the fire that grew out of control.

Andrew's fingers curled against his palms, his knuckles turning white as they strained, begging to be thrown into the nearest jaw. Both of his hands trembled as lava coursed through his veins, his spine arching into a position ready for violent action. Each step closer he took, his molars grinded tighter, his heart slamming in his chest like a sledgehammer against a brick wall.

Garret and Ben hadn't noticed Andrew when he closed in on them, nor did they predict the ensuing inferno that spread in their direction. The final word out of Garret's mouth was "anorexia" before he was launched back against the row of lockers. He groaned after smacking his back onto the metal doors, the contents of the upper shelf of Ben's locker spilling to the floor.

A hush fell over the students in the vicinity, who all were granted with the amazing grace that was a fighting show they didn't have to pay to see. Andrew wasn't focused on them, however, but on Garret, the snarl never leaving his face, his tight chest expanding and receding at rapid speeds.

"Andrew," Ben interceded, distracting him from shoving his fist into Garret's mouth. "Stop it."

Andrew's molten eyes singed as he turned them in his former friend's direction. "You have something to say to me, Ben? You fucking say it to my face."

Seeing an opening to flee the situation, Garret backed away, unwilling to step in on his friend's behalf. Unfortunately for him, Andrew saw him cowering the scene and lunged for him. Simply grabbing him by the shirt and yanking him back wasn't enough—Andrew had a message to deliver, and by God, he'd make sure he made it clear.

"Fuck!" Garret cried, his final call for help. For such a scrawny young man, Andrew packed a hell of a wallop. When his knuckles met the bones of his jaw, he lifted his palms in self-defense to block his face, protecting it from Andrew's unabated fury. Around them, students whooped and chanted, but the sound of the crowd was a hum within Andrew's reverberating ears.

Ben dove into the fray, yanking Andrew off of the trembling Garret, who spat a wad of blood to the floor. Andrew threw him off his back, spinning around to face him once and for all.

"Stop it!" Ben reiterated as his final warning. "It's not Garret's fault you and your father sucked face in public!"

Elevating his head, rolling his shoulders back, Andrew crowed, "Oh, *really*! You mean he just started spreading the news for my health? It's not his business! It's not *anyone's*!"

"Your daddy's the one that crammed his tongue down your throat." Repulsed by his own words, he leaned away from Andrew as though he smelled of rotting garbage. "He likes them young, I see. Too much of a loser to find someone his own age, so he rapes his—"

Thwunk!

Ben staggered back from Andrew's piercing knuckles striking his face. Before he could gather his bearings, he was covered in a mass of rage and black clothing, and soon the two of them were nothing but a cloud of fists, elbows, and knees slamming into one another, all while their spectators hollered and cheered.

Ben slammed him against a series of lockers, the crowd spreading like parting waves to give them room to brawl. Andrew kicked and thrashed, elbowing Ben in the jaw, only to have his gut punched in. The sounds of meat thudding and smacking vociferous, they tossed punches and kicks, trying to knock each other out before they were caught.

Ben locked Andrew's head in his elbow, but Andrew slipped out of it, slamming into him with his small frame, scratching and ripping at his shirt, jabbing him in the chest and ribs with his fierce and feisty punches. An unforgiving, unbreakable wrath grew deep within Ben, a place where the past rose up like the mindless undead, film reels of memories shuffling by. Andrew had turned him down for dates. He had rejected his gifts. He had insulted things that mattered most to him. And now this; hitting him, starting a fight with him, all because he told it like he saw it. Brimstone filling him from top to bottom, Ben didn't hold back, and clocked Andrew in the eye, sending him sailing onto the floor. As his face met the hundreds of wet, brown footprints, his shoulder smacked against the hard tile, and his nose gushed a crimson river onto the filthy ground.

Ears ringing, nose throbbing, lip torn and ribcage bruised, Andrew tried to regain his footing, but the pain was too great. In defeat, he collapsed, releasing a surrendering cry, a childlike whimper. The ache in his face was loud, a powerful, screaming jolt that pounded every few seconds. His shoulder pulsed, his back vibrated, and he groaned in torment.

Holding his black eye shut, Andrew began to weep, curled up on the floor like a broken human piñata. Ben, the victor of the battle, stood above his prey like a vulture ready to dig into its meal. Then, he heard the sound of Andrew's agonized tears, and lowered his fist, which loosened.

What just happened? A minute ago, he was standing by his locker talking to Garret. Now he was looming above a weeping Andrew, whose face was coated with fresh blood. Did he really just beat the living shit out of him? That couldn't have taken place. It wasn't possible.

No. He did it. He actually did it.

"Andrew?" he called down to him, his voice supple and blameworthy. Andrew only sobbed. Ben only got a glimpse of the amount of blood streaking down Andrew's nose and mouth, but it was enough to make him sick. "Andrew," he beckoned once more, mourning thick in his words. "Oh my god. Oh, *shit*." He didn't get the opportunity to help him up, or to make sure he was okay. A school security guard pushed through the crowd to the two students who just concluded their fight.

"Good lord," he gasped at the sight of the beaten Andrew bleeding upon the floor. He called the nurse's office on his radio, as well as the principal. The nurse and an assistant helped Andrew to the office, and they dragged Ben along as well to deliver his punishment.

The nurse lied Andrew upon the bed within the office, but he was too delirious and shaken to understand what was happening. Ben wanted to join him, to talk to him, to say anything at all to him, but he was ushered into the principal's office. His father would be called. He would have rather allowed Andrew to kill him than to face the wrath of that man when he found out he'd be getting suspended.

Kevin had reached his second mile on the treadmill when the alarm on his watch went off. Time to pick up Andrew. He slowed his speed and hopped off before running to the bathroom to wipe his face off, then to his bedroom and closet to put fresh clothes on. While pulling a T-shirt on over his head, the electronic ring of the cordless phone echoed throughout the house. He rushed to it, trying to slow his heavy breathing as he spoke to the caller.

"Mister Kevin Neil?" It was an older woman's voice, slow, but on edge.

"Yes," Kevin panted, tugging a pair of jeans onto his hips.

"Your son, Andrew Phillips, got into a fight at school today."

The phone cupped between his jaw and shoulder almost dropped to the floor, and he caught it before it fell. "What?! Is he all right?!"

"He's fine. He has a swollen eye and bloody nose, but nothing is broken."

"What the hell happened?!"

"All we know is that he and another student had a disagreement and got into an altercation. He's not speaking much right now."

"I… okay. I'm coming." He thanked her, then promptly hung up before dressing and running out the front door.

Despite the traffic streaming out of the school parking lot, Kevin made it there in less than a minute. Nearly slipping on ice on the way inside, Kevin raced like a marathon runner to the school office and told them why he was there. They guided him into the nurse's office where Andrew was sitting upon the tissue-covered bed, and he came to his side before anyone could say a word to him.

"Oh my god," he gasped, moving Andrew's hair out of his eyes to get a good look at the damage. His eye, red, puffy and swollen was half-open and dried blood caked his nostrils. In spite of the nurse's presence, he clutched Andrew's face in both hands. "Honey, are you okay?"

"Dad." Each breath he took was like sucking blades into his lungs. "I'm sorry."

"What happened?"

"Ben... I... I hit him. And he hit me back. A lot."

"You hit him? Why?"

He didn't want to talk about it now, especially with onlookers around. Later, when they were alone, would be more appropriate. "Can I come home now?"

"I'm taking you to the doctor first." He chose not to pay attention to the nurse's censorious huff directed at him. Kevin trusted that the nurse had given Andrew a thorough examination, but it was better to be safe than sorry.

Andrew groaned at the prospect of going anywhere but to the house, but he accepted his father's conditions. As Kevin pulled him in for a hug, he fell limp, his returning grip loose and indifferent. Even the bruises and twitching bones didn't hurt as much as Kevin's embrace at that moment. To be near Kevin was to remember that whooping crowd surrounding him and Ben, to hear those scathing words from Sarah, to see the revolted look on Ben's face.

Though Andrew didn't seem too interested in a hug at the moment, he stroked him on the back. "I'll grab your book bag. Can you walk okay?"

"Yeah, I'll be fine." Andrew slid off of the bed, rubbing his sore shoulder.

Before they could take their leave, Kevin heard the sound of shouting outside of the infirmary. Andrew had also heard it, but was less concerned with whatever was going on. If he had to look at another student or member of the school staff, he'd lose his mind. "Wait here," Kevin told Andrew, who obeyed reluctantly.

Leaning his head out of the infirmary, Kevin got a glimpse of the main office, which was vacant of a principal, but did contain Ben and an older man, who was pacing before him while he sat with his head hung.

Ben had heard his father shout more than any other sound since his childhood. He turned the channel on the TV, his father yelled. He came home five minutes after curfew, his father yelled. He forgot to do the dishes, his father yelled. There was very little his father didn't scream about.

Though he thought he had heard it all, nothing compared to this humiliation. The way he paced back and forth in front of him like he did whenever he was disappointed him, the way he burned with contempt, the way he spat every other word like firing bullets was something Ben could never get used to no matter how often he saw it.

"God damn it, Ben! What do I have to do to knock some sense into your empty skull?!"

"I know, sir," he appeased.

"Do I have to lock you in your room and never let you out of it?!" roared the beast of a man as he stomped back and forth across the room. "Do I have to put you in a cage like an animal?!"

"I'm sorry, sir."

"Don't. Don't even start your bullshit with me. Your telephone privileges are now taken away. You are not allowed to go out *anywhere* for a whole month. Do I make myself clear?"

"Dad…"

"*Do I make myself clear?!*"

"I'm not a kid anymore." Ben hastily changed his tone when cracking flames reflected off of his father's eyes. He swiped a tear away before it could be seen. "Yes, sir."

"You come out to the car when you're done whimpering like a girl." He charged out of the principal's office, leaving Ben alone to think.

Feeling someone gawking at him, he turned toward the nurse's office, seeing Kevin standing in the doorway, observing the spectacle. By the look of sympathy in his eyes, he could tell that he and Andrew were not about to have the same yelling match that he and his parent did. At that point, Ben didn't know how to feel about it. One voice in his subconscious asked him to be enraged at the injustice of it all. Another told him to let it go, and try to improve things before they got even worse.

Andrew didn't have to punch him. He was only stating the facts about Kevin. He didn't blame Andrew for whatever went on between him and his father, but he found it disturbing, and he couldn't help feeling that way. He certainly couldn't imagine loving his own father in the way Andrew loved his. If he thought something was wrong, he had a right to that opinion.

Dwelling on the aftermath of their brawl, Ben remembered Andrew's mangled face, and that he had been the one to smash it in. He didn't mean to hit him so hard, only intended to show him that no one struck him and got away with it. He might have hammered that lesson in a bit stronger than he had intended. He could admit, despite the tears Andrew had caused him, that he didn't deserve to be hurt like that.

Was it really Andrew's fault, Ben wondered? Would Andrew have ever tried to fight with him if he had accepted the facts earlier on? Now, he would never know. Despite how cold he felt toward both him and Kevin, he couldn't deny that the very thought brought him grief. That same smiling, happy face he once sat down with at lunch and loved to chat with was now gashed and bleeding because he shoved his fist into it.

Sometimes, it was too late for apologies, and he thought that by now, Andrew wouldn't accept one. If he had been Andrew, he wouldn't have. Alternately, he wouldn't be able to rest easy until he gave him one. He might not have liked the fact that he had Kevin there to lick his wounds when he had nothing but suffering to look forward to, but there should not have been any wounds to heal in the first place. He should have put an end to them before one of them lied bleeding on the floor.

Ben didn't join his father outside, but instead left the office to head to the doorway where Kevin stood. Kevin's posture stiffened when seeing him approach, but didn't instigate, only stood in front of the door like an impassive nightclub bouncer.

"Mister Neil," he acknowledged. Humble, he followed up with, "Nice to meet you."

Kevin nodded. "Ben." He said nothing else, nor did he reach for his hand, only filled the doorway with his stature.

Ben felt lucky that he got that much out of him. He wouldn't have blamed the guy if he grabbed him by the shirt and chucked him out. "May I speak to Andrew? I have a lot to say to him."

Hesitant, Kevin looked in at Andrew, who stood by, curious. "I don't know. Haven't you done enough to him?"

"I promise, Mister Neil, I don't want to hurt him. A-anymore." His teeth minced together as he twiddled his thumbs.

Lemons filled Kevin's mouth, and he sucked on his lower lip in concentration. "Fine. He needs to see the doctor, so make it quick."

Uncomfortable at the predatory loom of Kevin, he mumbled, "Thank you," before strolling past him and entering the office.

Andrew recoiled at the sight of him, so Ben got as close as he allowed him, which was at least five feet. "I got suspended," he told Andrew, hoping it would compensate for what went on between them.

"So did I. They took me off the school paper, too. So that's nice."

Ben slipped his hands into his pockets and felt around at the balls of lint inside of them as he stalled. "You're going to the doctor?" With the silence that followed, Ben figured that was the end of their conversation, but then Andrew spoke.

"Yeah. I guess Dad wants to see if I have a concussion or not."

"I… I hit you that hard? Jesus. Andrew, I…"

"Whatever it is you want to say, it doesn't matter now, all right?"

"Would you listen?" Andrew went silent, but eyed his father at the door to see if he was still keeping watch. Kevin had never taken his eyes off of them. "I didn't mean to hurt you like this, Andrew, I really didn't," Ben rambled.

Blood streaked onto Andrew's nose when he wiped it. "Yes you did."

"Okay. All right. At first, I did. I admit it. I was angry at you. Maybe you didn't mean to, but you just kept hurting my feelings."

"Look. I thought about inviting you to that Diode show, but my dad wanted it to be special between us. You got to go anyway, and I'm glad, because I felt bad you couldn't go with me." Ben bowed his head, kicking at the floor. "Ben, I wasn't lying when I said I liked you. I do. You're probably the coolest guy in this school. You're a hell of a lot cooler than me. But, there's no nice way of telling someone you're not into them. And I'm not into you. That's just the way it is. If you want to hate me for that, fine, but there's nothing I can do about it. I'm just me. I'm always going to be *me*. I can't change that. And you can't change yourself."

"I don't hate you, Andrew."

Andrew gestured to his black eye. "Could have fooled me." Ben lowered his head once again. "Switching our locks? Tripping me in the cafeteria? Insulting my father? I know I'm not perfect, but I never started any shit with you until you asked for it."

"I'm sorry for all that. I didn't know it would get this bad, and... I guess there were a *lot* of things I didn't know." Andrew looked away from him, so Ben persisted. "I know I fucked up. I just wanted us both to be happy."

"I'm sorry I couldn't be the one you wanted. But it needs to stop here, Ben. We're not children. If there's a problem, we should talk about it. Not pull this childish bullshit."

Ben took a couple of steps closer to him. The tension was thick, but Andrew allowed him to come near. "Andrew... I want to start over. If you'd let me. Just wipe the slate clean and start from the beginning; before we fought, before we hurt each other. Before any of this."

For a moment, Andrew said nothing to him, giving in some painstaking thought. Then, "Are you sure you want to be friends with someone like me?"

Ben didn't catch on to his hint. "Someone like you?" When Andrew tipped his chin in Kevin's direction, he understood. "Oh. That." He drew in a deep, cautious breath. "So it's true." An awkward silence filled the room, and he cleared his throat.

"I don't see a point in denying it now."

Another long pause. "You know that's..."

"I know how weird it is, Ben. You and everyone else were courteous enough to let me know."

"Illegal... right?"

Andrew squinted, ready for another fight if it came to that. "So what?" Ben's mouth widened, but Andrew cut him off. "And if you're going to accuse my father of raping me again, you'd better have some evidence to support it."

Ben's palms came up in a sign of surrender. "No. I don't think that. I said that out of anger, and it was stupid, okay? But that doesn't make your relationship any less wrong."

"In whose eyes?"

"Everyone's."

Unfortunately, Ben was correct about that. No matter how right it looked and felt to him, to any outsider it was deviant behavior worth punishing. All he could think to say to him was, "You really. Don't. Understand. And the way you're looking at me now tells me that you never will. Explaining it to you will do no good whatsoever if you've already made up your mind about how it makes you feel. I can't kill your instinct to react to it with disgust. I can only show you the facts."

Most of Andrew's words bounced off of him, but he tried to come to terms with what he told him. "What if someone presses charges against him?"

Assuming this was a threat, Andrew's icy irises expanded in fear. "You wouldn't."

First, he was shocked that Andrew would think such a thing. Then he was empathetic at his accusation. He would think the same thing in his position. "No. I wouldn't. But, Andrew, you really have to know that it's just…" He paused when Andrew sighed, weary and exasperated, rubbing a rough hand over his face. Given some deliberation, Ben changed his tone and voiced with sincerity: "Never mind."

Grateful that it was over, Andrew released his face and gave him a half-assed smirk. Ben smiled back, and they took a minute to review the conversation.

All hostility in Andrew faded, replaced by a hint of respect. After everything they had been through, Andrew was shocked that he vowed not to cause him any more grief. "Maybe I am willing to start over."

"Maybe I'm willing to not be such an overbearing asshole all the time."

Though Andrew could sense Kevin's urgency in getting him to the doctor, he turned and walked toward Ben once more, his head high, though the pain ripped through him like a knife slicing paper. "I'm sorry." Ben blinked in surprise. "I should have gone to that show with you."

"It's okay. You didn't miss much. You could tell that Ross was sober the whole time."

"Really. That's rare."

"Tell me about it."

When Andrew said nothing more on it, Ben kissed the side of his head. Andrew didn't mean to flinch, but it hurt, in more than one way. "I wouldn't ask you to change for any reason," he whispered in his ear. "I like Andrew the way he is. No matter who he's with."

Andrew hugged him around the neck, though his collar defied him. Ben's arms encircled his waist, and trembled when doing so. "Do we get to stay friends this time?"

"Yeah, buddy," he promised. "We do."

This very hug had been the one thing Ben had always wanted to share with Andrew, and in his view, it was a shame they now held each other under these circumstances. Regardless, it was a moment Ben relished every second it lasted, which were too few. The way in which Andrew clung to him told that he was sorry for more than decking him in the jaw.

Never will I meet anyone like you, Ben realized. *Please don't let this be the last time we speak.*

"Andrew," Kevin called. "Come on, we'd better get you there."

When Ben felt Andrew's arms loosen, he knew that it would be the final time they would share physical contact, and releasing him was tougher than it should have been. Knowing it was for the best, he let him go. Andrew unhooked his arms, bid him farewell, and joined his father at his side, walking with him out the door. Kevin cast a worried glance at Ben one final time, and Ben responded with a smile and wave, reassuring him that he could be trusted, that the news of their relationship would stay locked behind his lips. Giving Ben the benefit of a doubt, Kevin nodded to him and returned the open palm before hurrying Andrew out to his car.

As Ben watched them leave, his troubled thoughts cleared. His and Andrew's future personas could still meet up like he had imagined before, sharing a meal and talking about their day. Andrew would tell him about his photo shoots, and he would explain his independent movie to him. Andrew would answer his cell phone when it rang, smile, laugh, and wink at Ben, knowing he was in on his secret. He would invite the caller to their lunch, and Kevin would show up. It wouldn't bother him to see him, because Andrew was happy to be around him. Kevin would shake his hand, buy them all lunch, and offer Ben the creative rights to turn one of his books into a film. Andrew would be there, taking photos of him and his production for an online editorial, once again referring to him as "very talented." A smile spread onto his face.

To see Andrew happy; that's what he wanted. He wouldn't get the relationship he sought, but he would still get to be his friend, and that was better than nothing. That was better than tormenting him, and hurting him. It was better than slamming him in the eye. It was true that Andrew had started the brawl, and he could have told the school staff that he wasn't responsible and might have gotten the suspension revoked. He also might not have been yelled at by his father so much.

He would accept his punishment. In his mind, he was getting punished for much more than fighting with Andrew, and in the end, things could go back to normal.

At least, whatever they considered normal.

Andrew never liked going to the doctor. Kidneys hurt? Pour some water down your throat. Coughing and sneezing? Take vitamins. Fever? Make some tea and pour a ton of honey into it. Had it been Kevin that sustained an injury, he'd stop at nothing to make sure he paid visit to a doctor, but when it came to his own health, he'd rather suck a tail pipe than go anywhere near a hospital.

Kevin wanted to know the truth about what happened at the school, but Andrew knew that home was the only place to discuss it. For Kevin, their relationship was unaffected by the tribulations, but Andrew could only think of their future together now. How many more times, he wondered as the doctor checked his nose to see if it was broken, would he fight with people? How many more friends might he lose? How many taunts, names, looks, and accusations would lambaste him? He had to take into account whether or not it was worth the pain he may or may not suffer, and by the looks of it, he had suffered a lot more than Kevin had so far.

When they were alone in the room as the doctor left to ready their paperwork, Andrew slipped his jacket back on while staring at his father, who seemed to be trying to make light of the situation, as he always did. Now, Andrew felt, was the worst time.

"It almost looks fake, like a makeup effect," he said in regards to his black eye. "It sure adds to your style." He grinned and gave his shoulder a loving pat, but Andrew didn't react. Kevin's face fell. "I know you're probably upset about the suspension, honey. And you think I'm angry at you, too. I'm not, I just want to know what's going on."

"Dad…" He winced when he slid off of the exam table. Every inch of him was sore. Most painful of all, though not in the physical sense, was the tenderness in his ass. "I want to ask you something." Kevin waited. "Does Kyle know about us?"

Apprehensive, Kevin leaned back and forth on his heels, clicking his tongue a few times. "No. I never told him."

"Why?"

That was a good question. Why hadn't he told him? If he thought he would lose Kyle, that meant he'd have to question the nature of their friendship and if it was worth hanging onto. "I don't know."

"Yeah, you do."

"No, I don't."

"It was to keep him around in case we didn't work out. Wasn't it?"

"Andrew…" He rubbed his exhausted eyes. "What are you getting at?"

"What do you think I'm getting at? You knew from the start, didn't you?" When he broke into tears, Kevin went to touch his shoulder, but he withdrew it.

Now in desperation, a frantic Kevin questioned, "Knew what?"

"That we wouldn't last."

"What? No, I didn't assume that!"

"But it was in the back of your mind, Dad. It was in the back of both of ours."

Kevin couldn't argue with him on that. Perhaps it had crossed his mind once or twice, regardless of if he wanted to believe it or not. "Are you going to tell me what happened at school today? Or why Ben gave you a black eye?"

He sniffled, wiping his nose on his shirt sleeve, which already had dabs of blood on it. "I think you know what happened."

Kevin had come to the appropriate conclusions long ago, it was true. "I want you to tell me."

The doctor returned with the paperwork and a painkilling prescription for Andrew, who took a moment to wipe his nose and eyes before taking it. Kevin shook his hand and thanked him, though the atmosphere in the room had darkened between the time he had left and returned. After paying the expenses, Kevin took Andrew home to rest his wounds.

Andrew didn't rest, though. He was tired, and his whole body throbbed, but they needed to have a talk. Kevin asked if he wanted anything other than the painkillers, and Andrew said he just wanted to sit down with him. They went to the living room, since Andrew refused to deal with this in their usual comfort zone, and sat on the sofa.

"They knew," was the first thing out of Andrew's mouth.

"Who are 'they'?"

"Everyone."

Kevin sighed and leaned back, contemplating the matter. "I take it they weren't quiet about it."

"No. They weren't. At all."

"How…?"

"It doesn't matter. Somehow, they found out."

Kevin tried to make peace by putting an arm around him, but he shrugged it off and leaned away. His father looked at him as though he had just raked daggers through his heart, a sight Andrew thought he could handle, but ultimately couldn't face.

"I'm sorry, honey. Sometimes it's hard for people to…" He paused, seeing that Andrew wasn't looking for solace. He was looking to have a serious discussion about their relationship. "Andrew, it's not like they actually know anything. One kid says something, and they all listen to it because it's interesting. It's gossip, that's all it is."

The word "gossip" echoed from Andrew's dry lips as he shook his head. "It's gossip that's true."

"I've told you, not everyone is going to like you."

"I don't *care about that!* It was fucking *humiliating, Dad!* To look at them and think they know! They know that I kiss you, that I sleep with you, that I do sexual things with you!"

Bewildered by Andrew's attitude, Kevin attempted to calm him before another explosion. "Why is it such a big deal that they know? Do you care who any of them are?"

"Well, I can't get to know them now, can I?!"

They both fell into despaired silence for a few moments. "Andrew, I didn't know you were so ashamed of us. Why didn't you tell me this before?"

Andrew tucked his head down, putting both hands on the back of his neck. "I don't know. When we're alone together… I'm not ashamed. But thinking of other people seeing us…" A brief pause, then he added, "You feel the same way."

"I do not."

Andrew then shoved his hand into Kevin's right pocket, then yanked out his smartphone, holding it out to him. "Then tell Kyle." Kevin bit his tongue as he merely stared at the phone in Andrew's hand, and a partial smirk curled on Andrew's lips. "That's what I thought. You're just a fucking hypocrite." He tossed the phone onto the coffee table. Kevin was too upset to protest the mishandling of his objects.

"My situation with Kyle is a bit more complicated than you being teased at school."

Andrew rocketed off the couch, storming across the living room, but didn't vacate it. "Meaning you want him around to *fuck*. Maybe you planned to continue fucking him behind my back, who knows?!"

Kevin got up as well, following him around while he paced. "That's not why."

"Bullshit, Dad. You're so full of it. And how could you compare you and him to what happened to me? Have you seen my fucking eye?!" He shoved his face into Kevin's, pointing to the swelling engulfing his cheek. "Look at me!"

"I'm not the one that caused your injuries, Andrew. You did."

Andrew's knees locked, and he halted. Aghast, he stared up at him, mouth gaping, eyes bulged. "How could you say that?"

Kevin, now fed up, tossed a hand into the air. "Because it's true. I told you to let it go, didn't I? I told you to fix things before it was too late. You don't fucking listen to me. You just do whatever feels good to you. Ben harassed you because he was being an asshole, yes, that is true. But you allowed it to perpetuate."

His protruded lower lip shook. "You're blaming me? You were the last person I'd ever think would do such a thing."

Kevin sighed, running a hand over his hair. "I'm not blaming you. I'm saying you're not excused of guilt. You have a black eye because you hit Ben instead of walking away."

"Dad, he said that you *raped me*! I'm supposed to walk away from *that*?!"

"Yes. You are."

Unable to sort his thoughts out, Andrew growled and paced again. "It's easy for you to say all this shit when you sit here at home in your comfy, cozy office all day. You didn't have to see them all looking at you. You didn't have to feel their eyes all over you. You didn't hear them laughing."

"What do you want, Andrew?" Kevin finally asked. "You want to end it?"

That was the ultimate question, wasn't it? Ambivalent, Andrew didn't answer right away. It required some time to stew in his mind. Each time he thought of the two of them snuggling, kissing, having sex, it was tainted by the sound of cackling. It was poisoned now, void of grandeur, stripped of any and all harmony. He loved Kevin's touch, his sweet words, but his peers reminded him, even in his head, that it was wrong. The world would never be accepting. He would never find another soul who looked upon them with the respect he wanted. Even Ben was thoughtful enough to keep his disgust in check when promising not to call the police.

It didn't matter what he did to show his love for Kevin. There would always be those that judged. Every person he'd meet on the street, he'd be paranoid of the concept of them "knowing." He wouldn't be able to hold Kevin's hand in public. He wouldn't be able to introduce him as his father and the love of his life.

If the events of the day had never happened, would everything really would have worked out for them? Would they have stayed happy, in their precious bubble, for the rest of their lives? Something of this nature was bound to separate them eventually. To say that they could make it last was unrealistic.

Kevin was eighteen years older, and would be the first of them to reach old age. If they lived a risk-free life, Kevin would die before he did. Coping with losing a father was hard enough, but losing a father and a lover? How would he manage that? Would he even be able to sit beside him and hold his hand as he lay in his death bed? Would he even bother to continue living after such a loss? His father had told him it was too soon to think of things like that, but he had to consider it. Death was just as important as life.

Then there was Kyle. He had an attachment with Kevin he would never be able to reach, and he was certain that Kevin was also aware of it. For all he knew, Kevin had feelings for Kyle he never admitted. Maybe they wanted to be together, but felt trapped now that Andrew had come around.

Thinking of their relationship for the first time in a rational way, Andrew found few things positive about it. Being held by Kevin was the greatest feeling he had ever experienced, and the worst was being taunted by his classmates. Looking back on it, he wasn't sure he could handle the risks. He couldn't handle spending the rest of his life in secret. He would go back to the shadows where he belonged.

The shadows were safe. No one could hurt him there.

After mulling it over, Andrew prepared to inform his father of his decision. He held back, unsure of himself, but he knew it had to be done. "M-maybe I do want to end it." Grief-stricken, Kevin bowed his head, squeezing his eyes shut. "Dad, we didn't think this through before we got involved. We were so excited, so in the moment… we didn't give it time."

"We knew what we wanted. I'd say we gave it all of the time it needed."

"Not enough."

Kevin was more distraught than Andrew thought he'd be. He had to have predicted that something of this nature would occur someday. His soaking eyes deviated from that judiciousness. "I can't tell you how to live, Andrew. I can't force you to make a choice. But if this is what you want to do… if you want no relationship beyond father and son… you'd better be very damn sure that's what you want. Because I…" He tried to steady his voice, but couldn't. It cracked as he whimpered, "I won't go through this again."

Andrew turned away from him, feeling sick knowing he was causing him pain. "Neither will I. I should have listened to you the first time when you said it wouldn't work. I wouldn't be hurting you now."

"Andrew. Please."

This was the first time he had heard his father beg for anything. Perhaps their relationship was something more than a good feeling for him. He cherished it. They both did. Nevertheless, all good things came to an end, and was better for it to end sooner rather than later.

"I'm sorry, Dad."

"Don't do this to me."

"Dad, please! You're making it more painful than it needs to be!"

"*I'm* making it more painful?! You wanted this more than anything, remember?! Now that a few nobodies point their fingers at you at school, I'm not important to you anymore?! What the hell is wrong with you?!"

Andrew didn't dispute. It would only make things worse. He

rushed to the staircase and started heading up to his room, unable to deal with his tears and desperation.

"Andrew!" his father bellowed from below, pleading with him. He didn't turn back.

Andrew slammed into his bed and sobbed into his pillow. Despite living the event, he couldn't conceive that he had just thrown away one of the greatest things that happened to him in a long time. It was too late to go back now. It was over, and there was very little he could do about it now.

After crying for a straight half hour, Andrew could no longer form tears. He went into his bathroom to use up a whole roll of toilet paper blowing his nose. He had mourned the death of relationships before, but none of them stabbed him as hard as this.

Unlike Andrew, Kevin had lost many lovers over the course of his life, and unlike Andrew, he had specific tools he used to cope with the depression that followed a breakup. Alcohol was usually the first thing he went for, then several packs of cigarettes, and phone calls to Kyle, which he had to forego for now.

Kyle had been right when he assumed he had vodka in the house. He kept it hidden in the back of his icebox for emergencies such as this one. He rushed out to the garage, blinded by the rain streaming over his eyes, and cracked open the icebox, which required a bit of effort, as it sometimes did in the winter months. The bottle was almost filled to the top, thank goodness, and he rushed it inside to the kitchen, where he grabbed a tall glass. He filled a quarter of the glass with citrus soda, and filled the rest with vodka. He sloshed the mixture around a bit, but didn't waste time dumping it down his throat. The fiery burn as it went down was equal parts gratifying and callous.

The vodka was an expensive brand, top shelf, a favorite of his. It wouldn't be a favorite for long. With every gulp, he knew that it was one sip away from further associating the beverage with Andrew's words. He took the cup, as well as the bottle, to his office where he was commonly more comfortable than when he was in his bedroom. He rummaged around in his drawers for cigarettes, knowing he must have had some lying around somewhere.

None. Not a single cigarette was stored away. When he said he'd quit before, he meant it. "Great," he huffed, slamming the cupboards and drawers. He'd have to go out and get some. He stumbled out of his office and shoved his shoes on, but didn't bother with a coat, though it had to have been eighteen degrees out.

The drive to the convenience store was a quick one, as was the process of buying cigarettes. Since they didn't carry whole cartons of his favorite brand, he bought several packs, cleaning out their supply. He would smoke the shit out of those the moment he got home, and even they wouldn't be sufficient enough.

With his cigarettes and vodka, Kevin spent the rest of the evening in his office, only coming out to urinate and, later on in the night, vomit once or twice. Eventually, he passed out with his head on his computer desk, slurring to himself.

Upstairs, Andrew only had the energy to lay in bed and stare at the wall, crying off and on to relieve the pain of returning recent memories. He was so happy all weekend, and he couldn't believe how crazy with love he had been. What was he thinking? What were either of them thinking?

Neither one of them spoke to each other for the rest of the night, but each of them knew that they needed to find a way to deal with their living situation, as theirs was unlike any other.

CHAPTER TWELVE

In Which the Ladder Breaks

Sleep was impossible for Andrew almost the entire night.

Though he was frustrated, he worried about his father. He had seen him get emotional, but that was the first time he had witnessed him break into pieces, and it had been his fault. A compromise couldn't be made, and he knew that. When the show was over, it was over. Lights on, curtains drawn, and everyone went home.

The restless night crawled into dawn, and Andrew snuck downstairs, his stomach in knots and screaming for sustenance. Seeing no sign of his father in the kitchen, he crept to the fridge to rummage for a quick, light breakfast.

That's when he noticed the smell— burnt tobacco, mint, and lemon, all of which were stemming from the vicinity of the study. It had been about a month since Andrew had detected the scent of a cigarette in their house, and he had almost forgotten what they smelled like. The aroma escalated as he neared the door, which he nudged open to get a peek inside.

Sitting at the desk was Kevin, his head upon the oak finish, his shirt unbuttoned and hair scattered. He was out cold, sleeping next to an ashtray, where a mountain of cigarette butts were piled. In his hand, which was also sprawled upon the desk, was an empty glass. It appeared as though he had passed out after reaching for it. A puddle of drool had spread under his mouth, and even from where he was standing, Andrew got a whiff of his foul breath.

Andrew took a step inside, trembling all over at the sight of his father in such a ragged heap. His primary thought was to jump to his aid, to help him out of the chair, and to drag him to a hot shower where he could sober up; to apologize, to tell him that yesterday he had been a total idiot.

No more than a few minutes after that thought did Andrew decide against it. It was better to let the wound heal on its own. Anything he did now would give Kevin false hope, as much as it pained him to leave him lying in a puddle of sweat, tears, and sorrow.

He didn't manage to get a single foot out before hearing and seeing Kevin stir in his chair, knocking his empty glass to the floor, shoving his computer keyboard and mouse aside.

"Andrew?" whined the groggy and raspy voice of Kevin.

Andrew ducked away without a word, escaping the area before Kevin discovered him. Screw breakfast. He wouldn't be able to keep it down anyway. Back to his bedroom he hid.

Kevin turned his chair toward the door, which was cracked open, hopeful that Andrew wanted to speak with him. The doorway was vacant, and he was alone again. He clutched his head as it pounded, groaning, and staggered away from his desk and out into the hallway. He stumbled his way upstairs and to his bedroom, where he stayed secluded all afternoon.

Four days passed— all of which were suffered in silence. For each of the four days, they remained holed up in their rooms, miserable and full of regret. On the eve of the fourth day, Kevin decided to leave his room for something other than the occasional snack. His eyes burned as light pierced them, and his legs required more effort to move than normal. The first idea that coursed through Kevin's mind was making himself some tea. A fresh cup of chamomile and honey might warm his blood.

Kevin found one of the last remaining apples in the fridge, which he nibbled with his tea. As soon as it went down his throat, he wanted to lurch it back up again, but he knew better than to do that. Regardless of where he now stood with Andrew, he cared about his health.

While sipping his hot beverage, he rubbed at an ache in his neck, one that made turning his head difficult. How long had he slept?

Hours? Days? He had lost track. He wasn't even sure what day of the week it was. Wondering if Andrew was still in his room, and if he was okay, Kevin thought to go upstairs and knock on his door. Perhaps by now he had cooled off and was willing to talk again. Any kind of conversation would be sufficient enough.

After finishing his tea, Kevin left the kitchen and headed upstairs to Andrew's room. He placed his ear against the door, listening for any signs of life, then rapped on it three times. "Andrew?" he called, hoarse.

Inside, Andrew heard him, but he didn't budge from his spot on the bed. He wanted to talk to Kevin— Lord, did he ever want to— but he couldn't bear to look at him now. *I'm sorry, Dad,* he mouthed, but the words themselves were merely breaths. *Why can't I say it to him? We slept together for fuck's sake, and I can't talk to him?*

Kevin cracked the door open and peeked into the dark room, seeing Andrew curled up and breathing with his back to the door. For now, he would let him sleep, as long as he knew he was alive and safe. Heading downstairs now, Kevin knew that Andrew had to come downstairs eventually, and when he did, he'd be waiting for him.

Becoming fed up with spending so much time in his room, it also came time for Andrew to emerge from under the rock he had tucked himself beneath. Once reaching the bottom step, he heard activity in the kitchen, and froze. The smell of tobacco once again entered the room, and Andrew followed its trail to Kevin, who was sitting at the kitchen counter, smoking.

Andrew hadn't yet made a sound, but Kevin had an uncanny awareness to his proximity. His father turned his head to look at him, his eyes dark, his hair uncombed, his face covered in fresh stubble, and his lips cracked and dry.

"Hey," he said, a hint of a smile forcing its way onto his lips, filled with optimism.

Andrew felt like he was ten years old again, walking into a room after Star and David had finished erupting at one another. To this day, he didn't understand why they married in the first place. "Hey," he squeaked, then shuffled to the fridge, raiding it for something light to eat.

Kevin's parched knuckles tightened around the cigarette between his fingers. "How are you doing? You feeling okay?"

"I'm fine." He picked up the pace, snatching a bottle of chocolate

240

milk and some lunch meat, getting ready to prepare a turkey sandwich.

Kevin allowed the dust to settle for a few seconds, then he spoke up a second time. "Andrew, I remember everything you said. And I still understand your decision. But I don't want us to be this way. I want to see you. I want to talk to you. I know you don't want to be partners, but can't we go back to being friends?"

Andrew heard every word he said to him, but it only slithered between his ears as one garbled sound, incoherent. Just make this sandwich and get out of the blasting zone, and run. Run and hide.

Kevin's inflection had already been unbalanced, but shocked tears entered it now. "You're not going to talk to me?"

"Dad... I can't. I can't fucking do this right now."

"We haven't spoken in days. What are you planning to do, vanish from existence entirely?"

"I'm damn well going to try," he mumbled, not intending for his father to hear, but the moment those cold words slipped from his mouth, he heard a choke, followed by a fit of gasping and sniffing. Kevin's head lowered and he convulsed in a fit of despondency.

I'm a fucking monster, Andrew realized, staring at the mess of depression that was once a happy man. *How could I do this to him?*

You had to be cruel to be kind, Andrew recalled hearing once. He was doing them both a favor in separating them this way. The sandwich he had assembled looked just as disheveled and neglected as their relationship, but he took it with him anyway, pitying the worthless creation. Andrew, like he had before, ran away, about to break down at the suffering he had caused.

With nothing resolved, at least not in the way they wanted, Kevin and Andrew returned to their depressing routine.

"**You** okay, Kevin?"

Kevin had dialed Kyle, asked him how he had been, but couldn't manage to say much else, and not just because his throat was raw and worn out.

"I need to see you."

A sigh came from Kyle down the line, and Kevin flinched at it. It sounded rebuking. "I don't know."

"Kyle, I'm sorry if I hurt you before. I really am. I just... I need someone to talk to. I need to get out of this house."

"Why? Did something happen between you and Andrew?"

"S-sort of. I'll explain when I get there. If you want me there."

Their conversation wilted into silence, and Kevin thought he had hung up on him. He almost did the same, but Kyle answered him, still with the same coldness as used previously. "All right. Come on over."

After slipping his coat on, Kevin visited the kitchen where he grabbed the notepad that he kept next to the cordless phone. He ripped off one of the sticky sheets of paper and wrote a note on it for Andrew, letting him know where he'd be, then crammed a pair of boots on and sped out before he changed his mind.

Kyle didn't live far from Kevin. Since his late twenties he had been residing in the same place: an apartment building due far west of Kevin's neighborhood. It was a decent living, though inflated in price, but Kyle could manage it with his salary. He had been an inventory manager at a community college for the past few years, a job which he could practically get away with murder at, as long as he got the job done, and he was one of the few that did.

Kevin's phone call had left him feeling at a loss. When Kyle saw the screensaver of his smiling face on his cell phone screen, he was breathless when answering, hoping that his friend wished to revisit their talk about a possible romance between them. Hearing him so sad worried him, but it also disappointed him. As always, he was the crutch, the shoulder to cry on, and never the one Kevin shed tears for.

Fifteen minutes rolled by since the call, and Kyle busied himself with washing dishes before he heard the familiar knock he recognized as Kevin's. Upon opening the door, he staggered back a step or two. The fragrance of cigarettes and sweat hit him like a blast of a ruptured sewage pipe. If he hadn't seen Kevin's mournful face, he would have cracked a joke wondering why he didn't have flies buzzing around him.

"Jesus, Kev," Kyle gasped, letting him inside. "You look like shit."

"Feel like shit," murmured Kevin, inching his coat off. Kyle helped him out of it.

Hanging his coat in the closet, he came to his side and checked his face, which looked over-rested and tattered. He dragged a soft hand across the top of his head, where strands of his hair poked up like stubborn weeds. "What the hell happened to you?" Kevin planted his cheek upon his shoulder and engulfed him. Kyle hugged him back, but recoiled at the smell. "Kev, talk to me."

"I don't know where to start."

"Try the beginning."

Not amused, Kevin left their hug. "I think you should sit down for this."

This hadn't been the first time Kevin had news compelling enough to require sitting. The first was when he scored a publishing contract. That had been, until Andrew came around, the happiest he had ever seen him. Kyle obeyed him and sat, readying himself for the report, which was obviously negative.

Kevin didn't waste time before spewing out, "Andrew and I had a relationship. A romantic relationship."

Nothing, not even sitting, could have prepared him for that one. "What…?"

"I know you don't believe me. But it happened. I'll spare you the details, as I'm sure you don't want them, but a few days ago he, uh…" He stopped to steady his voice. "Broke up with me." With every word, Kyle's eyes got bigger and bigger until they nearly filled his whole face. "I know it sounds funny. Maybe it would be a little, if I hadn't been the one involved in it. Hell, maybe even Andrew finds it funny. I don't know what's going through his mind anymore." As he paused, he noticed Kyle's unchanging traumatized expression. "I know what you're thinking. You think it was purely sexual. It wasn't like that. It was… something more than that. Whatever it was, it's over now. Some kids at school found out, and he took it kind of hard. Now he won't even talk to me. Will barely even look at me. I don't know what to do. I just don't know what to do."

Kyle placed a sweating, shaking hand over his mouth and rubbed it until it started to itch and turn red. Silence washed over them, and Kevin fidgeted.

"Kyle… say something."

"I'm letting it sink in, all right?" Another pause. "So… you had sex with him?" Tearing up again, Kevin nodded like a kid with his hand caught in a cookie jar. "Oh my god, Kevin."

"What?!"

"You fucked your son? What the hell is wrong with you?"

Kevin stared his friend in the eye, incredulous. "Someone that you pick up in a bar for a night is someone you fuck. A groupie fanatic that follows you and everything you do is someone you fuck. I didn't *fuck* Andrew, Kyle. I made love to him."

With his eyes pinched in a chilling glare, he stated, "You know what I mean. Don't act high and mighty about this. You know what you did wrong." When Kevin appeared on the verge of shambling out the door, he calmed himself. "Okay, okay. Kevin, I'm sorry. But you have to understand this from my perspective. It's a little weird."

Drying his eyes, Kevin retorted with: "Is it about as weird as you wanting a relationship with me?"

Vacant of sentiment, Kyle spat, "It's *weirder.*"

"Not to me."

Knowing he wasn't going to get anywhere arguing with him, Kyle gave up for the moment, rubbing his now stressed eyes. "So… he broke up with you. You said he was teased at school, right? What'd you expect to happen? How long were you planning to keep it a secret? Especially from me, no less. You really thought that something that fucked up could be kept behind locked doors?"

Kevin didn't answer him, but turned away, hiding himself from Kyle's line of vision. He wasn't sure why he excepted his friend to understand any of this, as close as they were. Kyle had always been the judgmental type, the one to make wisecracks rather than make amends, but they always saw eye-to-eye on things. Since high school, Kevin had come to him for every problem, and he never once looked at him in the same manner he was now. Not even a bond of many years could stay connected when something of this nature was brought into the equation.

"I shouldn't have come," he told his friend, who softened his attitude at hearing the regret in his words.

"Kev…" He took a deep breath, attempting to relax his muscles, and his voice. "Look, I'm sorry. I don't think anything is wrong with you, or with Andrew, and I didn't mean to imply that. It's just sort of shocking for me. I mean, I suspected *something,* so it's not all that strange, but… I can see how much this is beating you up." He heard Kevin sniff. "And it couldn't have been easy telling me the truth."

"It wasn't."

"So… talk to me."

Kevin hesitated now, fearful of being judged, but Kyle stood and guided him to the couch where he sat with him. "Andrew ended up getting into a nasty fight with his friend. Gave him a black eye."

"Is he okay?"

"Other than locking himself in his room and treating me like crap, yeah, he's fine."

Kyle took a valuable moment to reflect on the information, not wanting to offend Kevin anymore, despite the fact that he felt they lived on entirely different planets now. "He might need some time. I remember when you got teased at school by Tracy Tucker when he found out you were gay. Kids are dicks."

"This is a little different, Kyle."

"I'm sure you don't need to be told this..." He kept his chills under control. "But he's a teenager, Kev. A lot of things about life, and especially about love, are pretty new to him."

"I know that. I knew it going into this. He seemed so ready for it."

"No offense," Kyle warned, and Kevin prepared to take offense anyway. "But he's too young for you. He's not ready to take on a relationship as serious as you want it to be. Have you considered that... Christ, this is going to sound harsh. Have you thought that maybe it's not you Andrew is in love with?"

"What? What do you mean?"

"Think about it. Star dumps him off with you, and you give him some room to breathe. With you, he could be anything, do anything he wanted. Which is good, don't get me wrong. I know you love him, and I'm glad you do. But before living with you, I don't think Andrew had that before."

"What are you getting at?"

Kyle rested a hand on Kevin's knee, offering him some lukewarm affection that he didn't seem to want right away. "I'm saying that maybe what Andrew really loved was his freedom. You gave him the freedom to love who he wanted, and naturally, because you gave him everything he wanted, he felt it for you." When he heard Kevin sniffle, he continued. "His priorities might be different than yours. Do you really think Andrew will be able to hold out the long-term relationship you want? Do you think he could stay in it for years like you could? He has his youth. Let him keep it. Otherwise... you're being unfair to him."

"I... I..." Kevin trailed off into a whimper, and he buried his face into his hands. "I didn't mean for Andrew to get hurt."

Draping an arm around him, Kyle pulled him close. "I know, Kev.

It's okay. He'll talk to you again. Just give him some space."

Tucking his face into Kyle's neck, he clung to him, letting the pain slip away while his friend comforted him. For a while, they sat like that, holding each other, Kevin's tears eventually coming to a stop.

"You want to use my shower?" asked Kyle, who couldn't bear to smell Kevin's funk any longer. "I still have some of your clothes here you can change into."

"Sure."

A warm shower was just the aid he needed on the road to recovery. He loved the brand of body wash Kyle used, and every time he inhaled it, he remembered many of the nights they shared, romping in bed and showering afterward. Maybe it truly was best that he and Andrew didn't work out. Nothing good could ever come of what they had together, no matter how amazing it felt to experience it with him. At the other end of hope and promise was only fear and desolation, where they might be holding hands, but they would be alone. All alone. No one would give a damn about them until they had remonstrations in mind.

Alone with Andrew. Would that really be so bad? It had to have been. If it were good, Andrew wouldn't be so upset with him now.

Regardless, Kevin thought of moving away from the city with him. They'd have their life together, and could leave the world out of it. They could hug, kiss, laugh, and play, without a care of what went on outside. No one would have to know, because it was none of anyone's business but their own.

He put it out of his mind to keep from crying again. He was tired of crying. His nose had been permanently stuffed up for days, and his eyes were red and dried out. Now wasn't the time to dream of possible futures. Now was the time to let go. Andrew was to be his son, and he was to be there for him in times of need, but that would be the extent of it.

After his shower, he got dressed in some of his old clothes and rejoined him in the living room, where they sat and watched television. Kyle offered Kevin a beer, and he took one, but after the adventure he had a few nights ago with vodka, he wasn't interested in drinking too much.

Hours rolled by into night, and Kevin's mind went back to Andrew several times, and many of those times, he almost called the house to check up on him. Kyle advised against it, however, and told him that it was better to leave him alone.

Andrew's way of relieving stress didn't involve phone calls to friends. Not even a wailing tune on the guitar abolished his restlessness. All he could think about was Kevin. He expected the attraction to hold firm even after their separation, but it wasn't helping him stay away from that which he tried to escape.

It took him hours to get to sleep each night without Kevin holding him. The judging looks still haunted his imagination, but he missed Kevin's arms around him, his warm body against his back, and needed them just to feel comfortable anymore. As he tossed and turned and struggled to get any rest, he questioned his own actions over the past few days.

He hugged himself, thinking of how tight Kevin would squeeze him, how safe he made him feel. He could still smell him on his skin— that hint of citrus, spiced cologne and aftershave, the very one that the interior of his car reeked of. Though it was almost like he was there with him, he still couldn't fall asleep. It wasn't close enough to the real thing.

I'm an idiot, thought Andrew, longing for those strokes to his back and face, those whispers of affection, and even being smothered halfway through the night. *What the hell am I doing? Is this really the way I want to live? Am I going to spend the rest of my life in this room, hiding from him?*

Regret pounded away at his wall of emotions. Over the past few days, he had allowed the both of them to suffer, and for what? Because a few kids at school paid attention to rumors? Maybe they didn't have to go through so much pain. It was possible that he had acted before thinking, that he and his father could go on as before, undisturbed by outside factors, as long as they managed it properly. He'd have to be twice as careful the second time around; to treat it like an incubating egg and allow it to develop, to make certain it was safe, warm, and untouched by the hands of others.

They could make it work, that is, if Kevin forgave him.

Step one was apologizing to him. Knowing their recent habits, he would be downstairs, possibly smoking or drinking. He dove out of bed, shoving his clothes on and doing a sloppy job of it, not giving a damn how wrinkled they were. When he went down the stairs, he jogged, calling out for his father with a desperate cry.

Kevin wasn't in the living room, the office, or the kitchen. Andrew opened the door leading to the garage, seeing his car was gone. A rapid sink of the heart followed, and he shuffled back into the house, which felt so much bigger and emptier when Kevin wasn't inside of it. Coming back into the kitchen, he saw a large piece of paper pinned to the fridge underneath a magnet with handwriting on it that looked like Kevin's. He scooted over to it, his socks slipping on the wood flooring.

Snatching the note from the fridge door, Andrew read it, muttering to himself:

Went to Kyle's. Couldn't stay here anymore.
Call my cell if you need anything.

As pissed off as Kevin might have been at him, Andrew was touched that he still managed to be a parent. Now, all Andrew wanted to do was hear his sweet voice, to hear the relief and love in it as he told him how sorry he was, that he wanted to rekindle the flame he permitted to burn out.

It'll be okay, Dad, Andrew prayed. *I'll make it better.*

Taking a moment to read the note over again, his stomach churned when he read Kyle's name. He hoped it didn't mean what he thought it did, not that he could imagine his father rebounding so frivolously. He had accused Kevin of it before out of anger, just another stupid thing he did in the heat of the moment. At the time, he meant it, but rationally, he knew it to be ridiculous.

Taking a moment to remember Kevin's cell phone number, he dialed it and waited, listening to it ring five times. His voicemail picked up, that apologetic message announcing that the caller had reached Kevin Neil, and that he was sorry he missed them. Andrew didn't leave a voicemail, but he hung up and re-dialed.

"Phone's ringing, Kev," called Kyle from the living room to his friend who was looking for a snack in the kitchen. A thump resonated from the area near the fridge as Kevin knocked his knee into a cupboard. Now hobbling, he limped his way over to the glass table between the kitchen and living room where his phone was sitting, plugged in.

On the screen of his smartphone was a picture of his house, the

248

word "Home" underneath it in bold, white letters. "It's Andrew," gasped Kevin to Kyle, who sat up the instant he mentioned it.

"Well, see what the kid has to say," Kyle advised, a hint of bitterness layering his tone.

Thinking the call might have been an emergency, Kevin answered it with concern. "Andrew?"

"Dad," breathed his son, in both relief and catharsis.

He sighed. "Yes?"

Everything that Andrew wanted to say to his father, he couldn't let out as well as he would have liked. "I… I wanted to talk to you."

Kevin paced the room. "Well. I'm listening."

"Not over the phone. I want you to hear this in person." Silence. "Are you going to come home?"

"I don't particularly want to, Andrew."

The conviction in his voice was strong. Andrew wasn't going to get off with just an apology in this case. "I just want us to talk. I've been thinking a lot… about the way I've been acting."

"Yeah. So have I."

Andrew had trouble telling if Kevin was angry or sad. It could have been both. "You're at Kyle's?"

"Still am, yeah."

The phone almost stuck to Andrew's ear from the gusts of cold he felt in his father's words. "Oh." They didn't seem to know what to say to each other, but they didn't hang up, either. "You guys… aren't… fucking, are you?"

A frustrated sigh, then, "What difference does it make?"

Gloss slid over Andrew's eyes, his nose clenching and twitching. "I… I don't know. I hoped that you weren't."

"I told him. About you and me."

Catching his breath a moment, Andrew felt the phone sliding around in his sweaty hand. "You did? Seriously?"

"Yeah. Seriously."

"O-oh." *I'm so glad you did,* he tried to say, but his brain refused to send the message to his mouth.

Unable to speak to him much longer without wanting to get worked up, he blurted, "I have to go, Andrew. I'll probably be home by tomorrow."

"Dad, wait!" The responding silence made him think that Kevin hung up, but he heard the sound of him breathing.

After a few seconds, he answered, "What."

"I... I'm sorry. I'm sorry, and, and I love you."

A hiss of static fizzled in the receiver as Kevin exhaled. "I'm sorry, too." He made no mention of whether or not he loved him.

"P-please come home tonight."

"Andrew, I can't see you right now."

"But, I..."

"I know you're sorry. That doesn't stop it from hurting."

"That's why I wanted to see you. I want us to feel better."

Kevin crossed the living room and walked down the hall, stepping into Kyle's bedroom where he could have some privacy. "Listen. I believe you when you tell me that you're sorry. I really do. But you gave me a lot to think about, and Kyle did, as well. You're not ready for a relationship."

"Yes I am!" Andrew disputed, but Kevin didn't accept it.

"Honey, I'm not blaming you for being upset about what happened to you at school. I'm upset that it happened, too. That's why you were right in leaving me. We can't hide forever. If it bothers us that much, maybe we can't do it after all."

"But, Dad, I'm over it. I don't even care anymore. After I graduate, I'm never going to see those people again. I don't care what they think of us!"

"Yes you do. And you should." He closed his eyes in grief at the sound of Andrew choking on the other end.

Andrew gasped and spluttered, "I know that I'm young. I know I'm stupid sometimes, Dad. I fucked up. I fucked up so bad and I want to take it back."

Lying down on Kyle's bed in the dark, he kept his voice as neutral as he could as to avoid upsetting both of them. "You don't understand, Andrew. I'm trying to tell you that you were right. It's not going to work."

"I don't know what I'm talking about!"

"You knew what you were talking about. It was in your heart, and you meant every word. You know as well as I do that we can't go on as we did before." He broke off for a moment to dry his eyes. "I can't trap you in a relationship like this. It's not fair to you."

Andrew released a pitiful sob. "Dad! Please, just listen to me!"

"Andrew, I'm sorry. The truth is that you're too young for me."

When considering the possible answers, he couldn't reply with any of them. Kevin still wouldn't believe him. "Give me another chance. I can do this, Dad. I promise I can."

Kevin lit a cigarette, the only thing that allowed him to cope with such a heavy conversation. Andrew's suggestion was tempting, one to give some serious thought. He missed Andrew cuddling up upon his chest, the taste of his sweet mouth, the tenderness of his embrace. Was it really "freedom" Andrew loved? The tightness of his arms around him, the sincerity of his words *I love you, Dad,* said that it might have been true that they had the real thing. All the same, Kevin had his reasons. "I'll still be me. I'll still give you everything you need. I just can't give you… that." He froze up when he heard Andrew wail on the other end of the line. Such a horrible sound, one worse than that of death. "Don't cry, honey. It'll be okay."

"No," Andrew whimpered. "It won't."

"I'll come home in the morning. We'll talk more about it then. Right now, I need some sleep."

"Come home and hold me," cried Andrew in desperation. "Please. I miss you, so much. It hurts."

Kevin wanted to hold his son, more than anything else in the world, and he wanted to do it for eternity. "We'll see each other in the morning." He paused, hearing Andrew moan. "Good night, Andrew." Andrew didn't answer; he only hung up.

Andrew dropped his head onto the marble kitchen counter. He had been too late, and too stubborn. *I should have given in when I had the chance. Now, we'll never have that closeness again. I let it go. I just fucking let it go.*

It would do no good to sit around wallowing in self-pity. Andrew looked through the numbers stored in the phone, scrolling through many names he didn't recognize, until he found Kyle's. Underneath his name was his phone number, and beneath that, his address. He wrote it down on a steno pad sitting near the phone, then ripped it off and took it to Kevin's office, almost keeling over as the pungent smell of menthol punched his nose in the same way Ben had.

He sat down at Kevin's computer and opened the web browser to search for directions to Kyle's house, specifically walking ones. The directions he printed out warned him that the walk from his house to Kyle's apartment would take at least thirty minutes. Initially, that mattered little to him. He had walked for longer distances when trying to run away from home as a kid.

In spite of his readiness to take the journey, a winter storm had blown in, one of the worst of the season. Ruthless winds rattled the panes of the windows, caused the house to creak, and sheets of ice sprayed the roof with raining crackles. The blinding snow not only came down in curtains, but fell at a rate too fast for Andrew to determine. If it wasn't considered a blizzard, Andrew would certainly call it damn near close to one.

For at least ten minutes, he paced around the front door, staring out at the mess of white and silver, debating his travel methods. What if, when he finally got to Kyle's, they didn't let him in? What if they slammed the door in his face, told him to walk all the way back home, in that furious weather? Kevin would never do that, he reminded himself. If he believed Kevin was the type to slam the door in his face and toss him out into a storm, he wouldn't love him as much as he did.

Not only did he have the snow and ice to worry about, but the dark. If someone managed to slip on the road and crash into him, it would likely be the less damaging outcome of his walk in the night. He and Kevin were arguing, but he doubted he wanted to end up with a dead son that evening.

Taking a deep breath, watching the wall of flakes crash down on their neighborhood, he thought of him, on the other side of that storm. At the end of the treachery, of disaster, Kevin was waiting for him. Kevin, with all of his love and glory, his warmth and compassion— his guiding light in the blanket of darkness. Where Kevin was, he belonged there. Where they were together, they were home, whether it be in his cushy, expensive house, or a tattered cardboard box beneath a dripping gutter in a dank alleyway. It wasn't home if Kevin wasn't there. Home was where he wanted to be now.

If Kevin wouldn't come to his home, Andrew would go to him.

He opened the coat closet, grabbing one of Kevin's coats, which was way too big on him, but well insulated, complete with a thick, furry lining that traced the inner stitching. The outer material was faux leather, thick and impenetrable. It was the sort of thing Andrew imagined a survivalist wearing, let alone some shut-in author. Unfortunately, Andrew had no boots to wear. He'd have to wear his dilapidated rubber-soled sneakers. He grabbed the house keys from the key rack on the wall, reading the directions in his hand several times before folding them and tucking them into the pocket of

Kevin's coat. As he opened the front door, a gust of wind nearly knocked him back, but he pushed against it.

After locking the door, Andrew began his expedition.

The first body part to get stiff was his ears, which throbbed as the wind slapped into each of the waxy canals. He hadn't even reached the main road before he thought he had lost the ability to hear. Tiny particles of microscopic ice shards pierced his cheeks, stinging him with every strike. The relentless winds simultaneously chilled and burned his skin, numbing it to the point of making movement difficult.

The snow was deeper than it looked. Whenever Andrew took a step, he thought it would land on solid ground, only to plummet through wet dust up to his knees. At several points, he tripped, soaking himself from top to bottom. The ice in his hair had frozen it in sections, stiffened it like cardboard spikes.

Halfway there, Andrew needed to take a break. He was exhausted from lifting his knees so high, from fighting against the winds, which seemed determined to knock him over whenever it got the chance. He took a seat on a tree stump near the road side, which was also covered in snow and ice, catching his breath. There he sat, shivering, for at least a few minutes. He wiped the snot from his nose, only to feel a burning scrape on his skin afterward.

The trip was so tiring that Andrew almost thought to turn back. Then he decided against it. He was going to finish it, whether or not he'd suffer the whole way. He could make it if he persisted, and continued to think of Kevin as he pushed on. He stood once again, then crossed the street, moving on with his journey.

The winds were so powerful that his eyes stung and watered, and as his salty tears moved down his face, the cold chafed his skin, sticking them to his cheeks. He was close, so close. Just keep moving. Don't stop. Keep a steady pace, and don't let up. He stood underneath the beam of a street light as he pulled the directions out one more time, checking the street names. He was there, on Williams Street, where Kyle's apartment building was located. Just a few more kilometers. He could see Kevin again. Kevin was there, and he would feel his embrace, hear his heavenly voice, and he would be safe once more.

When he reached the apartments, a dreaded fact dawned on him: he didn't know what number Kyle resided in. He slid over to the front doors, pulling on them. They were locked from the inside.

Oh, God, no, Andrew fretted, his heart hammering, though it barely had the blood to do so. He looked to the left of the entrance, seeing a panel of names and buttons. He looked over them one by one through raining eyes, which he needed to blink several times before his vision cleared. Under number two-sixteen was the name K. Phillips. Andrew jabbed his thumb onto the big red button.

Kyle, who had been occupied watching television, heard the call for the intercom. Curious, he stood up and wandered to the panel next to his door and pressed the "Call" button.

"Yeah?" he asked into the speaker.

Static at first, then a panting, heaving voice said, "It's A-Andrew. Is my dad there?" Teeth clattered and clicked together.

Stunned, Kyle recoiled, thinking some sort of joke was being played on him. "Andrew?!"

"P-please... I just want to see m-my dad..."

"How the hell did you get here?!"

"I w-walked. Could you open the door? It's f-f-fucking cold out here."

Kyle hesitated, thinking of leaving him out there to freeze. Kevin would probably castrate him for it, so he changed his mind. He buzzed him in.

Andrew yanked the door open, flinging himself inside, the door closing behind him. He pushed his way up the stairs, shivering the whole way, his soaking clothes sticking to him. When he reached Kyle's floor, he was almost too exhausted to make it to his door. If he had chosen to eat more than bread that day, he might have had less of a problem with his trip, but it was too late to make up for that now. He saw the apartment number come into view and knocked with his numb hand.

The door swung open, and he stumbled inward, shivering. Small piles of snow dropped onto the welcome mat, water dripping from his hair and clothes. As he stood there clutching his own chest, shivering, his inner ears pulsing and throbbing, Kyle shut the door and wandered down the hall to retrieve Kevin. From the living room, Andrew heard his father's voice.

"He *what?!*" Some mumbling from Kyle followed.

The door down the hall sailed open and Kevin emerged, hauling ass toward his frozen son in what looked to Andrew like slow motion. The first thing Kevin did was peel the soaking coat off of him, only to see that the clothes underneath it were also soggy.

"Andrew, honey," he whispered, his hand shaking as he moved frozen hair out of Andrew's eyes. "Are you all right?" Andrew used what little energy he had to lift his chin and lower it in a listless nod. "What the hell were you thinking, walking in that?"

"I didn't want us to be apart."

Kevin, defeated by Andrew's persistence, accepted the terms. He stripped Andrew's dripping shirt off, then removed his own, pulling him against his chest to heat him up. It was like huddling a pile of snowballs against his bare skin, but it helped to stop Andrew's shivering. To help further warm him, Kevin moved his palms over his back and arms.

Kyle, who had been watching from the hallway, leaned against the wall with crossed arms. Kevin glanced at him, overwhelmed by his disconcerted aura. "Could you run a hot bath for him, Kyle?"

He thought he heard Kyle reject him with a growl, but nevertheless, he replied to him. "Yeah. Sure."

"Thank you," Kevin told his friend, despite the sour look on his face. Kyle only nodded at him, then disappeared into the bathroom.

"Something could have happened to you out there," Kevin whispered to Andrew as he heated him up. "Could have slipped and broken your leg. Could have been hit by a car. Do you think I would have wanted that?"

Clicking his teeth, Andrew stammered, "I-I'm fine. I'm so happy to see you."

Clinging to him, Kevin tightened his clutch, the lovely squeeze that Andrew had grown to adore. "I'm happy to see you, too. Regardless of the circumstances."

Kyle came back into the room to let him know the bath was ready, and Kevin guided Andrew into the bathroom where he helped him remove the rest of his frosty clothes. Andrew climbed into the tub as soon as it was possible, eager to stop shivering.

Steam rose up on all sides of him as he sank into the basin. Though the water was a moderate temperature, it felt boiling to Andrew's frozen appendages. Soothing his frail bones, Andrew took a few moments to unwind. He peered at his father, who stood by the kitchen sink, facing the tub and keeping an eye on him. When he saw that Andrew was feeling better, he opened the door and began to step out.

"Dad. Don't go."

Kevin lingered by the door, ambivalent. Then he shut it again and reentered, taking a seat on the floor in front of the tub, saying nothing. For a while they stared in one another's indistinguishable azure irises, making no sudden moves. The first of them to speak was Andrew, who could now do so without gnashing his teeth.

"I haven't slept in so long."

"Neither have I," confessed Kevin.

"I thought I could get used to it being this way. I thought it'd be easy to go back to simply being your son. It's not working. I miss you."

"I miss you too, Andrew."

"We don't have to... do we?"

"Have to what?"

Andrew sat upright, resting his elbows on his knees, arms dripping as he raised them. "Pretend not to love each other."

Kevin relinquished his sorrow with a sigh. "I don't know. Are you sure it's me you love? And not the freedom I give you?"

Andrew's brow wrinkled and his nose scrunched up like he smelled something foul. "What? What are you talking about?"

"Kyle made a point to me earlier." Though Andrew rolled his eyes, he went on. "I didn't think of it before. Star treated you pretty poorly, but when you lived with me, you were given a life you didn't have with her. You saw that you had more freedom with me, and I think it was natural for you to attach to me the way you did. Maybe it isn't me you love. Maybe you just want that freedom back."

Water dripped from his marble hair as he swayed his head back and forth, chuckling with incredulity. "Is that what you think? Dad, you've got to be kidding."

"I'm not. And I don't appreciate you mocking me."

"I'm not mocking you. I just can't imagine such a silly idea coming into your head."

"It made sense when Kyle explained it to me."

"Well, Kyle doesn't know me! I know you two are close, and he knows you, but he doesn't know me, and he never will if he keeps talking about me like he does. It's okay that you trust him, but god damn it, Dad, you have to trust me, too."

Kevin's head tipped, a frown tugging his mouth. "I do. I just hope you want me for the right reasons."

His eyes brimming, Andrew whispered, "You're the reason for everything I do. That includes loving you." Kevin smiled at his sincerity. "Even if you weren't my father, you'd still be the greatest man I've ever met in my whole life. You make me want to try. You make me want to work hard. You make it so that I have something to work *for*. Without you, there just isn't a reason for any of it. I love you. Because you're wonderful, Dad. You're my hero, and you always will be."

Kevin looked not into his eyes, but through them, where he saw more than just a possible future. There, he saw more than a bleeding heart, but hope, chance, and best of all, honesty. "I love you too, sweetheart."

"I'm such a shit head. I'm so sorry I hurt you." His tears made it impossible for him to continue, but he didn't need to. Kevin lunged forward and pulled him into his arms, squeezing him and loving on him like he used to.

"Shh. It's okay." He kissed his damp cheeks, once again drying them with his hands, easing his pain. "Everything will be all right." Andrew started to lift his arms to hug him back, but he lowered them when realizing they were covered in water. Kevin then grabbed one of his dripping limbs and pulled it around his neck, invoking a laugh from his son as the collar of his shirt got wet.

Andrew made a familiar request: "Get in with me." Kevin didn't hesitate to remove his clothes and climb into the tub behind him, pulling him into the safety of his embrace and securing him there while he relaxed against him, every once in a while running his damp palms over his chest.

After about fifteen minutes of Kevin preening and washing Andrew, who giggled whenever he snuck in a tickle, there was a knock on the door.

"Shit," sighed Kevin, climbing out of the tub. He grabbed the nearest towel he could find (which didn't look all that clean), and wrapped it around his waist before pulling the door open. On the other side was a confused and disgruntled Kyle.

"Are you naked?" he inquired, staring at towel.

"Yeah," Kevin said with a secretive smile.

Kyle leaned around him to look inside the room at Andrew, who had a blissful grin glued to his face, and surmised that the two of them made up. "Kev, I love you, but… keep your playtime at home, okay?" He quavered, breaking eye contact.

Wincing, Kevin nodded. "Sorry. Yeah. I'll be out in a sec." He shut the door for only a moment to turn to Andrew, who looked like he tasted some of the sourest grapes in the world. "It's okay," Kevin reassured him. "Give him some time."

"Does he hate me?"

Kevin shook his head. "He's just…" He shrugged. "Not used to it. He'll come around." Before leaving, he set some towels out for him to dry off with. "I'll get you some dry clothes. Come into the bedroom when you're done."

Andrew nodded to show he heard him, then he was left alone, basking in ecstasy, a fresh glow brightening his features. Suddenly, the many nameless faces laughing at him seemed so distant, and at long last, they faded into the background until they could no longer be seen or heard. It was just a bad memory. Nothing more, nothing less.

As soon as Kevin stepped out of the bathroom, the daggers of Kyle's stare, sharpened and pointed at his back, hovered around the air ready to strike. Feeling uneasy, Kevin skulked into the bedroom, finding some clothes for Andrew, some that he had left there years ago. He recognized the black T-shirt with the yin-yang symbol on it right away from his days in community college. He once loved that shirt, and wore it everywhere, including Kyle's house. He brought the cloth to his nose and inhaled, the scent of marijuana imbued in the fabric. It really took him back to his twenties, when life was simpler, and drama didn't ail him. The days of lazing about smoking pot and having endless sloppy sex were good ones, but ones best left in the past where they belonged.

Though he had moved from place to place over the years, Kyle never misplaced his things. He had to respect him for that. After laying the clothes out on the bed, Kyle entered, looming in the doorway. When Kevin turned, he jumped at the sight of him. "Jesus, man. You scared the shit out of me." He thought this would make him laugh, but it didn't. "What's the matter?"

"So. The first time around, you didn't learn anything?"

Kevin moved toward him, but he stepped back. "It's okay, Kyle."

"This always happens with you, Kevin. I don't just mean because he's your son. That..." He squirmed as though insects were crawling beneath his skin. "I'll get past it, eventually. You know he's just going to pull this crap on you again."

Keeping his tone, civil, Kevin accused, "You seem upset."

"I *am* upset. I don't want to see that hopeless, crushed look on your face again. I can't watch you break down like that."

"Kyle. We'll be okay. And if not... I'll handle it on my own."

Swallowing the acidic flavor in his mouth, he mitigated his stance. "You can't hide him from the rest of the world. He deserves to go out, screw up his life, sleep with strangers, wake up with hangovers. You know, the shit we did at his age. Give him the chance to live."

"That's *living* to you? Getting so smashed you puke all over yourself, doing embarrassing shit you can't remember, and possibly catching STDs? What about drugs? You think I want him doing that? I hate that I did those things. I always wished I had done something more productive in those years, rather than wasted them away."

With a roll of the eyes, Kyle argued, "You know what I mean."

"Kyle, I understand, but he's an adult. If he chose to live his life a different way, I wouldn't stop him. Andrew will probably leave me someday. We're both going to get older, and I can't stop that from happening. I'm just going to make the most of our time together while I..." He bit down on his lip. "While I still have him." Kyle fell silent, knowing he wasn't going to get through to him. "This isn't really about me and Andrew, though, is it?"

Kyle refused to look at his friend. "What else would it be about?"

"You were hoping he and I would stay separated."

First, a sneer, then: "I don't know what you're talking about."

"Kyle, don't treat me like I'm an idiot."

He scanned his friend with smoldering eyes, which were narrow and crimped. "Then don't act like one."

Ignoring his animosity, he said, "Why did you wait so long to tell me how you felt about me? We had been sleeping together for years. Several times you made it clear that you wanted to stay friends. If that wasn't true, then why did you keep it from me?"

Wanting to get away, Kyle climbed onto his bed and lied down on his back. "Why do you think?"

Kevin watched him from over his shoulder. "Is it because you thought I'd reject you?"

"Of course I thought you'd reject me. We grew up together."

"We're like family, wouldn't you say?"

Kyle dragged an arm over his face, hating the irony of it all. "Yeah. I guess I would say that."

Kevin, standing and maneuvering to the side of the bed, articulated, "You must have some understanding of the way I feel about Andrew." He leaned his back against the wall and pocketed his hands.

"That's different. We're not blood related. You and Andrew are."

"So what? He shares my blood, and he's been in my life for the past two months. You don't share my blood, and yet we called each other 'blood brothers' all the time when I was nine and you were seven. I still consider you my brother."

"Okay. I get it, Kevin. You made your damn point."

Kevin dropped it, and Kyle stewed. Before Kevin could vacate, Kyle muttered to him, "You're my brother, too. But sometimes I have to wonder what the hell you're thinking. Andrew might be an adult, but he'll always be a kid. Your kid. You can hug him and kiss him all you like, but that's not going to change. He's not mature enough for you."

"And *you're* acting mature right now?"

"Compared to him? I'd say so."

The door creaked open, and there stood Andrew with a towel around his waist. Kevin waved him in.

"Sorry," Andrew said, mostly to Kyle. "I didn't mean to interrupt."

"I was leaving, anyway," Kyle grunted, stepping off of the bed, brushing past Andrew and shoving his way out the door. He took one look at Kevin and snarled, "Not in my bed."

Kevin swirled his eyes toward the ceiling, his face tinted cardinal. "We won't." Kyle breezed out, shutting the door behind him.

"What the hell is his problem?" Andrew grunted.

"Don't worry about it. He'll be all right." He passed him the dry clothes, and Andrew dressed in them. "We'll go home tomorrow, when the ice melts a little."

"As long as we're together," Andrew said whilst giving his father a loving hug. "I don't care where we are."

Kevin's arms came around him, and their mouths crashed into one another's. Not since their first kiss had they experienced such concurrent delight and reprieve. Kevin hoped like hell it would last, and if it didn't, he'd cherish it with all his heart while he had it.

Andrew didn't only swear an oath to his father, but to himself: he'd be as careful as he could now that he had him back. For years to come, he would be judged; Kevin was right about that, and he knew it. However, he would do his best to look the other way. In the opposing direction was someone he saw his future in, someone who would never turn a blind eye to his pain and anguish. Someone, who despite knowing how strange and different they were, would never abandon him, and would love him regardless of the things he had done. No one else would give him that serenity.

He didn't need to flee to the shadows any longer. Safe was what he was now.

Loved was what he would always be.

Chapter Thirteen

In Which the Helix Turns Eternal

"*Keep* 'em closed!" buzzed Kevin for the fourth time in the past minute.

Andrew had done as he asked, but Kevin had some reason to believe he was peeking, a reason that had not become apparent to him. Kevin ducked into his office, and he heard the sound of typing and clicking, which kept him intrigued as to what surprise he had in store for him.

"Come on, Dad, what is it?" he chirped, bouncing up and down, unable to wait any longer.

"You'll see, you'll see!" Then, with one more click, he took a hold of Andrew's hands and pulled him into the office with him, lowering him into the chair at the desk, then wrapped his arms around him from behind. "Okay. Now."

A quick flutter of the eyelids, and Andrew's eyes opened. He tilted his head, confused at what he was looking at: a wide photo of a massive log home surrounded by a thick forest of trees. It sat undisturbed and isolated next to a clear lake. "Uh… it's… a picture. Of a house."

"Mm-hm. What do you think of it?"

"It's beautiful." He still hadn't caught on.

Beside himself, Kevin grinned. "Would you like to live in a house like that?"

With stretched eyes and a drumming heart, Andrew now perceived the situation, and he had to take a moment to remember to breathe. "Where is it?"

"Highland Lake. That's the best thing. We're going to have to take a little road trip to get there. It's about two hours away."

"Dad," Andrew said after his tongue managed to loosen. "Are you buying this house?"

"That depends."

"On what?"

"Whether you like it or not."

Andrew, clasping his hands together, gasped, "Can we go check it out?!"

"Absolutely." He took Andrew's hand and stood him up. "After your graduation ceremony, that is."

With his bottom lip jutted out, he huffed. "I don't actually need to go to that. They make you do it because it's traditional. Just tell them to mail my diploma."

Kevin swayed his head, presenting a stubborn simper. "Won't you do it for me, at least?"

With a groan, Andrew shambled out of the office. "Okay. For you."

"Oh, it won't be that bad. It's a beautiful day."

"Beautiful *hot* day." If it was one thing Andrew hated more than being social, it was humid, sticky summers, and New York had its fair share. The heat would only be exacerbated by wearing a long, black robe on top of his clothes. Just thinking about it had him perspiring.

Kevin followed him out of the office, wrapping an arm around his shoulders. "We've got time before we have to go. What shall we do?" He didn't need to glance at him to know he had that mischievous leer plastered on his face, the same one he always got when they climbed into bed together every night. "Again?" He whistled, incredulous. "What the hell are you running on? Nuclear power? I don't have the energy you do."

"You always say that," Andrew teased. "It doesn't stop you."

He couldn't contradict that point. Andrew never ceased to be appealing, even when he suffered from heat exhaustion. "You win this one," he chuckled, smacking Andrew on the rear. Andrew laughed and skittered up the staircase with Kevin following. Whatever energy Kevin claimed not to have, he did indeed manage to find it once they were alone in a bedroom together.

The graduation ceremony was held inside the stuffy high school auditorium, where Andrew was crammed between two students he had never met before, who were each fanning themselves with pamphlets to keep cool. In the middle of the stage, where they were all seated, was a podium where the valedictorian stood to give speeches that Andrew almost fell asleep to.

I finished my damn classes and passed them, isn't that enough? Groaning at the stifling heat smoking from within his robe like sitting a steaming sauna, he also fanned himself with paper.

After a drawn-out process of staff members droning on about how high school was an important road to the path of life, they got to the diploma handouts. As they went down the list of names, he heard Ben's name called, and watched him walk to the stage, take his diploma, and grinned with pride to his spectators, including his cheering parents. Andrew joined them in their enthusiasm, and Ben shot him a look of a surprise before smiling at him. He returned to his seat with a strut.

When his name was called, he approached the podium with a slight limp. During his earlier erotic gambol with Kevin, he managed to pull a muscle in his leg, which had not healed itself by now. The moment he walked across the stage, two whooping voices rooted for him: Kevin and Kyle, who sat side-by-side in the front row, throwing their fists into the air and shouting his name as if they were attending a sports game.

Andrew took the diploma from the teacher handing them out, and he grinned at his father, blowing him a kiss, unconcerned about whoever might see it. Kevin beamed with pride and blew one back.

When Andrew walked off the stage and back to his seat, Kevin sat back down as well, turning to his companion. "We're going to look at the house later. He's really excited."

Kyle moved his mouth to Kevin's ear, whispering, "Do you really have to move two hours away?"

"We're not going away forever. You know we'd visit. We'll see each other about as often as we already do."

Kyle wasn't satisfied. "Why are you moving, anyway? What's wrong with the house you have now?"

"Nothing. You want it?"

"Yeah. Sure. Let me just round up a million dollar budget and I'll move right in. Oh, maybe I can put a fountain out front." He rolled his eyes. Kevin smiled in that charming way he always did. Kyle killed the sarcasm. "You don't have to hide from me, if that's what you're doing."

"It's not you, Kyle. You're the only reason I'd even want to stay in Queens. It's everything else. It's so noisy here, so busy. I can't walk outside for a breath of fresh air without hearing an ambulance siren, or the neighbors' kids screaming. I want to be able to work in a quiet place, to relax. New York City just isn't for me anymore. It seems Andrew doesn't feel he fits in here, either." He glanced at Kyle, whose face was partially obscured by shadows. The half that Kevin could see was twisted into an expression of worry. "We'll be all right. More than all right. We don't need much more than each other."

Kyle nodded, accepting that as a suitable answer. "I'll miss you, Kevin."

"It's not goodbye."

"I know." That wasn't the kind of "missing" he meant. For months, he had longed for his nightly tumbles with Kevin, the laughs they shared afterward, the reminiscing while lying side by side wearing nothing but grins and sweat. To say he "missed" that closeness with Kevin was an understatement. What he felt was a lifetime of affection, years upon years of building the foundation of a wonderful kinship, only for it to be broken by the most bizarre of wrecking balls. Andrew was Kevin's son, and he had accepted that. But why did he have to come into his life and take everything away, and so fast? If asked by Kevin if he resented Andrew for this, he would guffaw, tell his buddy how ridiculous it was, but the torment would only grow, and so too would the hostility.

Kevin placed his hand on Kyle's knee and gave it a few gentle pats, jolting him back to reality, wrenching his heart. "I'll miss you, too."

Concluding the ceremony, the students tossed their caps into the air, all except Andrew, who didn't want to lose his tassel, knowing Kevin wanted to keep it. Then, the students were allowed to disperse and meet up with their families. Andrew watched Ben as he joined his parents, seeing them for the first time. His father, a tall, burly man with a ragged silver beard and full cheeks, slapped him on the back in congratulations. His mother was more equipped with fondness, who hugged and praised him. Andrew then wondered what Star would have done had she attended the ceremony.

She sure wouldn't hug me like that, he dwelled.

Spacing out for a moment, Andrew hadn't noticed Kevin and Kyle approaching him. "Congratulations, Andrew," said his second cousin, lacking the approval that Kevin was overflowing with.

"Thanks." He reached out for Kyle's hand, who stared at it for a moment before taking it and giving it a flimsy shake. Before he could say much else, he was engulfed by his father's arms.

"I'm so proud of you!" he sang.

Andrew didn't think that graduating high school was that much of an achievement, not compared to some of the goals he strived for. Now that he was done with school, he could look into taking photography courses and start doing what he really loved.

"Thanks, Dad," he said, sneaking a kiss to his cheek. "Now, please take me home and get this thing off me." With the corner of his mouth, he added, "*Rip* it off me, even." Kyle raised an eyebrow at them.

Kevin chortled. "You got it." As they headed for the exit of the auditorium, Andrew heard his name called.

"Andrew, wait up!"

He paused, as did Kevin and Kyle, seeing Ben jogging over to them. Since their fight during the winter, it took some time for their friendship to return to its original state, but Ben had managed to let a lot of things go that Andrew probably wouldn't have if he were him. While keeping his relationship with his father a secret, Ben was still skilled at avoiding any mention of it even when alone with him, and even tried to change the subject when Andrew would bring up things that he and Kevin planned to do together. He accepted it in time, but he never really got used to it.

Somehow, it didn't affect their continuing friendship, though Ben didn't want to discuss his feelings on it, perhaps out of fear of offending him. Whatever the reason, Andrew didn't ask. If Ben wanted to stay friends with him in spite of how "icky" he might have felt, he was okay with it, as long as he didn't tease him.

Andrew didn't get to film Ben's movie, but when the film club showed their projects after school one day, he and Kevin attended to watch it, unbiased, from start to finish. Somehow, a subplot about a father and daughter entered the story out of the blue, to which Kevin and Andrew scratched their chins at. There were some unmentionable, hush-hush similarities to a certain father and son couple that existed in reality, but only the three of them were aware of such things. This subplot broke the mold, and abolished the unoriginal system of the Ben's first draft, and was what the club called for in filmmaking: originality. Ben didn't accept his prize without giving an over-the-top speech, thanking the high school for letting him create his first film, and thanking his friend, who remained nameless, for giving him the inspiration he needed.

Garret, who still hadn't been able to subdue the nausea he felt when remembering that kiss he found Andrew and Kevin locked in, had a pretty difficult time forgiving him for the trouble he caused. When Ben tried to talk him into forgiving him, Garret had no part of it. It was then that Ben grasped how little Garret was interested in talking to him anymore. He couldn't say it was any great loss to be rid of him, and he was happy to have Andrew back.

Since coming around to being his friend again, Andrew spent more time with Ben than he did before, and when he wanted to stay home, Ben was a bit more understanding of his situation. In the spring, Ben invited both him and Kevin to come see the school play, and they were more than happy to attend. The performance was dazzling, and Andrew got to see Ben really shine at what he was best at. It could have been the lighting, the other stage performers, or the atmosphere, but he could already see a touch of fame and fortune in Ben's every dancing step and bellowing note.

"You guys throwing a party?" asked Ben, bringing Andrew back to the here and now.

"Nah," Andrew answered. "I didn't want one. Dad's taking me to Highland Lake, though."

"Highland Lake…" He looked up to the rafters in thought. "Where the hell is that?"

"Two hours from here. That's all I know. He's showing me a new house."

His triumph took a sudden plunge. "New house? You're moving away?"

Andrew grew uncomfortable at the sadness in his voice. "I might be."

"Wow." He rubbed his taught shoulder. "That's… heavy."

"I would have told you sooner, but I just found out this

afternoon. Dad sort of surprised me."

With a shaking chin and jaw, Ben asked, "Will I see you again?"

To be honest, Andrew wasn't sure. "Of course. I'm not going that far."

When the mood became a bit too drab, Ben tried to improve it with sunnier news and a positive outlook. "I wish you guys luck. Really." Andrew smiled at that, touched. "I'm going to NYU's School of Arts for film classes as soon as I'm able. Maybe the next time you see me, it'll be my name on the big screen." He was almost blown back when Andrew gave him an unexpected hug.

"It'll be sooner than that, Ben," he told him while patting his back. "I promise."

Ben closed his eyes and swung his arms around him. "Tell your dad I'll hunt him down if he doesn't take good care of you."

Andrew, chuckling, squeaked, "I'm in good hands."

"I'd better get going. My parents *are* throwing me a party. Too bad they wouldn't let me hire strippers, though." Ben didn't depart without giving Andrew a kiss to the cheek, which he glowed at. "Take care, Andrew."

"You too, Ben." As they went their separate ways, Andrew wondered how different things might be if he had been attracted to Ben and they ended up together, rather than him and Kevin. Somewhere in the back of his mind, he acknowledged it as a more "healthy" relationship. On the other hand, he and Kevin were so happy together that he couldn't imagine sharing it with anyone else. Kevin was simply the one, regardless of the scientific facts.

They didn't get the chance to leave, because once again, they were stopped by someone calling for him. This time, the voice belonged to Sarah, who was toting a hefty book under her arm as she hobbled toward him, weaving in and out between students.

Since the incident at school, Sarah had apologized to him once the gossip had died down to a dull hush. Though Garret was a friend of hers, she said that it was possible that he misconstrued the situation, though not intentionally. Underneath her excuse, she might have believed all along that he and Kevin were intimate, but she didn't let her disturbance seep to the surface. It could have been, Andrew hoped, that she may have just accepted it for the "gossip" it was and believed it for a lie.

When she approached him, she gave him a hug, which he returned with gratitude. "What are your plans now?" she wondered. "Tell me you're going to keep up the photography."

"Without a doubt," Andrew voiced with confidence.

"Maybe we'll see each other at the same school again."

"You might not. I'll probably be taking online courses."

"I was wondering…" She unhooked the book from beneath her arm and passed it to Andrew. "Would you sign my yearbook?"

"Really? You want my signature?"

"Why wouldn't I?"

Shrugging, Andrew took the book from her, as well as a fancy fountain pen from his father, and wrote the following on the third page in, since the first two were covered in handwriting from various others:

For what it is worth, Sarah, I really do care what you think. Thank you for so much encouragement. If it hadn't been for your words, I might not have considered a career in my craft.

I wish you luck, wherever your heart takes you.

~With love and respect, Andrew "Conrad" ~~Phillips~~ Neil.

When he passed it back, his face was alight with amusement, which Sarah couldn't work out. She would certainly have a laugh when seeing his signature.

Then, after she strolled away, the three of them took flight before anyone else could stop them. On their way out, Andrew took Kevin's hand. Kevin was surprised at how public his affection was, but accepted it as one of the positive changes in their progressing relationship. He smiled down at him, linking their fingers together, a cord unbroken. Andrew smiled back, all signs of fear gone from his eyes. He was ready to live the rest of his life, in the best way possible, with the best person for him.

When they got home, Andrew rushed to his room to change out of sweaty clothes and into something more his style and combed his hair. It had gone back to Kevin's natural black color, and he was glad it had, but he missed the neon blue look. He'd let Kevin dye it a second time. He enjoyed sharing that time with him, and would love having it again.

Running back downstairs, Andrew noticed that Kyle hadn't yet left, but was hovering by the garage door while Kevin grabbed something from the kitchen. Apprehensive at being alone with Kyle, he veered toward the kitchen to help his father do whatever it was he was doing.

"Andrew," Kyle stopped him.

Letting out a soft curse, Andrew turned toward him. "Yeah." Kyle waved him over with his finger. Compelled to obey him, Andrew stepped closer.

"I wanted to have a little talk with you."

From experience, Andrew knew that "little talks" were hardly ever so. "What about?" Even when in the same room as Kyle, he kept his distance.

For almost a minute, Kyle froze, barely blinking or moving. "I'm glad you're in Kevin's life."

The tone of Kyle's voice implied that this declaration might not have been very honest. Andrew expected the "but" to come along any minute now. "I am, too."

"I'm happy to see him happy."

Was he trying to make him uncomfortable? If so, it was working. "So am I."

Kyle appeared identical to the bronze statues Kevin kept around the house. It startled Andrew whenever he spoke. "He says things are going pretty well with you both. And that's good. I'm glad to hear that."

"They are." Andrew wiped dabs of sweat from his neck.

When Kyle shifted his posture, Andrew folded his arms over his chest. "And they'll continue to go well. Right?"

Hearing threats in Kyle's requests for reassurance, Andrew took a timid step back. "Of course."

"Good." Tipping his head down, keeping his eyes pointed upward, he looked past Andrew into the kitchen where Kevin was still rummaging around, determining if he could hear him. "I still talk to your mother. Keep that in mind."

Andrew's fear melted into aggression. If anyone ever tried to take him away from Kevin and return him to that woman, he'd spend the rest of his life plotting the worst revenge. "What's your problem, Kyle? If you hate me, fine, but be a man and admit it."

"I don't hate you. But I don't like you, either."

He did not see that coming. "Why? What'd I do to you?"

"It's not what you did to me. It's what you did to your father."

"You're still—!" He changed pitch, lowering it so that Kevin wouldn't hear. "Really? You're still pissed about that? We got over it. I'm sure you can."

While continuing to cast a silent wrath upon his second cousin, he chuckled. "I am over it. I just have a vivid memory, that's all. I don't forget things as easily as your father does."

"Sounds like a personal problem to me."

"It's not my problem. It's Kevin's. At least, I'm sure it will be. I'm just waiting for the day you hurt him again."

"Oh, and you don't hurt him? Telling him shit like I don't really love him? I just love my 'freedom'. You know what? Fuck you. Don't talk of things you know nothing about."

Kyle snorted billowing smoke and took a few steps toward him, and Andrew staggered back, ready to run to his father for cover if it came to that. Their conversation, and potential knock-down-drag-out, was interrupted by Kevin bringing Andrew a piece of chocolate cake on a plate in one hand and a guitar case in another.

"Dessert for the high school graduate!" Kevin announced, passing it to Andrew, whose appetite had slackened since speaking with Kyle. Regardless, he took the plate from him and nibbled. He smiled and nodded at his father to let him know how good it was. "And your gift." He showed him the case.

"I thought the house was my gift."

"The house is for *us*, silly."

Once he sat his cake down on a table, he took the guitar case from him and unzipped it. Inside was a brand new acoustic, fashioned from dark, polished wood. Also inside the case was a new set of picks. In thanks, Andrew curled his arms around his father's neck, and Kevin told him to bring it along for their trip.

For the most part, Kyle was quiet until it was time for him to leave, including when sharing some cake with them. When it came time for him to head home, he told them both to enjoy their walk-through of the house, and to keep him posted on the news. When he went in to give Kevin a parting kiss, Kevin retracted, then shook his head at him, reprimanding. Dejected, Kyle slinked out with his tail between his legs. Then he was gone, and Kevin and Andrew had the house to themselves once again, giving them time to prepare for their adventure.

With driving directions and bottles of lemonade in hand, Kevin and Andrew hit the road. Andrew whipped out his new guitar and tuned it, getting a feel for it in his arms. Kevin made a few requests, which Andrew played for him to the best of his ability. Andrew told him he'd have to write him some new songs, which Kevin encouraged.

"Make me a whole album!" he suggested. "It'd be a great way to get your name out there, too."

While Andrew appreciated his fervor, he was a tad more cynical than his father. "I don't know if many people would be into acoustic love songs about my dad."

"You never know."

The evidence didn't need to be presented for Andrew to actually know, but he enjoyed having the support. "Maybe I will. For you, at least."

Right away, Andrew loved Highland Lake, even before he got to see the house. The hamlet, nestled in the town of Highland, was small, almost barren of population, and the drive through the canopy of trees around the lake to the property was awe-inspiring. Andrew couldn't keep his eyes away from his window, where he got the best scenic view of the two hundred and fifty acre body of water encompassed by spruces and pines.

Kevin pulled his sports car up the drive of the isolated, two-story red cedar log home, which looked even bigger in reality than Andrew surmised from the photo. He had never seen so much wood arranged in such a beautifully symmetric fashion. In the driveway was another car, white, which had an ichthys magnet on the rear bumper. In front of the obscure, hidden house was a tiny realty sign.

When Kevin stepped out of the vehicle, Andrew did as well, and Kevin took his hand when walking with him along the cobblestone path to the front door, which was also made of wood with hand-carved designs on it. Andrew had to crack a smile when he saw it was painted black. The roof was pine green in color, as were the window shutters, and a large deck followed the outer walls around the home. His breath had been stolen at the sight of it.

Kevin pressed the doorbell, and someone hurried to answer the call. A tall, brunette woman pulled the door open, flashing them a set of coffee-stained teeth. "You must be Mister Neil," she said, shaking Kevin's hand.

"That I am. You can call me Kevin. This is my son, Andrew."

Andrew tossed her a shy wave, but she seemed eager to shake hands, so he did.

"Jennifer McIntire," she told them. "Come on in." With a wave of the hand, she granted them access to the house, and they followed her. She toured them through the living room, kitchen, dining room, and master bedroom, all of which were furnished with hand-carved wood, and large enough to house ten people, let alone just the two of them.

Jennifer approached them with the notes in hand. "What do you think? It's very modestly priced for such a big place, isn't it?"

"Where's the nearest hospital?" asked a paranoid Andrew, poking at the wooden pillars he thought he heard creaking. He ducked out of the way, thinking they might fall any second.

Jennifer swallowed, delaying the answer. "Only a little less than twenty miles away."

Andrew fixed his worried look on Kevin, who comforted him with a stroke to the shoulder. "We should be okay," he eased, though Andrew wasn't buying it off the bat. Regardless, he loved the house, and everything in it, a lot more than Kevin's original home. "Would you give us a moment to discuss it?"

"Of course." Her heels clopped upon the wood floor as she strolled out of earshot.

"Well?" Kevin asked Andrew, now that they were alone. "Like it?"

Andrew smiled and nodded. "I do."

"You want it?"

Smiling wider, he nodded again. They hugged, Kevin kissing his face, where his taught facial muscles were still tugged into a grin. "It's great, Dad. I'm so excited."

"No one will bother us. People will keep to themselves, mind their own business. We can relax, and just be us. No interferences."

"Can I take some online photography classes?" He beamed and bounced on his heels.

"You know you don't need to ask for that. I'll do whatever I can to help you."

Unable to contain his overexcitement, Andrew cheered, drawing the attention of Jennifer. He cupped a hand over his mouth, burning crimson. "When can we move in?"

Kevin turned back to Jennifer and walked toward her. "I'd like to have it inspected before I sign, but I am interested in purchasing."

Stunned, but pleased, she laughed out, "Great!" She handed Kevin a business card with the words "Reed Realty" stamped to it in blue ink with a fax and phone number, telling him when to call with his offering price and when to sign the contract.

The drive home seemed so much longer than the trip there, so Andrew decided to take a nap. Without Andrew chattering to him the whole way, the ride back was lonely for Kevin. He loved hearing Andrew talk, no matter what it was about. Coming to a halt at a red light, he glanced at his son as he slept, whose lips twitched now and then as he dreamed, his nose wiggling like a rabbit's. He giggled at the sight of it. While he still had time before the light changed, he ran his palm over his silken hair, brushing some strands away from his nose to prevent it from tickling it, only for it to slip back down again. Kevin clicked his tongue at how hopelessly stubborn Andrew's hair was.

Throughout life, Andrew's dreams were as normal as anyone else's, but prior to meeting Kevin, he had an abundance of nocturnal hallucinations revolved around flying. He could take off whenever he wanted, wherever he wanted, sail through the trees and clouds, join the birds on their venture through the forests. Since coming into Kevin's life, those dreams ceased.

Replacing them were ones of an unidentifiable nature. That afternoon, he was walking down the street— one vacant of all life, where the temperature was moderate and the sound muted. On the corner was a blinking light, the signal he needed to cross to the other side. No cars were coming, either up the street or down, but he looked anyway. As his toe reached the road below the sidewalk, he heard the sound of a motor speeding in his direction. Jumping back to avoid getting hit, he watched as a vehicle as black as night drive up to the curb. The windows of the car were tinted, and Andrew could just barely make out what was inside.

Then, the passenger window rolled down. Andrew hunched over to look inside, but he saw no one. No driver, no passengers— there was nothing but a faint scent of meat. He pulled on the handle, popping the door open, curiosity getting the better of him. There! Something in the backseat! He turned to look, expecting to see a person. What he saw instead was a bird. A raven.

Alarmed, Andrew gawked at the enormous avian visitor, which

274

perched upon the seat as if the car belonged to it, head tilting to the left, then to the right, its beady eyes studying every inch of Andrew. The raven made a squawking sound, deep and vibrating, then followed up with a few clicks of its beak.

"Trip," it said in a robotic sing-song voice too uncanny to resemble anything human or raven alike. "Trip. We're going on a trip!"

"Where?" Andrew wanted to know.

"Home! Get in, get in!" The raven, now excitable, bounced from one clawed foot to the other. "Get in!"

Home? Wasn't he home already? No. He was on his way home. He supposed it couldn't hurt to accept a ride from a raven that owned his own car. After all, he seemed friendly enough. He stepped into the passenger seat, lowering into it and shutting the door.

"Yay!" cheered the raven, tilting its beak up. "Home! We're going home!"

Outside of his mind, Andrew felt himself smile. The childlike joy of his feathered friend reminded him of his youth, when he would wish and dream of meeting Kevin, of being carried away from harm, given a happier life. Such wishes were all he had to keep him going, and now they had become reality.

"Home" was something Andrew never called his place with Star. That was "a house he lived in." With Kevin, he would always be home. Nothing could take that away from him now. Not even the demons of his past.

As Andrew's eyes opened, it was like they had for the first time in his life. Meeting him was the burning glow of a distant sunset, striking him from outside the window. They were close to the house now, off of the highway and traveling down the main roads. As he woke, he turned to his father, whose face was serene, filled with endless bliss.

Seeing him awake, Kevin looked at him and smiled like he had just witnessed his birth. Andrew mirrored that look of happiness, loving him in silence, a love he knew would not rest, a love that not even death could take away. A love from that of a son, a best friend, and partner for a lifetime.

A love that Andrew would feel forevermore.

Other Works by Mel Thorn:

For the Sake of Happiness
Gay Romance

When Cory Anderson receives the first of many letters from a secret admirer, his initial reaction is fear and anger. When he discovers more about his stalker, he learns that the person is more than just unsettling notes and awkward desires. Hoping to understand the meaning of how it all began, he sets out to learn from his pursuer, not only about why they followed him, but also to learn about life itself. In time, he finds that life is much more complicated for some as it is for others.

US: http://www.amazon.com/dp/B00ICL9LCM
UK: http://www.amazon.co.uk/gp/product/B00ICL9LCM

Author Website and Blog:

www.thorncreations.com

www.ingramcontent.com/pod-product-compliance
Lightning Source LLC
Chambersburg PA
CBHW072224190626
46809CB00016B/459